PRAISE FOR A[...]

"Wilson (*Midnight on the River Grey*) weaves a splendid tale of murder and deception in this fun, suspenseful Regency . . . The main couple are well matched in spunk and intellect, and Wilson strikes a nice balance between intrigue and gentle romance. This delightful story is sure to entertain."

—Publishers Weekly on Masquerade at Middlecrest Abbey

"From the very first page, I was enraptured! Ms. Wilson delivers a timeless story made even better by a hero who epitomizes generosity of love like no other I've read before. *Masquerade at Middlecrest Abbey* has intrigue, mystery, and suspense beautifully enhanced by the vulnerability revealed through memorable characters making this story impossible to put down. A must-read recommendation, this story is exactly what makes me love reading!"

—Natalie Walters, author of the Harbored Secrets series

"Murder is far from no one's thoughts in this delicious new romantic mystery from Abigail C. Wilson. With scandal dodging every turn of the page, mystery hiding behind the visage of each character, and a romance brewing with an English rake of the worse—and best—sorts, readers will find nothing lacking! I was entranced, mesmerized, addlepated, and not a little bit bewildered as I wandered the halls of Middlecrest Abbey. While it was easily cemented before, it is now forever set in stone, that I am a loyal fan of all things Abigail C. Wilson."

—Jaime Jo Wright, author of Echoes Among the Stones and the Christy Award-winning novel, The House on Foster Hill, on Masquerade at Middlecrest Abbey

"Suspicion shades the affluent grounds of Middlecrest Abbey in this riveting novel by Abigail Wilson. The artful balance of mystery and romance cleverly blends with the Gothic tones of Regency England. With exquisite prose and a layered plot, *Masquerade at Middlecrest Abbey* is a compelling story not to be missed."

—Rachel Scott McDaniel, award-winning author of Above the Fold

"With a wonderfully suspicious cast of characters, intriguing clues, and lush backdrop that readers can easily get lost in, *Midnight on the River Grey* is a captivating novel."

—HISTORICAL NOVELS SOCIETY

"Abigail Wilson's debut novel is a story rich in detail with a riveting mystery . . . With enough jaw-dropping plot twists to give readers whiplash, it would be a severe oversight to pass this story up."

—*HOPE BY THE BOOK*, BOOKMARKED REVIEW,
ON *IN THE SHADOW OF CROFT TOWERS*

"Readers who enjoy sweet romances, gothic settings, innocent heroines, and mysterious heroes should enjoy this read."

—*HISTORICAL NOVELS REVIEW* ON *IN THE SHADOW OF CROFT TOWERS*

"Abigail Wilson's *In the Shadow of Croft Towers* is the kind of novel I love to recommend. Well written, thoroughly engrossing, and perfectly inspiring. I honestly couldn't flip the pages fast enough."

—SHELLEY SHEPARD GRAY, *NEW YORK TIMES*
AND *USA TODAY* BESTSELLING AUTHOR

"Mysterious and wonderfully atmospheric, Abigail Wilson's debut novel is full of danger, intrigue, and secrets. Highly recommended!"

—SARAH LADD, AWARD-WINNING AUTHOR OF *THE WEAVER'S DAUGHTER*

"What a deliciously satisfying debut from Abigail Wilson! *In the Shadow of Croft Towers* is everything I love in a novel: a classic Gothic feel from very well-written first person storytelling, a regency setting, a mysterious hero . . . and secrets abounding! *In the Shadow of Croft Towers* is now counted as one of my very favorite books, and I can't wait for more from this new author!"

—DAWN CRANDALL, AWARD-WINNING AUTHOR
OF THE EVERSTONE CHRONICLES SERIES

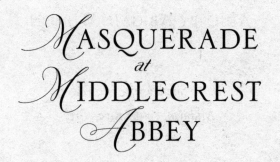

MASQUERADE at MIDDLECREST ABBEY

ALSO BY ABIGAIL WILSON

In the Shadow of Croft Towers
Midnight on the River Grey

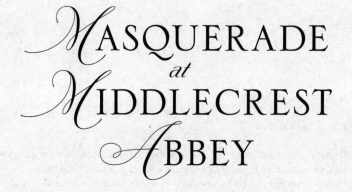

MASQUERADE *at* MIDDLECREST ABBEY

ABIGAIL WILSON

THOMAS NELSON
Since 1798

Masquerade at Middlecrest Abbey

© 2020 Abigail Wilson

All rights reserved. No portion of this book may be reproduced, stored in a retrieval system, or transmitted in any form or by any means—electronic, mechanical, photocopy, recording, scanning, or other—except for brief quotations in critical reviews or articles, without the prior written permission of the publisher.

Published in Nashville, Tennessee, by Thomas Nelson. Thomas Nelson is a registered trademark of HarperCollins Christian Publishing, Inc.

Thomas Nelson titles may be purchased in bulk for educational, business, fund-raising, or sales promotional use. For information, please email SpecialMarkets@ ThomasNelson.com.

Publisher's Note: This novel is a work of fiction. Names, characters, places, and incidents are either products of the author's imagination or used fictitiously. All characters are fictional, and any similarity to people living or dead is purely coincidental.

ISBN 978-0-7852-3307-7 (trade paper)
ISBN 978-0-7852-3296-4 (e-book)
ISBN 978-0-7852-3301-5 (downloadable audio)

Library of Congress Cataloging-in-Publication Data

CIP data is available upon request.

Printed in the United States of America

20 21 22 23 24   LSC   10 9 8 7 6 5 4 3 2 1

For my son, Luke
My joy, my heart, my favorite scientist.
Thank you for your endless smiles, your witty humor,
and your infectious love of adventure. You teach
me every day to see the world in a new way and
to enjoy every precious moment. I love you.

CHAPTER 1

1815
SOUTHEASTERN ENGLAND

I blinked a few times and took a deep breath. Apparently I'd survived.

Shaky, I pressed my hand to the wet gash on my temple as the world around me swirled into focus.

Gunshots. Highwaymen. The carriage crashing to its side. The whole awful encounter raced through my mind like a runaway horse.

The blazing afternoon sun filtered in through a window of the overturned carriage, illuminating disheveled squabs that slumped to my right and left. Dust lay suspended in the air, oddly seasoned by the scent of my lavender perfume. The bottle must have broken when the carriage crashed.

Wedged between the door and the seat, I attempted to sit up, but my muscles ached in response.

A faint cry took flight on the wind, and my eyes shot fully open. "Isaac!" I clawed at the splintered wood around me. "Isaac? Mama's here." I could hear my cousin's words resounding in my mind as I struggled to get my bearings. *"You really should be more careful with the boy."*

I thrust a loose bandbox from my legs and forced myself semi-upright. The movement sent a shooting pain like lightning through my head, and I cried out. My stomach rolled in answer as blood throbbed its way to my forehead. What was left of the carriage I was pinned within swam around me in circles, but nothing would keep me from my son.

Several heart-pounding seconds passed as I pawed through the disheveled interior. Finally I located Isaac's curly blond head in the far corner. Black spots crept into the sides of my vision as I stared at his motionless form. Was he injured—or worse?

I stretched out my trembling hand just as his eyes popped open. He let out a frantic cry and his gaze found mine. Gasping for air, I screamed, "Oh Isaac!" Tears spilled down my cheeks as he crawled over the various pieces of luggage and into my lap, my fingers sliding over every inch of his precious body.

"Madam, are you hurt?" A deep voice echoed from somewhere above, but I couldn't maneuver around to see its owner. My ears buzzed as I drew Isaac close, reveling in the feel of his warm arms.

We had a rescuer, but what now? My entire body throbbed in pain. And—the Palmers! They were expecting us in Dover. Tonight. The horrid highwayman had ruined my carefully laid plans.

Blood trickled down my wrist as I pressed the wound on my forehead. "I don't think anything is broken, sir . . . only, my head . . . I believe I hit it rather hard."

"It was a ghastly accident, I'm afraid." The voice was that of a gentleman, a passerby perhaps? "I'm afraid your coachman has suffered greatly. I've bound up his leg, but he has not yet regained consciousness."

I clenched my jaw. "Indeed, it was ghastly! Did you see the devil who ran us from the road?"

A pause. "Well, yes." A metallic squeak sounded, and the equipage jolted. "I've the door open above you now. I think it best if I come in and assess your wounds before lifting you out."

Unable to take the sudden flash of bright light, I shielded my eyes with my hand. "That sounds reasonable. My son seems unharmed, though I'm not certain I can move at present. My head is awfully tender."

The carriage shivered as the man dropped safely into the coach. He pushed my valise out of the way and knelt at my side, bringing his face into view at last. I stifled a gasp as an icy wave filled my chest.

It was him—the highwayman. I clutched Isaac against me.

He held up his hand, his voice tender. "Don't be frightened. I'm only here to help."

"Is that so?" I pushed through the burning twinge inching down my neck to dip my chin. "A highwayman with a conscience. What a comfort."

His hand retreated to the rag covering his nose and mouth, and he mumbled under his breath, "I forgot I still had this thing on. Guess there's no denying it now."

"Certainly not."

He reached up to lower the mask but hesitated as he gripped the cloth. "Perhaps it would be best if we remain as we are—two strangers, nothing more."

I shrank against the cold glass of the side window, the memory of my terror at the approaching robbery charging my nerves once again. "What is it you want? We haven't any money . . . or jewelry for that matter. I was on my way to accept a position as housekeeper." I gave him a hard smile. "You've risked our lives for nothing."

He shook his head, his voice grim. "This entire mishap was just a shocking misunderstanding. I'm dreadfully sorry to have involved you and your son."

My gaze flicked to the broken window. "And our driver?"

"Unfortunately, he will need a doctor straightaway." The highwayman gestured to my bent legs lying lifeless among the loose items that had fallen during the collision. "Considering we haven't much time, it is imperative I check your injuries at once. May I?"

I flinched as he extended his arms.

His voice softened. "You know you'll have to trust me if I'm to get the three of you out of this."

He sounded reasonable enough, and someone else might not come along for some time. But I'd not let a man this close to me . . . not since Brook. My muscles stiffened before I forced a nod. After all, what other options did I have?

The highwayman felt along my feet and knees before moving his hands to my arms and around my shoulders. His touch was gentle yet assured and eventually brought a pair of pale-blue eyes a few inches from my face. We assessed each other for a quiet moment. The man's steady gaze was familiar somehow. Did I know him? Surely not.

He gathered Isaac from my chest, then strong-armed me into a sitting position close to his side. "There. Does it pain you terribly to move?"

At first I thought the worst was over, but my ears soon buzzed to life, my stomach churning in response.

Unaware of what raged inside my body, he went on. "I believe there is an inn a few miles ahead—"

All at once my face felt hot, and a black veil dropped over my vision. I tried to warn the man, flitting my hands in the air, but there wasn't time before I tipped over—straight into his lap.

The unexpected caress of the man's fingers at my back and on my arm startled me as I woke, and he guided me once again into a sitting position. I thought his subtle touch at odds with the villainous robber he presented on the road moments before, but I was far too preoccupied to remark upon it.

He moved quickly to assess the wound on my head. "I begin to fear you might be concussed."

"Actually, I feel a bit better now." But I'd spoken too soon. The carriage seemed to tilt, and I felt the man lower me back onto the side of the coach, which served as the floor at present.

"This is a bit more complicated than I thought. I'm greatly concerned you've— What the deuce?" He sprang to his feet and cast a quick glance out the window above before ducking back into the shadow of the coach, Isaac wriggling in his arms. A muscle twitched in his cheek. His voice, however, was composed as he said, "It appears we're to have company. There are horses approaching."

The roar I'd heard before swelled within my ears, and I feared I might slip from consciousness once again. The highwayman sought to avoid my stare but couldn't entirely manage to do so. I wondered if he shared my concern or if something else drove his actions. And those eyes. They were indeed familiar. Struck by a sudden notion, I motioned him near. He leaned toward me and, cautiously, I scrutinized every last curve of his exposed face.

Could it be? Brook? When he'd broken my heart and refused to acknowledge my son about a year and a half ago, I thought I'd never see him again. Yet here he was—stooping beside me as if he owned the world. I shifted to mouth his name, but my lips wouldn't cooperate. Perhaps I'd already fallen within a dream. As I continued searching the eyes that focused on mine, I realized they were not quite as familiar as I'd thought.

The man's hand was at my chin, his voice urgent. "Stay with me. It won't be long now till help is upon us." Footsteps pounded somewhere beyond the black tunnel of my vision. The highwayman shouted up at the open door above us, "We're in here. Make haste! A woman is injured."

Then he whispered to himself, "Oh God, what have I done?"

It was not Brook Radcliff speaking beneath that mask. No, the voice was deeper, more refined. In a curious haze, I tugged the rag from the man's face just as voices crested the open door of the carriage.

"I say! Is everyone all right in there?"

Darkness circled my vision. As the buzzing in my ears drowned out all other sounds, I lay stunned at what my fingers had unwittingly revealed.

It wasn't Brook who forced my carriage from the road and yelled, "Stand and deliver!" It was his disreputable older brother, Lord Torrington.

*

My fingers curled around a soft blanket as I nestled into a pillow. A dull pain hovered around the depths of my eyes, but it remained at bay by what I came to realize was a cool cloth across my brow. For a moment I allowed my mind the space to rest before the whole terrible nightmare of the carriage accident forced me into consciousness.

The room around me stood dark and unfamiliar. A solitary

candle guttered on a small table beside the bed. Voices and laughter resounded from beyond the walls. I squinted, peering into the looming shadows that lingered about. I'd never seen the sparse furniture that dotted the room or, more importantly, the figure seated in a nearby chair and slumped forward on the eiderdown.

It seemed my rescuers had found a way to recover me from the coach, after all. However, they couldn't have taken me far. The highwayman had mentioned a local inn.

I swallowed hard against my parched throat. I was in great need of water, but I didn't dare move for fear the staggering pain would return to my head. So I gently reached to awaken whoever had been appointed as my nurse, but my hand froze in midair inches from a rather large and muscular arm.

It was a man.

My heart stilled. The doctor?

Whoever rested on my bed must have sensed a change, because he stretched out his arms and lifted his head for a long yawn before turning to face me. His voice was a little above a whisper. "You're awake. Good. How's the head?"

I stiffened at the sight of the highwayman himself only to regret my hasty movement. I forced a measured breath. "What on earth are you doing in my bedchamber?"

A practiced half smile crossed his face, which the feathering wave of candlelight made only more pronounced. He leaned forward, his thick, copper-colored hair dipping in and out of the darkness. "You wouldn't believe me if you tried."

For once I was speechless. Never in all my life had I imagined such a moment with Brook's impressive elder brother. My thoughts spun as I tried to make sense of what he'd said. What brought him here alone? To be certain of my recovery? To alleviate his guilt? In the coach he declared the accident a misunderstanding, yet how could that be true?

I caught a probing look within Lord Torrington's unnaturally pale eyes. He wasn't here to ravish me. At least, I didn't think he was. But that he had come with a purpose in mind was utterly clear.

My voice cracked. "Where is my son?"

"He's asleep with the innkeeper's daughter in her room. She seems a redoubtable girl with good sense. He will be well cared for in your absence." He leaned back against his chair and folded his arms, which afforded me the first glimpse of his attire. A dressing gown of all things . . . better yet, *my* dressing gown.

I jerked the blanket beneath my chin, and my stomach tightened. Had I been wrong about his intentions?

"What do you mean by all this?"

He ran a finger under the lapel. "Not my color, is it?"

"Don't be ridiculous."

His eyes softened as he adjusted the cloth that had slipped to the side of my forehead. "The doctor will be quite vexed with me if I rile you. He prescribed rest and quiet, and I assured him I would follow his instructions." He paused. "The cool cloth, however, was my idea."

"How thoughtful." I couldn't hide the bitterness in my tone. I angled my chin, waiting for something else, some kind of explanation for his intrusion into my private room. "Well?"

A furrow formed between his eyebrows. "You're quite right. Undoubtedly you deserve an answer for my being here. Goodness knows it was not my intention from the start; nevertheless, I'm afraid I've a bit of a story to impart. But considering the doctor's implicit instructions, I'm not certain you are well enough to hear the whole of it now."

I eyed the closed door. How could I possibly sleep without knowing everything? "What time is it?"

"One in the morning. Do you require some water? Your voice sounds hoarse."

I nodded and watched as he crossed the room to a table near the door. With my initial shock subsided, I swallowed my pounding reservations and appraised my overnight intruder. Torrington certainly had an intelligence about him, even while wearing my robe. His commanding presence, though, was thankfully absent of the overbearing nature of many of his peers.

I squinted into the dim light as he finished filling the water glass and turned back to face me. Though he and Brook favored each other in looks, Torrington had inherited his father's broad shoulders and regal bearing, whereas Brook had always been lean and more relaxed.

Torrington slid once again onto the straight-backed chair by the bed. Instinctively, my fingers curled tight around the blanket. I had only seen him across a crowded dance floor, but Brook had been right. His brother possessed a daring look. A flawless angle to his face, a firm chin. Years ago Brook labeled him a libertine. Goodness, I'd heard countless stories of Torrington's conquests, which I remembered all too well—like the time Brook was forced to leave town to pay off one of his brother's many mistresses. My throat burned at the thought.

Torrington leaned forward and pressed the water glass to my lips, careful not to spill it on the bed. "Easy now. Not too much at once." After I drank, he settled the glass on the bedside table and rested his elbows on his knees, his eyes suddenly somber. "I owe you a rather insufficient apology for what I've put you through today. And yet—" He offered a tentative smile. "I feel ridiculous doing so in my current state of dress. Of course, this was the only thing in your trunk I could possibly wear."

"My trunk, huh? And where, may I ask, are your breeches?"

"Being cleaned at present, although I doubt they shall be able to get out the blood, let alone return them in any reasonable length of time." He shot me a quick grin. "I have come to learn there is a particularly interesting cock fight in the area. The ostler's words, not mine. Hence, the White Lion Inn has been crushed with people and the help sadly unprepared." He motioned to the chair. "Thus, here I sit and wait."

Hesitation laced my voice. "In my bedchamber? For what purpose, my lord?"

He gave a lighthearted shrug and stood to cross the room, speaking over his shoulder when he reached the fireplace. "Rest assured, I did all I could at the outset, demanding two rooms from the proprietor of this backwater establishment, but there was just the one available. And since he thought we, uh . . ." He propped his arm on the mantel, a nervous laugh hovering on his breath. "Regardless, it was imperative that I speak to you alone."

Alone. Only one room available? The thought sent a fresh wave of nerves tingling across my shoulders. "Then, by all means, speak at once. I've never had the patience for pleasantries or the least qualms about screaming for rescue, if need be."

He turned, a hint of amusement about his eyes. "Touché." His smile faded. "I'm afraid there is much you must be made aware of, and hastily at that. You are Miss Cantrell, are you not?"

A faint tremor accompanied my answer. "Well . . . yes." He knew me. From his brother? There was a moment of strained silence. "And you, I am well aware, are Lord Torrington."

He tapped his fingers on the mantel. "It appears my instincts proved correct. I had a feeling you recognized me in the coach." The flame from the fire dipped, and he moved to rub his forehead. Tiredness lay beyond his practiced façade. "Though you and I have never been introduced, I am well acquainted with a few members of your family: Mr. and Mrs. Sinclair."

I paused, my heart drumming in anticipation, certain he would add that his brother was once in love with me, but he didn't acknowledge the connection. Perhaps Brook had faithfully kept the secret he thought so necessary at the time. Of course, such a strict confidence had benefited him and only hurt me. Isaac's bright smile and curly head came to mind—so like his odious father.

The hurtful memories tainted my voice. "When can I see my son?"

"I suggest for now you focus on your recovery and—"

"I do thank you for your concern." I gave him a pert smile. "However, I shall do no such thing. I expect Isaac to be brought to me as soon as can be arranged."

Torrington covered a smug grin with his hand. "As you say, *my lady*. I'll be sure you see him first thing in the morning. But at this very moment, it is urgent we decide between the two of us what is to be done."

"We? I assure you, my business is none of your affair." The last thing I wanted was further connection to Brook's family, particularly with the highwayman who had run my carriage from the road. "As soon as I am recovered, I shall continue on to Dover and assume my position as housekeeper. I will not permit you to feel responsible for me in any way."

Torrington made his way to the bedside. "If only it were that simple."

Clearly the man was accustomed to barking orders and having them performed immediately. By the look in his eye, he had a plan, and considering his presence in my room, it must involve me. A chill swept over me, but I shook it off, adding hurriedly, "Allow me to remind you, this is not a game. I am not some chess piece to be moved at will, my lord."

He plunged his fingers into his hair, which drew my attention to a small patch of gray residing just above his forehead. "I do apologize if I gave you that impression. I have never been one for tact. In fact, I have spent the last hour or more calculating the best way to tell you what has transpired since the crash. I don't wish to upset you, however—"

"It is a bit late for that. Be assured, you have upset absolutely everything—my plans, my future." I sighed. "Simply give me the whole of it, if you please."

He slumped into the chair beside the bed, his words achingly slow to come. "You have already made the connection that I was posing as a highwayman when the accident occurred."

"How could I not? You pointed a pistol at me through the window. Did you think I could forget such a thing? And my coachman, dare I ask how he fares?"

Torrington ran his hand down his face as I'd seen my brother, Lucius, do a thousand times when his back was against a wall. "He has a few broken bones, but the doctor assures me he will heal. I've paid the staff to see to anything he needs."

Torrington waited for me to fully digest what he'd said, the shadow of pain evident in his eyes. "Is he a friend of yours?"

"No, although he was quite close with my brother, Lucius, at one time."

The muscles in Torrington's jaw clenched, and he shook his

head. "As I said before, the whole blasted robbery was a mistake. Listen—" He lifted his finger to point at me, then crushed it into a fist and pressed it against his chin. "I can see you have no intention of making this easy—gawking at me like that." He took a long breath. "And you had to be Curtis Sinclair's cousin-in-law. Convenient." He tapped his fingers on the bed first one direction then the next. "I do realize you deserve more than a well-constructed lie, yet . . . Tell me, has Mr. Sinclair ever mentioned me before?"

"Mentioned you? Good gracious no. Why should he?" The words were out rather quickly, but as I met Torrington's sharp gaze, my thoughts took a wild turn, back to a year and a half before when Curtis spent time as a British spy. He'd posed as a highwayman to gather information. Could Torrington be involved in something similar? Brook had never revealed anything of the sort.

Torrington dipped his head, watching me with a keen eye for several seconds, then smiled impulsively. He knew I knew.

If only I wasn't such a terrible liar, I might try to deny what was probably written across my face. My shoulders slumped. "You worked with Curtis?"

A slow nod. "You could say that."

I narrowed my eyes and took the bait. "For the crown?"

Torrington paused to appraise the coverlet, then abruptly looked up. "You must realize it goes against my very nature to discuss something I have kept well-hidden for nearly fifteen years."

I didn't move.

"On the other hand, if Curtis saw fit to entrust you with his own secret, and considering our situation, I believe I have little choice but to do so as well." Something shifted in his countenance.

Concern? Confidence? It was hard to read Torrington's slight emotions in the candlelight. His voice, though, took a dangerous dip as he gripped my hand. "What I am about to say must be kept in the strictest confidence."

I met his steady glare. "You have my silence. Go on."

"At present and in secret, I work as an agent for the British government." His eyes flashed. "Moreover, I'm a spy."

An odd mix of emotions struck me as I processed his confession. Half shock, half interest. I'd always thought of Curtis as selfless and good. How on earth had Brook's scandalous elder brother become involved in such a noble endeavor?

Torrington glanced down at his hands as he folded them on the bed, his voice low but rushed. "I was sent by a secret division of the government called the special office to rob your coach. You see, the authorities in Dover uncovered information that a document was being moved across England in a carriage matching your coach's description. I was told this missive, whatever it may be, is of vital importance to the war effort." He steadied his gaze. "I've single-handedly put Wellington in a difficult position after I held up what I can only deduce was the wrong coach."

"It most certainly was the wrong coach. I haven't the least notion of any document, and I've never had any love for France."

He closed his eyes. "I'm well aware you are not a part of the spying network we have been playing cat and mouse with over the last few years. My blasted error has ruined everything. For you, for Britain." He lowered his head. "And when your cousin-in-law finds out what I've done . . ."

The silence of the room pressed against my ears. He was right. I could only imagine Curtis's reaction to all I'd experienced. He was currently in London unaware I'd even left his home, let alone traveled without warning to accept a housekeeping position for a friend. Of course, I planned to write them when I had settled and there was no question of fetching me back.

I cleared my throat. "Your words do have merit, my lord. Curtis can be quite protective of his family. Yet . . ." I glanced up. "He may also be kept in the dark if need be."

Concern crept into Torrington's eyes. "Unfortunately, there is more, a great deal more." He adjusted his position on the chair, and for the first time I thought him genuinely nervous. He forced more of a grimace than a smile as he rested against the seat back. "You see, when the second carriage arrived at the scene of the accident, you'd already removed my mask. I said something to protect my identity that I have now come to regret."

The dull headache threatened to return, so I waved him on.

His voice dipped into a sort of comical apology. "I, uh, told them you were my wife."

CHAPTER 2

Your wife!" Panic wrapped my heart.

Torrington held up his hand, staving off a slew of searing words poised to spill forth. His face remained a maddening mixture of integrity and arrogance, yet his tone sounded defensive. "I acknowledge what I said was brash and foolish, but you must try to understand. I was inside the carriage and neither you nor your coachman were conscious when help arrived. It was imperative that I protect my identity. I had no idea who they were or what they'd seen. And without your words to refute me, I carried the lie at length, even into the inn and your very bedchamber."

I drew away from him, cringing as the reality of his declaration echoed into the gloomy corners of the room. What might come about from such a simple statement? My head swam, yet I attempted to push myself into a sitting position. I could not fully digest this development lying on my back. Torrington sought to help me, but I thrust him away, completing the shaky transfer within my own power. "Exactly how many people heard what you said?"

His voice was firm as he flexed his fingers. "Only a few. However, I wasn't expecting to meet an acquaintance of mine in the receiving area when I arranged for our room." He looked up. "He

16

knows me. He knows you. The damage is done. I had no choice but to continue in my deception."

I huffed a cynical laugh as Torrington sat there regarding me like a cursed statue, probably uncertain what to do or say next. He had made a mull of everything. Whatever was left of my failing reputation would be nonexistent in a matter of days. An assignation in the country with Brook's elder brother . . . Oh, the dratted Radcliffs!

Of course, there were likely few who had connected Brook to my son, but another scandal on my part had the distinct possibility of ruining any chance I had to work as a housekeeper—even for a friend. I had planned so well for Isaac and me. A small country village, space for him to grow in the freedom of anonymity. Now it was all lost. And so close to Dover? This little escapade would not go unremarked.

I buried my humiliation before giving Torrington my own scorching glare. "How do you plan to go about setting this man straight—and the others, my lord?" All at once I had the feeling money would be involved, and a flame lit my tone. "I don't want anything from you, not a solitary farthing if that is why you are here."

He seemed taken aback, his gaze flitting between me and the dismal recesses of the room. The ease surrounding his earlier conversation died away. It was only then I took note of his previous words, *"Continue in my deception."*

I braced myself. "What precisely did you tell your friend?"

He opened his mouth, then faltered. It was as if a shroud dropped between us. His face fell emotionless, his back stiff. The keen light in his eyes became a probing dagger. He managed to say drily, "I gave him the gossip he was so eager to uncover—a plausible reason for my sudden flight into the area, why I had been in your coach and your room unescorted."

My eyes widened.

"I told him I was deeply in love and decided to marry you on a whim by special license but a day ago." He swallowed hard. "And I have no intention of taking back that statement."

His words burned with far more venom than I could have imagined. Slowly, I shook my head, the heavy ropes of truth binding my chest ever tighter. He meant marriage. To me.

Torrington allowed me a quiet moment before his fingers rested on mine. "I am well aware we are strangers, and I am a poor offering for any lady, but I would ask you to entertain the possibility. Please, do not dismiss me out of turn." He lowered his voice. "As my wife, your position in society would be secure, your purse full. Though neither of us set out this morning with any idea of such a ridiculous arrangement, I find on further reflection that a convenient marriage might fit both our needs."

"You seriously mean to continue this, this farce?"

He didn't flinch. "To the signature on the marriage document and beyond. I care a great deal about my country as well as my two daughters. I won't attach another scandal to their names. I've had some time to think on this while you slept. Marriage is the only way to satisfy not only my vow to the crown, but my honor as a gentleman. I would never leave you in such a fix."

My chest felt heavy. "You don't even know me. Rest assured, there will be no scandal, not for you or your family." Brook's utter betrayal came to mind, and I found I could barely look at Torrington's face. "I have already had a child out of wedlock . . . You owe me nothing."

He turned my hand over in his, his focus following the flurry of shadows across my skin. "I am well aware you are unwed, but if you are concerned for your son, please, do not be. There can be no better situation for him than under my protection at Middlecrest Abbey. He will have opportunities there and, with my financial backing, the ability to achieve more than he could anywhere else."

I closed my eyes, picturing little Isaac curled up asleep in the other room and what his life would be like as a housekeeper's son. I could not dismiss Torrington's proposition so easily. My heart squeezed. My response would affect the rest of Isaac's life. But could I do it? Could I marry Brook's brother after their father forbade Brook to marry me? The thought was absurd yet oddly satisfying at the same time. The Radcliff family did owe me, so to speak. How Brook would squirm if he knew.

I narrowed my eyes. After all, I had given up any thoughts of romance or love over the past year. Torrington's emotionless offer was nothing to me, but what of my independence? I'd worked so hard to find a place where I could simply . . . disappear. Could I bear to lose my freedom as well?

Torrington angled his chin. "I can see you working through the advantages and disadvantages of such a match, so let me add that I do believe marriage the optimal decision, not only for Britain, but for us as well. I have two nearly grown daughters at eighteen and sixteen who are in need of a woman to guide them, and more practically, a chaperone to escort them to balls and parties and whatnot."

His tone eased, the rugged confidence returning to his face. He possessed a rather attractive grin and used it to his advantage. "Who better to do so than my wife? I've never been a solitary creature, and with my eldest daughter engaged to be married and my youngest in all likelihood not far behind, I daresay it would be to my benefit to have a person with a well-informed mind residing in my house."

The thought of me inducing what he considered intelligent conversation drew a smile. "I am not a bluestocking, my lord."

"That is not what I intended to imply nor what I desire." His eyes flashed. "Perhaps what I should have said was a refined woman."

So he meant to remind me of my six and twenty years. I was well aware of my age. What he and the rest of the world couldn't possibly understand was that all I really craved was simplicity and solitude.

Silence settled between us, and I was left suddenly aware of my own heartbeat. He rested his arm on the eiderdown, and for a whirling second I imagined what it would feel like to be held by such a man.

I shook myself back to the present. What would he say when he learned of Isaac's parentage? *If* he learned of it. If the gossips were to be believed, Brook had stayed away from Middlecrest Abbey for years.

I cast a sideways glance, the outrageous offer swaying like a pendulum in my mind. What if I agreed?

I forced the questions circling my mind at bay, allowing myself the freedom to fully consider how my life would change—what it would feel like to be near this man daily—to be intimate with him. Though he said it would be a convenient marriage, we would still be thrown together a great deal. He was handsome to be sure and a well-practiced flirt. I'd allowed myself to fall into Brook's arms so easily. A girl in the throes of her first love, I'd believed all of Brook's impassioned declarations. But I was older and wiser now, and Torrington was offering me the exact opposite of what his brother had two years before—security without love.

He didn't bother pretending not to notice me staring at him. He knew quite well I was measuring his worth. He leaned forward, a knowing edge to his voice. "Well?"

With the ghost of a laugh, I turned away, quick to squelch any misplaced attraction. Torrington was not to be trusted, and I was hardly myself at present. It was the late hour, the dipping candlelight, the emotive stillness . . . and my prior relationship with Brook. I suppose some sort of love for him still resided deep within, buried somewhere in the recesses of my mind. I was merely transferring the feelings to his brother. How alike they were, but at the same time so different.

Torrington also seemed determined to shake off the moment. He was all business now, a solicitor enacting a deposition. "Do you think you can manage a decision? Unfortunately, we haven't much time to quibble."

Quibble, indeed. I knit my brow as all kinds of questions popped into my mind. How old was Torrington? I could see the laugh lines branching about his eyes, a cultivated jawline that could only be gained with experience. He rode his horse exceptionally well, his seat as good as any I'd ever seen. He had years on Brook, that I knew, but how many with two nearly grown daughters at home? I cleared my throat. "If I may, what is your age, my lord?"

He eyed me for a moment. "I am not in my dotage, if that is what you think."

"The number, please."

He chuckled. "Will it affect your decision?"

"Possibly."

"Seven and thirty." He seemed to be choosing his next words carefully. "I was married and widowed quite young."

Very young.

"Do not distress yourself." Diversion crept into his words. "I fully intend to provide you with a jointure if in fact you do end up wearing the widow's weeds as you seem to think likely."

I shot a look up at the ceiling. "I didn't mean to imply you were near death."

"No?" He adjusted the ruffle on the dressing gown he'd borrowed as a newfound reticence entered his voice. "Though I do feel I've lived a long time in many ways."

"As have I."

He searched my eyes before looking away. "Then all that is left, my dear, is for you to agree to marry me by special license and pretend to the world that you were swept off your feet by my allure."

I pursed my lips, a curt refusal aching to slip out.

He laughed. "I said pretend, not to actually fall in love with me." He checked himself. "In fact, I am beginning to wonder if you possess such an ability at all after I've tried quite deliberately so far to draw you in."

"Is that what that was?" I dipped my chin. "And yet I am unmoved."

"All I ask is for you to feign affection in public, my dear, and we shall get on quite well with one another. Think of our marriage as a rather pleasant masquerade."

I nearly laughed aloud. "But I will still have to live with you."

"Ah, the one drawback to my little scheme."

"And a big one it is."

He grinned to himself. "I daresay you are correct. My habits may not be to your liking." As if it was entirely natural, his fingers found mine once again. "I enjoy my country estate as well as my girls, so I fear you may see much of me about the house. I love music and dancing and riding . . ." He brushed his thumb across my wrist. "I prefer to find my way home most nights for supper, and I entertain often in the neighborhood. You, of course, would be expected to play hostess. So the question is, my dear, will you jump? Is this a life you might find tolerable?"

A sudden warmth flashed across my cheeks. Could I believe him? The Radcliffs were awfully good at persuasion, the kind that got under one's skin. I daresay Torrington with his easy manner and enticing smile could get anyone to do anything. In all likelihood, he had taken one look at me and assumed where my desires might lie. How little he knew the woman who had grown out of Brook's abandonment. "You ask me to make a life-changing decision at a moment's notice."

"Marriage is life changing. And a decision not to be made lightly. However, it is imperative that you do so quickly, as I have."

I sucked in a breath. "Then you are completely decided—to marry me, just like that?"

"I assure you, any vow I make, I take seriously." His confidence was intoxicating, but he pulled away. "Perhaps it is best if I leave you overnight to come to a decision on your own. I'll return first thing in the morning with the special license."

The wretch. He already knew my answer. "You are awfully confident of what I will decide."

He shot me a wink. "Merely prepared." He crossed the room, but his wide stride ceased at the door as he rested his palm against the doorframe. A laugh emerged.

"What is it now?"

He whirled around to face me, then rested his shoulder against the door. "I cannot leave."

"Why ever not? Just go quickly. No one will be out and about in the hall so late."

"You forget." He folded his arms. "This is also my room . . . *wife.*" He watched me cringe as he strolled back over to the bed, all the while doing his best to hide that maddening smile. I set my jaw, but I was unable to hold a frown as there was something annoyingly appealing about Torrington's engaging yet uncertain countenance.

He pressed the mattress to see how soft it was. "Not bad." His eyes found mine. "Do you think . . . Well, considering our pending arrangement and how blasted tired I am, perhaps you might allow me to make use of the empty side of the bed? In a strictly business way, mind you."

I launched my pillow at his head. "You presume too much, my lord."

A muffled groan escaped as the pillow made contact with his face, then flopped onto the rug. He smoothed his hair back into place. "No bed. Understood." He reached down and swiped the pillow from the floor before cradling it against his chest. "My name is Adrian, by the way. You'd best start calling me that." He raised his chin. "Since we are madly in love and to be married tomorrow. And don't fret, I shall find a spot here on the rug until then." He smiled. "*With* the pillow."

CHAPTER 3

As with so many previous events in my life, my marriage proved the complete opposite of my dreams. Lifeless. Rushed. Apparently Lord Torrington had little imagination where the ceremony was concerned. We simply gathered before lunch the following day in the small back room of the White Lion Inn, surrounded by the shredded remains of stained wallpaper and the lingering scent of ale.

The only attendees were the local rector and his wife. As one would expect, the mood of the service matched the dull ache in my head.

The whole dreadful thing felt more like a wayward dream than reality, with the unsettling thought of Brook never far from my mind. Of course, when the rector turned his piercing glare on me, I said and did what was expected, providing a shaky answer when prompted. It was only later in Torrington's crested carriage that I found myself able to breathe, able to sort through the startling truth that I was indeed married—and to Brook's brother no less.

The atmosphere within the coach held a balance of the cold spring morning and the heavy silence of thought. I suspect we were both a bit dazed by our impulsive decision. Especially Adrian, who sat on the edge of his seat as if he anticipated something.

Finally I heard him sigh. "You look done in."

I forced a weak smile as I adjusted Isaac's sleeping form farther up my chest. "I'm afraid I am."

He leaned forward. "Is it your head that plagues you? Or me?"

I hesitated. "My head . . . among other things." I retreated to the window. What did he expect me to say to that? He only wanted to make light of our situation. Well, it didn't feel light to me.

The persistent March sun flashed in and out of a string of errant clouds and extended its sharp fingers one streak at a time through the glass. My squinted gaze roamed the far hills and beyond the dithered valley in the direction of the home I would not see for some time.

A creak of the bench, and I turned just as Adrian crossed over to Isaac's and my side of the carriage. Gently, Adrian wrestled him from my hands, his eyes softening as he regarded Isaac's rosy cheeks.

"I believe your mama needs a moment to herself. She has been most accommodating up until now." He stole a glance at me as he placed my sleeping son against his far shoulder without so much as a squirm, then smiled. "Don't forget, I've had two of these already." He gave a light chuckle. "But not one of this variety, I'm afraid. I fear I shall have much to learn. Tell me, will my estate ever be the same?"

"Not likely." I allowed a grin but couldn't hide the pain that persisted behind my eyes.

Adrian sighed. "It is unfortunate that we had to leave for Middlecrest today, but when you seemed somewhat recovered earlier, I thought it best . . ."

"Please, don't concern yourself. It was my decision to leave. The doctor declared me fit to travel, and I wanted nothing more than to be rid of that horrid inn. It is not so far to your estate; as I understand, it is close to Plattsdale. I shall do my best to bear the journey."

"Indeed. We should be there within the quarter hour." He motioned down with his head. "In the meantime, my other shoulder is free if you are in need of a *pillow*."

I ignored his jab. If his light snores were to be believed, he'd slept quite well on the thin carpet while I lay awake in misery pondering my fate.

Giving in to fatigue, I choked back my pride and rather awkwardly settled my head on his shoulder while my fingers sought the gold band on my hand. My wedding ring. He bought it this morning from a local craftsman when he left to acquire the special license. It was not a perfect fit, but it would do. "How did you know?"

The tension in his muscles eased. "Know what?"

"That I would agree to this outrageous idea."

He paused to peek at the bundle on his chest. "Isaac." His voice relaxed, his words sounded like the notes in a song. "I could see it in your eyes from the moment I met you. You would do anything for him."

He fell silent, his gaze on Isaac's curly head. "In that, we have much in common. I feel the same about my girls." I felt him turn away from me, and I wished I could see the look on his face, because when he spoke next, his tone had turned grim. "I sent word of our arrival ahead of us to Middlecrest by way of my valet." Again, that hesitation. "I daresay the announcement of our marriage will be something of a shock for them all; nonetheless, I decided it best for everyone to be made aware of our, uh, situation before you arrive. It will be easier that way."

My mouth felt suddenly dry. "I understand." Did he mean our marriage or the fact I had a son?

"My daughters really are good girls. They have simply had a level of freedom in the house that might need some adjustment. Though change is difficult at times, it is also necessary."

My eyes widened. "Oh?" So his daughters were likely spoiled. Our little *arrangement* might be more involved than I originally thought.

He added, "Timing is also a bit delicate at present. You see, a large party has arrived at the house."

"A large party?"

"I should have told you before, but there has been so much to discuss and arrange . . ." He gave a little shrug. "You see, my eldest daughter is to be married at the close of the week."

I sat up to face him, my hands clenched in my lap. "You mean to tell me we've stolen a march on your own daughter?"

He seemed a bit surprised by my reaction, moving to pat Isaac's back to ensure his sleep. "No, not precisely. This is my second marriage, and I assure you, Juliana is as practical as she is serious. She will hardly regard it."

I blinked. "Will she not?" Then lifted my eyebrows. "Perhaps you don't know women as well as they say you do."

He stilled, but he didn't refute my words.

All at once the coach slowed, and what appeared to be a gatehouse loomed large in the side window, blighting out the sun. The conversation fell away as red bricks, weathered by the hands of time, peaked from beneath a curtain of ivy and followed a curved arch and narrow opening. Three rectangular windows faced the road, but the building didn't seem to be occupied as the coach only reduced its speed to traverse the entrance.

Adrian lifted his chin, motioning to the far side of the coach. "Middlecrest Abbey is just beyond."

Thick forest cluttered the window for several seconds before opening up to a lush, rolling landscape generously spotted in wildflowers and small shrubs, which soon flattened to a sheet of manicured lawns. The carriage followed the hedgerow before turning along the base of a small hill, where I got my first unobstructed view of my new home.

Breathtaking. The rectangular, storied structure stood artfully symmetrical, adorned by stretched chimneys and white carved gables, balanced on all sides by the hands of a masterful gardener. My heart deserted me. Perhaps I had been a bit hasty in my earlier assessment of the *arrangement*. A lovely house could certainly help me tolerate a pair of willful daughters.

It took several minutes to navigate the road that led to the front portico, and I kept my eyes fixed to the structure for the whole of the approach. The horses drew us to a staggered halt, and slowly I turned back to Adrian, who seemed pleased by my wonder. He motioned to the door. "Our country seat. I hope you approve."

Regardless of how the marriage had come about, I couldn't help but take a small delight in the word *our*. I'd not had a place of my own since my parents passed on, and the magnificent structure before me was beyond anything I could have imagined. His word choice continued to dance around in my mind as I accepted his outstretched arm and descended the coach's steps one at a time.

Across the front drive, Adrian passed Isaac to a young maidservant, instructing her to put him down to nap, before leading me to the group awaiting us near the front door.

An elderly man dropped his watch fob and stepped forward

to meet us. "My lord, my lady. So good to have you home. Your daughters are awaiting you in the drawing room."

Adrian smiled wide, a sense of pride evident in his eyes. "Thank you, Young." Then to me. "Young here is butler at Middlecrest, and"—he pointed to a thin, fragile-looking creature lurking beside the man—"Mrs. Coombs, our housekeeper. The two of you shall have much to discuss in the days ahead." He nodded to the two of them. "Will you see that Lady Torrington's things are delivered to the blue bedchamber?" Adrian spun toward the door, but I was a step behind and in the perfect position to catch a momentary flash of astonishment glint in the older woman's face.

She started forward, then lifted a quivering hand, her fingers curving and extending like a small claw before retreating to her side. "You cannot mean the *blue* bedchamber, my lord?"

He paused. "As I said."

I felt his arm stiffen as he drew me away, waiting to speak till we'd climbed the steps. "I daresay you will feel much better once you have a cup of tea in your hands." His voice, however, was at odds with the lingering tension. "We won't remain long in the drawing room. My daughters will understand."

His steps were assured, his smile encouraging, but the house-keeper's rapid movement had set me on edge. I narrowed my eyes. The bedchamber in question would have been in all likelihood his first wife's, but why the hesitation from the housekeeper after so many years? Was it me? Did she disapprove already? Though subtle, something lay hidden within that unsteady voice, something more than the awkward arrival of the second wife. A wriggling prickle scaled my back as I gripped Adrian's arm, and the elation I'd felt driving through Middlecrest's gates faded to uncertainty.

Adrian thrust open the large front door and led me into a

squarish room, elongated by white plastered walls and a tall ceiling. A scrolled fireplace ran along one side and flanked a wide, curving staircase. For an instant the house stood motionless, as if holding its breath to appraise me; the atmosphere was so still and hollow that if I called out, I thought I would receive an echo back.

Adrian's deep voice warmed the air. "The drawing room is right this way."

We navigated an extensive hallway ornamented by paintings, white wainscoting, and a long, thick rug before Adrian drew us to a halt and leaned close to my ear.

"I know we are practically strangers, but throughout this entire ordeal I have detected your good sense. A quick greeting and then we shall make our escape."

I nodded, but he didn't release my arm.

"Everything about this situation is uncomfortable, and I know you have been under a great deal of stress, but I need a little more familiarity from you than you were able to manage at the wedding."

I flinched. "Familiarity?"

He turned me to face him, his hands on my shoulders. "If our story is to be believed, I ran away from home a week before my daughter's wedding to marry *you*. I went against years of my own declarations that I would remain a bachelor forever because I have fallen in love with *you*. Don't you see, my daughters know me better than anyone. I cannot do this without your help."

Defeat laced my sigh. "I understand."

"Do you?" His eyes were sharp. "Whoever was transporting that missive is still out there, possibly harboring suspicion of whether I was really in your carriage to marry you. I have put everyone in this house in danger, including you and your son. It is imperative that we convince them this was a love match. Everything hinges on the next few moments."

I met his eyes and my muscles tightened. "You are not alone in this. I will do my part."

His fingers encircled mine, and he whispered a hurried "Thank you" before pushing the door ajar.

A collective murmur christened our entrance, followed by a rustle of movement as the two occupants made their way across the well-lit room. Empty stares accompanied wide eyes as the younger of the girls slid on her spectacles.

The taller one smiled as she came forward and was promptly embraced. "Papa, we are so pleased you have returned."

She slanted a glance at me as she stepped back, and I smiled, expecting her to do so in return. However, she did not lift her tight gaze. Adrian had been right. His daughters were already scrutinizing me. I swallowed hard.

Adrian wasted no time enacting the charade, his natural charm and wide-eyed affection for me springing to life. Like a doting suiter, he kept me close, his hand so tight against mine the warmth tingled my skin. It was all so easy—for him. I belatedly fumbled to produce the loving regard my new husband thought imperative to our safety.

Though I batted my lashes and affected a loving smile, not even the merest acquaintance of mine would have thought my affections real. Yet as I forced myself to look up and meet Adrian's clear blue eyes, my heart betrayed me for one full beat of silence. Goodness, I'd stared at my husband several times in the last two days, but had I ever done so in just this way? Here was the rake Brook had warned me about, the one who could sway any woman's heart. And I had gone off and married him.

Quickly I turned back to the ladies, hoping to appear at ease yet at the same time anxious to meet them. I took a measured breath and allowed my heartbeat to return to a more manageable rate. Why were men always so good at deceit?

A squeeze of my fingers and Adrian motioned to the young lady he'd embraced. "My eldest, Juliana."

Deep-brown curls lay atop a heart-shaped face. She remained poised as she deemed a nod, but her eyes betrayed the hint of discomfort. "Welcome to our home."

I thought the words stilted, yet I was glad she produced some sort of a greeting.

Adrian directed my attention to his other daughter, a chestnut-headed young lady who was waiting rather impatiently beside her sister, bouncing up onto her toes. Now here was the true beauty of the family. Phoebe possessed a happy openness to her nature, and when she responded with an enthusiastic grin, I thought it a genuine one. At least one of the girls seemed pleased by my arrival.

Juliana arched her eyebrows. "We were quite surprised to receive the letter recounting your, uh, attachment." Standing like an adder waiting to strike, she was the natural leader of the two siblings. And if her welcome was to be believed, she did not regard my arrival with the easy equanimity Adrian had thought likely.

On instinct, my own bristles popped to the surface, and I willed them away. "As I am certain your father related, it was a hasty decision, yet one I am quite pleased we made."

Adrian was quick to echo my sentiment. "Yes, it was rather brash . . ." He flashed that smile of his—perfection. Heavens, he could win anyone to his way of thinking with that look. He shrugged. "But you know me."

His hand came to rest on the small of my back, and I tried

again with his daughters. "I do look forward to knowing each of you better in the coming days."

Juliana snapped a sideways look at her sister. "We were just discussing something similar about you, weren't we, Phoebe?"

Phoebe jumped as if she had been pinched, her eyes widening. "Why, yes."

Juliana ran her finger along the arm of the sofa, the bend of her lip contrary to her conciliatory tone. "I daresay you shall be equally pleased to meet my fiancé. The gentlemen are due to return from a short hunting expedition at any moment. And then, naturally, you will need to be introduced to everyone else who has come for the wedding. It is curious that none of my friends knew who you were. At least, they had never seen you at Almack's during the season."

I cringed. I hadn't received vouchers to Almack's in years. Of course, Juliana probably already knew that. I clasped my hands at my waist. Perhaps it was a good thing that Adrian's eldest daughter would be departing at the close of the week. She was shrewd, yes, quite shrewd. Yet she had probably seen very little of the world. In many ways, she reminded me of a younger version of myself. The thought rankled, but I measured my response as my cousin Sybil would have done in the same situation. "I shall look forward to meeting all of your guests."

Adrian touched my arm. "Yes, thank you, Juliana. I shall be pleased to introduce your new mama to the party tomorrow, but as I stated in my letter, she has been in a terrible accident and must not be kept up for much longer."

Adrian helped me to a seat by the fire to await the preparation of my room as Phoebe hurried to bring me a hot cup of tea. My shoulders relaxed as the warm, floral aroma filled my nose, and

I looked about. Middlecrest's drawing room was a pleasant one with muted purple hues and thick brocade curtains. Juliana's selections? Possibly.

The girls found adjoining seats on the long sofa and watched me with a mix of interest and caution until Phoebe sprang to life, agog with questions about our courtship.

"Won't you please tell us where you met?" and "How long did you know one another?" was followed by Adrian's lively version of our "love story." Apparently we met by accident at an inn, and he was immediately smitten—not far from the truth, at least the inn part, but there was no mention of our recent highway robbery.

Phoebe's curls bounced as she spoke. "Is that why you have been sneaking out of the house at all hours, Papa? How romantic."

I looked up at Adrian only to be silenced with a diverting glance. He'd cleverly leaned against the fireplace mantel where he could watch me out of the corner of his eye, his arms folded neatly across his chest. Goodness, he was handsome. I was forced to steady my heart once again. He was amused, that was certain, but I wouldn't allow it.

I raised my voice. "It was not clandestine if that is what you imply."

Adrian coughed back a laugh. "Not at all." Then he sobered all too quickly. "I simply knew how irretrievably lost I was the moment I saw her. Elizabeth and I decided it would be senseless to wait any longer. I knew *I* couldn't wait any longer."

Juliana raised her chin, her next words layered in ice. "Yet the scheduling of this liaison was a bit odd, would you not agree, Papa?" No one could have missed the glance she tossed at my stomach, and I shrank back against the cold chair.

Adrian lowered his arms, the undertone of his voice suddenly callous. "You surprise me, Juliana—"

Footsteps reverberated in the hall, followed by the music of voices and laughter, which saved Adrian from completing his sentence. Juliana's face brightened, and she pushed to her feet. "Never mind, Papa. The gentlemen have returned."

Within seconds, a tall, lanky man strolled through the door, his skin flush from the spring air, his jacket a bit dusty. Before he ever bothered to assess the rest of us, his eyes focused in on Juliana and a bright smile overtook his features. Yet, when he peered over at me, the astonishment in his face echoed my own. "Why, Miss Cantrell! What a surprise to find you here."

He strode across the room, and I rose to greet him. "Giles."

Adrian drew up behind me. "You are already acquainted with my wife?"

"Indeed, I am." Giles's eyes widened, his smile doing likewise. "Your wife? Well, that's famous. Famous, indeed. Miss Cant—er, I suppose I mean Lady Torrington. We know each other quite well. We spent several fine summers together as children. Well, not exactly children, I suppose."

I couldn't stop the heat that stormed into my cheeks. He'd made our innocent play sound as if the two of us were involved somehow. And after what Juliana had implied, I could have hit him. Goodness, it was my cousin Evie he had always cared for, not me. I stole a glance at Adrian, hoping the comment had gone unnoticed, but he had cleverly turned away. Considering Isaac did not have a father publicly, I certainly did not want anyone to think—

Giles took my hand, clearly missing the awkward exchange. "I assume you've heard the news about Miss Radcliff's and my betrothal, but I know nothing of you. Tell me everything. How is Lucius? I've not seen him around town in months."

Great, another person unaware of my brother's absolute betrayal and his arrest for smuggling. My favorite topic of conversation.

I took a deep breath. "Lucius is in Newgate at present."

His mouth fell open. "You don't say."

My shoulders felt heavy. "He was caught smuggling goods to France."

Adrian was no doubt aware of Lucius's misdeeds, or perhaps he noticed my discomfiture, for he routed the conversation at once. Thankfully the discussion turned to Giles and Juliana's wedding, and I was spared the uncomfortable conversation of explaining my brother's fall from grace. It wasn't long until Mrs. Coombs arrived to announce the readiness of my room.

Astute to my headache or more than likely ready for an escape, Adrian begged our leave at once and headed to the door. Giles, however, delayed me near the fireplace. It was almost as if he had been waiting for just the right moment to speak with me without being heard by the others. Juliana had moved to the far side of the room, but I could feel her eyes bearing down on us.

"Elizabeth, I—"

I shook my head. "Tomorrow, Giles. I am not well."

His voice was a mix of necessity and resolve. "Dash it all, Elizabeth. You cannot know what it means to me that you are here. There is something I simply must discuss with you." He paused to look back at the room. "Perhaps you are right. Tomorrow then, but it's terribly important, mind you, and I'm not certain whom I can trust. Juliana is a good girl, but I don't want to burden her so close to the wedding." He dipped his chin. "Your sudden arrival is nothing short of a godsend." He moved in close. "Tomorrow, after the garden party, meet me in the south woods behind the rear wall. Will you promise to come?"

My chest tightened. "But why?"

He shuffled in place as his glare settled on Adrian and the door. "Can't say right now. Just please, tell me I'll find you in the woods after the party." There was a palpable urgency to his words.

I nodded slowly and then quickly as if to reassure him, but a fresh wave of anxiety washed across my arms. As if to appease me like he'd done as a child, he nudged my chin before walking away, leaving me to gather my nerves before facing my new husband.

Slowly, I turned back to Adrian with a smile fixed neatly across my face, but I knew in my heart that whatever Giles meant to tell me I did not want to hear.

CHAPTER 4

The housekeeper was right to cringe at Adrian's room selection. Though the bedding had been replaced and the room
hurriedly gone over, I could sense the depressed state of the blue
bedchamber. It was almost as if the furniture itself had retreated
to the room to be lost and forgotten.

A slender wardrobe hid behind the poster bed, an empty
desk sat to the side, and a settee was angled perfectly beside the
newly lit fire in the fireplace. Yet it all felt cold somehow, as if
hovering beneath the watchful eyes of the powder-blue printed
walls.

I had slept a few hours at least, yet I hardly felt rested after
waking to the distant sound of dogs barking beyond the walls.
The gray haze of late afternoon had taken over the lonely room.
Eventually I rose, crossed the well-laid carpet, and thrust open a
pair of heavy chintz drapes. Far below, Juliana and Giles strolled
the front lawn as Phoebe dutifully trailed behind, busy amusing
two large foxhounds. I watched them until something alerted the
dogs, and the happy group headed out of view.

It seemed a long time before I stepped away from the glass and
retreated into the silence of my thoughts. I had been isolated many

times in my life, but this forced intimacy with a family of strangers did nothing to relieve the tightness in my chest. I moved quickly to tidy my dress and hair. Isaac would be missing me by now.

Earlier in the day, Adrian showed me to my room to rest; however, he had only indicated the direction of the nursery. While I was certain many would be willing to guide me, I set out unescorted down the wide hallway from my room in the family wing.

Floor-length windows lit my path on one side while large paintings of men stared at me from the other. Adrian's family, no doubt, and a stern lot at that. I rounded the corner and heard a cluster of giggles, which to my delight I knew could only belong to my son. I followed the laughter down a narrow corridor, all the way to an open door.

There in the center of the rug stood Isaac, quite pleased to have pushed himself into a standing position, one hand grasping the rim of a tiny table. A young maidservant knelt at his side and smiled.

"I think you look quite smart, Master Isaac. What a wonder you are at only eleven months old." She gave his tummy a tickle, and he laughed once again.

It was only a moment before he saw me lingering in the doorway, and an immense grin spread across his face. He plopped to the floor, crawling as fast as his little knees and pudgy hands would allow. I met him halfway and scooped him into my arms before giving him a flurry of kisses.

"My lady." The maid curtsied then smiled. "Ah, what a good lad you have there. He has been showing me all the things he knows how to do."

"Did you hear that, Isaac? She thinks you are brilliant." I rubbed his nose with my own, drinking in his scent before turning back to the waiting maid. "I must thank you for looking after him so well."

"It has been my pleasure."

"And you are?"

"Forgive me. I'm Miss Alice Barton, my lady."

Isaac appeared rested and quite recovered from our little adventure. He wriggled in my arms, and I set him back on the floor. "Isaac is a busy boy these days. No time for his mama." I took a moment to glance about the room. "Will you be the one who is to look after him every day?"

"Oh yes. Well, only till you employ a head nurse and she agrees to my help, of course."

"I see." Lazily, I ran my finger across a book of poems on the table. "Finding a head nurse will be a difficult process, I'm afraid, for Isaac was quite close to his last one." I sighed. "She was like a member of the family and so good with him."

"I understand. Long ago, my mother was head nurse here at Middlecrest. She was always quite particular with 'her boys,' as she called them."

"You grew up on the estate?"

"I did, your ladyship. And I assure you, there's no other place like it. Life took me away for a short time, and I was never more glad to come back. No other place would feel like home to me."

Tension ebbed from my muscles as I regarded Isaac playing on the floor. My darling boy was in good hands. "You seem to have put Isaac at ease after a difficult time. I thank you for that."

"Isaac and I have had a grand afternoon. In fact, I was just thinking it time to head to the kitchens to arrange his supper. Does he have a schedule you'd like me to follow? It might assist with the transition."

I nodded. "Certainly. Allow me to pen it out for you, as I assume there will be several nursemaids watching over him in the coming days." I started across the room, then hesitated. "You do read, Miss Barton?"

"Oh, yes, my lady."

"Wonderful. Have you a quill pen?"

She scurried past a slew of Isaac's luggage to a desk before motioning me over to the seat. I settled in the chair before reaching into Isaac's little brown bag where I knew I had a few pieces of scratch paper. Securing a loose page, I took prodigious care to pen out Isaac's daily routine.

Waking time, eating time, nap time, playtime, bedtime.

Miss Barton watched as I finished the last line with eight o'clock. "There now. Where shall we put it?"

She scanned the room. "Oh dear. I've never been a nursery maid before. Wherever you think is best."

I followed her searching gaze to a blank space on top of a dresser and left the schedule there. "This shall do nicely. It will keep everyone informed of my expectations."

"Yes, my lady, and don't you worry. I'll do my best to see the little master taken care of."

"Thank you, Miss Barton. It is a great relief to leave him in your capable hands." I turned to the door, all too aware I couldn't hide in the nursery forever, not on my first day at Middlecrest, not when Adrian and I had so much to discuss and there were people I had to meet.

My stomach clenched at the thought. How many guests had

come for the wedding? And more importantly, how many would I have to deceive?

✲

"But what shall we do?"

I heard Phoebe's gentle voice from the hall, a few steps before the sitting room doorway. Her question was immediately followed by Juliana's swift words.

"There is nothing to be done now. Father made his choice without even consulting us. I suppose we must live with the ramifications. Well, *you* must live with them. I have never been happier to be departing in a few days."

I stood in the shadow of the wall as the ugly truth dawned. It seemed Adrian's daughters had gathered for a meeting about their new mama. I knew full well I shouldn't remain hidden, but I desperately needed to know what I would be dealing with in the coming weeks—even if their words proved painful.

Phoebe spoke next, her voice much more conciliatory. "But with Papa in love, I don't believe he would bother asking what we thought. After all this time, don't you think his sudden attachment romantic?"

"Ha." Juliana gave a harsh laugh. "Is that what you think? That they are in love? I don't believe it for a second. Did you see the way she flinched before taking his arm? I would never act that way around Giles. I cannot help but think something is going on that we are not aware of."

So, I had indeed failed Adrian's request. Figures. Intimacy with him would not come easily. Not after Brook.

Phoebe piped up. "Perhaps she is only shy. I thought—"

43

"Not everyone is a mouse like you, darling," Juliana said. "And I don't find her the least bit shy. Conniving more like."

"Why do you say that?" I could hear the disappointment in Phoebe's voice.

Juliana's tone dropped as if she spoke between her teeth. I had to take a step forward in order to make out what she was saying. ". . . that son of hers. I have it on good authority that she has never been married."

I pressed my eyes shut, my shoulders heavy with the mistakes of my past, waiting for the inevitable condemnation. I'd heard it a thousand times before. Trollop. Wanton. Bird-of-paradise. The names I'd been called were never far from *decent* people's lips.

Phoebe broke the silence. "Then who do you suppose is the poor dear's father?"

"Wouldn't we all like to know?" I heard light footsteps within the room, and Juliana began again. "I thought it only right to ask Giles that very question this afternoon, but he is uncertain. She's had several seasons, mind you . . . and several admirers. I don't know what Papa was thinking bringing a woman like that into this house. The scandal will surely follow her to Middlecrest. I'm only glad everything between Giles and me is firmly settled. But for you . . ."

Phoebe's voice shook. "Are you implying that Father's marriage might have an impact on my upcoming season?"

Juliana's answer was sharp and quick. "That is precisely what I'm saying. How could it not when there is so much more you don't even know? Giles's mother swore me to secrecy, but I daresay you should be made aware of the whole. You are the one who must live with it, in any case. I would be remiss as a sister to withhold such vital information." She paused. "What I am about to tell you does not leave this room. Do you understand?"

I tipped my head back against the wall. Fanny Harris, Giles's mother, was at Middlecrest as well and already running her wide mouth. How different she had always been from her kindhearted son. My feet itched to flee down the hall, to take the first stagecoach bound for Dover. How could I live in Adrian's house knowing what his daughters had decided about me?

My toes curled in my half boots as Juliana's next words splashed a fresh dose of embarrassment and disgust over my wounded pride. Yet what did she say that wasn't true?

"You heard earlier that our new mama's only brother is a prisoner in Newgate, having been caught smuggling goods to France. As if that wasn't bad enough, years ago their illustrious parents died a pair of debtors, leaving their children to attempt to gamble their way back into solvency."

One gasp, then a second echoed, each hitting my ears like a musket ball. Slowly, I retreated from the door, nursing the emotional wound that never seemed to heal. The ghosts of my past had set up residence in my new home before I even arrived. Would I ever be rid of them?

I crept back up the grand staircase and stumbled down the hall of the family wing, certain that time alone would prove the best medicine for my battered soul. Steps from my closed doorway I felt the callous eyes of the corridor's darkened corners, followed by a sudden puff of shifting air. A flash of unease filled my chest, and I cast a quick glance behind me. Had someone followed me? Surely not. The conversation I overheard had only set me on edge, nothing more. I looked over my shoulder once again. No one was there.

Fighting the niggling fear that I was being watched, I thrust open my bedchamber door and escaped into the sanctity of my room—yes, *my* room. The wretched blue bedchamber with its sparse furniture and lonely walls. I collapsed against the door's hard wood, realizing too late there was really no escape from my mind.

I pressed my hands to my face. What on earth had possessed me to agree to Adrian's preposterous proposal in the first place? Isaac's future could never be protected at Middlecrest, not even when I bore the Torrington name.

Once again, I'd made a terrible, terrible mistake, and my innocent, wonderful little boy would pay the consequences.

CHAPTER 5

I begged leave of supper that night, claiming a headache. Although the dull pain still lingered, it had faded considerably and was certainly not my sole reason for avoiding Adrian's visitors. No, if I intended to find my place at Middlecrest, I had to be honest with myself: Juliana's cutting words and the gossip likely to follow had instigated the tray in my room.

I ran a finger along the brocade pattern of the settee. Naturally, Adrian's daughters were suspicious of me, considering my sudden arrival and Isaac's unknown parentage. But it was all too apparent now that my cousin Sybil had sheltered me from the full censure of society regarding my family's transgressions. That addition to Juliana's argument only deepened the scar Brook conveniently left exposed.

I rose from my seat by the fire and walked to the window before parting the heavy drapes and revealing an already blackened night. Beyond the recessed glass, darkness lay thick over the rolling hills as a touch of moonlight glinted off the silhouette of treetops—the motionless beauty of the countryside at rest.

Flickering in the glass, the remains of my evening candle rendered my faint reflection visible—my lifeless hair, my lean face. I tucked a stray lock behind my ear. How much I had changed in so short a time. The radiance of my last London season came to mind. Brook had declared me his personal ray of sunlight dropped from heaven only for him. He had always been a master of flattery. Too bad his words proved empty.

I clasped my hands together and closed my eyes, my thoughts darting unbidden back to the present and the realities of my new life. Adrian had promised to return directly after supper. It would not be long before I heard his steady knock at the connecting door.

Adrian. His name was but a whisper on my breath. He was a stranger to me in every way. My gaze drifted to the door beside the fireplace that led to our shared sitting room. The distracted gentleman who'd left me in a rush to tend his family might not be the same one who returned.

I tightened the ribbon around my dressing gown. At the inn I had been shocked to find him alone in my room. I was quite recovered now. I tugged the drapes closed, daring the uncertain depths of the night to unnerve me, but my fingers tarried on the thick fabric. From the start Adrian had labeled our arrangement a convenient one, yet I could not stop a chill from sliding across my shoulders. What if the Baron of Torrington intended more? He had no heir after all, only the two girls. Many would expect a woman in my position to oblige him. I snapped my attention once again to that closed doorway, and all at once the room seemed smaller . . . warmer . . . far more unfamiliar.

Restless, I stood and paced the available space, my heartbeat driving my furtive steps. It wasn't as if I knew nothing of such things. However, I had been so deeply in love with Brook at the time. Then . . . disaster.

Movement sounded through the adjacent wall and arrested my steps. Adrian had returned. I whirled first to the fire, my eyes fixed on the flickering flames, then back to the settee. Surely he would merely pop in to check on me before taking himself off to bed—if he came at all. I had a headache for goodness' sake. Yet we *were* newly married.

I'd hoped the severity of the accident and my injury would quiet the servants for a few days, but Juliana's maid had worn an infuriating smirk when she left me to dress for the night.

Minutes passed as hushed voices rose and fell beyond the wall, followed by a set of footsteps, then an uncomfortable silence. Adrian's valet must have departed. I straightened, moving only to ensure my robe was just as I thought it should be.

A knock and I jumped. The connecting door latch popped open. For a breathless moment, I thought the wretch intended to enter before I'd had a chance to respond, but Adrian only whispered through the crack. "Are you awake, Elizabeth?"

I cleared my throat, concealing my throbbing nervousness with placid disinterest. "Why yes, do come in."

The door swung fully open, but Adrian lingered in the shadows of the threshold. I angled myself defensively toward the fireplace, the embarrassment of the situation fighting to overcome me. How I wished I could read his face so I might know where I stood.

"Are you well enough for a visit?" His voice was warm. Slowly, he advanced into the firelight where I was momentarily relieved to see a look of concern. But was it real or forced? I wasn't certain. He'd discarded his jacket, waistcoat, and cravat, leaving his white shirt loose at the waist. Of course he should be at leisure in his own home. I was the intruder.

The air in my chest felt strangely thin and I crossed and un-crossed my feet before forcing myself to meet his eyes. "My head-ache is much improved. Thank you."

He cast me an altogether too attractive smile but said nothing as he secured a poker from its iron holder near the fireplace and jabbed the smoldering logs. The fire leapt on cue, sending a wave of heat rolling into the room, but it did little to squelch my tingling nerves.

After a brief glance at the door, Adrian turned back to the grate and pressed his free hand against the mantel. His thin shirt revealed broad shoulders and a muscular back. I wondered how long he meant to stand there facing away from me when he sud-denly turned, a curious look about his eyes. He relaxed his jaw as if he meant to address me yet chose instead to make his way over to me and ease down onto the rug, his back against the settee.

I'm not certain why Brook flashed into my mind at that mo-ment, but I was fairly certain I'd never seen him relax in such a way, let alone command a room with little more than a look.

"I am glad to hear you've recovered." Adrian propped up one leg on which to rest his elbow before angling to look at me. "And I'm happy to report the deed is done. I daresay we shocked them all. Mrs. Harris gave a rather credible gasp, but after I assured the table of my utter devotion, the astonishment passed." He patted the floor next to him, a smile tugging his lips. "Why don't you join me down here? It's a great deal warmer closer to the fire."

Warmer indeed. My eyes widened, but I didn't move. Not yet.

"You needn't look at me like that. I only wish to talk. We have much to discuss, and I'd rather not do so with you glowering over me like the Queen of England."

I stared down at the empty space on the rug. Adrian was

simply trying to ease me out of my reticence, nothing more. If only he wasn't so infuriatingly handsome, I might have a moment to think.

He laughed as he seized a cushion. "Surely I'm not all that repulsive." He lowered his head in mock condescension, then grasped my hand.

Glaring at him with faint amusement, I shifted to the edge of the settee. "I suppose I shall do as you wish this time, but only because I find this settee rather uncomfortable." There. I angled my chin. I could play his game if need be. Considering I'd survived three London seasons with more fortune hunters than eligible gentlemen, I only needed to keep my wits about me.

Careful of my robe, I slid down beside him on the floor, aware all too quickly that he had coaxed me into a distinct disadvantage. My irritating husband waited only long enough for me to adjust my seat before he extended his arm across the cushions behind my shoulders.

"You know, I believe I am in complete agreement about this horrid piece of furniture. Never could stand the thing. It shall be gone as soon as it can be arranged."

I blinked. "Swift justice here at Middlecrest, I see. A lump here or there and out the door you go. I hope I am not so easily tossed aside."

He eyed me but gave no response, instead motioning into the air with his fingers. "Feel free to make whatever alterations you wish. Little has been done to this room since my wife passed sixteen years ago. It's about time someone freshened it up a bit. In fact, I'll be sure to send Mrs. Coombs to discuss the particulars with you in the morning."

It took great effort not to sound defensive. "Thank you. I

should very much like to speak with Mrs. Coombs regarding several things, but please do not send her to me first thing tomorrow. With Juliana's wedding in a few days, I am in no rush to make further disruptions."

Adrian smiled to himself. "Now why do I find that interesting?" A flicker of light drew his gaze to the ring on my hand. "Somehow I'd imagined you commandeering my entire household as soon as possible."

I cocked an eyebrow. "Shows how little you know me."

His hand went to the back of his neck. "I daresay you are more than aware I know nothing about you." He offered a smile and the hint of a dimple danced in and out of his cheek. "Yet I continue to get the feeling you've heard something of me."

The bend in his voice made me look up. "Surely you cannot be ignorant of what the matchmaking mamas have to say about you in London. You've been a bachelor for some time . . . and a busy one at that."

He chuckled as if we were old friends, but I wondered if I detected a trace of unease. "Yes, and gossip in London can be rather vicious. Wouldn't you say?"

My heart constricted. Was he insinuating something about me and Brook?

He touched my hand. "Listen, if I'm to keep up our love story around the household, I'll need something more with which to entice their waiting ears. Believe me, I was hard-pressed to do so tonight at supper. In fact, my mother-in-law, Mrs. Ayles, who also lives here at Middlecrest, gave me the oddest sense she didn't believe one word I said." He leaned in close. "It is imperative I know a few niceties about you—prior loves, that sort of thing—for the masquerade, of course."

Heat filled my cheeks, and I drew my hands into my lap. If Adrian meant to allude to gentlemen in my past, there had been no one besides Brook.

"There's not all that much to tell really."

"All right. What about your family? I don't know much about the Cantrells."

"There aren't many of us left. My parents are both deceased; my brother is locked away awaiting transport to the colonies, which you already know."

"I confess that I do." A line crossed his forehead. "But not the details of his arrest. If we were truly in love, you would no doubt share such things with me." He paused. "I do realize the situation must have been quite difficult for you."

I took a long breath. "Yes, it was, but not for the reasons you may think."

"What then?"

I fidgeted with my robe's satin ribbons. "As you can imagine, Lucius had high hopes I would marry well. Our parents left us so very far in debt, you see, but then he learned about Isaac. It was my unfortunate situation that made him desperate. He took risks I don't think he would have otherwise. Smuggling was just so blasted lucrative. I'm afraid he got in too deep with his good friend, the late Lord Stanton. Do you know of him?"

"A bit. I know he was exposed after his death as a rather infamous French spy. If I remember correctly, Curtis never did completely uncover that network of informants, certainly not at the highest level. I heard Stanton may even have had people in Parliament."

"I wouldn't know. Curtis and Sybil rarely discussed such things with me. I had my own troubles."

Silence fell between us until Adrian nudged my arm. "Anything else? About you, I mean. I shall need a great deal more than your brother's sad story, or I'll be found out before the week's up. You see, you've yet to meet my mother-in-law. She can be rather persistent. I need specifics."

"Specifics?"

"You know, something personal."

Caught in one of those unreadable looks of his, I shifted on the rug. What was he fishing for? "Well, I adore horses and the color green."

He raised his eyebrows for a long moment, then laughed aloud. "That's the best you can come up with for your husband?" He tipped his head back against the settee's hard cushion. "I'd hoped for more than simple drawing room conversation that I could pick up anywhere. It goes against my nature, but I see I shall have to pry." He cast me a wary glance, but I could not have anticipated his next words. "Tell me about Isaac."

My mouth slipped open. "I suppose Juliana spent the evening guessing."

He pulled back. "Guessing what?"

"Who his father is, of course."

Adrian froze for a moment, then managed a sharp breath. "First of all, I would never allow her to do so. Convenient or not, if this marriage is to have the least chance of success, we must support one other—in everything. I have been forthcoming about my spy work, and I've agreed to provide for the boy. Why keep me at a distance?" He paused as if lost for words. "Rest assured, my question about Isaac's parentage has nothing to do with spreading gossip or relieving some misguided curiosity."

He added gently, "As I said before, I would like to make a go of it for him. I need to know what obstacles might arise. Just me. No one else."

I sat there for some time, my fingers worrying the fringe on my dressing gown, but I could not bring myself to give any sort of answer. Regardless of Adrian's assumed sincerity, it was far too great a risk. My allegiance would always be to Isaac. His very future lay in my hands. I didn't know how Adrian would react if he learned Isaac was his nephew. And moreover, it would affect how Adrian interacted with Brook. They were brothers, after all. They would inevitably speak or write at some point. I would do anything to keep from enticing Brook back home.

Far too much was at stake—too many buried hurts that would do no one any good if the truth came to light.

Adrian moved to still my restless fingers. "Clearly someone hurt you."

I drew away. "Yes, and I would rather not relive it." Particularly with him.

We sat in silence a moment longer, Adrian tapping a finger against his knee, before he finally leaned forward and faced me. "We all have demons in our pasts we'd rather keep locked away. Since the world remains ignorant of this man's identity, I can only assume he abandoned you to your fate."

I nodded. Tears burned, but I would not allow a single one to fall. "I have no intention of ever seeking out Isaac's father again, which I assure you will be best for my son."

Adrian hesitated, then nodded. The twist in his voice told me far more than I wanted to hear. He didn't entirely trust me. "At present, I won't press you any further. You may keep your secret, but promise me this: if a time ever comes that I should know Isaac's parentage, you will tell me. Understand?"

I agreed far more quickly than I should have, relieved to feel the tension ebbing from my shoulders. In all likelihood Isaac could be a grown man with his own family before Brook ever returned to Britain. I managed a whispered "Thank you" before looking away.

Adrian went on. "There is another thing we need to discuss." He took a deep breath. "I do not relish the task, but I must write Curtis first thing in the morning. I cannot be certain how he will receive the news of our hasty marriage. He might very well call me out."

"Don't be ridiculous."

"Perhaps if you were to enclose a note as well . . ."

"Naturally, Curtis will be concerned by such a rash decision on my part. I suppose a letter from me would be helpful."

Adrian ran his finger along the edge of the rug. "And what will you tell him?"

My gaze fell and lingered on the fire's thick flames. "That I am happy."

I felt Adrian's arm tighten. "I understand how this whole arrangement must be difficult for you. Goodness knows, I've experienced the same concern and regret, but I also recognize how necessary it continues to be, how vital it is that we convince the household of our undying affection. We've begun a dangerous journey that we must see through to completion. However uncomfortable, Britain needs us. I've already had further instructions regarding the missing document."

I too sat up. "Oh?"

He met my movement with a swift turn. "Remember, no one here at Middlecrest knows of my dealings with the government. I've kept them all in the dark for their own safety, even my girls. I must trust you to do so as well." His face betrayed a layer of distress, but the concern lifted when our eyes met. "You know, it is of some relief to finally share this side of me with another person—to speak of my dealings out loud without fear. I've been isolated in my work up until this point, and it has been something of a lonely road."

I paused to digest his words, understanding the heart of his difficulty in a completely different yet all too familiar way. Of course, there would be no similar liberation for me. I gave him a wan smile. "Rest assured. I shall help in whatever way I can, and I promise to guard your secret."

Adrian cast me a fleeting look, the word *secret* likely reminding him of the mystery of Isaac's father. He chose not to press me any further, however.

"Thank you. I intend to keep you clear of this blasted trouble as much as I can. You have done a great deal to aid the cause already. Just continue to work on pretending to love me, and I'll take care of the rest." He inched closer, diversion slipping into his voice. "We could practice, you know."

I shrank back and managed a choked, "Practice what?"

"Oh, I don't know—you could tell me how utterly handsome I am, fall into my arms, swoon when I whisper your name. You know, the normal bit."

I couldn't help but shake my head and laugh. Who had I married—Don Juan?

For a breathless moment I thought I might be grabbed and thoroughly kissed, but Adrian didn't move.

"All joking aside, I have been informed by the admiralty that they believe the missive has not been delivered to the courier who was to take it on to the coast, which must mean it is still in the area."

He paused, allowing me a moment to process his words. "We

have a local informant, who has uncovered intelligence that the transfer will take place under the guise of Juliana's wedding. We've long suspected the traitor resides somewhere nearby. It would make perfect sense for him to use the wedding party to dispose of sensitive information with so many people in one place. If I can maintain my anonymity, the French spies will have no idea they are walking into a trap."

"Won't that be dangerous for the household?"

"No more so than usual, but I agree the situation is not ideal. I would prefer to apprehend him somewhere besides Middlecrest. The risk this man is taking tells me he must be frantic to dispose of the document." Adrian stood and assisted me to my feet. "Considering we know neither when nor where this man will appear, there can be no headache for you tomorrow, my dear. You have a garden party to attend. I am not certain who has been invited, but once again, the ladies must be utterly convinced of our affection for one another. I don't want anyone the least suspicious of my sudden marriage."

My shoulders sank. "And where will you be?"

"Shooting with Giles. They've decided to get up another hunting party." As if he knew I'd overheard his daughters' conversation earlier in the day, he went on. "Can you manage with Juliana and the others?"

I angled my chin. "Certainly." I was no simpering miss; I'd been handling people like Juliana for years.

"Good. I knew you had backbone the moment you ripped off my mask in the carriage. Perhaps this masquerade of ours might work out for the best." He peeked behind him to the connecting door, a slow smile making its way across his face. "What do you think? Have I stayed long enough?"

"Long enough?"

"To satisfy the servants, of course. I'm afraid you shall have to bear my company in the evenings for the next few days." He shrugged as he walked to the connecting room door, then cast a quick glance at the bed. "Of course, it would be even better if they found me there in the morning. I could always—"

"Out." My sudden response surprised even me.

He offered an irritating final shrug, managed an "As you say," and walked through the connecting door without looking back.

My new husband was proving to be nothing but a handsome, exasperating tease. I shook my head, unable to keep the picture of his keen smile from forming in my mind.

Oh, no. Never again would I fall for a member of the Radcliff family. I was far too shrewd for that. Brook and Adrian were savvy when it came to women, but I had something far more valuable—experience.

CHAPTER 6

The morning of the garden party dawned light and fresh. An artist could not have painted a prettier picture of Middlecrest in the throes of spring loveliness. The lush greenery was blessed overhead by puffy white clouds and the occasional burst of sunlight that warmed the gentle breeze. Flowers filled the air with a sweet fragrance, as they popped into view along the hedgerows. The event stood poised to be a glorious affair, one I would have adored at any other time.

Tents had been erected on the lawn, tucked back at the corners by pink and white ribbons. Liveried servants slipped effortlessly in and out of the various groups of ladies, who stood chattering with enthusiasm, smiles fixed across their faces. But none were as brilliant as Juliana, who set up her court in the center of them all, her parasol perched nicely on her shoulder.

I inhaled a long breath, conscious of how tenuous my role remained. I looked back at the house, wishing I could have brought Isaac down with me. His happy laugh soothed so many awkward situations, but I knew he would not be welcome. No, Miss Barton would find a quiet spot for him to play away from all the excitement and knowing looks. I had to face this moment alone.

Phoebe must have seen my advance down the winding path, as

she drew up beside me, gasping. "A glorious day, is it not, Mama? I've never seen its equal around these parts." She frowned at my odd look. "Do you mind me calling you that? Papa insisted, and I do like it."

It seemed Adrian had already been busy. I took her arm, smoothing over my misplaced shock. "I am more than pleased to have you call me Mama."

The tension in her face relaxed. "Since you did not come by the breakfast room, Papa also tasked me with introductions. He's afraid Juliana may be less than attentive, and there are several ladies waiting to meet you."

Ogle me, more like. I forced a smile. "I shall be glad of your assistance. And your father is right. Juliana shall be far too busy to worry with me—as it should be."

Phoebe chuckled. "I daresay Juliana is too preoccupied with Giles to think of anyone else at all. Giles this and Giles that. You'd think he was in line for the throne."

"Giles is a good man, and I am glad to know he has found a wife who adores him."

Phoebe's smile froze in place. "Yes, well . . . Oh look. There is Grandmama. You must meet her at once. She has been asking about you incessantly since you arrived."

I had been informed by Juliana's maid that Adrian's mother-in-law, Mrs. Ayles, had been at Middlecrest since her daughter's death. With no other family, Adrian insisted she make her home with them. As I made my way over to her chair, I couldn't help but wonder how my sudden presence might affect such an arrangement.

A woman of advanced years, Mrs. Ayles was plump around the middle, yet bone thin in her arms. She was seated in the shade beneath the large tent, her arthritic fingers gripping an ebony cane, her hooded eyes withdrawn beneath a sallow brow. Her lips sank into a grimace, which only dipped farther upon Phoebe's enthusiastic introduction.

Wavering, she lifted her head. "So you caught yourself a husband at last. Convenient I'd say."

The last part was mumbled, but I had no trouble deciphering her meaning.

She swung her cane back and forth as if it were a pendulum. "I daresay more than a few young ladies shall be in quite a pet when they hear the news." A bubbling laugh escaped her lips before she swallowed it. "Each one all but certain to be announced as the next Baroness."

My arms felt heavy. I'd not been to London for the season in years. Had Adrian a court of admirers? "I don't know what you mean."

Her wrinkled brow shot up in a challenge. "Don't you?"

So there was to be no pretense between us. Mrs. Ayles was not pleased I was here to take her late daughter's place. Luckily I was saved an answer to her pert question by Giles's mother, who ambled into our little circle, adding a huff. Almost as an afterthought, she met my eyes. "Why, Lady Torrington, what a surprise your arrival has been."

"Mrs. Harris." I nodded, choosing to ignore her waspish glare. Mrs. Harris and I were well acquainted. Of course, she'd chosen to spend my last season in London ignoring me. She had always been an opportunist, and Adrian must have been quite convincing at supper the previous night, for she eased the tone of her voice.

"Are you all settled in at Middlecrest?"

Mrs. Ayles's face blanched before she looked away. I directed my answer to Mrs. Harris. "Yes, all settled." Then I motioned to Juliana, standing a few yards away from us and happily entertaining a group of young ladies. "But we are here for Miss Radcliff today. If you will excuse me, I would like to give her my good wishes." I nodded. "Glad to meet you, Mrs. Ayles. Good day, Mrs. Harris."

I took a few steps into the sunlight, intent on shaking off the chill the elder guests had bestowed before approaching Juliana. The sudden pounding of horse's hooves, however, jerked my attention to the horizon and charged my nerves once again.

What on earth? A horse was approaching—and fast. The playful voices around me vanished into hushed silence as each person turned to confront the rider streaking like a black bolt of lightning across the near rise. In only a second it was clear the man had lost control of the animal, and the pair was barreling straight toward us.

Juliana's strangled voice rang out seconds before the wild beast crashed headfirst into the furthermost table. I realized the rider was not in the saddle as I'd first thought, but rather draped precariously to the side, his foot trapped in a stirrup. Nothing but a limp doll, the dangling rider bounced back and forth as the horse bolted first one direction then another, the man's arms flailing like loose ribbons in the wind.

A motionless second passed as we all stood in disbelief before the lawn erupted into chaos. Ladies screamed; chairs crashed to the ground. Mrs. Ayles had barely pushed to her feet when the animal plowed through the middle of the party, thrashing and covered in sweat. Fixed to the spot, I stared at the limp passenger, who repeatedly banged against the horse's powerful flank. My stomach turned as I caught a glimpse of the man's face. Giles!

Desperate, I raced forward, my heart thundering. Such a

beating could not be endured for long. Oh, Giles! Uncertain what to do, yet equally certain I must do something at once, I snatched a napkin from a nearby table and turned to the horse, my arms extended. It was not difficult to feel the horse's panic. He only wanted a calming hand. Foam drenched his black coat. He tossed his head, but little by little he allowed me to hedge him into the corner of the tent.

My steps turned cautious as tears pricked my eyes. Half on the horse, half on the ground, Giles's twisted body lay stock-still. Phoebe drew up beside me, and I whispered for her to be careful. Horses could sense fear and there was enough commotion behind me to send him bolting once again.

"Easy, boy." My voice came out shaky as I tried not to focus on Giles's inert body and what it meant for my friend. I grasped an apple from a nearby table and held it out.

"It's all right, Midnight." Phoebe too edged forward, and at the last second gripped the horse's reins as he hesitantly reached for the apple.

More horse hooves pounded in the distance, and we both looked up. Phoebe flew to grip the bridle with her other hand as the riders bore down on the lawn, and I turned to Giles's lifeless form. It took all my strength to disengage his warped boot and ease his body onto the grass. My heart sank as I knelt and touched his chest. Carefully, I closed his eyes before looking over my shoulder for Mrs. Harris, then belatedly at Juliana.

She was but a few steps away, terror written across her face. Like a frightened doe, she met my troubled look and stumbled backward. She already knew—her fiancé was dead.

A terrible wail bubbled out of her throat, greeting the men as they swung from their saddles and rushed into the morose group gathered near the central tent. Mrs. Harris's reaction was just the opposite; shock stole her voice, then transformed her face. Someone helped her into a chair. Another second and I was fairly certain she would have swooned.

Adrian pushed his way through the crowd before dropping to his knees at my side and slinging his hat to the ground. He shot a look at me.

"He simply slumped forward in the saddle, then tipped over." His fingers found Giles's forehead. "Oh, Giles. I cannot believe it." He motioned for a servant to take the horse, then looked back at me. "The sudden movement must have spooked Midnight. There was no time to react—no time to help him."

Another young man around Giles's age knelt beside us, his curly blond hair wet with sweat. "Shall I send for the doctor?" I noticed a slight deformity on the man's left hand.

Adrian shook his head. "It is too late, Ewan." He paused and Juliana's sobs filled the uncomfortable silence behind us. "But others might need his assistance."

The gentleman nodded. "I'll send someone at once."

I managed to stand, disbelief numbing every muscle in my body, and backed away, clutching Phoebe's hand. "We should see to Juliana and Mrs. Harris."

Phoebe struggled to speak. "Y-yes."

Adrian stopped me as I turned to leave. "I shall be by to speak with you as soon as I can get away."

There was a question in his voice, and I whirled back to Giles's still form. It had been an accident, right? He fell from his horse, nothing more. Why did Adrian sound so puzzled, so wracked with . . . guilt? Did he have something to do with the accident? Surely not. But . . . Giles did look strange. I refocused my attention, taking in what I hadn't noticed before. His skin had an almost purple tint to it, his mouth was open, and his tongue—

"I need you to go to Juliana. I will be there as soon as I can." Adrian's hand pressed my arm. "Elizabeth, you must trust me." His voice held a pleading tone. "It will do you no good to memorize something so horrific."

I shook my head. I had seen it now and could do little to rid my mind of the terrible truth. Adrian was right to be disturbed. Something had indeed happened to Giles—something other than a simple fall from his horse. A quiver scaled my back, the hairs on my arms prickling beneath Adrian's strong fingers.

Why I kept standing there, I did not know. But Adrian allowed me a quiet moment. Giles had been a good friend to me.

Eventually, instructed by her father, Phoebe urged me from the tent, across the lawn, and into the house. There we found Juliana collapsed on the sofa, a small party gathered around her unconscious form. The gentleman Adrian had called Ewan waved a bottle of smelling salts beneath her nose.

Though several years younger than Adrian, Ewan had a sort of wisdom in his eyes. He cast me only a cursory glance as I approached, then bent back over Juliana.

"Juliana. Juliana."

He used her Christian name.

Another whiff of the salts and Juliana coughed, her eyelids fluttering open. She lay like a porcelain doll for a breathless moment before her face scrunched up and the tears returned.

"Giles! My darling Giles! He cannot be gone. He cannot. I forbid it!"

"Shhh." Ewan took her hand.

"No!" Her voice was frantic. She thrust herself into a sitting position. "He knew, I tell you. He had to. Something was wrong—yesterday."

Ewan seemed taken aback. "What do you mean?"

She pointed at me. "You. Tell them. I saw him whispering with you."

All eyes in the room shot my direction. "I-I have no idea what she is referring to."

Juliana shrieked and slammed back down, pawing at the sofa, thrashing her head back and forth. "Giles. My darling, Giles. He cannot have left me."

Phoebe touched her sister's head. "She's hysterical. Have we anything to give her to calm her nerves?"

The room offered a collective shrug, and I stepped forward. "Where is Mrs. Coombs?"

The willowy housekeeper wafted out of the shadows. "Yes, my lady?"

Irritated she had not offered her services sooner, I spoke a bit more forcefully than I intended. "Have you any soothing syrup?"

"Not at present. Although, I could mix some hartshorn and water to provide her some relief."

"That will have to do for now." I turned to Ewan. "Miss Radcliff should be in her room. Would you be so kind as to carry her to the first floor to await the doctor?"

There was a lightness about his movements, a fastidious respect as he lifted her into his arms. When he turned to the door, his soft gaze fell on her distraught face. My steps faltered.

Who exactly was this Ewan? And why had he come to the wedding?

It took the length of an hour to mollify Juliana into a restless quiet, though she didn't truly settle until the doctor had given her a dose of laudanum. I was grateful to Mrs. Ayles for attending Mrs. Harris during the same time.

Phoebe and I remained at Juliana's bedside until she finally slept, the both of us too tired and ill-affected to rally much conversation. She never asked what Juliana meant in the drawing room when she pointed to me. That sudden accusation, however, had already taken root in my mind.

Giles *had* intended to tell me something—something important—right after the garden party. I could still see his face in the drawing room the previous day. He had been happy, yet edgy, and relieved to find me in residence. But what had he meant to say? Could it have something to do with the French spies and the danger Adrian had brought upon the house?

Giles had always been so easygoing, so incredibly affable, and more than anything else, a strong supporter of Britain—his grandfather was a British general. How could Giles possibly be involved? I couldn't imagine him spying for either government. He was just so—how to put it? So incredibly honest.

I wiped a tear from my cheek as I traversed the hall by my room. Giles was a good friend in my youth. If only my cousin Evie had given him half a chance, all this might have been avoided.

I heard Isaac's lively babbling before I crested the door to the nursery. After an emotional hour with Juliana and Phoebe, I'd intended to seek the solitude of my room but at the last moment turned to the nursery instead. I needed to feel Isaac's soft curls.

Miss Barton held him propped on her lap, playing with some wooden blocks on a table. She smiled as I moved into view, then her smile faded.

"My lady. Can it be true? Was there really a commotion at the garden party?"

I took a seat at her side. "Far more than that, I'm afraid."

"And Mr. Harris?"

"Is no longer with us."

The same confusion I'd battled the past hour fought for control of Miss Barton's face. "The gentleman fell off his horse—just like that? What a terrible accident."

"He did fall, but his foot was caught. I—" I hesitated to say more, troubled by what I suspected. Thankfully, Miss Barton seemed a steady girl, calm and methodical.

She cocked her eyebrows. "You were there? You mean, you saw the whole thing?"

"Yes. Giles's horse dragged him straight into Juliana's garden party."

Clearly troubled, her hand found her forehead, but her voice came out strong. "And Miss Radcliff, is she . . . ?"

"Disturbed . . . disordered . . . distraught. Dr. Knight has given her something to help her sleep. She has a long road ahead, I'm afraid." It was then I noticed the state of the nursery. I took in all the little details I'd not noticed when I walked in a few minutes earlier.

Papers lay scattered on the floor of the room's small alcove. Isaac's bag had been moved across the rug to the bow window and emptied. The escritoire drawers pushed at angles, hastily closed.

I motioned to the mess. "What's all this?"

Miss Barton hopped to her feet. "Isaac and I entered only moments before you and found the disarray. Is it not surprising? I had only just begun to clean it up."

Tiring of his game stacking blocks, Isaac wriggled into my arms. "You mean this happened today?"

With an empty lap, Miss Barton crossed the room to tidy up. "It must have. A bit odd, don't you think? It's possible the housekeeper or one of the maids was searching for something, but to leave it all just so?" She shrugged. "Well, at any rate, I'll clean it up as soon as I've half a chance, and I'll be sure to have a word with Mrs. Coombs."

"Thank you. I've far too much on my mind at present to worry with a little disorder." I stood to leave, but I couldn't help glancing back into the room. Someone had certainly been looking for something.

CHAPTER 7

Late in the afternoon I entered our shared sitting room to await Adrian. I wasn't certain when he would seek his bed-chamber to dress for supper, but we had much to discuss, and I meant to speak with him before he did so.

Though the sun still hovered above the horizon, it had dipped behind the house, leaving the east-facing rooms to lonely shadows and a gray haze. I stoked the fire, warming the small space as best I could, but a stubborn chill persisted. I rubbed my arms beneath my shawl and sat in the wingback chair a few feet from the fender.

It was a comfortable seat, cranberry red with two faded armrests—Adrian's chair. On first inspection, I hadn't imagined he used the sitting room all that much, but on second glance I noticed what I hadn't before: signs of life—a rumpled paper tossed onto the Hepplewhite desk; a small leather book that cradled a pair of spectacles; the scent of Adrian's cologne, a pleasing mix of lavender and citrus, pressed deeply into the chair's fabric.

I rested my head against the chair's wing and breathed it in—one more reminder of my intrusion into Adrian's private world. Of course he had been the one to push the idea of marriage. I was simply doing as he wished. I ran my fingers along the rim of his wire spectacles. They weren't something I'd expect my notorious husband to wear. But one never does know a person, do they? Giles had once called me the ice queen, and I was never icy, not really, just extremely careful. And Brook. I'd never have guessed he would abandon me. What little good my wariness had done me over the years.

I heard footsteps through the wall and my gaze shot to the door.

Adrian pushed his way through the door, a sluggishness to his walk and his shoulders weighted down with fatigue. He paused in the firelight where he almost looked a stranger. He had changed so much over the course of a single day. Grooves lined his face. His eyes told the story of a grueling few hours.

He remained silent for a moment, his eyes finding mine in the dim light before he walked to the nearby sofa. He eased down and rested his elbows on his knees then his head in his hands. "I've just come from seeing Juliana."

I left the wingback chair to join him on the sofa, lifting my hand to comfort him, only to hesitate, his easy demeanor never far from my mind. Was it a good idea to extend any familiarity between us, particularly when we were alone? The last thing I wanted was to complicate our arrangement. "Is she awake?"

Adrian eyed me for a long moment, and I wondered if he'd seen my hasty movement. "She is still overcome, but Phoebe says there is much improvement from earlier." He reclined against the cushions and placed his hands behind his head. "I can only thank you for your help. I'm not certain what I would have done if you weren't in residence."

"Nonsense. Phoebe showed great fortitude of mind. She would have handled everything in my absence."

"Yes, well, she surprised me. I've been far too busy this past year to see what is right in front of my face. I daresay she and Juliana have grown into women while I've been pulled away by my work."

I offered a small smile. "Your daughters do you proud."

He nodded but his agreement lacked enthusiasm. I suppose he was only making conversation for my benefit, his mind pre-occupied by darker thoughts.

"Did they decide anything? Anything about Giles, I mean."

He brushed a hand through his hair. "Nothing of any con-sequence. The general consensus is that his death was an accident. A heart condition perhaps. Or something else that caused him to fall, which in turn scared his horse." Adrian's fingers then worked at his cravat, tugging the knot open.

"And you don't believe them."

His hand stilled. "That is not what I said."

I scrutinized him. "I will remind you that I am not without some experience in the world. We both know Giles's body did not look as it should have."

He succeeded in unfolding his cravat and launched it onto the floor. After a pause he started on his waistcoat buttons. "Then we are in agreement."

I pressed my lips together. "What do you think could cause the discoloration of his skin?"

Adrian slipped his waistcoat from one arm then the other. "Ewan may not have been so far off when he suggested an illness or a chest complaint. I don't have much knowledge or experience regarding such things. I could hardly speculate." He laid his waist-coat over the arm of the sofa, and I watched with a wary eye as he moved to the ties on his shirt.

Almost as if he felt my discomfiture, he looked up. His fingers stilled. "I do apologize if this makes you uncomfortable. It's only my neck. I think I may have done something to it when I rode after Giles."

"Indeed."

He kneaded the muscles around his hairline and his eyes slipped closed. "I sent my groom into Plattsdale to retrieve a friend of mine, Mr. Lewis Browning." He peeked open one of his eyelids when I didn't respond right away. "I'd like him to take a look at Giles before they take the body away."

"Why him?"

He tilted his head to stretch his neck only to wince at the movement. "Browning spent some time in China where he studied under a man who taught him a great deal about the deceased." He took a long breath. "I don't know why, but Browning finds such knowledge fascinating."

"You mean he studies dead people?"

"Not exactly. He has simply familiarized himself with what certain types of dead bodies look like. He has this book—"

"And you think he might be able to tell us why Giles appeared so strange?"

Adrian tapped his leg with his free hand. "I'm hoping so."

"Do you think . . . If it might help, I told Mrs. Coombs I would take a turn watching over Giles's body. They had already divided most of the night among the female servants, as the girls are too affected to take up such a responsibility. I'm to sit with him for a few hours starting at six in the morning."

Adrian tossed a glance at the door. "That is good of you." He continued to rub his neck. "Yes, I believe that would be a great deal easier than explaining our intrusion to a servant." He paused, lowering his arm, and I wondered if he'd meant to say something else. "How well did you know Giles?"

"We were great childhood friends, as he mentioned." A quiet moment settled and I drifted back into distant memories, ones I'd not wanted to relive until now. "We used to roam the woods between our estates every spring. You see, my parents would send Lucius and me to our house in Kent when the weather turned warm while they went to London for the season. We had little supervision in those days. Giles, Lucius, and I climbed trees and explored the rolling hillsides. We never thought such happy times would end. But look at us now. I can scarce believe what has become of each of us."

"I'm sorry for your loss. I— Ow."

I'm not certain what he meant to say, but his hand flew once again to his neck. Without thinking, I scooted close and reached out. "Perhaps I could try to ease the pain?"

The fire popped in the grate. The small clock on the mantel ticked off several seconds. Adrian shot me a rather curious smile.

"I-I didn't mean to presume . . ." I froze, my fingers tingling. After all, what had I just decided a moment earlier—to stay away.

He breathed a laugh. "I would appreciate any aid you can render."

He took his time turning his back to me, in all likelihood enjoying the fact that he left me little choice but to press my thumb into the spot he indicated. I hesitated, all too aware of my thumping heartbeat, then raised my hand to the base of his neck. I closed my eyes for a brief second. His skin felt warm under my fingertips, his muscles tight.

He let out a sigh, and I smiled. How dangerously easy it would be to fall under his spell. As my fingers made their way up his neck, I couldn't help but notice the attractive flecks of red buried deep within his thick copper locks. No one would notice how they glistened in the firelight, unless they were quite close.

It took some time for me to relax the knots beneath his skin, but confident I'd done some good, I eventually pulled away.

He sat rather still, then tugged his shirt forward before settling once more against the sofa. "Thank you."

I smoothed out my gown, hoping my heartbeat would return to normal. "I hope I helped."

"You've the touch of an angel."

I darted a glimpse up, expecting to see the mischievous look in his eyes I'd grown accustomed to, but I found an honesty in his gaze I wasn't prepared for. I tucked my arms at my side. "Yes, well . . ." Goodness, what could I possibly say to that? "I um . . . I waited for you tonight because I need to tell you something about Giles."

"Oh?"

My mind was muddled. "Giles said something. Yesterday, shortly after our arrival, before you showed me to my room. He was terribly anxious to speak with me alone."

Adrian narrowed his eyes. "About what?"

"I don't know. He arranged to meet me after the garden party. He promised to tell me then."

"And he never made it." Adrian lifted his eyebrows. "Convenient."

"And then Juliana said something earlier. I daresay the little group in the drawing room thought her out of her wits, but she pointed at me and declared I knew something about Giles's death. Of course, I don't. Giles told me he didn't want to worry her, but I do wonder if Juliana might know something—something that might prove valuable."

A muscle twitched in his jaw. "It is possible."

"I'm not certain it should be me who questions her, but we must do so as soon as you feel she is ready."

His voice sounded strained. "You do understand that Giles was a far cry from my personality. He was no spy, and I can't see him involved in anything nefarious."

"But I also cannot see him murdered for no reason at all. Surely there must be a clue . . . something that might lead us to the truth."

Adrian stared for several seconds at his hands in his lap. "Elizabeth, you surprise me by all this. I hope you'll not give me cause for concern. Remember, we don't know anything for certain, not till Browning can tell us more. Giles's death might very well have been an accident. Moreover, if what we fear is true, that would be far more disturbing. It would mean that someone residing within this house is a killer." He took my hand. "Let that sink in. A killer. Here at Middlecrest. And the murderer did the gruesome act right under our very noses." He pushed to his feet. "I am solely responsible for bringing you and Isaac here at such a time, putting you both in danger." He paced the rug. "Fifteen years I've kept my work and my family separate, and I don't intend to change that now. I know you've a mind for answers, but I don't want you getting involved."

I sat forward. "I only want to help. Didn't you say it was nice to finally share your burdens with someone?"

He crossed over to the door before resting his hand on the latch. "I promise I will discuss anything I learn with you, but please, leave the investigating to me. This latest development may prove a delicate matter." He took a long look out the window. "The last thing I want is someone else getting hurt."

I was slow to nod, but I did so for his benefit. He only wanted to keep me safe, yet I had no way of turning off my mind, playing the helpless wife so many other simpering females enjoyed. No, I'd been making decisions for myself and Isaac for far too long. I'd not relinquish the reins now. If there was any way I could figure out a possible motive or a working list of suspects, I would absolutely look further into my friend's death . . . with or without my husband's explicit permission.

After all, at six and twenty I was no longer in the habit of asking permission.

CHAPTER 8

Sleep came slow and fitful that night. I was forced to head to the parlor as promised at six o'clock the following morning, far wearier than the day before. Mrs. Coombs met me in the hall to inform me that Adrian's orders had been carried out. Giles's body had been washed and dressed by the undertaker's associates late into the night.

I nodded and watched her calculated departure, one hand clenched at my waist, the other frozen on the door latch. I was suddenly loath to open it. As a child I had sat with both my parents while we awaited arrangements for the funeral. However, something felt different about Giles's death, something far more sinister.

A surge of nervousness christened my entrance, but I was relieved to see one of the chambermaids sitting watch. Her arms were tucked close to her chest, her profile devoid of emotion. I could only imagine how long the night had been for her.

Thick drapes snuffed out any hope of morning sun as a string of candles dripped into their holders on the sideboard. The servants had placed thick vases filled with lilacs around the room to mask the emerging odor, but there was no denying the march to the grave had begun.

I touched the young lady's arm. "I'm here now. Please, go get some sleep."

Her reaction was a bit delayed, but she looked up and nodded before moving toward the door. A whoosh of air and it silently swung closed behind her, leaving me alone with the remains of my friend.

The gloominess felt absolute. I forced my feet across the wooden floor. Giles lay in his coffin, which was draped in a wool shroud and placed on a long table in the center of the room. He appeared as I had anticipated, but the sight of his still form arrested my thoughts. Motionless, I digested all that had happened the previous day that led us to this awful moment.

Who could have done such a thing to good, kind Giles, if indeed it was intentional? I inched backward into the chair the chambermaid had vacated at his side. There would be hours for prayer and reflection, and I had much to say.

Slowly, I intertwined my fingers on my lap as the utter emptiness of loss settled on my shoulders. Silence reigned, all the clocks having been stopped the previous day, a reverent tribute to Giles. The calm did little to ease my frantic nerves. I closed my eyes and bowed my head, seeking comfort.

The pop of the door latch sent my eyes blinking open. Disconcerted, I pushed to my feet and turned to the door.

A sliver of light illuminated the crack before Adrian pushed through, his expression grave. "Elizabeth, I didn't mean to frighten you."

"No, please." I motioned him over. "You startled me is all."

He pulled off his beaver hat, the clump of gray in his hair far more noticeable in the dim light. His eyes looked pinched, his movements dulled. Perhaps Adrian had managed less sleep than I had.

He motioned back at the door. "Mr. Browning has just arrived. Would it be convenient to allow him to look at Giles's body?"

My instincts flared, and all at once I didn't want the man to enter, to invade Giles's privacy. But the truth of Adrian's heart was all too evident across his face. He meant the best for Giles. And any information we might learn would help us understand his sudden and surprising accident.

"Yes, but please, do be discreet." I inched away from the table.

Adrian eyed me for a long second, then thrust the door fully open.

A tall man with windblown hair and astute eyes advanced into the room, a book clutched in his fingers. Adrian moved in next to me and rested his hand on my back. "May I present Mr. Browning?"

I nodded, taking in every inch of his friend's attire. Though he dressed well, he possessed a sort of careless air. An ill-fitting jacket, a cravat loose about his neck. So different from Adrian's perfectly cut clothes. Adrian went on. "Browning, my wife, Lady Torrington."

The man gave me a rueful look. "How do you do?"

I dipped my chin. "As well as can be expected."

Adrian tugged me gently to the side. "Would you rather wait outside? This cannot be pleasant to observe."

I swallowed hard. For some reason I felt the need to protect Giles, almost like a sister would. "No, I would prefer to stay, but I don't believe I will watch."

Adrian thought for a moment, then rubbed his wrist. "All

right, but if it proves to be too much for you—I mean, if you need me, please don't hesitate to speak up."

The concern in his eyes bolstered my wavering resolve. "I will."

He moved my chair to the far corner before eyeing Mr. Browning with a hard look. "Shall we get on with this?"

Mr. Browning laid his leather book on a side table before carefully pulling back Giles's shroud. The acrid smell intensified for a moment, then settled into the pervasive odor saturating the room. My hands quivered as I turned away, intent on merely listening to the men talk.

It was several minutes before Mr. Browning's deep voice broke the silence. "You say his mouth and eyes were open when your wife found him."

"That is what I understand."

I heard the flap of pages and then the hard clunk of a book on the table. "See here."

A pause. "Yes."

There was a shuffle and Adrian's voice intensified. "His fingernails are black as well."

Browning quickly responded, "And here, look how his skin is cracked."

"Then you think it was indeed poison?"

I gasped, but the gentlemen did not seem to hear me.

Mr. Browning went on. "With the tongue swollen, protruded, and blood in the mouth, I would find it hard to believe anything else."

"Is there any way to ascertain exactly what type of poison it was?"

"No." Browning took a deep breath. "Not really. Not unless you were to find some other evidence."

I heard the sliding hush of the wool shroud being replaced, and I made my way back over to the gentlemen. Adrian offered me his arm. "It seems we were right. Someone is indeed responsible for Giles's death."

I shook my head. "But who? How? And more importantly, why?"

The men glanced at one another, then Adrian touched my hand. "I'm not certain at present, and it may take some time to gather the information. As of yet, no one has come forward with any proof of wrongdoing."

I touched my neck. "Well, it must have been someone with the knowledge and the means to complete such a terrible act."

Mr. Browning stared down at Giles's form. "I can remain at Middlecrest if I can be of some assistance, but I'll need to send word to Rebecca."

"That would indeed be helpful." Adrian led the way to the door. "We'll have to move quickly if we are to question everyone at Middlecrest before they leave. Elizabeth, I may need your help with the ladies."

Adrian was already willing to go back on his declaration to keep his family out of the hunt for the murderer. Of course, he needed me now, and by the looks of it, he knew I wasn't to be excluded.

He must have followed my thoughts, for he fought a grin as he went on. "If you would, ask each person what they saw yesterday, if they thought anyone was acting out of their usual way. There was quite a bit of commotion in the house before the garden party. Someone may have seen something."

"Or someone looking for something."

"What do you mean?"

"Yesterday Miss Barton and I found the nursery in disarray, like someone had been pawing through Isaac's things."

Mr. Browning and Adrian shared a long look. "Interesting . . . We shall certainly keep that in mind." Then he squeezed my arm. "Please, whatever you do, don't take any unnecessary risks. We'll do this carefully, thoughtfully, and together."

Mr. Browning closed his leather book and paused to examine it before speaking. "It is none of my affair, but I must say, Torrington, I don't think Curtis would appreciate Lady Torrington—"

"Curtis does not have to be told everything." Adrian shot me a knowing glance. "And I am not so foolish as to make the same promise you did regarding my fair lady. He'll find his way to understanding. I daresay Curtis knows as well as anybody that Lady Torrington has a mind of her own."

CHAPTER 9

I joined some of the ladies in the drawing room that afternoon to prepare the funeral gifts. After a long morning of watching over Giles then questioning several guests, I struggled to fill the hostess role I was no doubt expected to assume.

A nervous hush roamed the air, the drapes drawn tight, our whispered conversation clipped at best. Seated between Mrs. Ayles and Phoebe at a four-person card table, I focused on the rosemary in my hand, tying each black silk ribbon around a scented sprig.

I attempted conversation. "A few more and we shall have plenty to give the mourners."

Phoebe looked up, her eyes weary. "What of Mrs. Harris? Should we not do something special for her?"

A voice rang out over my shoulder. "I have already made arrangements for Giles's mother." Juliana was standing in the doorway like a specter. She forced a half smile as she advanced into the room, but she couldn't hide her lingering shock and pain. It was as if every muscle in her face held perfectly still, her eyes dark mirrors for the flickering candlelight. She held out her hand. "I brought a lock of Giles's hair to be placed in a brooch."

Touched, I rose to console her, but Phoebe warned me off with a shake of her head. I accepted the small tangled clump in silence. Though it went against my nature to remain so, I was still a stranger in this house, and Juliana was a complicated young lady.

Mrs. Ayles grasped my arm as we watched Juliana make her way to the window and peek between the heavy chintz curtains. "Poor girl. Far too young to don the mask of death."

I inched onto my seat at the table. "Giles was a good man. I—"

Mrs. Ayles thrust out her cane. "Yet death is a necessary part of life, wouldn't you say? We have all lost people dear to us and found a way to move on. Tragically, it is Juliana's turn to mourn this time . . . and Mrs. Harris's."

I wondered if Juliana heard her grandmother's callous words. "Grief is never easy, nor the same for any—"

"I daresay the gel takes after her father. He's worked nearly twenty years to appease his own restless soul."

I hid behind an uncomfortable pause. "Oh? I did not realize."

She angled to face me, the merest bend to her lips. "Didn't you?"

It was a challenge, and though I'd promised Adrian to protect our secret, I hadn't the fight in me to defy his mother-in-law, not with the loss of Giles so heavy on my heart.

A sickeningly triumphant smile creased her wrinkled cheeks. "I don't believe Torrington has ever got over my daughter's death, let alone taken a fancy to a lady like you."

My chest felt heavy.

Juliana jerked her attention to the two of us. "Please, Grandmama, feel free to speak up. I am not a child to be handled with kid gloves. I am well aware something terrible happened to Giles, something you all are keeping from me. He was not himself earlier this week. I—"

Mrs. Ayles held up an arthritic hand. "My dear, we would

not be so indelicate. Giles has not even been laid to rest. Let us not speak ill of the dead." She cast me a sideways glance. "Lady Torrington merely asked me about your late mama."

I braced myself to deny the assertion when Juliana released an odd little sigh. "Oh."

Mrs. Ayles positioned her cane to rise, her satisfaction palpable as she pushed her old bones into motion. She'd made me look a fool. Of course she couldn't know her words did little to hurt me. So Adrian was still in love with his first wife. Why would I care? Affection was never part of our arrangement. She met my wary gaze as she extended her arm toward Juliana, a look of derision filling her eyes. Mrs. Ayles had no inclination of giving up whatever power she currently possessed in the house.

"Will you assist me back to my room, Juliana? We've enough tokens here for all of Plattsdale." Her tone sounded far more pitiful than it had seconds ago.

Juliana wavered for a moment but then crossed the room and took her grandmother's arm, leaving me to swallow any retort to defend myself.

L

The funeral procession was to start after nightfall, and though I'd heard a great many stories about the dangers they posed for women, I couldn't help but feel a twinge of disappointment that ladies rarely participated. I should have liked to walk to the church and say a prayer for my friend.

Twilight had descended on my blue room when I entered to rest before supper. A suffocating grayness remained. I blew a stray lock of hair from my face only to stop short a few paces onto the rug. There, in the middle of the coverlet on my bed lay a folded piece of paper. I paused to peek at the connecting door.

Had Adrian left me a note? A numbing concern crept its way up my neck as I inched forward. Somehow I knew it wasn't from him.

A faint pop snapped beyond the wall. The air in my room seemed to shift like a northern wind. A sea of tiny bumps washed across my arms.

I shook my head, my eyes trained on the bed. The note was probably left by a maid. I was being silly. I took the last few steps across the rug and picked up the paper, slowly unfolding it.

I know what you have in your possession. Time is of the essence. Leave it in the crook of the old oak tree in the church courtyard by midnight, or I'll be forced to take further steps to secure it. Tell no one. I'm watching you.

For a moment all fell utterly still. Then the room's furniture began to take shape beyond the paper in my hands. My heart thundered, and I stole a glance at my bedchamber door.

I'd been terribly afraid after my parents died. After all, who was to take care of Lucius and me? The fear came again when I was pregnant and abandoned by Brook. But nothing could have prepared me for the terror that coursed through my veins when I read those words. *I'm watching you.* The image of Giles's motionless body clambered into my mind. Someone had been in the house, in my very room—a person who thought I possessed some sort of information.

Suddenly I could hear every creak in the house. The subtle shake of the wind playing with the windowpanes. The predatory hum of silence that stole into the room between gusts. A shuffle sounded through the connecting room wall and I jumped.

A low mumble, then pounding footsteps. I let out a trapped breath. It was Adrian. Thank goodness. Without another thought I tore through our sitting room and made my way into his bedchamber. If anyone could help me make sense of the threatening letter, it was my husband the spy.

Traces of a smoldering fire met my nose as I pushed the door aside and proceeded into the heart of his private space. I found his room a bit grander than I'd expected, the dark furniture foreboding—almost as if I'd wandered into a secret part of the house, reserved only for the master of the estate. Servants had already drawn the heavy crimson drapes for the evening, leaving a slew of candles flickering about the room.

My steps turned sluggish as I caught sight of Adrian and his valet standing in the shadow of his wardrobe. Though I immediately began to question my rash decision to enter unannounced, I had no time to contemplate the intrusion.

Adrian dismissed his man at once with a wave of his hand. "Give us a few moments if you would, Forbes."

It took all my reserves to wait patiently for the valet to leave before I dared reveal why I'd come. As the door clicked shut and Adrian alone angled to face me, I found the words I'd been itching to say slip wildly from my mind.

I'd seen my husband dressed at the height of fashion more than once, but for some reason as he stood there appraising me with his arm crooked at his elbow, his black fitted jacket just so . . . The feel of the room turned suddenly intimate.

I managed a whispered, "I'm sorry to rush in like this."

He crossed the crimson rug beside his bed, his questioning

gaze tight on my face. "You startled me, is all. What on earth is the matter?" He led me to a chair by the fire and waited to take a seat at my side. "You look ill, Elizabeth. Shall I pour you a drink?"

"No, thank you." I thrust out the letter, my hand still a bit shaky. "I discovered this on my bed but a few moments ago."

He narrowed his eyes as he took the letter, opening it slowly near the firelight. The muscles in his jaw tightened as he scoured the short missive, then cast a sharp glare over the paper's edge.

"Have you any idea who might have written this?"

I swallowed. "None at all. The handwriting is foreign to me, and I've seen no one about my room save my maid."

Carefully he smashed the folds of the paper back together, a hard look in his eyes. "Or what it could possibly be referring to?"

"No."

He pressed his forehead. "Tell me, how many people did you inform of your plans to leave Croft Towers?"

"Well, no one, really. Even Curtis and Sybil were ignorant." I bit my lip. "What exactly are you getting at?"

"I'm not entirely certain at present. Just a hunch . . ." He stood and stalked over to the fireplace, then perched his arm on the mantel. "It's well past time I spoke with that coachman of yours. He's likely still recovering at the inn."

"My coachman? I can't imagine him involved in all this. What do you hope to learn?"

"Maybe nothing, but there was a great deal of confusion after the accident. So many people were on the road and in and out of the White Lion that day—too many opportunities for vital information to be misplaced, passed around, or worse, planted for safekeeping. And since we know the Frenchman in Plattsdale is still awaiting the intelligence—"

"Do you mean to suggest I might possess something I'm unaware of?"

"This note would certainly imply just that." His voice held an uncertain tone, but there was a quiet urgency to his words. "Think back. Did you overhear anything before you left the Towers or maybe at the inn that might have seemed insignificant at the time but on second thought could prove to be important?"

My mind churned for answers. "I wish I could say I did, but I haven't the least idea what the person who wrote this note thinks I have."

Adrian paused to think, leaving a grim silence between us, then turned once again to the fire. "All I know is this threatening letter proves Middlecrest is no longer safe for you and Isaac."

My chest tightened as I read the unspoken words on Adrian's face. "Please don't send us away. If the French spy found a way to get to me here under your watchful eye, he could very well find me anywhere."

I was right, and Adrian knew it. This whole terrible business had spiraled out of his control. He balled his fingers into a fist, then released them. "Somehow I'd convinced myself I was helping you by proposing marriage." There was a change in his countenance, a softening of his features, almost as if he'd let down his guard and I'd been permitted a rare flash of vulnerability.

My heart stilled. "Regardless of whether or not I should leave Middlecrest, we still need to come at a decision about tonight. I have nothing to leave in that tree."

Slowly, he leaned back against the scrolled edge of the fireplace and crossed his arms. "And there's more. Don't forget you've the role of hostess to play here at the house before the funeral procession. We haven't much time." He ran his finger along the edge of the note, staring for an agonizing moment into the fire. "Leave the rest to me." A sharp sigh and he slipped the letter into his jacket pocket.

"And, you mustn't worry. I have every intention of acquiring answers for you by tomorrow morning."

L

Answers by morning indeed. Adrian would be far too busy with the funeral possession and burial to have any time to investigate tonight. I, however, had no obligations once the men left the house in the procession. A feigned headache that took me to my bedchamber would leave me free to find my own answers, one way or another.

First and foremost, whoever wrote that note planned to visit the tree before morning to retrieve whatever they wanted me to leave, and I meant to discover whom we were dealing with. I allowed a small smile as I knelt onto my bedside rug. The opportunity for answers was too good to pass up.

I folded Adrian's great coat and tucked it under the bed where I'd already stashed a pair of his trousers, a shirt, and one of his beaver hats. Everything was ready for nightfall. I only had a few more hours to wait. Twisting my wedding ring on my finger, I thought one last time through my plans.

No one would guess I wasn't one of the paid attendants contracted by the undertaker for the funeral procession, or more importantly that I was actually a lady hiding under Adrian's long coat. I would merely slip away from the procession at the right moment, plant a fake note in the tree, then find a hiding spot to wait and watch for someone to fetch it.

My plan was complete.

CHAPTER 10

Night descended on Middlecrest, riding on the back of a rolling wind and chilly fog. Phoebe and I scurried to present the mourners the rosemary springs we'd prepared, while Mrs. Harris, Juliana, and the other chief mourners were given gloves. Giles's coffin had been moved into the black carriage and draped with a black velvet cloth.

My nerves had been raw all evening but never more so than when I made my last round as hostess. Itching to escape, I watched from the front hall as Juliana took Mrs. Harris aside to give her the brooch she'd made. The pair embraced before slowly making their way upstairs for the evening. I imagined Mrs. Harris and Juliana would watch the procession depart from their bedchamber windows.

A great deal of commotion clambered in the entryway and spilled out onto the front drive as the men of the house began to gather for the funeral procession. My breathing stilled as I set my empty rosemary basket on the rococo side table by the door. The moment to make my escape had come at last. I whispered a quick word to Phoebe about retiring to my room, and she nodded in understanding, exhaustion written across her face.

I took my leave of Mrs. Ayles before making my way to Adrian. My steps felt almost clumsy as I approached the group of gentlemen by the door. It would take all my acting skills not to alert him to my plans, and so far they had proved abysmal.

He walked forward to meet me. "Is something amiss?"

I shook my head, but he held my hands a bit longer than usual, peering into my eyes with that probing look of his. Did he guess my secret already? Or was this simply part of our love act? He didn't take his gaze away from my face. "I asked Young to keep an eye on the house while we are at the funeral."

"Thank you. I shall sleep better knowing he's up and about."

"Yes, well . . ." A perfectly placed pause. "Then I suppose I won't speak with you again till morning."

"I suppose so." Cautiously, I slipped my fingers from his grasp and turned away, ascending the grand central stairs with as much grace as I could muster, my legs quivering beneath my skirt. Time was terribly short if I was to join the procession. Once out of sight of the lower floor, I tore down the family wing, the drafty corridors quickening my steps.

Plowing into my bedchamber, I raced to the bed, then scrambled to retrieve the clothes hidden beneath. One by one, I wriggled into the trousers and shirt. Thank goodness I was tall, but I still had to tuck and tighten the various strings and extra fabric to look presentable. Adrian's large coat hid anything that might have given me away.

I heard the low grumble of voices beyond my window and paused only long enough before the looking glass to secure my hair within the beaver.

I took the side stairs two at a time, thankful I'd found a vacant path, and departed Middlecrest beyond the east wing. The damp night air felt heavy in my lungs, the darkness looming ever closer. All the while the clawing reminder of what could happen grew in my mind. What would I do if I was exposed—an unprotected lady out so late?

My brother told me once about the rampant thefts in funeral processions. He'd called the crowds a pickpocket's dream. Only a few years had passed since the Duke of Bedford's procession was attacked as the coffin was carried into the church. In that instance, one of the attendants was knocked down and trampled.

An uncomfortable chill scaled my back, but I forced the dark thoughts away. Joining the funeral procession disguised as a man was still preferable to journeying alone at night, which I would be forced to do if I didn't slip into the group in time. Either way, I needed answers—for Giles, for Isaac, for me. None of us would be safe until the French spies were locked away, particularly if one of them proved to be the murderer I suspected.

Hurrying around the far corner, I pulled Adrian's coat tight about my neck. The carriage lamps did little to illuminate the large gathering of men shifting about on the front drive. Horses sidled one way then the other, and voices echoed off the stone walls. The six bearers with their black sashes made their way to the front of the group as I ducked through the shuffle of horses and men. When I spied the stables, I allowed a small sigh of satisfaction. I had been right. No one took the least notice of an extra attendant.

My next challenge was to secure a horse. The confusion near the stables, however, aided my cause. One of the young grooms offered to help me saddle a brown mare located in the third crib. Dashing to and fro, the lad was clearly too overwhelmed and distracted to doubt my story. After all, not all of Giles's family was known to the staff. And I knew just enough to make my statement plausible—a distant cousin of Fanny Harris, arrived late in the day by stage. When the reins were finally in my hand and a horse trailed in my wake, I took a deep breath. I'd nearly done it.

Free of the stable yard, I used a low stone wall as a step to mount astride and urged my borrowed hack toward the departing group. I caught sight of Adrian at once, sitting tall in his saddle, his black cloak flapping in the breeze. Mr. Browning and his mount stood right beside him. I thought it best to keep my distance and meandered into the group several yards behind the front vehicle.

Four black Friesian horses with their black ostrich plumes pulled the carriage housing Giles's body as we made our way the short distance from Middlecrest to the parish church. The rest of the mourners followed behind, and I did my best not to draw any attention to myself as I directed my horse to keep in line.

It wasn't long before I realized the paid attendants had enjoyed more than enough to drink earlier in the night. Loud and terribly vulgar, the men barked out round after round of coarse words and jovial exchanges as we plodded past the shadowed fields and turned onto the main road to Plattsdale. I wondered if the group was brought in from Dover, as they seemed far more interested in their own entertainment than lamenting my dear friend's untimely death. I gritted my teeth. Giles deserved better than this.

Thankfully the resounding clang of the church bell rent through the cold air, and the men seemed to sober as the church appeared out of the mist, its grand spire disappearing into a sea of blackness. I cautiously reined my horse back, allowing her to fall farther and farther behind the last rider. That was when I saw the English oak the letter had referenced take shape in the darkness, the sole tree standing watch over a dewy courtyard. My pulse snapped to life, sending tingles shooting through my arms and legs. I was almost there. I urged my horse to take a slight turn in silence, then drew her into the nearby glen of trees.

Water droplets shook loose from the low-hanging branches, littering my coat and trousers. I pushed my way into the center of the grove and slipped from the saddle. After tying the horse, I scurried to a far tree where I could make out the entrance to the church as well as the stately oak. I had several minutes to wait as the funeral riders dismounted and entered the building. Once empty, the glen around the church fell to utter silence. Not a cry of wind or a bird in the air. Just my own erratic breathing.

My gloved fingers quivered, but I located my coat's pocket and fished out the stack of papers I'd tied with a string. Inch by inch, I crawled beyond the shelter of the trees. Far above, the stars were tucked neatly behind a thick blanket of clouds, yet the lonely white light of the moon wound its way through the insidious darkness.

I kept to the shadows until I was as close to the tree as possible, then bolted across the open courtyard. I dared not glance back, fearing someone would materialize from the gloom. A scream crept up my throat, and I fought it back.

I was out of breath when I reached the massive, round trunk of the tree. As far as I could tell I was alone, but someone had penned and left the note in my room, and he would not be far away. The oak had a rather large opening at the base of its first branch—the perfect hiding spot for a secret message. I pushed the papers as far in as I could, then crept around the corner of the church. If the spy was indeed watching me, I wanted him to think I meant to join the funeral, though I had no intention of doing so. Out of sight of the tree, I stood for some time in the alcove of the door, planning a path back to the small grove where I could watch with far more ease.

However, a sudden crack sounded behind me. The heavy wooden door of the church swung open with a whoosh, effectively trapping me in the corner behind it. I recognized some of the paid attendants as they strolled onto the front lawn. I retreated into the shadows and held as still as possible, praying they wouldn't turn around.

At first I thought I'd escaped notice, but one of them happened to glance over his shoulder.

The lanky man had dark hair, his eyes ghostlike in the thin moonlight. He rubbed his chin as he squinted back at me. "No stomach for the service either, eh, boy?" He angled the hat on his head, moving back toward the church, ever closer. I might have believed his casual conversation, only he motioned to his friends with a pop of his chin. "You ain't from around here either, are you, boy?"

I shook my head, my muscles growing tenser by the second. I extended my hand toward the church door.

The other two attendants circled me, and the first man glanced at each, then laughed. "I believe we 'ave found ourselves the very person to fill our pockets with coins." He turned back to me. "The night's still young, and we've not drank our fill."

I attempted to sound as much like a boy as I could, but my voice shook. "I haven't any money."

The man eyed me, then scrunched up his lips. "That coat you're wearing says otherwise." Another pump of his chin. "I know quality when I see it."

"Like I said, I don't have any money." I realized too late that

I'd been unable to fully disguise my voice. Desperately, I clutched the door handle, but one of the men's arms was already there to prevent me from opening it.

He stared down at the hand I'd used to grasp the handle, then shook his head like a father disciplining his son. "You know? I don't think you're a boy at all." He knocked the beaver from my head, and my blond locks spilled onto my shoulders.

The other two men's mouths fell open. "Cor!" one shouted. "What the devil?" the other echoed.

Utilizing their sudden shock as a distraction, I scrambled down the steps and sprinted for my horse. My heart thundered, driving my scrambling pace. I gasped for air as I angled straight for the trees. I hadn't all that far to go, and then it would be a horse race—one I was fairly certain I could win.

Steps from the tree line I felt a grubby hand at my neck, and all too easily I was yanked from my feet. My back slammed into the cold ground so hard my vision swam. Hands assaulted me, pawing my body, dragging me into the trees. I could smell the ale on the men's breath as I fought for control. A scream erupted from my throat, but a clammy palm was slapped over my mouth.

Why had I ever thought the funeral procession would provide a layer of safety? I had been so terribly, terribly wrong.

A great deal of shouting sliced through the haze, then pounding footsteps approached. Suddenly the brutal hands vanished from my body, the crushing pressure relieved. I forced myself upright in time to see Adrian drive a blow into the dark-headed man's face as his two friends swarmed away. Adrian motioned with his chin, and Mr. Browning wrestled my assaulter to his feet, then asked, "And the other two?"

Adrian never took his eyes off me. "They won't get far. We can identify them. Right now I must see to my wife. You may take this foul excuse for a man to the magistrate with my blessing."

Mr. Browning dragged my attacker away as Adrian dropped to his knees at my side, tenderly sliding his arm around my back, his words awfully slow to come. "How badly did they hurt you?"

Emotion fought for control of my voice until I managed to clear the thickness away. "You arrived in time."

He closed his eyes for a long second. "Thank God."

My voice still wrestled with various levels of panic. "I don't know what I would have done if—"

"Shhh. There is no use reliving it. Just breathe for a moment." As if exhausted he shifted his legs and collapsed back against a nearby tree, his hand at his brow, a harrowed look about his eyes. He beckoned me over beside him, and I tried to do as he'd said—to simply breathe—but my skin burned with tingling disgust.

He tilted his head against the tree, his voice almost teasing as he asked, "How the devil did you manage to get out here?" A lengthy pause followed as he looked me over. "And in my clothes, of all things?"

There was a gentleness to his touch as his hand rested on mine, and I had a difficult time focusing on anything beyond the warmth of his fingers. He had reacted so differently from what I expected. Lucius would have been livid to find me in such a position, particularly when I'd taken such a dreadful chance in coming out alone. I patted my—or rather his—trousers.

"Well, after you borrowed my robe at the inn, I thought it only fair."

He released a breathy laugh. "I suppose that means we're even now."

"Yes, even." Afraid of what I would see in his eyes, I dared not glance up, yet I found myself doing just that. "I'm sorry, Adrian. I only came tonight to learn who wrote the note."

He seemed lost for words as he opened his mouth, then closed it. He plunged his fingers into his hair. "What the deuce did you think I had planned for the evening? No, don't answer that. I daresay this whole thing is my fault."

I blinked. "*Your* fault?"

"Oh, Elizabeth. I knew that twinkle I saw in your eyes earlier had to mean you were up to something." He gestured at my clothes. "I just never would have guessed this. You've a bit more pluck than I accounted for." A wayward smile snuck onto his face, but it faded all too quickly.

"I should have told you my plans from the start. Thank goodness my man recognized the coat and I left the church when I did." His thumb made a path across my skin as he gripped my hand. "What a way to start a marriage. Both of us dodging and weaving when we should be working together. I guess I've just always had a difficult time trusting people, and we haven't known each other all that long. You see, when I . . ." His hesitancy was followed by a sudden and far more difficult lapse into silence.

I waited patiently for him to finish his thought, but he seemed reluctant to do so, and the look on his face made me question the connection I'd felt moments before. Was he about to reveal something from his past but thought better of it? I looked away. Perhaps we both possessed more than our fair share of invisible demons. Me, most of all, or so I'd thought. Something about Adrian's abrupt hesitation made me wonder just how many he had to slay.

Complex men in my past had only made my life more complicated—first Lucius, then Brook. But was Adrian really their equal? Something in his tone this evening—his honest tenderness—had given me reason to pause. Perhaps there was more to Adrian's attractive confidence and unending charm. Had I ... misread him? My skin smarted beneath his touch, and I hated how quickly I found myself responding. Attraction could be so deceptive. Adrian was a Radcliff at any rate. A fact I could never allow myself to forget.

I drew up my legs to stand, masking my tone. "Don't be absurd. I should have told you what I meant to do."

He held out his hand to stop me, then motioned into the shadows. "You did leave something in that tree, right?"

"Of course I did. It was only some blank paper."

He reached into his pocket. "Well, I'd prefer we leave this." He held up a folded bundle.

"What is it?"

"False intelligence for our little courier to take back with him to France."

Voices ripped through the crisp air. My heart seized. The mourners were already on their way to the gravesite burial. Adrian pushed to his feet. "We haven't much time."

We rushed through the courtyard, flying to the base of the tree. Adrian eyed me as he stuck his hand into the small opening in the rugged bark. A severe look swept over his features.

"What is it?"

"Absolutely nothing. The note you left is already gone."

CHAPTER 11

The events of the evening gave me much to ponder as I rocked Isaac alone in his dark chamber suite in the late hours of the night—the attack at the church, the disappearing note, Giles's poison . . . Goodness, how would Adrian and I ever discover who was involved?

Isaac's soft breathing against my chest had settled into a regular pattern, his sweet muscles twitching within his sleep. I wasn't ready to lay him down, not after I'd heard him crying while I was in the hall by my room. Exhaustion, however, was creeping over me.

I'd reached his bedside before Miss Barton and sent her away for a much-needed break. The household staff had been so preoccupied with the funeral preparations I doubted anyone had relieved her from her duty as of yet.

Isaac was happy to see me when I arrived, squirming into my arms and tucking his hand beneath his chin. Once I settled in the chair, he fell asleep in seconds. When I stood and carried him back to his bed, I realized his favorite blue blanket was gone. That was why he awoke crying. Crawling all about the house, he must have forgotten it somewhere, as was his tendency. At least, I hoped so.

A cold sensation filled my core. Had I seen the blanket since the carriage accident? I thought back over the last few days. I'd suffered such a headache at the time I couldn't even remember if he had it our first night at Middlecrest; he'd fallen asleep before I made my way to his room. Did I remember seeing it in his bed? I thought I had.

There was so much confusion at the inn. I could only trust we hadn't left it there.

Regardless, I hoped he wouldn't wake again tonight. Of course, Miss Barton would be there to comfort him.

I heard the door open in the adjoining room and silently slipped from Isaac's small bedchamber. Miss Barton had returned to the nursery, a candle in her hand. She looked distracted.

"Back already? I anticipated you would hunt a book in the library. I meant for you to sit and read for a bit."

She placed her candle on a nearby desk and made her way to the fireplace to stoke the fire. "I set out to do so, my lady, but there is a definite chill on the air, and the only other room with a fire is the drawing room. After seeing the Friday-faced Mrs. Ayles, I did not wish to disturb her, or Mrs. Harris for that matter."

Mrs. Ayles had not stayed in her room as I'd expected. I was surprised as she had looked ready to drop. Mrs. Harris must have needed her. She would be the only one to seek her out.

Miss Barton moved over to the sofa. "There's something else. The rattle is missing."

"The rattle? Isaac doesn't have—"

"It was mine, your ladyship. We had so little to do that first afternoon, I brought it for him to play with. And now it's gone."

Another missing item.

Her eyes were wide, her fingers busy at her waist. "I'm terribly concerned I won't be able to find it, and it meant a great deal to me. I've searched the house throughout the day and again tonight. No luck."

"That's odd. Isaac's beloved blanket is missing as well. Perhaps when you are looking for the rattle tomorrow you would keep an eye out for the blanket as well?"

She paced across the room. "Of course."

"They could really be anywhere, particularly with everything so unsettled in the rest of the house." I filled the resulting silence with a yawn. "I daresay I should have been in bed long since, but Lord Torrington left to meet his friend Mr. Browning in the village. I was all alone, and when I heard Isaac's cry I just couldn't stay away."

"It's been a long day for all of us. I suppose his lordship is off to Plattsdale for some ale."

"Goodness, I hope not. They—" I stopped myself. "They had business to attend to."

Miss Barton possessed a ready smile that I rather liked. "His lordship seems a decent sort of gentleman and has always been so very handsome and kind to me. In fact, he came by the nursery this mornin' to ensure Isaac had everything he needed. He stayed for several minutes to help the lad line up his blocks."

My eyes widened. Adrian came to the nursery and stayed? "I will admit, Miss Barton, I'm a bit astonished to hear his lordship visited the nursery, but after the last few vile days, I suppose nothing would surprise me."

"Nor I, your ladyship." Her fingers went to work on the arm of the sofa. "Was it so very dreadful arranging all the details for the funeral?"

I closed my eyes a moment. "Indeed, and rather shocking."

"Oh." She adjusted the sleeve of her dress. "After sitting with Mr. Harris's body, some of the chambermaids said his death looked rather mysterious. I was hoping they were wrong and it was all a hum, but since then I've talked to Duff in the stables . . ."

"And what did Duff say?"

"Just that his lordship's been asking questions about the death as well."

Miss Barton seemed to be a good friend to many of the staff. Perhaps she could be of some assistance in my search for the murderer. I leaned forward. "His lordship and I have come to suspect Mr. Harris was possibly"—I lowered my voice—"poisoned."

"Poisoned?" Her voice squeaked. "I cannot believe it. The poor, poor gentleman." She pressed her fingers to her mouth. "Who might have done such a thing?"

I couldn't tell her anything about Adrian's spying, but I could get her thinking. "It must have been someone with access to the house. In fact, I'd like you to do something for me."

"Certainly, my lady."

"If you hear anything further from the servants, you'll come straight to me."

She nodded, then rubbed her arms, her face ashen in the firelight as she glanced about the room. "Do you find it frightening that we could be in the same house as a killer?"

"Yes, I do. But there have been so many people in and out of Middlecrest for the wedding, we cannot be certain the person responsible is still in the area."

"I suppose not, but it does make one nervous just the same. And Miss Radcliff? How is she faring?"

"Not well. Grieving."

Miss Barton lowered her lashes. "To be expected." I could hear the pity in her voice, and I knew we were both exhausted from a long day.

"I will leave you now to get some sleep, which is something we are all in desperate need of at present." I crossed the room but paused at the door, suddenly fearful of what my careless words might bring about. "I do hope what I revealed will not make you afraid to work at Middlecrest. Isaac adores you, and more than anything else, he needs constancy right now. I can promise you that Lord Torrington will do everything in his power to uncover the truth, and I am confident the murderer will be brought to justice."

I only hoped I was right.

L

I knew Mrs. Harris would leave Middlecrest for her own estate, but I was surprised to find her packed and ready to depart on our return from morning services at church. She was sitting at a small desk in the yellow salon, tidying up the last of her correspondence.

Pausing in the doorway, I cleared my throat. "You mean to leave us already?"

She fumbled with the papers on the desk as she bobbed a hasty look up. "Yes . . . I . . ." She whirled to face the window, but I saw her wipe a tear from her cheek. "No reason to stay, really. My dearest Giles has been laid to rest. I . . . find I would rather be at home."

I stepped into the warmth of the room, breathing in Mrs. Harris's light rose scent. "You do know you are always welcome—"

"Yes, yes, of course." Her fingers went to the brooch Juliana had made for her with Giles's hair. "Lord Torrington has already begged me to stay, but I feel the time is right, and the Meadows is not really that far away. I'm afraid Middlecrest has simply become too difficult to bear."

I wondered if Mrs. Harris had any remaining family now that her son was gone. Her husband died years ago. In town she was known as an interminable gossip and enjoyed the company of several like-minded friends. But out here in the countryside, isolated as we were so far from London, she would likely have few visitors.

She eyed me as if she anticipated the question poised to spill from my mouth, but I said it nonetheless. "Will there be anyone for company at your house?"

She sucked in a breath. "I'll have my maid. She is a great comfort, I assure you. And my cat, of course. No need to worry your head about me."

Yet I was worried. I knew quite well what it was like to be alone. "Perhaps you would allow me to visit you in a few days? I mean, once you're all settled. I'd love to see the house you've spoken so fondly of."

For a moment I wondered if my tainted reputation might keep her from accepting my offer, until she reached out and touched my arm. "That would be very much appreciated, thank you. The days may prove longer than I am expecting." She stood to move past me but hesitated, almost as if she was lost as to what to do next. "Please, Lady Torrington, when you do come to the Meadows, will you promise to tell me if you hear anything? About Giles's death . . . anything at all."

I wondered how much Adrian had apprised her of as I met her pained gaze. Did she know we suspected murder? Or perhaps there was something else hidden behind those words. The owlish look to her eyes faded as quickly as it had come. "You were always a good friend to Giles. I will not forget that."

"He will be greatly missed."

She moved to respond, but overset by tears, she turned to the door, mumbling to herself as she left. I stood there for several seconds, processing her departure, but it was not until I made my way down to the breakfast room that I realized I'd heard and understood part of what she'd uttered beneath her breath.

Danger. She'd definitely used the word *danger.* My hand retreated to my mouth as I ceased any further movement. Not only had Mrs. Harris's sudden parting been wrought by her grief, but she had also been afraid to stay.

CHAPTER 12

I watched Mrs. Harris's carriage depart Middlecrest's front drive from beneath a nearby willow tree, hiding from sight until the rear of her coach disappeared around a bend. The dust settled and my chest tightened. Never before would I have entertained such a thought, but I realized I would miss Mrs. Harris.

An unnatural restlessness plagued the wind as it tugged on my bonnet, and I glared over my shoulder at Middlecrest Abbey's seemingly idyllic structure. The house was certainly a handsome one, surrounded by lush trees and thick hedgerows, a credit to the neighborhood, but in many ways it was also a fortress. After what Mrs. Harris had said, I was loath to go back inside and face the unknown.

Adrian's estate had proven itself to be a place where anything could happen. Goodness, within those old redbrick walls I'd assumed a life I hardly recognized, certainly one I'd never dreamed of. And Giles—I could still barely think of the accident without pain.

Middlecrest's bold shadow sent a chill snaking across my shoulders. The thick shade had crept forward in silence while I wasn't paying attention. Shrugging off the uncomfortable feeling, I darted into the sunshine. But I could not be easy. Mrs. Harris

MASQUERADE at MIDDLECREST ABBEY

had felt something—something that sent her home to an empty house. I'd received a threatening letter. Had she?

Had I been a fool to come to Middlecrest so hastily, to marry a man I barely knew? Could we keep my son safe? My eyes slipped closed for a brief second. From now on, everything about the current inhabitants of Middlecrest needed to be questioned. More importantly, I needed to figure out whom I could trust.

A bumblebee buzzed by my ear, making its way from the daffodils of the front gardens to the white blossoms that lay like a carpet across the far hillside. My shawl slipped from my shoulders to the crooks of my elbows. I'd forgotten over the winter how delightful the sun felt on my bare skin.

A voice broke through the gusty breeze. "You look like you are in want of a ride."

I squinted into the bright light, surprised to see Adrian standing with his arm propped against a nearby tree, his riding crop gripped in his hand. A look of mischief filled his face. How long had he been standing there . . . watching me? It was the first time I'd seen him since he rescued me, and I was still a bit off stride.

I followed the curve of the drive until it brought me nearer to where he stood. He raised an eyebrow. "Well?" There was a bend to his voice, the one I'd come to recognize all too well.

"A ride, you say?" Time on the back of a horse might be just what I needed to settle my bound nerves. "I suppose I would consider it." I wrinkled my nose. "But only if you have a horse up to my standards."

He laughed as he tapped his riding crop on his leg. "I didn't realize you were a bruising rider."

"Captain Garvey declared me the best seat in the county three years ago, but I have had little time for indulging of late."

A pause. "Captain Garvey, you say?"

"Yes. Lucius bought my horse, Aphrodite, from him years ago. He keeps a very fine stable in Sussex, you know."

Adrian moved in close, blocking the piercing sun from my eyes. "As a matter of fact, I do know. He keeps a very fine gambling house in London as well, among other things. What the deuce was your brother thinking introducing you to him?"

My shoulders slumped. Of course Adrian would know about a gambling house when I did not, and it would be just like Lucius to keep such company. I crossed my arms. "Very little, I assure you."

"Well, if . . ." Whatever Adrian meant to say drifted off as we caught sight of Ewan Hawkins leading Juliana around the corner of the house. There was a rigidity to his gait, and he'd tucked his left hand in his pocket, hiding the deformity I'd noticed the day Giles died. Their heads were bowed deep in conversation.

Like a bolt of lightning, Adrian grasped my arm, tugged me against him, and slid his arms around my back. He spoke quickly into my ear. "Sorry to be so sudden, but Juliana has had far too many questions about you and me. We need to make this look good."

Every muscle in my body twitched beneath his touch, the shock of his sudden movement arresting my heart. Something had changed between us since that moment in the woods—something I was quickly losing control over.

Carefully, he drew his hand up to the nape of my neck and I was left to stare awkwardly at his chest, a flash of cold on my skin, then warmth. His voice was gentler this time, like a whisper on the wind. "Look up at me. We're supposed to be in the throes of love, remember?"

My heart pounded, but I lifted my chin.

He answered with an all-too-attractive smile, amusement tinting his voice. "Why are you so bad at this?"

My fingers clenched, and I narrowed my eyes. "Better yet, why are you so good at it?"

Adrian's grip slackened for a moment, then he motioned back at the house. "I believe they've both seen our little tryst. There's no use to continue." He stepped back. "Why don't you go change into your habit? I'll meet you at the stables for our ride."

He followed the statement with a kiss on my hand, but I couldn't help but wonder if I'd heard a bit of grit in his voice.

"I shouldn't be more than ten minutes. You will be there waiting for me . . . at the *stables?*" I focused over Adrian's shoulder as I spoke, trying to see Juliana and Mr. Ewan Hawkins. "I'll—" No more than a second had passed before I glanced back at Adrian.

He'd control of himself now. "I find that a bit hard to believe."

"What?"

"Ten minutes—for a lady to change?"

"Oh . . . right." I shook my head. "Then I'd best get to it."

$\mathscr{L}$

The cool breeze tickled my ankles as I hurried across the paddock, the heavy merino fabric of my riding habit brushing against my legs. I stopped and paused at the stable door before clearing my throat to get Adrian's attention. "Ten minutes, my lord?"

Standing beside a large black horse, Adrian gave a tug at his saddle's girth. His fingers stilled, but he did not look up. "Twelve."

I huffed. "I beg to disagree . . . my lord." I rose onto my toes to get a better look at him. "I daresay your watch is slow."

"Perhaps." He shrugged, and his lips twitched into a smile. "Or perhaps not."

The wretch. "Well, where exactly is this horse you've selected?"

He gestured to the corner of the stable. "Duff, one of the grooms, is getting her ready."

An older man popped up from behind the far crib, a gentle smile across his wrinkled face. "Good morning, your ladyship. I've got Flick all right and tight. She's a high stepper and a bit flighty at times, but I'm told you've the spunk to handle her."

I cast Adrian a pert look as the groom directed the sleek, gray bay from her crib to meet me near the door. The mare tossed her head as if in greeting.

"What a beauty." I ran my hand along her soft neck before turning back to Adrian, my voice far more conciliatory since I'd seen the selection of my horse. "Thank you for inviting me to join you."

Adrian gave me a hard stare, then glanced at Duff before making his way to my side. "Always, my love." He leaned in and kissed my cheek, our prior intimacy still on his breath. "I know how you adore riding." We shared a passing look before he cupped his hands to assist me to mount.

My face burned. How many times would I forget to put on the love act? I was quite possibly the worst spy Britain had ever seen. Or was it my infuriating husband? I forced a wide smile, my next words nauseatingly sweet. "You are so very kind and thoughtful."

I thought I saw him cringe, but he moved close to my ear, his voice a tight whisper. "Not too thick now." Then in a singsong tone he added, "Or they'll never believe you."

My hand itched to slap his face, but my maddening heart

pounded just the opposite. Oh, my husband was good—too good. I glided my half boot onto his laced fingers without further retort.

Adrian lifted me comfortably onto the sidesaddle, and I took a moment to adjust my skirt and hopefully my performance. "Adri—darling . . ." So much for that. I darted a look away. "What do you call your horse?"

"Atlas has been with me for several years." He gripped the reins and pulled up, swinging his pristine riding boot to the far side of his horse.

"An Arabian?"

He spurred Atlas forward with a soft kick before looking over. "Indeed, he is."

I urged Flick to follow, and we departed the paddock for the back side of the house. Atlas shook his head and pawed the ground as we walked. Adrian held him under bit until we crossed the manicured lawn. Flick was light and fresh but manageable in a dull sort of way. I suppose Adrian did not wish to see his wife unseated on her first ride. How I missed my own horse back at the Towers. Aphrodite had been the perfect mix of strength, elegance, and speed.

Adrian gave me a hasty nod as we approached the east field, and we allowed the horses a manageable trot. It wasn't long before he drew Atlas in close. "I'm glad you agreed to accompany me. I've been hoping to have a word with you all day."

"Oh?" My cheeks burned.

"It's about Juliana."

Not what I was expecting. I shot him a quick look.

He pressed his lips together. "I'm concerned about her."

I measured my voice. "Yes. I'm sure you are. She's had a great shock."

"I've not had any luck speaking with her regarding what happened. It's only natural for her to grieve, but this strange silence of hers I find worrying. I thought that perhaps, since you are a woman, you might have better luck . . ."

The muscles in my back tightened. Had he not witnessed Juliana's complete revulsion of me? Goodness, his mother-in-law would be a much better person to ask. "I'm barely even acquainted with Juliana, and you know I've had little encouragement from her."

He allowed a small chuckle. "She has always been a bit guarded, far more so than her sister, but her emotions also run deep." He paused for a glance, then carried on, surprisingly in tune with my thoughts. "And I don't think Mrs. Ayles the right person to help her through this difficult time. She possesses little sentiment. I'd rather Juliana be advised by you than anyone else."

I paused for him to say more, but he was waiting for me. "I can certainly reach out to Juliana, but I cannot promise she will be receptive." I brushed Flick's mane with my fingers. "I daresay she sees me as a threat to your affection."

"Does she?" He seemed to straighten in the saddle, but I couldn't read his expression, only the feel of it.

The reins turned heavy in my hands, and I forced myself to focus on the path ahead. Goodness. I thought I'd managed some sort of control of my emotions, but without warning—there I was, back in the grove reveling in the safety of his arms and . . . what else?

If Adrian noticed the flush that warmed my cheeks, he made no remark. "Your being here at Middlecrest has turned out to be, shall I call it—providential." Atlas sidled in place, breaking the tension. Adrian grinned. "I think it time we turn them loose."

Without so much as a thought, an answering smile tore across my face. "I only hope you may keep up."

"A challenge? To the crest of the hill?"

"I most certainly—"

Adrian's lustrous black stallion plunged forward with magnificent strength, and I jerked Flick to follow with a quick swipe of my crop.

Trees sprang up around us then drifted away, the vast field of daffodils passing under flying hooves. The mare proved smooth and fast, a joy to ride, but without my beloved Aphrodite, my husband would remain fixed out of reach.

The cool rush of air sent my bonnet flapping at my back as the cutting breeze ripped through my hair. A laugh bubbled from my lips, and I reveled in the familiar sensation of flying. It was several minutes before I came upon Adrian who had reined his horse in at the crest of the hill.

"You're nothing but a horrid cheat," I said breathlessly as I pounded up beside him, grappling with my bonnet.

He shook his head. "My dear wife, how else could I possibly beat you? Cad or not, Garvey was right. You're amazing on the back of a horse."

I rubbed the nape of my neck. "I daresay if you hadn't cheated, you still would have beaten me."

He eyed me for a long second before giving me that lazy shrug I'd seen from him before—the one that meant nothing and everything at the same time. "Perhaps, but I had to be certain."

"Well." I huffed. "I would demand a rematch if my Aphrodite were here." I patted Flick's head to appease any rumpled feathers. "She is the fastest horse I've ever had the pleasure to ride."

"Aphrodite? Is this pillar of horseflesh presently at the Towers?"

"Yes, but I share her with my cousin Sybil, and I would never have the heart to take her away."

"I see." He motioned to my horse. "Flick here must be a sad replacement."

I leaned forward and covered her ears. "Shhh. She'll hear you. And I don't agree at all. She's lovely. Just not as fast or as smooth as Aphrodite."

"I can see plain as day I shall have to make a trip to Tattersall's."

My eyes widened. "Heavens, don't go out of your way on my account." I'd intended a definite refusal, but I couldn't hide a hopeful expression as I considered a new horse.

"Follow me. I've something to show you up ahead." Adrian continued along the curve of the land, a comfortable silence between us. The path narrowed, and I pulled Flick behind Atlas as we followed a little-used trail hidden delightfully among the thickening trees.

Bushes lined the rutted dirt, the tips bursting with small white flowers. Beech trees rose and spread their branches over our heads, providing a welcome shade. Before long, the lane straightened to parallel a small brook, which was hard at work sloshing over rocks and muddy sides on its way to the large and sometimes torrent River Grey.

Adrian averted Atlas from the brook, heading instead for the base of a large hill. He cast a quick look back before urging his horse up the incline.

I directed Flick to follow, leaning forward in my sidesaddle. "Come on, girl. Surely you aren't tired already." Several well-placed strides and we crested the rise where I could only gasp at the breathtaking view.

We could see for miles beyond—the earth a kaleidoscope of

greens and crisscrossing hedgerows. Far below, a stately clump of oaks stood at the center of the wide valley, encased in sumptuous grass for many yards. Smallish trees and puffy bushes provided the perfect spotted backdrop.

Adrian was slow to speak. "This is my favorite spot on the estate. My brother and I used to play here as boys in the trees and along the hillsides."

My heartbeat faltered. Brook.

He must have sensed my involuntary glance as he responded rather fast with one of his own. "I miss him sometimes. Particularly when I remember how close we were as children. I know Lucius's arrest was the beginning of a difficult time for you, but do you ever miss your brother?"

I forced my breathing under control and managed a wan smile. "I do. Lucius took prodigious care of me for many years. I miss that time. However, my memories are also tainted now with the truth. In the end he thought of no one besides himself."

Adrian looked down. "You've had much to bear."

"Yes . . . as has your own family, particularly Juliana." I adjusted my position in my saddle, unable to think of Lucius's deception when Giles's death was so fresh on my mind. "Have you learned anything new about the poisoning? I cannot seem to fully grasp what happened, what the murderer could have used. I mean, the poison must have worked rather quickly. We both saw him well the night before his death."

Adrian sat in silence. "I too have pondered that very question. Browning is researching a few different drugs. Apparently there are many possibilities for what our murderer could have utilized. Camphor can cause difficulty breathing and convulsions, but it would have required a large dose. And it has a sour taste and smell. I can't imagine Giles ingesting such a thing without knowing something of it."

"What about hemlock?"

"Browning says it tastes like parsnip and has a mouse-like smell."

I bit my lip. "I think I read something in the paper about laurel water. Has Mr. Browning considered it?"

"Again, a rather odorous smell. I considered prussic acid as well. But death occurs almost instantly with that poison. Giles rode and shot with our hunting party for at least an hour before the effects began, assuming the poison was administered at the house. I can see no other way."

"I suppose it couldn't have been a gas of some kind since you were all out of doors."

"No. What Browning and I believe we are looking for is a poison Giles could not detect as well as something that would take a few hours before rendering him unconscious. It is my belief that the murderer meant for us to think his death nothing but an accident. He had no way of knowing Giles's horse would bolt straight for the garden party, or that Lewis Browning would know something of the causes of death. And Ewan saw Giles slump over in the saddle." Adrian leaned forward, his expression fading further into a look of uncertainty.

"Well, we can't come to any conclusions out here." I dipped my chin. "I have an inkling to visit Middlecrest's vast library. Shall we make our return?"

Adrian nodded, but as he directed Atlas away from the hill, the piercing crack of a gunshot sliced through the air. Flick's knees buckled at first, then flexed. In a whirlwind I crashed forward onto Flick's neck then back into the saddle. Shock coursed through my nerves as I felt the sudden loss of control, my fingers scrambling for the reins.

Flick's powerful muscles jolted as she reared up, and I screamed. It was all I could do to maintain my seat as I gripped the side-saddle with my right leg. I was lifted into the air, then slammed down hard.

Atlas shuffled in place, grinding against Adrian's tight control. Adrian jerked him around, intent on reaching Flick's head, but his desperate move was too late. Flick bolted.

The crash of wind pounded my face as my eyes stung with tears. "Flick! Oh Flick, stop!" My voice was lost to the thrashing of hooves.

The image of Giles erupting into the garden party leapt into my mind. Had I been marked for the same fate? The reins proved useless as I jerked back, the muscles in my arms screaming with each thrust. Flick was consumed by instinct.

I heard a shout from behind me and peeked over my shoulder. It was Adrian in pursuit, his arm outstretched. What was he pointing at? I'd never been to this part of the estate and my eyes were blurry with tears. Unable to release the death grip I had on the reins, I couldn't wipe my eyes. It took several of Flick's long strides before I made out what Adrian was so desperate for me to see.

A sudden drop in the land. And Flick was heading straight for it.

My heart deserted me at first, then pounded its way back into my chest, shooting quivers down my arms and straight into my fingers. Despite the sweat gathering on Flick's coat, she showed no sign of tiring. A near stumble only charged her panicked flight, but it brought my father's voice into my mind.

He'd been in the same situation long ago. What had he said? *"Ease up on the reins. It makes no sense, but it works."*

Ease up on the reins! I forced my locked fingers to open, allowed the thin leather straps to slide forward. "Relax," I said to myself. I was clinging to Flick like a cursed mountain lion and causing her even more fear.

I can balance. I could do this. "Oh, God, help me." I prayed aloud.

Seconds passed. My breaths came shallow and fast. One by one, I forced my muscles to relax. Several wild strides more and Flick lowered her head.

"That's right, girl. Everything is all right."

Her frantic pace slowed enough for Adrian to overtake us a few measly yards from the cliff's edge. He directed Atlas to Flick's head and gradually turned us all to safety. Gently, he pulled her to a stop. My ears buzzed and I don't even remember Adrian springing from Atlas's back. But his arms were around me just the same, lifting me from the saddle to the ground.

My legs shook, and he kept his arms tight around my waist.

Gasping, I choked out, "A gunshot? So close?"

"A hunter perhaps." He sounded remarkably calm, yet deep within those blue eyes I saw anger. He drew me near. "If you were not such an exceptional rider, Flick certainly would have unseated you."

I glared back at the cliff's edge. "You don't think?"

His voice turned icy. "We can talk more at the house." His tight gaze swept the rolling land around us before he regarded me. "Right now, I don't want to linger." He moved me in front of him, his eyes a bit softer. "Do you think you can ride?"

On instinct I nodded, but as soon as I turned back to Flick, my stomach churned. I felt Adrian's hand at my back. "Why don't you join me on Atlas?"

I sighed, feigning nonchalance. "I'm fine. I mean, I'll be fine. They say to get back on the horse, right?"

"That's what they say, but saying and doing are two separate things."

I tilted my chin. "Well, I'm not a quitter."

"No, but we'll need to move fast." He tied Flick's reins to his saddle. "Up onto Atlas with you."

Adrian cupped his hands beside his horse, and I placed my boot in his solid fingers. He thrust me in front of his saddle, my leg crossed awkwardly against Atlas's neck, before swinging up behind me. We settled into place, and Atlas held perfectly still as if he wished to make the whole thing easy on me.

Adrian reached around me to secure the reins. "Are you comfortable?"

I wanted to laugh. Comfortable? I was a mess. A bit fearful of the horse but far more so of my own heart. Adrian felt warm and solid at my back, his strong arms the perfect refuge. Tears threatened to spill onto my cheeks.

Whether I could continue to fight it or not, I had to admit to myself I'd developed feelings for my convenient husband—the same man I knew to be a flirt and a rake. Of course, he had proven he wanted to protect me. Of that I was certain. I sighed as I leaned my head against his chest, and I felt his arms tighten around me.

Love had never been part of our arrangement, and I'd best remember that.

CHAPTER 13

I awaited Adrian in our connecting room again that night, my nerves raw, the feel of his arms still fresh on my skin. I gathered my feet beneath my dressing gown and snuggled farther into the sofa. The sun had dipped below the horizon, relinquishing the roll of night guard to the moon. The scent of woodsmoke tinted the air as the steady crackling of the fire broke the emotive silence around me.

When the door latch clicked, I turned to see Adrian enter the sitting room, his gaze fixed to the floor. Weariness had wound its way into his eyes, his jaw tense. He tugged at his tight-fitting jacket as he crossed the rug, then stopped at the fireplace without a word, avoiding the vacancy on the sofa to jab at an already roaring fire. After perching his hand on the mantel, he finally stole a glance my direction.

"Have you recovered from earlier?"

"As well as can be expected." Was he angry with me?

He shoved the poker back in its place on the iron rack with a resulting clang. "I rode all over that blasted hillside after I returned you to the house. Whoever took that shot was long gone. At first I thought it was the result of that cursed letter—that someone meant to do you harm, but Browning arrived a few minutes ago.

He had a run-in with one of the French couriers he's been tracking and got a shot off with his pistol. It seems they were rather close to where we were. It's possible it was the same shot that startled your horse." He glanced up. "But here's where it gets interesting. When Browning came upon the man he was following, he recognized him. The spy was none other than one of your attackers from last night."

I sat up. "What?"

"Browning injured the man, but he ducked beneath a bridge in the fog and eluded him. Browning doesn't believe he can get far with such an injury. He'll likely need shelter and medical attention."

"They must have been watching me from the church the whole time. The group was there for the letter."

Bitterness entered his voice. "We cannot be certain until we've captured him, but we would be fools not to assume so. Either way, I've come to a rather difficult conclusion. First the funeral, then the stray shot in the woods . . . I think it best that you and Isaac leave for my townhouse in London first thing tomorrow morning."

The air left my lungs. "Leave for London, now?"

The sharp lines on his face softened, and he crossed the room to take a seat at my side. "I know you'd prefer not to face the society waiting for you there, but it is no longer safe for you to remain here."

I considered his words as Isaac came to mind. Was the townhouse secure? How could we be sure? Fear gathered in my chest. Whatever I decided, Isaac was my main priority—he must be protected at all costs. "How can you know we will be any safer there?"

Adrian balled his fingers into a fist, opening his mouth to speak, then hesitating. "I cannot."

More to myself I added, "Isaac and I would be alone at the townhouse." Then to him, "I wouldn't know who to turn to if I needed help. I have no friends in London, and I know you won't leave Middlecrest until the intelligence is discovered."

"And the murder investigation is concluded." He released a sharp sigh. "There's more."

"What is it?"

"Mrs. Ayles. She has begun to question whether you and I are truly in love, putting me in an awkward position, particularly when she already suspects I'm hiding something." He raised his eyebrows. "Unfortunately, she came upon me one night a few months back when I'd just returned from one of my late-night rides." He rubbed his temples. "I handled it badly. Rumors have been swirling in the village for some time regarding my many excursions from the house. The carriage accident and our love story solved so many problems for me. I had been looking for a way to dodge the rumors for some time."

He held up his hand. "I know what you are thinking about Mrs. Ayles, but I've investigated, and I don't believe her involved with the French; however, she has a great many friends and a far-too-busy mouth. If she thinks you and I are hiding something, she could ruin everything."

I sighed. "She said something to me as well regarding my indifference. I'm afraid I've done a poor job of pretending to love you."

"If you and Isaac leave now, it would put an end to the charade. I will warn you, however, the move might open us up for censure. I do not pretend to know what would be said, but if we did not marry for love, my being in your coach as well as your room in the inn would not go unnoticed nor unremarked."

He sat perfectly still, staring at the same corner of the room for several minutes. "Whether *you* stay or go must be entirely your decision. I have mistakenly arranged your life into the very danger you must now escape." His hand was in his hair, a somber glint in his eyes. "I could never live with myself if I forced you to London or asked you to stay and something happened to either of you."

I laid my hand on his arm, driven in part by a sense of loyalty and respect . . . but what else? My response burst forth before I'd really had a chance to ponder it. "I choose to stay—with you. I will not abandon you or your mission. Britain needs my help. I truly believe we can work together to uncover the truth *and* protect Isaac at the same time. I owe Giles as much. And regardless of where I am, neither of us is safe until we find this murderer and bring him to justice. Whoever wishes me harm could reach me just as easily in London. And here at Middlecrest we have each other."

A slight smile accompanied his words. "I should say you surprise me, but I would be lying. I've never met anyone quite like you." He ran his finger across my skin, then stopped as he drew back, a wave of tingles following the path. "Perhaps we've both seen too much of the good and bad in this world. If character is shaped by experience, I daresay we've both had our fair share."

"I suppose it is." My chest felt tight. I couldn't help but think back about myself just a few short years ago, how arrogant I had been, how unfeeling to everyone but Brook. Then life had dealt me a bitter blow, and Brook's utter betrayal had changed everything.

Yet for the first time since it all happened, I finally realized that the sum of my choices as well as his had sent me down a particular path, one I could only look back on now and be grateful for. I was not the same person today as I had once been. Had Adrian gone through something similar?

Something made me look up, and I was startled by Adrian's watchful gaze. Of course, I still had a long way to go if I meant to understand the depth of my heart and, more importantly, how much I was willing to risk.

♣

Deep into the night I awoke, my mind stirred by the events of the day. Utterly still, I stared at the shadowed canopy above my bed as the gusty arrival of a spring storm clamored against my bedchamber window. What perfect company for my incessantly dark thoughts. Gathering the eiderdown beneath my chin, I took a long breath.

The memory of the attack at the funeral fought for control of my mind. One of the men who'd participated was a French spy. Likely, they all were. A chill caused the hairs on my neck to rise, and I couldn't help but glance at my bedchamber's locked door. Could Giles's killer be involved with these men? Granted, I couldn't see any sort of connection, but the two incidences had to be linked in some way. No one could dismiss such a thing as mere coincidence.

Adrian had mentioned before he left the sitting room earlier in the night that he and Mr. Browning would continue researching possible poisons before they retired. Huddled alone in the gloom of my bedchamber with sleep elusive, I decided to hash out once again what I knew of Giles's death and how it might relate to me or Adrian.

The poison had to be one of the keys. Who gave it to Giles, and how?

The guests still in residence from the party had been free to move about the house all day just as they had been the morning of Giles's death. Each one had come to Middlecrest to be a part of the wedding—to partake in the joyous celebration. Yet someone had come with a far different purpose in mind. But who? And why?

Mr. Ewan Hawkins was invited by Adrian himself, so I didn't think him a likely suspect. Of course, he was present in the house when the poisoning happened. I found it interesting he'd not left the estate yet. And he seemed to be spending a great deal of time with Juliana.

Speaking of Juliana, what of her and Phoebe? I ran my fingers along the smooth coverlet as I examined the details I'd compiled over the last few days. Anything might prove vital. How well did Adrian know each of his girls? He seemed distracted at times, busy with his work for the crown. He could easily miss something important, especially something a father would never believe about his own child. Juliana had a darkness to her character. Of course, she was grieving and much of her behavior could be laid firmly at that door.

Was it indeed my husband's spy work that brought a murderer into his home? Moreover, did I honestly think Giles was somehow involved in the French threat? Slowly, I shook my head, dismissing the thought as hastily as it had come. Not Giles. Not silly, affable Giles. He could never betray his country.

My mind shifted back to the poison. Whatever had been used to render Giles unable to manage his horse had to be ingested somehow. Assuming it wasn't tasteless, the murderer would have had to be extremely careful when he slipped it into some type of food or drink. Otherwise, Giles certainly would have regarded it. And what about everyone else in the house? How could someone be certain Giles and Giles alone would take the poison? It could hardly look like an accident if someone else fell ill. And what if Giles wasn't even the intended target?

No one had been in the breakfast room when I arrived the morning of his death. Of course, I had been avoiding most of the houseguests that day and arrived rather late. Really, I'd given the killer an easy go of it. By the time I made my way to the garden party, the men had left long before. I would get nowhere along this line of thinking without finishing the interviews Adrian had asked me to complete. I still had several people to speak with.

I plumped my pillow and rolled onto my side. Busy or not, the cook, Mrs. Jennings, would have to be next. First thing in the morning I'd head to the kitchens. She alone knew just what Giles had eaten prior to his fateful ride. I pressed my hand to my forehead and flopped onto my back once again. Anyone could have presented him his last bite of food or drink. At any rate, somebody saw something, and I was determined to flush out the truth.

The first ray of morning light sent my eyelids fluttering open. Had I even slept? It was quite a chore, but I was able to drag myself out of the bed at last and pull the bell for my maid, Lilley.

My bedchamber window framed a misty morning. Though sluggish, I still hadn't much patience to wait for my maid to arrive, so I wormed my way into my morning gown of jaconet muslin and sat at the looking glass long before she appeared with a cup of hot chocolate. She had proved to be a proficient lady's maid as well as a help to Miss Barton in the nursery.

"I see you're up already. Any plans today, my lady?" She had a soft voice and easy manners.

"Not really. I shan't be leaving the house. However, I do hope to spend some time looking into the running of this estate."

Lilley's hands hesitated in the air as she moved to gather up my hair. "Would you like me to tell Mrs. Coombs to expect you? Mrs. Ayles usually meets with her in the green salon late in the morning to discuss the various things that need to be done."

I wasn't surprised by her disclosure, only concerned. Mrs. Ayles had obviously stepped in over the years as lady of the house, and it would be a delicate process of dethroning her. I had purposefully avoided stepping on the grand dame of the house's toes until now, but such a thing could hardly be avoided for long.

"Thank you. I shall plan to see both of them at some point today." My eyes shot to the looking glass just in time to catch the look of surprise that flitted across her face. "Of course, that is . . . after I meet with Mrs. Jennings."

L

I stumbled upon Adrian near the servants' quarters on my way to the kitchens. It seemed he'd come to the same conclusion as I—whatever Giles ate and drank the morning of his death could very well be the key to answering so many questions. Adrian's eyelids looked pinched with heavy shadows under his eyes. He held the kitchen door wide for me to enter first but whispered in my ear as I passed.

"Be careful what you say."

I paused, shooting him a sideways glance. "I'm always careful what I say."

My words were drowned out by the cook's booming voice reverberating across the busy space. Pans clattered. People laughed as they worked. The fresh scent of bread and spices met my nose. Mrs. Jennings saw us immediately and wiped her hands on her apron as she spoke.

"Your lordship!" The room fell silent.

Adrian smiled and addressed the room. "Please, do not let us interfere. Continue with what you are doing. Her ladyship and I just need a moment to speak with Mrs. Jennings."

Heads nodded in all directions, but the feeling of concern was evident across their stricken faces. They were probably disconcerted to find their employer suddenly watching over them, fueling an undercurrent of anxiety in the room.

Mrs. Jennings barked a few orders at the scullery maids, then led us around the corner to a small apartment down the back corridor. As I stepped into the room, I noticed a large cabinet and a circle of keys that hung on the far wall, while a desk and chairs filled the bulk of the remaining space. I took a seat as instructed, the cold wooden slats pressing against my back. Adrian pulled the door shut behind us. Mrs. Jennings twirled her fingers one direction then the next, finally plunging them against her apron.

"What can I help you with, your lordship, my lady?"

Adrian took a quick glance at me, then spoke. "Please, be at ease, Mrs. Jennings. There is nothing amiss. Quite the opposite actually. The staff has been nothing short of exemplary these last few difficult days. I wanted to thank you for that."

Her broad shoulders relaxed, and she offered me a wan smile. "The staff'll be glad to hear of your approval. 'Pon my word, it's been a beast of a few days."

"Yes, it has." I leaned forward. "Which brings us to another reason his lordship and I have come to see you." I paused. "Would you mind thinking back to the morning of the gentleman's accident? Do you remember anything out of the usual happening that day in the kitchens?"

Her eyes widened. "Unusual? I cannot say that I did."

"For example, did anyone come to the kitchens that morning who isn't usually in the area?"

Her face flushed red, her eyes darting from Adrian back to me. "Can't say I remember exactly. We were quite busy with the garden party, your ladyship. I'll be the first to admit I took any help I could get that day."

Adrian lifted his hand. "What about the guests then?"

She shook her head, then froze as if she'd remembered something. "Wait . . . There was someone . . . Mr. Hawkins popped in to see what I might give him to eat. He had missed breakfast, and I was obliged to offer him a small sandwich."

My nerves were pricked. "Did he perhaps take any other food with him? For anyone else?"

"Cor, no. He shoveled the sandwich in his mouth and was on his way."

"What about the servants who were working that day?"

"Nearly everyone in the house was expected to help out. We could have hardly done otherwise. Even your maid, Lilley, spent some time kneading dough and passing plates. Goodness, we had a time holding everything together. One of the footmen even had to chase a rat from beneath my feet. They've been quite awful of late." She scrunched up her lips. "I can't say I remember too much else—just lots of hard work."

Adrian rubbed his chin. "Do you know if Mr. Giles Harris ate in the breakfast room with the rest of the guests?"

"I believe he did. Yes, I remember clearly, Jerome"—she glanced at me—"one of our footmen, said Mr. Harris was the last to leave the room. As I was delivering the cake to the garden party, I saw him m'self trotting across the lawns to the stables. Enjoyed his food, he did."

Adrian drummed his fingers on his knee. "Over the next few days, I may find it necessary to speak with each and every person you can remember entering the kitchen that morning."

"'Pon rep.'" She stiffened, turning a roving glare about the room. "That will include quite a bit of people."

I gave her an encouraging smile. "Perhaps you could make us a list. And I would appreciate it if you would include everything that was served in the breakfast room as well."

She nodded, a scowl taking over her face. "I've plum tarts to attend to now. I'll get to it as soon as I can."

Adrian pushed to his feet and opened the door in one quick swoop. "Thank you, Mrs. Jennings. I do realize we're taking you from your work. We appreciate all the help you can muster."

"Humph." She bobbed her chin as she left the room.

Neither Adrian or I spoke on our way back into the main kitchen area, and we were met by a room just as quiet as before, the staff standing like his majesty's soldiers at attention. It was just as Adrian and I were about to take our leave that everything changed.

A loud crash resounded behind a nearby door.

One of the scullery maids jumped near to the ceiling. "Heavens, if that was another rat, it's the loudest I've ever heard."

Mrs. Jennings's eyes grew round. "That was no rat." Her gaze circled the room as if to ensure everyone was accounted for. "Probably just one of the servants in the dry larder."

Did she really believe that? Adrian stepped forward, a curious glance at me. "Perhaps we should take a look."

He followed Mrs. Jennings to the dry larder and waited as she pumped the handle. The door held tight.

"That's odd." She repositioned her hand. Suddenly the latch released, and the door crashed open. A volley of movement and Adrian was forced to dive out of the way as a large shape collapsed forward.

Cook screamed. One of the scullery maids fainted. Adrian fell into silent contemplation as we all stared down at what appeared to be a dead body slumped over on the floor.

CHAPTER 14

He's alive." Adrian rolled the man onto his back before darting a sharp glare at me.

My heart pounded into my throat as my gaze followed his. It was one of my attackers from the funeral.

Mrs. Jennings toddled forward, her hands as restless as before. "Heaven help us. Who is that?"

Adrian shook his head, his voice at odds with his hard stare. "I don't know." One more shrewd glance at me. It seemed our knowledge of his identity was to be a secret.

A moan from the man on the floor drew my attention to a brown stain across his midsection.

"He's wounded." Mr. Browning's shot, of course. He had indeed hit his target.

The spy grunted as he worked to move, his hand flopping onto his stomach. "J'étais sur mon cheval . . . une branche d'arbre."

Adrian pulled back. "It seems we have a Frenchman in our midst." Irritation laced his voice. We were already losing control of the secret. "What the devil is he doing at Middlecrest?"

Beneath a tangle of wet, black hair, the injured man had a slender face and even longer nose. Another agonized moan, and he blinked open his eyes, revealing a marbled glaze that covered two dark-brown pools. Sweat dripped from his dirt-stained temples, but his limbs trembled as if he were cold. I knelt at his side and touched his ruddy forehead, which was burning hot.

"Should we send for the doctor and the police?"

Adrian shouted for Mr. Young, the butler, and one of the footmen took off running to fetch him. Carefully, I lifted the bottom of the man's shirt, relieved to find the wound free of any fresh blood. The terrible bruising, however, extended up his chest.

Unable to focus on either Adrian or me, the man's eyes slipped closed, his head lolling side to side, and Adrian gently nudged his shoulder. "Tell me, sir. Do you know where you are?"

Dry and cracked, the man's mouth opened and closed, but no words came forth.

There was a strange severity to Adrian's voice when he leaned near the man's ear. "We will assist you with your injuries, but we need to know just why you are here."

The man's eyes rolled up beneath his eyelids, and I reached for Adrian's arm.

"I don't think he's lucid."

Adrian pushed to his feet, turning like a dragon on the servants who had gathered to watch. "Does anyone recognize this man?"

No one moved an inch.

"Don't take me for a fool." Adrian spread out his fingers on the counter, his voice in full control, the master of the house. "Someone helped this man into the kitchens."

Mrs. Jennings's plump neck jiggled beneath her chin as she shook her head. "My lord, no one's been in the larder for hours." She looked anxiously about the room. "Trust me, we're all as shocked as you." The bend to her voice lent an aura of truth to her words, but Adrian and I both knew someone must have seen the man take refuge inside. A few tight breaths and Mrs. Jennings addressed each staff member one at a time, each repeating his or her own adamant denial.

Adrian mumbled. "I suppose it's in the realm of possibility that the man got himself in there somehow to hide without anyone seeing him."

Footsteps pounded beyond the kitchens louder and louder until the door swung open. Several men poured into the room, Lewis Browning at the head of the crowd, his intelligent eyes scrutinizing the scene. Adrian motioned to the injured man on the floor.

Mr. Browning squinted, then knelt. "He was in the dry larder?"

"Curious, isn't it?" The two of them were so calm and cool, I couldn't help but wonder how many times Adrian and Mr. Browning had been forced to conceal something like this before. "I'll go for the authorities as soon as you no longer need me."

Adrian turned to Mr. Young. "Send my groom into Plattsdale to fetch Dr. Knight at once." Then he beckoned the footmen over. "I'll need your help to move this man to the conservatory. There's a large sofa there where he can be both private and secured. See if you can find something we can carry him on."

I didn't like the look in Adrian's eyes, and I moved in close beside him. "Darling?"

His eyes flashed to mine, clearly startled by my term of endearment. It was the first time our little charade had fallen from his mind.

I gave a tight smile. "Won't moving this man so far in his present state cause further pain or injury?"

"I'm afraid we have no other choice at present."

The footman burst back into the room with a long board from

the stables. The group assisted the battered man onto it with as much delicacy as they could muster. The man tolerated the movement better than I expected—or perhaps he'd slipped from consciousness. I raced to hold the door as the four men maneuvered their way out of the kitchens.

The initial pass down the servant's hall was quiet and swift. But by the time we got to the main hall, the commotion had alerted the other residents of the house, who joined the group in haste to lend their own opinions of things.

"Don't tilt the board so." Mrs. Ayles seemed far more spry than usual, barking orders as if she'd studied medicine in her spare time.

"He doesn't look very well, Papa." Phoebe ducked and weaved to get a look at the injured man's face. "Oh, the poor dear. Do we know him?"

I pulled her aside. "Listen, I need you to gather whatever medical supplies are in the house and bring them to the conservatory as soon as possible." She hesitated, then nodded.

Middlecrest's conservatory was situated on the eastern corner of the house and boasted the same solid roof as the rest of the structure. Rows of magnificent windows lined one wall and met a piped stone floor. Though quite a few plants dotted the open space, clearly the room had been designated for a purpose other than gardening.

I blinked away a puff of dust as I breathed in the overwhelming scent of fresh paint.

It was artwork that covered the adjoining walls—a lone tree, Middlecrest at sunset, landscape after landscape of rolling hills and lush valleys. Dodging to stay out of the men's way, I shrank against the window's edge, close to an intricate portrait of a beautiful woman.

Phoebe plowed into the room with the medical kit, belatedly catching me staring at the work of art. She thrust the supplies into Mr. Browning's hands before making her way back over to me, her nose scrunched up at the bridge. "Do you like it?"

Surprised by the question, I quickly nodded. "The painting is lovely."

But Phoebe's attention could not be held for long. "Do you think the man will pull through?"

"We'll have to wait for the doctor." I, however, was distracted by the picture. Somehow the woman looked familiar. "Is this your mother?"

"Oh, yes." She spared only a cursory glance at the portrait. "She doesn't look anything like me, does she?" A nervous laugh. "She was beautiful. I enjoyed painting her likeness from a small picture Papa has." Phoebe rose up onto her tiptoes as the flurry of movement continued across the room. "Heavens, why are they tying his hands?"

"For safety." I drew her away, but my mind was elsewhere, flashing back to Mrs. Ayles's words in the drawing room. Was she right? Was Adrian still in love with his dead wife? I'd originally branded him a hardened rake, but now that I knew him better, the label felt uncomfortable. Perhaps he was indeed heartsick. "You have quite a talent, Phoebe."

Her attention, however, remained fixed on the commotion in the room. The best she could muster was a distracted, "Thank you."

Neither of us heard Adrian when he drew up behind us. "What a ghastly business."

His hand was at the small of my back. "Dr. Knight should be here shortly, and Browning intends to watch over our guest as soon as he returns from Plattsdale. Mrs. Coombs has arranged for one of the manservants to clean him up. There is really little more the two of you can do here." There was a pointed ring to the undertone of his voice. He meant to speak with me in private. I nodded.

Phoebe piped up as we moved to the door. "Please, Papa, I'd like to stay and help in some way."

Adrian peeked into the busy room before shaking his head. "This is not a place for young ladies."

Phoebe gave him a pert frown and crossed her arms. "I am not an idiot, nor a hoyden. I only mean to help Mrs. Coombs."

"Not this time. Off to your room. I'll be by to speak with you all shortly."

I could tell she thought about pouting. One last hard look at Adrian and she turned to leave.

He watched her departure with an odd expression before extending an arm to me. His voice came out tight. "I cannot be certain, but I suspect we have found our murderer. Although I cannot believe he acted without help."

"And the household—"

"Is not in any danger at present. Our unexpected guest is hardly in a position to make an escape, and he will never be left alone."

I peeked behind me to be certain we were out of earshot. "What leads you to believe he's the one who murdered Giles? There is more to this business than simply being a Frenchman."

Adrian quirked a smile. "Most definitely." He motioned with his chin. "Browning found a bit of grayish-white powder in the seam of the man's boots."

"Could he possibly be the same man you were supposed to have robbed that day on the road?"

"That is precisely what I think."

I paused for a moment, my thoughts running wild. "But if that is true, why on earth would he murder Giles?"

"Clearly there is more to this mystery than we have ascertained, which is one of the reasons why I've moved him into this back room. Browning and I need to question him. We shall send word to our people in the admiralty as well. If at all possible, I'd prefer Browning be the one to take him to our people in London. That is, as soon as the man is well enough to travel. I simply don't trust the authorities around here. We shall have to let them question him, but I don't want them taking him into custody. It shall be a delicate affair."

I looked up in faint surprise. "That is quite risky, don't you think? And in the meantime? Is he to remain here in our house?"

He gave that roguish shrug of his as if such a gesture was all the reassurance I needed. "Do not be anxious, Elizabeth. He'll be bound and watched"—his eyes found mine—"very closely."

L

I found Phoebe near the landing the following day, gazing out a window. I called her name, but she was so distracted I was forced to touch her arm to gain her attention, and then she staggered backward as if I'd caught her doing something naughty. She gave me some ridiculous story about watching a bird and then hurried on her way, leaving me a bit cold and confused. I looked out the window myself but saw nothing untoward on the east lawn. Whatever she had been watching with such intensity was long gone.

Equally disconcerting, I later stumbled upon Juliana perched in a nearby alcove laughing with Ewan Hawkins, who knelt before her in some sort of dramatic display. Of course, he popped up off the floor as soon as I approached, pretending all too easily he'd not been enjoying himself.

"Pardon me." He stifled a chuckle, his right hand hard at work wiping the smile from his chin while his left one ducked behind him. "I didn't realize you were there, your ladyship." Decorum crept back into his face.

Juliana stood as well and swept over to my side, belatedly taking my arm in a way she would never have done if Mr. Hawkins were not in our company. "Do not regard my dear Ewan. He is nothing but a tease." To him she said, "Perhaps it is best for you to go." A lingering laugh accompanied her words. "I'd like to speak with my new mama alone."

Ewan bowed and made his escape, clearly unconcerned by what I must think of their improper behavior. I, however, could not but remark on the familiarity between them, the use of their Christian names. This was the first spark of life I'd seen from Juliana since Giles's death.

She turned to me, her earlier reticence returning. "Will you accompany me to the sitting room?"

I was wary of Juliana's newfound charity, but I had promised her father to forge a friendship. "Certainly."

Adrian's daughters frequented a large sitting area on the upper floor most afternoons. I was surprised to find the room empty as Juliana led me through the door. The small room, though a bit dark, housed a well-tended fire and comfortable seats. It didn't take me long to see why the girls enjoyed the space. It was a relaxing affair with yellow walls trimmed in white, accented by thick, damask drapes that fell like waterfalls on either side of two spacious windows.

I relaxed in a wingback chair while Juliana took a nearby candle to light the wall sconces.

"There, that's a bit better." She eyed the door, then took a seat in the chair across from me. She smoothed out her skirt first once then twice before finally clearing her throat. "I brought you here because I don't want you to misunderstand about Ewan. It would only cause trouble for him. We grew up together, you know."

"No, I didn't." I delayed any further words, trying to make sense of what she had said. "What do you mean, grew up together? I thought he was Giles's friend, here to play best man at the wedding."

"He was Giles's dear friend, but he is also ours. You see, years ago Papa found him in London in a workhouse. Dear Ewan was only ten years old and I nine. Maybe it was the disfigurement of his hand or something else, but Papa's heart was touched. He grew angry with how Ewan was being treated, and what do you know, but Papa brought him here. Ewan was tutored at Middlecrest alongside Phoebe and me—like a brother—until he was ready for Cambridge." She adjusted her back. "Papa made it quite clear there is to be nothing romantic between us, and there never will be. I could not consider marrying a man of questionable birth, if you get my meaning."

Though she was only echoing the sentiment of every other well-bred female as well as her father's, I could not help but think of Isaac and my cousins, Sybil and her twin brother, Harland, who had grown up in their own mix of questionable circumstances. I had discovered years ago that in many cases, life should not be so easily labeled. "I understand . . . a little."

I must have sounded irritated, for she shot me a pointed glare, the earlier joy vanishing from her face. "Then you must think I disrespect Giles's memory by enjoying another's company."

"Juliana, that is not what I said or meant."

"Didn't you?"

She intended to goad me into an argument, and I would have none of that. "I can see clear as day you loved Giles and he you. I would never suggest such a thing."

She choked back a tearful breath, and I handed her my handkerchief. She perked up at the offer, her eyes glistening with tears. "Giles and I cared for each other a great deal, even though we knew each other such a short time." She stole a peek over the handkerchief. "Did he by any chance say anything about me?" A sniff. "The night before he died?"

All at once I wondered if she was running her own investigation into Giles's murder, or if something else spurred the question. "He did tell me he wanted to protect you." I lifted my eyelashes. "He told me he was worried about something."

She shifted in her chair, her voice rising an octave. "Why on earth would he say he needed to protect me?"

"I haven't the least idea. I thought perhaps *you* did after what you said just moments after he was killed. Tell me, did something happen before your father and I arrived at Middlecrest? Anything in the days leading up to the garden party?"

Her flippant confusion turned to anger. "I suppose Phoebe put you up to these questions."

"No." I scanned the room. "Why would she?"

Juliana fiddled with her fingers in her lap for several seconds, and it was almost a surprise when she jerked her attention back to me.

"Phoebe thought Giles's sudden disappearance was somehow my fault."

I froze. "What disappearance?"

"Oh, it wasn't anything to remark, really." She sniffed and dabbed her cheek. "He left the house a few days before you arrived. We'd quarreled about the wedding, and he told me he needed a few days to think everything over. Phoebe said I'd been far too overbearing. I didn't mean to order him about, but I wanted everything to be perfect. He was not himself when he returned. I grew anxious he wished he could call the whole thing off, but he would never do so as a gentleman. Such a task would have been left to me."

"Did he tell you where he went when he left?"

"No, but he could not have gone far. He was only absent for one night."

Surely someone in the stables could fill me in on the missing details. Of course, his groom and valet had already left the estate, but others would have some idea. I looked up. "What about the morning of the garden party? Did you see him then?"

She shook her head. "After speaking with Phoebe, I had decided to carry on with the wedding as planned, unless Giles asked me to do otherwise."

I clenched my teeth. Was it possible that Giles simply wanted to talk over his impending marriage that day he'd asked for a private meeting in the garden, or was there something else that drove him to speak so urgently to me the night before? How I wished I had not put him off.

Juliana leaned forward. "You don't think of me differently now, do you? I could not bear for anyone to think of me in such a way."

There was an earnest truth to the tone of her voice, and I more than anyone understood embarrassment. I gladly took her hand and whispered, "Not at all." But as I met her gaze one last time before rising to leave, my heart stilled. There was something in those green eyes of hers. Was it guilt?

Adrian was right. Juliana's grief had several layers, layers that might hold the key to her fiancé's death.

CHAPTER 15

I spent the following afternoon in the nursery with Isaac, hard-pressed not to pour all I had learned from Juliana into Miss Barton's willing ears. Isaac's nurse had proved something of a friend since I'd arrived at the house, but servants tended to talk. And I needed to protect Juliana's privacy.

Isaac was his usual happy self, darting about the room for hours, picking up and putting down everything he came in contact with. That is, until it came time for his nap. I gathered him up in my arms and looked about to do the same with his favorite blue blanket, but it was not on the nursery room floor, nor tucked in his bed where he left it sometimes. I'd noticed it missing the night I heard him crying, but I'd forgotten all about it.

I called out to Miss Barton as I scoured the room and the hall, but the well-loved scrap of fabric was nowhere. Isaac's pudgy fingers repeatedly clenched, then released, as he added his own pitiful wail for the familiar soft fabric. Finally he smashed his chin into my shoulder, tears spilling down his cheeks. Miss Barton poked her head in the door on my third trip across the carpet.

"I guess the blanket has still not turned up."

She splayed her hand across her chest. "Is that all? You had me worried. With all the commotion of the house, I'd forgotten to tell you I've still not found it."

"How have the nights been with it gone?"

"I was terribly anxious Isaac might take a pet as he is doing now, but the poor dear has been so exhausted from our adventures of the day, he's fallen asleep at once."

I glanced first at the clock, then the doorway. "Well, I'm afraid he's going to be a bear to put down today. I can't remember the last time I've personally laid him down for a nap without it."

Miss Barton caught my arm, speaking in that soothing voice I knew so well. "Please, my lady, don't let yourself be overly concerned. Isaac and I shall manage well enough this afternoon as we have for the last two days. He only needs a little extra love. I'll help our darling boy to bed."

I passed Isaac's wriggling figure over to Miss Barton's outstretched arms, and he clutched her neck. "I cannot understand why the rattle and blanket have not turned up. Though he frequently lays his blanket down, he always comes back to claim it."

"Nor I. It is the strangest thing. Don't worry, I shall get him to sleep without too much of a fuss."

I kissed Isaac's head before sending a hand ruffling through his soft curls. "You must be a great deal better at getting him to do the difficult tasks than I am."

She shot me a determined smile, then turned to Isaac. "Come along, Master Isaac. It's high time you had a rest . . . with or without your beloved blanket."

"Miss Barton." The sound of my voice halted her steps. "Before you go, would you tell me where the two of you have spent your days? I've a mind to aid in the search at once."

A fleeting wrinkle crossed her forehead. "All over, actually.

There was the garden and the library, as well as the nursery, of course."

"Of course." I tapped my cheek. "I suppose I shall simply have to search the entire house till we find the items. But it does give me a place to start. I'll be sure to notify Mrs. Coombs as well." I shook my head. "What a time to lose something so dear. First the carriage accident, then the new house. Isaac has been through so much."

Miss Barton angled her chin. "Take heart, my lady. Even if we never do find it, which I doubt very much, all he needs is right here."

❧

A thorough search of the drawing room, the front and rear gardens, and the chapel disappointingly turned up nothing. Somehow Isaac's blanket and Miss Barton's family rattle had simply vanished. In fact, Mrs. Coombs acted like she'd never even seen such offending articles and added a mumbled, "Children and toys should be kept in the nursery at all times," as she walked away.

Mrs. Ayles spoke up from her seat on the sofa as I flew through the drawing room to add her own waspish comments about Isaac's disturbing behavior that had been permitted in every room of the house. As far as she was concerned, such disruptive behavior included laughing, speaking, and moving any quicker than a walk. Goodness, with those restrictions, Miss Barton was the worst nursery maid she'd ever met.

I choked back a retort, preoccupied with the growing fear that we would never find the blanket. I decided to seek out Adrian and ask if he had any idea where it had gone.

One of the chambermaids scurried by as I turned to descend the grand staircase, and Young greeted me on the ground floor. With a keen eye, he directed me to the library. Apparently Mr. Browning and Adrian had spent the length of the afternoon within those four walls.

My thoughts shifted as I traversed the east hall intent on the corner room. Adrian certainly seemed to trust Mr. Browning. The gentleman had been helpful in ascertaining the cause of Giles's death, but I didn't know him from Adam. Should I not be a bit cautious where he was concerned?

My hand settled on the library's heavy mahogany door and my heart constricted. Brook's betrayal had taught me to be cautious. People unfortunately were not always what they seemed. My eyes slipped closed for a brief moment. I wondered how much Adrian had told his friend of our arrangement. Either way, I knew what I must do yet dreaded it at the same time. With Adrian and Browning ensconced in the library, I would have to display my newly refined acting skills once again. I only hoped they'd improved.

My fingers curled into a fist, and I tapped the door with as much gusto as I could muster.

"Come in." It was Adrian.

I thrust open the door to find two inquisitive faces turned to mine, both quickly fading to surprise. Thankfully, the library was awash in a warm candlelit glow. Mr. Browning bowed from where he stood near the back shelf, a glass in his hand. Adrian sprang from his relaxed position in a chair by the fire, swinging his leg over the armrest.

"Elizabeth?"

"Darling, please, be at ease." I flashed a smile as my gaze fell to the stacks of books gathered haphazardly on the floor. "What's all this?"

Adrian offered me an arm and led me over to the sofa. "Browning and I have been doing a bit of research."

I looked to Mr. Browning. "And?"

After waiting for me to take my seat, Adrian dutifully took the chair at my side. "I'm afraid we have little to report."

Browning chuckled. "Except the possible poison."

Adrian flicked his fingers in the air. "Well, I guess there is that."

My eyes widened. "You mean, you've uncovered what Giles was given?"

"Possibly." Adrian tipped his head back against the chair. "And possibly not. Browning thinks Giles was given arsenic, but—"

"Such a poison fits all the symptoms." Browning crossed the room with a book in his hand. "Hours to take effect. Intestinal complaints. Loss of consciousness."

Adrian held up his hand. "The only problem we've run into with our little theory is delivery. Giles ate nothing but a serving of meat and a few vegetables before his fateful ride. Not a soup or a drink that the killer could deposit the powder into. We are at a loss as to how he could have ingested it."

I pressed my hands together in my lap. "And you're sure that is all he ate?"

Adrian retrieved a piece of paper from his jacket pocket and held it out. "Cook gave me the list but a few hours ago."

I accepted the paper and studied it for a few seconds. Adrian was right. Giles had ingested only a luncheon of meat and vegetables.

I slumped forward. "Where would the killer get the arsenic in the first place?"

"It's available at the apothecary, among other places."

"And I assume you have checked with all the local apothecary shops?"

Adrian peeked at his watch fob. "Browning plans to head to Reedwick and Plattsdale first thing tomorrow, but I doubt the killer would leave such an obvious trail."

"And you say it is a powder?"

"Yes." Adrian's voice had slipped into disinterest.

"Could the vegetables have been dipped in it in some way?"

He tapped a finger on his knee. "Such a thing would hardly have gone unremarked."

I imagined the food in the kitchen, the way it might look on the plate, how it would be served, then sat up, the hairs prickling on my arms. "But what about . . . marinated in it?"

Adrian jerked his attention back to me. Mr. Browning stopped cold and pressed his hand to his face. "Could it be that easy?"

Adrian blinked, then grasped my hand. "Did I not tell you my wife is brilliant?" He slapped his leg. "The meat! Of course. The arsenic could have simply been dissolved into olive oil—in effect, soaked in it. Why didn't we think of such a thing?"

I flashed a smile. "I couldn't say."

Adrian kissed the back of my hand. "Where have you been all afternoon, my love? If you knew how long we've been working on this. Well, never mind." He turned to face his friend. "So, what now?"

Mr. Browning dipped his chin. "Now, we ask the right questions."

CHAPTER 16

The ladies decided to retire early to their rooms after supper, as no one in the drawing room seemed the least interested in a game of whist or a song on the pianoforte, least of all me. The gentlemen had been long at their port every other night, so I imagined I'd have some time to await Adrian.

Inches from my bedchamber door he popped out of the shadows of the hall.

I thrust my hands into the air, sucking in a tight breath, ready to scream. Luckily, I managed to choke it back at the last second, gasping out a more ladylike, "What on earth are you doing?"

Adrian pressed one finger to his lips, an odd expression on his face as he motioned me inside.

I waited for him to seal the door to my bedchamber, my heart still drumming its way up my throat, before beginning again. "Why were you skulking in the hallway outside my room? You frightened me out of my wits."

"I do apologize." An infuriating hint of a smile emerged as he raked his hand through his thick hair. "I promise you I hadn't the least intention of doing so. However, it is good to know a crack exists in that maddeningly stoic demeanor of yours. Such

154

indifference—shall we call it—can be a trifle disconcerting at times."

"You know very well I'm trying my best."

"True." Gently, he reached out and touched my hair. "And were recently attacked. I haven't forgotten." Almost as an afterthought, he shrugged. "Well, I'm glad to see you are human at any rate."

"Human, indeed." Still shaken, I took a hasty step back. "And your inadvertent wife, if you've forgotten."

He darted a look up, that playful smile about his lips. "Don't worry, I've not forgotten." There it was again—that bend to his voice, the curious mix of humble servant and arrogant lord that left me questioning what I thought I knew of him. Shying away from any sort of an answer, I crossed the rug to the other side of the room. My maid had left us a snapping fire, and all at once the room felt uncomfortably warm. I took a seat on the settee.

"How is our spy in the conservatory?"

"Still in and out of consciousness. He's nursing a rather high fever at present. We must wait for it to break for answers." He looked up and added, "Someone is always with him, and he's in no shape to cause any trouble. The authorities will be back as soon as he is able to talk."

"Why were you waiting for me outside my room?"

Adrian softened his tone as he made his way onto the rug. "I had an idea, and I wanted to catch you before you'd had a chance to undress."

"Oh." All at once I felt foolish, my voice betraying a spark of uneasiness Adrian couldn't possibly understand. It was left to me to break the uncomfortable silence. "Tell me about this idea of yours."

He hesitated to speak at first. "We need proof linking Giles to the French spy and anyone else involved in his murder. I had the servants gather up Giles's things, and they are to be shipped to his mother's estate on the morn. What do you think about the two of us taking a look at them before they're removed?"

"You mean tonight?"

He propped his shoulder against a nearby wall, his arms intertwining across his chest. "Why not? It affords us the perfect opportunity to do so without the watchful eyes of the house."

"Then you intend this to be a secret search."

"Listen, you probably knew Giles better than anyone, even Juliana. That knowledge could provide us the important information we're looking for, and"—he cocked an eyebrow—"I trust you. There are few here at Middlecrest I could say the same about."

Was he hinting at Mr. Browning?

"If we work together, I do believe we can find a connection. Then and only then can we put this whole messy business behind us and get on with our lives."

Adrian's hand faltered as he reached for the bedpost, the confusion on his face echoing the thoughts charging so suddenly into my mind. What would our lives be like after everything settled down? I caught his perceptive look in the dim candlelight, and something fluttered in my chest.

The cursed Radcliff legacy crept into my mind, but was my deep hatred of the family already fading? Adrian was complicated, but he was nothing like Brook. At the end of the day, everyone makes mistakes. Goodness knew I had. And if I'd learned anything from my time at Croft Towers, it was that God does not reserve forgiveness for a select few. Still, could I trust my heart when it had led me astray before?

Adrian was handsome to be sure, his words so smooth and

controlled. He was so good at acting. Could I take such a chance with my fragile heart? With Isaac's?

Adrian motioned to the door, and I concealed my thoughts as best I could. "To the search, then." He offered a cursory nod and ushered me into the gloomy abyss of the wide corridor. What little moonlight bathed the outside wall of the estate lay hidden behind a row of heavy drapes. I kept close to Adrian as he led me farther and farther down the hall. Eventually we crossed the landing into the northern wing, and Adrian drew us to a halt beside a closed door. He spoke in a whisper. "This was Giles's room while he was here."

I heard the merest click and the door swung inward without another sound. Adrian took my hand and tugged me inside behind him. I leaned in close, the scent of his cologne meeting my nose. "How are we to see without a candle?"

He released my hand, and I listened to his heavy tread as he paced across the room. A whoosh of the drapes and a large recessed window appeared on one side of the room. Though hazy, little by little the white fingers of moonlight crept into the darkened bedchamber, making over every inch of the dismal space with various shades of gray.

Adrian turned back to me. "Better?"

"Yes, much better. Thank you." The large central bed took shape, and I saw Giles's trunk near the far wall. "Is it all in there?"

"As far as I know. I'll push the trunk over to the bed so we can lay everything out to examine it." Adrian knelt beside the chest and gave the corner a careless shove. The thick wooded box moved but an inch, and he sat back to assess his lack of progress. A smile wound across his face, his voice betraying a whisper of a laugh. "Well, that was a bit disappointing."

"I don't suppose you'd care for some assistance?"

He gripped one of the handles, his eyes finding mine. "If you would be so kind."

I did little to aid our plight, but we managed to slide the trunk nearer the bed.

Adrian wiped his forehead with his jacket sleeve. "What has he got in here, rocks?"

I fiddled with the latch and swung open the lid. The first layer looked to be mostly clothes, which Adrian wrestled onto the bed. "I daresay we need to check each piece. Anything could provide some sort of clue."

I reached for the first of a cluster of white shirts, then paused. "You don't think we are breaking Giles's trust in some way? Invading his privacy?" I lifted the garment, turning it first one way then the next.

Adrian did the same with the waistcoats he found, checking each pocket with his fingers. "Don't be absurd. Giles would have wanted us to uncover the truth. Don't second-guess yourself."

I reversed the shirt in my hands, then stuck my arms through the sleeves just in case, surprised to find no opening for the head. "How would one wear this? Oh . . . silly me, I suppose these are pantaloons. But goodness, they are awfully short." I flipped the thing over. "And what are these little ties for?"

I looked up to see Adrian's hand planted on his chin, a hint of mischief about his eyes. "To keep them in place, of course."

I moved the garment into the moonlight to get a better look. "I don't think I've ever seen pantaloons quite like these. Do you have a pair like this as well?"

He managed a casual, "Certainly," but I noticed the slight shake of his shoulders.

I flopped the short pantaloons over my arm and tilted my chin. "All right. Out with it. Clearly I've amused you."

A tap on the cheek and he flashed that insidious smile, his teeth gleaming in the moonlight. "They're, uh, not pantaloons."

I bunched up the item into a fist before flicking it about. "Then what is it?"

The laugh he'd held off till now burst forth as he collapsed against the wall. "I, uh, can't imagine Giles would appreciate you manhandling his drawers in such a way."

"You mean his undergarments?" I flung the clothing from my hands as if it had burned my fingers. Unfortunately, I'd been a bit forceful in my sudden movement as Giles's drawers splatted straight onto Adrian's face.

He peeled off the unmentionables, blinked a few times, then leveled a glare, which I returned with one of my own. We were able to hold our straight-faced gaze for a full second until the undergarment slumped over on the floor in a sad little lump, and we dissolved into hushed laughter.

"And I put my arm all the way in. Oh dear!"

"Like a champ." Adrian snatched up the drawers from the floor. "At least we know Giles didn't hide clues anywhere intimate."

I slapped his arm. "Stop your teasing at once. I've never even seen a pair like that." My hand retreated to my side. "In fact, Broo . . ." A flash of heat filled my cheeks. I'd been about to mention Brook, but what a shocking thing to declare. And Isaac's secret! I'd nearly given everything away in a pool of laughter. If Adrian learned the truth like this, it could change everything between us. The thought sobered me posthaste, and I whirled to face the bed. "Browning . . . Mr. Browning would not think us very clever investigators, do you think?"

"Not at all." Adrian's arm brushed mine as he slid back in beside me to rifle through the rest of the clothes, amusement lingering on his breath.

"Perhaps I should stick with the jackets and cravats."

Adrian echoed my sentiment. "I'm fairly certain Giles would prefer it that way as well, particularly if you mean to launch each one of his unmentionables onto my face. Here." He passed me a light blue jacket. "Make sure you check all the pockets."

"Shall I run my arms through the sleeves as well? That is, assuming this is not some thick undergarment men wear in secret. Perhaps at one of your clubs?"

He shook his head, laughter twitching his lips. "Not that I am aware of."

I shot him a pert look before diving into the jacket's inner pockets. "What do you suppose we are searching for?"

Adrian shrugged. "I haven't the least idea. A slip of paper, an envelope."

"You mean like this?" I pulled out a small folded piece of paper.

"Precisely." Adrian watched as I smoothed the scrap of paper and held it into the dim light.

THE ROSE INN
REEDWICK

I lowered my arm. "Have you heard of it?"

Adrian shook his head. "I don't recollect any place by that name. And there is no date . . ."

"Wait." I grabbed his arm. "Juliana said something to me earlier about Giles. Did you know he left Middlecrest for one night a few days before we arrived?"

"I did not."

I narrowed my eyes. "What if this is where he went? The two of them had an argument or something. Juliana was worried he was having second thoughts about the marriage."

"And he stayed a night away?"

"Exactly. Perhaps at the Rose Inn."

Adrian leaned his shoulder against the wall. "Have I ever told you that I admire the way your mind works?"

"Not at all."

He smiled. "Well, I do. I daresay Browning can add a little visit to the Rose Inn tomorrow, while we . . ." He settled his hand on the small of my back.

A flash of heat scaled my spine. "We what?"

"Do a little more snooping around here."

CHAPTER 17

The following morning I once again caught Phoebe acting peculiar when I looked out the library window.

Like a sprite she was darting back and forth across what I could see of the eastern lawn, a squarish bag and something rather long tucked beneath her arms. Adrian's second child was nothing but a joy to have in the house, always full of silly quips and easy forgiveness. Goodness knew she was a welcome difference from Juliana's relentless fatalism and the cantankerous jabs of Mrs. Ayles.

However, since our strange meeting in the hall yesterday, I'd been watching her. There was nothing precisely I could put my finger on regarding her behavior, but I'd begun to detect a hint of duplicity, as if her never-ending optimism was something of an act. After all, she was the only one who swept about the house in a flurry of good spirits, then fell into the sullens when alone.

I observed her that morning for a long while, my vantage point from the library window excellent. She seemed undecided in where she meant to go until abruptly she stopped, a mischievous smile spreading across her face. Hmm . . . I leaned my forehead against the cold pane. What exactly did Miss Phoebe have to grin about?

I tapped my finger on the glass. Perhaps she would welcome a bit of company. I pulled back. Or perhaps not.

Either way, I whirled about, grabbed my shawl, and began my flight from the house. Something was churning in that sweet mind of hers, and I was determined to discover what it was.

The clouds hung low and thick, blighting out the sun's warming rays and in some places plunging all the way to the earth—hardly a day for walking the grounds. I pounded down the back steps, scanning the nearby woods and open fields. The air felt unnaturally still like a bitter, lifeless soup as I hurried across the lawn.

"Phoebe," I called but received no answer.

She'd been heading toward the conservatory when I last saw her, so I set out at once in the same direction. She wouldn't go far, not in this rolling mist. Hurrying off the side path, my half boots swished through clumps of low grass. The moisture in the air smelled of stale leaves and tilled earth. I pulled my shawl tighter about my shoulders as the damp breeze sought to crawl over every inch of exposed skin.

No one would want to stay out in this weather long. A volley of birdcalls materialized from the gloom. Well, almost no one.

Staying as close as I could to the redbrick side of Middlecrest afforded me no response, nor did my frequent calls. A few more steps and the long, twisted silhouettes of oaks and shrubbery took shape within the shadows of the mist. Here and there, the tethered darkness of the woods broke the landscape. My heart constricted as I hesitated. Nothing could tempt me to enter the backwoods, not after the wayward shot and the attack. I was curious, not foolish, and Phoebe could be approached another day.

I was about to abandon my hunt when the conservatory

emerged from the mist and I heard a trill of laughter beyond—not from the room itself, but from behind it. Perhaps I had not taken such a disconcerting walk in vain. I followed the sound around the windowed room to find Phoebe alone in the middle of a small grove. She'd set up an easel and sketchbook of some kind. She saw me approaching over the top of her easel. Before I had a chance to speak, her hands flew to the paper, flipping it over in an awkward dance.

She paused, then laughed at her ridiculousness. "All right. You found me, drawing away when I should be working on my needlepoint. Did Grandmama send you to fetch me?"

I didn't know the least thing about any needlepoint, let alone Mrs. Ayles, who I tended to avoid at all costs. I simply shook my head and motioned to the picture. "What a day to be sketching. May I see it?"

Her eyes flashed to mine. "Certainly not. An artist never reveals her work until it's finished." She cast a fleeting glance at the nearest conservatory window. "I'm not at all certain I shall even finish this one."

"Is it a landscape? This little grove is quite beautiful."

She wrinkled her nose, her focus still tuned to the window behind me. "Something like that."

Did she think I didn't notice? Finally I turned to the conservatory but found nothing except empty windows. "I wonder if our guest is faring any better today."

She seemed to shake off a deep thought as I looked back at her. "Oh yes, his fever broke this morning. Dr. Knight believes he'll make a full recovery. He's even been able to eat some gruel today."

She must have been by to see him. Inwardly I cringed. What

would Adrian do if he knew she was venturing there after his explicit instruction that she not?

"I imagine the authorities will be speaking with him as soon as he is able."

Phoebe returned her attention to the easel. "I suppose so."

I homed in on her words but detected nothing hidden in either her answer or her mannerisms. "Have you spoken with him?"

A pink flush filled her cheeks. "Certainly not. Papa would never allow such a thing. Besides, someone is always with him."

I stepped forward. "But you do find him interesting?"

"Of course, I do. Who wouldn't? In a sinister sort of way, I suppose. How do you think he got into the house without being seen?" As if she didn't expect an answer, she moved to retrieve her sketchbook from the easel and placed it in her bag. "I had hoped to sketch for some time, but I find I am too cold to linger. Shall we head back into the house?"

A chill ruffled my shoulders. "This dreary morning is certainly not the right weather for an artist or her observer."

Phoebe chuckled as she folded the legs of the easel together and tucked it beneath her arm. "I daresay needlepoint is sounding better and better by the minute. I only dread the comments from Grandmama. Though she admires my artwork, she thinks I should spend my time on my less proficient accomplishments."

"I imagine so." I held out my hand, and Phoebe relinquished the easel. "Come along. We can face her together."

We hurried from the grove, side by side. However, steps away from the corner, I gave in to the urge to glance one last time at the row of conservatory windows. In a flash a dark figure melted out of sight. My heart sank. At some point someone had been there watching us.

Adrian pulled me aside later that morning, but I couldn't bring myself to disclose my newfound questions about Phoebe. As a loving father, he'd leap to her defense, and I wasn't even certain anything was amiss. I'd need far more information before broaching such a delicate topic. Instead I gladly agreed to visit the stables with him to see what we could turn up there concerning Giles—particularly if the Frenchman had help.

The swirling mist still held Middlecrest firmly in its clutches. I was glad for Adrian's strong arm as we crossed the drive. We followed the sweep of a treed path until he abruptly tugged me into the shadows. His voice was all business.

"I wanted you to know that I questioned our prisoner this morning."

My eyes widened as I considered that Phoebe and I were in the grove at the same time. Perhaps Adrian was the figure I'd seen in the window. "And did you learn anything?"

"He betrayed nothing regarding his journey into the house, but he did seem eager to tell me what I already knew—that he was on his way to France."

"So he was escaping Britain."

Adrian leaned against the trunk of a nearby tree. "Browning was certain of the man's identity, and I believe our little French friend already knew that. I daresay he means for us to believe he might turn on his comrades and provide us with information—*if* I make it worth his while. But I don't trust him at all."

I adjusted my shawl. "If he was on his way to the coast, why enter Middlecrest?"

Adrian smiled. "Why indeed?"

I arched my eyebrows. "To contact the person he's working with in the house."

Adrian crossed his arms. "My thought exactly. As I said before, the murderer could not have got to Giles alone."

I paced in front of the tree, then stopped. "But the Frenchman did find a way into the kitchens. He could have done the same the day of the garden party and added the poison to the oil with no one the wiser."

"True, but there were a great many people in the kitchens that day. Hiding in a rarely used room is one thing. Overseeing the careful administration of the poison is another. Not to mention, no one else turned up dead." He picked at a piece of bark. "I'm convinced they meant Giles's death to look like an accident. If we hadn't noticed his coloring looked strange and asked Browning to come to Middlecrest, we would have had no idea poison was used. After all, the inquest declared Giles's accident the result of a sudden heart complaint."

I bit my lip. "And you are certain you trust Mrs. Jennings?"

His arms fell to his sides. "I do admit she can be a trifle flighty at times and a good deal too sensitive for her own good, but yes. She has been with my family since Brook and I were in short coats."

I angled my chin. "Of course, that would mean something happened right under her very nose."

"Or in the stables." He extended his arm. "Could Giles have been offered something right before his ride?"

"And there's still the question of where and why Giles fled the house for his night away. I'm not convinced it was to separate himself from Juliana for a day or two."

The sweet scent of hay filled my nose long before the face

of the familiar clock tower peaked over the hedgerow. A grand two-story affair, Middlecrest's stables boasted the convenience of a large archway, which permitted the easy entrance and departure of any sort of carriage. Adrian and I passed beneath it to access the central door.

The main stone building was a long and wide structure with the coach house that finished off an elegant L shape. The sound of the stable door must have alerted Duff, the groom, who wandered out from the nearby tack room with a leather harness in his hand. His mouth fell open at the sight of us.

"Your lordship, my lady. May I fetch you a horse?"

"No, thank you. Her ladyship and I came to speak with Mead. Would you mind fetching him for me?"

The young man nodded, then bowed, his lanky legs a bit unstable as he twisted to leave. "Mead's upstairs in the coachman's room. I'll get him straightaway."

Adrian leaned down to my ear. "Mead is head groom here. He knows everything that goes on. If anything happened that morning in the stables, he'd be aware of it."

It was not long before I heard the pounding of footsteps on the stairs. A middle-aged man in brown trousers and a jacket marched down the narrow aisle between the cribs, giving a jovial greeting on approach. Adrian seemed pleased as well.

The man's smile lengthened as he took us in. "What can I help you with on this fine mornin'?"

"Her ladyship and I have come hoping you might be able to shed some light on a few questions we have regarding the day Mr. Harris had his accident."

The warm smile faded from the older man's face. "Such an unfortunate tragedy. And the man so young."

Adrian's tone echoed that of the head groom. "If you would, think back on that morning. Do you remember seeing Mr. Harris?"

Mead rubbed his chin. "Indeed, I do. Passed his horse straight into his hands myself that very day. He was late, you see, and I waited for him with Mr. Hawkins."

I couldn't help but pipe up. "Mr. Hawkins?"

Mead cast me a quick glance. "The two gentlemen spoke to one another before mounting their horses and departing the court-yard."

I went on. "Did Mr. Harris seem different to you in any way?"

Mead shook his head. "Couldn't rightly say. Didn't know the gentleman. Only spoke briefly with him once before, a few days prior. He seemed natural enough to me."

I stepped forward. "A few days prior? Was that the night he left the estate?"

"'Twas."

Adrian met my gaze for a moment, then turned back to the groom. "Did he happen to mention where he was going or why?"

"Not to me he didn't, but if I remember right, he did have a coze with young Johnny." Mead turned and shouted across the aisle. A boy popped out of the far crib, a look of concern across his face. Mead motioned him over. "Easy now, lad. All you need to do is tell his lordship what the gentleman said to you the night he left the estate."

The boy crept forward, his hat in his hand. When he was near enough, Mead thumped him on the back. "Get on with ya. Don't keep his lordship waiting."

The boy's big eyes tipped up to mine almost in pleading. "Pardon me, your ladyship, your lordship. All he said was he didn't know when he'd be back. He asked me where he might stay in Reedwick."

"Did you happen to recommend the Rose Inn?"

He smiled. "I did. Me pa is an ostler there."

I knelt to the boy's level. "And did the gentleman mention why he meant to visit there?"

Johnny scrunched his lips, the dirt on his face creasing into lines. "The gen'lman did mumble somethin' before he left."

"And what was that?"

A sheepish look overtook his face until he tilted his chin up to Adrian.

"He told me to always listen to me rector."

CHAPTER 18

W hat about a poem for our new mama, Ewan?" Juliana smiled from across the drawing room rug, but there was an inquisitive curve to her lips that I couldn't like. "She must not be left out of all the fun. Besides, she is not that much older than the two of us."

I'd been paying little attention to Ewan Hawkins's silly recitations and Phoebe's prattling, but my ears perked up at the mention of my new name. Juliana probably meant to fluster me with such a ridiculous declaration, but I was not so easily overset.

"You are a poet, Mr. Hawkins?"

Phoebe bounced where she sat on the drawing room sofa and clapped her hands. "Oh, yes! Yes, indeed. Ewan is so good at describing us. His poem for Juliana has grown to seven stanzas over the past few weeks. 'The Determined Swan' is most definitely my favorite. See, look how she blushes."

Juliana turned to the window as Mrs. Ayles rapped her cane on the floor and grunted beneath her breath. Clearly the self-appointed matriarch had little use for Ewan's artistry. Earlier in the evening she'd perched herself in a large winged chair near the fire, her back straight as a board, her eyes cunningly sharp as they took in the room.

She had chosen to wrangle Middlecrest's dwindling group of people into the drawing room following dinner. Since Giles's death she'd encouraged just the opposite, and I wondered what prompted her to push for us to be together now.

Initially I too fought the idea of any sort of evening entertainment, worrying it might put undue stress on Juliana, but she had blossomed amid an evening of conversation, particularly with Ewan Hawkins right beside her. Perhaps I had been wrong to agree to the isolation. Time in the drawing room also afforded me the perfect opportunity to observe the family at their leisure. Beyond everything else, the murderer could very well be in this room, and I was determined to fish him out.

I began to gracefully refuse Juliana's little suggestion and relieve Ewan of the awkward moment when Mrs. Ayles startled me into silence with a tight-lipped, "Well this should be entertaining," under her breath.

I don't know what I expected her to say, only it wasn't that. I took a sip of tea to hide my surprise.

No doubt sensing my discomposure, Ewan dutifully crossed the room and stopped a few feet in front of me, his eyes narrow, his gaze direct. "But can I do her justice?"

Adrian, who'd kept quiet throughout the exchange, cleared his throat, the hint of a laugh christening his words. "I highly doubt it—as far as your talents are concerned. She's beyond poetry." He flicked his wrist before resting his arm on the mantel. It was a subtle movement few would notice, but I did.

I forced myself once again to join the act. "Thank you, darling." Ewan made a production of kneeling on the carpet for his performance, but Adrian walked over and laid a hand on his shoulder. "Any poetry for my wife will most assuredly be composed by me."

Great. More playacting. I wanted to melt into the sofa.

Phoebe clapped. "How romantic."

Then the room fell silent as Adrian knelt and took my hand in his, his gaze so terribly astute. It was all I could do not to look away, to sit so very still, to allow my heart free rein.

He raised his chin.

"Beauty of the rarest form,
Hair like a golden flame;
A man could bear most anything
If she would but speak his name.
So call to me, my angel,
Quench my never-ending thirst.
Yet a captured heart can be a fickle demon,
The highest pleasure, the deepest curse."

His words descended onto the room like the start of a summer rain—sudden, interesting, and wholly unexpected. What did he mean by such a poem? My hand grew cold in his grasp, but I leaned forward with a forced smile.

"That was quite beautiful."

Phoebe stood. "It was nice, but not at all like Byron. What do you mean by a curse, Papa?"

Adrian laughed as he rose to meet her. "My dear, what would I do without your levelheaded assessments of my artistry?" Then he turned back to me, adding almost absently, "I suppose love can be a curse if it's unwanted, unrequited, or unattainable. Thank goodness that is not the case with your new mama." He flashed me a brilliant smile, one I could almost believe, but my heart whispered caution.

Phoebe swept past me on her way to the seat in the bow window, her earlier enthusiasm stripped away. "I don't want to think any more about curses. Perhaps someone would play a song on the pianoforte?" Her eyes looked different as she gazed back into the room. "Juliana? You are far better than I am."

Juliana shook her head. "I don't believe I shall ever feel the desire to play again."

Mrs. Ayles wrapped the floor with her cane, rumbling out a quick, "Don't be ridiculous. You're still young. The end of your story has not yet been written. Mark my words, your head will be turned again. All this foolishness. Death is not the end, my dear."

Ewan circled behind Juliana, running his finger along the back of the sofa. "Grandmama speaks the truth. Come along, Ju, I would love to hear you play."

Ju?

Juliana hesitated to stand, but who could refuse Ewan anything? He possessed such a friendly nature and kind eyes. But was it all a performance?

Juliana capitulated and took a seat at the pianoforte, rolling through a scale before securing some sheet music.

She chose a beautiful song, but a sad one, the melody built on emotion but incomplete, like a leaky dam driving the listener ever forward to what could only be a bitter end. I fought back the tears I'd kept firmly in place since my arrival.

Phoebe seemed to be fighting the same sentiment as she let out another pointed sigh. I watched as she stroked the edge of the drapes. Such a wild turn of emotions over the course of one evening. Happiness at a silly poem then sudden despondence. Was this becoming a pattern? Something was eating at her, and I didn't like it.

The settee inched forward as Adrian rested his hands behind me at the back. I hadn't heard him return to my side of the room. He leaned down near my ear as if to share a pleasant secret, but his words startled me. "I cannot help but wonder what you are thinking."

His whisper tickled my neck. Unsure how to respond, I allowed Juliana's poignant melody to fill the space between us for a moment.

"Nothing exceptional, I assure you. I was only pondering the composer of this song. Whoever wrote such a haunting melody must certainly have loved and lost. Such feeling cannot be created without depth of experience."

He considered his answer. "Mozart did lose his mother, whom he was quite close to."

"That is not what I meant."

I glanced up over my shoulder. He returned a smile.

"And I think you knew that."

He motioned with his chin toward the pianoforte just as Ewan reached over Juliana's shoulder to turn the page for her. "What do you make of this?"

"I am glad she chose to play." I shrugged. "Rest assured, I have found Juliana to be a strong and shrewd young lady who means to be quite careful before she allows any man to touch her heart again."

His voice held a hint of surprise. "Yes, well, Ewan is not one of her suitors. I have no concerns there." His gaze clouded as he focused on the far wall. "But if he was, you make it sound as if love is simply a choice. That Juliana could squelch such emotion at will." He took a quick breath. "I suppose I'm glad to know there are those who possess the power to do so." He pushed away before crossing the carpet to join Mrs. Ayles by the fire.

My chest felt heavy as I considered his words. We were talking of Juliana and Ewan, right? Not something far more complicated—something he told me was not a part of our arrangement. Yet how could I deny the hint of emotion lurking behind such a hasty withdrawal?

The truth was I couldn't . . . because against my better judgment and completely out of my control, I felt something too. Adrian and I had come to a crossroads in our marriage, and it seemed neither of us knew the best course to take.

My confusion over Adrian's behavior followed me upstairs for the night, even as I stopped by the nursery. Miss Barton couldn't help but pepper me with questions about the family that I loathed to answer mainly because I didn't know what to say. I found Juliana still grieving, Phoebe distracted, and Adrian a far cry from the man I once believed him to be.

She must have suspected my duplicity in regard to my husband as she flashed me a keen smile. "His lordship is so very kind."

I pursed my lips. "I see he has won you over."

A blush tore across her cheeks and she dipped her head to smooth out her skirt. "I will admit, he cuts a rather dashing figure when he comes to see Isaac. The two of you make a fine pair."

I didn't know why her casual remark about Adrian visiting the nursery panicked me as quickly as it did. Isaac was indeed under his protection, but why had he taken such an interest in him? My muscles twitched.

"Lord Torrington comes here often?"

"Most mornings I 'spect. Isaac crawls right up to him now. They've become great friends."

"Oh." I looked away, hoping I'd not betrayed my unease. Adrian and I were supposed to be in love. Why wouldn't I want him to be around my son? If only Brook wasn't Isaac's father, everything would be different. I changed the subject as quickly as I could.

"Has the missing blanket turned up? Or the rattle?"

She shook her head. "No sign at all. I'm beginning to worry we might never find them."

"They do seem to have vanished."

Miss Barton motioned to the adjoining room. "Poor little dear, he cried himself to sleep once again tonight."

"Which only breaks my heart. Do you think someone like Mrs. Ayles might have dispensed of the items on purpose?"

"Oh dear. You don't think?" A flame lit her tone. "I wouldn't put it past that odious woman. She's had nothing but ill words for Isaac. But rest assured, whatever happened, our little man will find his way past the loss soon enough. A few more nights and the blanket shall be forgotten completely. Trust me. He's young. He'll forget it in due course."

"I hope you're right. There is really nothing to be done." I squeezed her fingers, thankful for their strength. "I shall leave you to rest."

Tired and agitated from the day, I ducked into the darkened corridor with far more on my mind than Isaac's lost blanket.

Shadows roamed the halls of Middlecrest, each wide passage painted black by the gloomy hands of night. Sounds came alive as well, transformed by the hidden interior of such an old structure—moaning, popping, howling wind jiggling rusty hinges. It reminded me of the Towers in many ways. But Middlecrest was altogether a different animal. Almost as if Adrian's ancestors had covered up an infamous past with the white plaster designs and high ceilings. However, there are some things no one can hide completely.

I was but a few steps from my bedchamber door when the hairs on my arms prickled to attention and the pale light betrayed my eyes. My muscles tightened. My jaw clenched. Was there a person concealed by the darkness at the end of the hall? Surely not. The threatening note I'd received had merely sparked an already overactive imagination. Little by little, the eerie feeling swelled as I approached my door.

Someone was there—watching my every move like a wraith, standing unearthly still. I could just make out the merest glint of moonlight reflected in a toothy smile. Numb with shock and indecision, I reached for the door latch, my pulse throbbing. Would the person follow me inside? Should I not turn and run? Or scream?

For a second my arm froze. My fingers twitched.

Then I burst into my bedchamber, overtaken by a sudden wave of intense fear. Someone had been waiting outside my room. To do what? A split second before I smashed the door shut, I shot a furtive glance through the diminishing crack.

My heart turned cold. It was in that terrifying moment I knew exactly who had been staring me down in the darkened hallway.

Mrs. Ayles.

My vision had adjusted enough to make out the black crepe

gown and single ostrich feather she'd worn earlier in the day. I locked the door, my fingers shaking. What on earth was she doing in the family wing? And why hadn't she declared herself?

I stumbled back into my bedchamber, relieved to find Adrian walking through the connecting door.

His steps slowed at first, then pounded across the carpet. "What the devil is wrong? Are you injured?" He gripped my shoulders, his eyes wrought with confusion.

It took me a bit to find my voice. "I am well enough, only I've had a fright. There was a person hiding in the shadows of the hall just now. It alarmed me, and I didn't know what to do. I rushed in here, but—"

"Out there? Just now?" His voice was commanding and swift.

I nodded and he darted through the door only to return seconds later. "There's no one in the corridor or on the stairs."

I swallowed hard. "That cannot be possible. It was Mrs. Ayles. I'm certain of it. She was standing so deathly still beside the drapes, I . . . I don't know what I thought."

His brows drew in. "Mrs. Ayles? You must be mistaken. How could she manage the stairs with her cane?" He paused. "Moreover, how could she have escaped so quickly?"

I shook my head. "I cannot say how she managed it, but I know it was her."

He led me over to a chair by the fire. "You've had nothing but one trouble after another since I brought you to Middlecrest. Anyone would be on edge who'd experienced what you have. Perhaps you mistook her for someone else. A servant perhaps, someone with a cause to be here."

I raised my voice. "I know what I saw." But my shoulders slumped. He was right. How could it have possibly been Mrs. Ayles?

"I suppose it could have been any of the ladies of the house. We are all in black."

He moved to poke the fire. "True, but what possible reason could anyone besides the girls have to be lurking in this part of the house? And to leave so quickly?"

"I couldn't say." My voice dipped, and Adrian jerked his attention back to me.

He knelt beside the chair and took my hand. "You have every reason to be shaken by this."

His touch felt different after our interaction in the drawing room, my skin alive beneath his. Did he care for me? I took a deep breath, willing away the butterflies swarming in my belly.

"I am glad you walked in when you did." I said it almost as an afterthought, but the resulting smile that inched across Adrian's face sent me reeling back to that moment in the grove when he held me so gently, when I'd been granted a rare glimpse of the real Baron of Torrington. My toes curled in my half boots.

The real Baron of Torrington? I was fooling myself. Really I had no idea what was truth and what was an act.

He must have sensed the emotions at war within me, for he pulled away, then took a seat on a nearby chair. "I came to tell you I received a letter from Curtis Sinclair."

I sat up at once. "Oh? What did he write?"

Adrian gave me a shrewd look. "Much I will not repeat. Let me just say, he means to see you protected."

My mouth fell open. "Was he angry with me?"

"*You?*" He chuckled. "Certainly not."

I couldn't help but smile. "Oh."

He tapped his finger on his leg before slanting his eyes up at me. "You're enjoying this, aren't you?"

"A little."

"I suppose I deserved such censure." He leaned his elbows onto his knees, resting his chin in his hands. "Suffice it to say, Curtis very nearly called me out."

"Good."

"Good?"

I narrowed my eyes. "You do remember manhandling me in the coach, forcing me into an unwanted marriage, and bringing me to this horrid house to face a murder?" I couldn't hold the serious face I fought so hard to retain.

"Well, when you put it like that, I'd call me out too."

We both laughed and I was happy for the emotional release. That is, until I met his gaze and the fluttery feeling took a sharp turn into something else entirely. Goodness, his eyes were so bright in the unsteady firelight . . . and so close.

I sucked in a breath as Adrian feigned interest in the far window. There was a slight flush on his neck. I was not the only one affected by our continued intimacy. He was a man after all, and one who had made many conquests.

The thought made my stomach turn, and I looked away, irritated by how easily I could be drawn in. His hand, however, came to circle my wrist. "I would like to . . . ." He glanced at the door, then turned back, his eyes on our hands, a subtle smile on his face, the merest lift of his shoulder.

My heart stilled.

". . . spend some time with you tomorrow." A thoughtful pause. "To continue investigating the murder. I still believe our little Frenchman intimately involved; however, he had help . . . and more than once. I've continued to question the man, but he refuses to give any answers that might be of use. Mr. Browning will escort him to London as soon as he's strong enough." Adrian snuck a glance at me. "After Johnny revealed that Giles mentioned the rector on his way out of Middlecrest that day, I think it prudent to ride into Reedwick to meet with Mr. Baxter. And since you already know the gentleman from your time at Croft Towers, he might be more at ease with you along. Unfortunately, an off-handed remark may prove to be our only hope in directing this investigation."

I nodded quickly. "I agree." But what had I thought he was about to say? My throat felt dry, and I expelled a little sigh of relief. Or was it disappointment?

I dared not answer such a thought.

CHAPTER 19

Adrian met me at the front of the house the following morning with a particularly handsome grin and the distinct air of a man ready for an adventure.

I forced myself to slow my pace as I descended the steps, intent on focusing wholly on the task at hand and not on the growing attraction between us. But goodness, one dratted look at my waiting husband and all was lost. Unbidden, thoughts of the previous night sprang to mind. The honesty of his eyes. The curious turn of my heart. We'd shared some sort of an emotional exchange in the privacy of my bedchamber, and we both seemed a bit changed by it. Him, with his grin and rakish charm, and me, suddenly filled with the same anticipation I experienced before my first London season.

"Duff is bringing the horses around." Adrian tucked his riding crop under his arm, and I couldn't help but notice he wore a fine green jacket I'd not seen before with his black mourning band around his arm. The cut to his jacket was on point—Adrian certainly knew how to dress—and matched perfectly his trim pair of beige pantaloons. He propped one Hessian boot on a nearby ledge, his eyes focused on the path to the stables.

I wondered if he was as concerned as I was about our ride.

Last night I agreed to his idea easily enough, but the thought of getting back on Flick haunted me. My muscles felt like ropes in my legs and my palms were wet, but I had always been an accomplished rider, and I'd not allow anyone to take that joy away from me.

Adrian shot me a swift grin. "Ah, here they are now."

My stomach lurched at his words, but as I squinted into the bright morning light, warmth filled my chest. "Aphrodite!"

Duff led over my beautiful, prancing chestnut mare, and I ran my fingers down her silky neck. "Oh, my dearest one. If only I had a carrot to give you." I felt Adrian behind me and spun around. "However were you able to bring her here?"

His face looked a bit flushed. "Oh, I might have happened to mention to Curtis how much you missed the mare in my letter. And considering he and his wife are presently in London, I arranged to have my man bring her here."

"But—"

He touched my arm. "Rest assured, they wanted you to have her."

I looked back at Aphrodite. "What on earth could you have told them?"

He drew up at my side. "Let's just say, I can be persuasive when needed."

My breath caught. "You didn't say I was desperate, did you?"

"Are you?"

"Certainly not."

He tossed that irritating shrug of his and cupped his hands at the horse's side. "Then let us say no more about it and get on with our ride."

I certainly didn't relish another mystery, particularly one that involved my family. I knew quite well it must have taken a good bit of persuasion to get Sybil to relinquish Aphrodite after she'd ridden her all those months I was with child. Curtis had also spent no small amount of money to retain the horse when I had no other choice but to sell her. He acted as if we could share her between us, but I'd always known she really belonged to them. Yet here she stood like a fragrant breath from my past. My heart squeezed ever tighter.

I stepped forward and thrust my boot into Adrian's waiting hands. He swung me effortlessly into the sidesaddle before turning to mount his own horse. I took the moment to watch him as he eased onto Atlas, a peculiar sensation taking hold of my heart.

"I daresay there was more to Aphrodite's sudden arrival than a simple letter, so I thank you."

A slow smile spread across his face, but he said no more as he flicked the reins. Aphrodite and I were simply forced to follow in stride.

*

Mr. Baxter lived in a quaint little cottage on the west side of town but a short walk from the church. Middlecrest Abbey was situated much closer to Plattsdale, where the Radcliffs had always attended church, so Adrian had never met Reedwick's well-liked rector.

Adrian hesitated at the cottage door, then checked his jacket before finally reaching up to knock.

"Don't be nervous."

He shot me a vexed look and lowered his hand. "I'm not."

"Well, you seem to be." I pushed by him.

He allowed a small laugh. "I simply wish to make a good impression. Curtis speaks so highly of—"

"Mr. Baxter shall like you very well." I reached up and knocked in his place before adding, "If I can tolerate you, so can he."

"Tolerate! Hmm . . . I suggest you put on a better show than that. We're madly in love, remember?"

He slid his arm around my waist and pulled me close. "That's better."

Was it? My pulse raced as I faced the door pressed tight to Adrian's side. Perhaps I could manage to convince my old rector of our so-called love match, but should I do so with a man of God? I swallowed hard. And worse, it was becoming more and more clear it was my own heart that needed to remember Adrian had called our marriage a masquerade.

We heard footsteps and the door swung open to reveal a familiar middle-aged woman in a dark-blue dress. Mrs. Baxter had grown rather thin in my absence, but her face was round and inviting. "Ah, Lord and Lady Torrington, come in at once. Mr. Baxter is expecting you."

A delightful splash of cinnamon and apples met our noses as we were ushered into the center of a comfortable receiving room. A fire crackled in the corner, but the chimney must have had a draft, because the room looked a bit hazy in the dim light. My steps faltered as I took in every inch of the familiar room.

The sofa had been just so, the paintings hung in all the same places.

Adrian took my arm as if he detected something stirring within me. Perhaps he did. It was strange how buried emotions surge so uncomfortably close to the surface when you least expect them. I'd not been to the Baxters' cottage for nearly two years, but I stood here then with my cousin Sybil, my bonnet in my hand, a soon-to-be unwed mother yearning for the merest scrap of approval. The forgiveness God granted me freely had not been so easy to come by outside my small family. That is, until I met Mrs. Baxter. She was the first lady of the neighborhood who chose to acknowledge my impending confinement, and to do so with the grace and dignity I needed at the time.

She was just as friendly today as she ushered us past the sitting room and down a short hall. She paused to tap on a closed door.

A cheery "Come!" filtered through the wood. Ah, Mr. Baxter. I was glad to see him too.

Mrs. Baxter lifted the latch and took great pride in announcing our names to her husband, who made a show of shuffling to his feet and pushing a stack of papers to the side. He bowed, then moved to fetch a pair of slat-back chairs.

"Mrs. Baxter, some tea if you would." His wife smiled as she withdrew, closing the door behind her with one last kind look for me. She was glad of my marriage. Of course, she didn't need convincing that it was a love match. Why else would the Baron of Torrington consider me?

Though Mr. Baxter had earned a few more wrinkles since I'd last seen him, his happy face and eyes were as bright and inviting as ever. "You said in your letter that you came to speak to me about Giles Harris." His hand quivered as he rested it on the desk.

Adrian eyed me as if to be certain I wished to proceed. He must have sensed my fleeting discomfiture. Odd how easy it was to retreat to an older version of myself when returning to a place from long ago. Adrian turned back to Mr. Baxter.

"Her ladyship and I are in the difficult process of learning all that happened to Mr. Harris before that fateful day."

Mr. Baxter's jaw clenched. "I see."

"Quite by accident, your name was mentioned to us by a boy in my stables." Adrian's chair creaked as he adjusted his position. "Perhaps we have journeyed all this way for nothing, but we were hoping to learn if Mr. Harris met with you prior to his death."

Mr. Baxter held unusually still, then nodded, the wisps of gray in his sideburns bobbing in turn. "You are correct. I did speak with Mr. Harris for some time one afternoon. He came seeking my advice. But I'm not exactly certain what you have come for . . ." His fingers were busy at the edge of the desk, rubbing, scratching.

Adrian lowered his voice. "My good friend, Mr. Sinclair, speaks quite highly of you." There was something about Adrian that always made people perk up and listen, and Mr. Baxter fell easily under his spell.

"I think the world of Mr. Sinclair."

Adrian nodded. "Be assured, whatever you have to tell us will be kept in the strictest confidence regarding Mr. Harris."

The door cracked open and Mrs. Baxter shuffled in with a silver platter filled with tea and cakes. She set it on the desk, and the rector waved her away. No one moved. We were awaiting Mr. Baxter's answer, but he only spoke once the door was fully sealed.

"You must understand that I don't wish to bring any danger here."

Adrian stiffened. "Neither do we, but we all know a terrible thing has happened. As a man of God, I hoped you would do your best to see justice served."

Mr. Baxter's eyes flitted about. "Yes, yes, certainly. I only meant . . ." His fingers stilled. "I know you will use discretion. It's only . . ." He cast a quick glance at the door, then rubbed his chin. "Mr. Harris arrived that afternoon quite overset. I've known him since he was a boy, and I've never witnessed him act like that. He was pacing like a caged animal."

I leaned forward, my voice soft. "I also spoke with Mr. Harris—the night before he died. Something was very wrong."

His gaze flicked to Adrian, a grim line across his brow. "In my opinion, the boy was afraid."

Adrian seemed taken aback. "Of what?"

"He didn't say exactly, but he did come to ask me a question."

I could feel an imperceptible pull as we awaited his next words.

"Mr. Harris told me he'd learned something, something terrible about . . ." His eyes snapped to Adrian's, and he tugged a bit at his shirt collar. "I mean you no disrespect, my lord. But Giles told me he'd learned something frightening about . . . well, about the girl's family. He was lost as to what was best to be done."

My mouth slipped open.

Adrian froze. The small casement clock on the bookshelf filled the distressing silence.

"*My family?*"

The rector folded his hands atop the desk. "That is all he would confide. I, of course, encouraged him to speak with you directly as soon as possible. But he seemed hesitant to do so."

Adrian dragged his hand down his face.

The rector went on. "I prayed with Mr. Harris, and he did seem a bit better when he left. But the entire encounter did not sit well with me, not well at all."

My skin tingled as I digested all Mr. Baxter had said. *Afraid? Giles?* Of course, he had every reason to be. Suddenly my chest felt cold and all I really wanted was to be alone to process the wild thoughts circling my mind. I shook myself inwardly.

Giles had told Mr. Baxter, a trusted friend, that he'd learned something about Juliana's family, but everything up to this point had seemed so straightforward about all the Radcliffs. And Giles sought me out right after I arrived. How easily I dismissed his desperate pleas simply for the comfort of my bed.

A chill crawled down deep into my core as Mr. Baxter's probing glare settled on me.

What if Giles came to me with such heartfelt relief because I was the only one in the house he could trust?

CHAPTER 20

Adrian chose to forgo his routine visit to my room that night. It was the first time he'd stayed away since the wedding.

I was not entirely surprised, though I did wait for some time in the connecting room before retreating into my bedsheets with nothing for company but a jumble of dubious thoughts. Why had he stayed away when we had so much to discuss about our visit with Mr. Baxter?

By morning I realized I was certain of only one thing. There was still much to discover about the infamous Radcliff family of which Adrian was the head. What if he had withheld important information from me? Even inadvertently. Trust is personal and dangerous and terrifying, and I had to think of Isaac. Adrian would have to prove himself if we were to take our relationship any further. And I wasn't at all certain he would do so.

In this state of confusion I came upon the very two men who had consumed every waking hour of my thoughts these past few days sprawled out on the back lawn on a yellow blanket, immensely enjoying each other's company. I'd fled the house in search of Miss Barton and Isaac, but as I ducked around a low-hanging branch of a nearby oak, I realized that Isaac's nurse was nowhere in sight.

Adrian saw me before I had a chance to retreat. He smiled and waved me over as if he hadn't chosen to abandon me the previous night. Of course, the truth was he hadn't, which only vexed me anew. We'd had no fixed engagement. Our being together in the evenings was merely a show for the servants. Perhaps he had decided that we'd performed the act long enough.

And on second thought, I agreed. Though I was his wife, it was in name only. The rest was all an act. Goodness knew I'd never sought his attentions. I'd taken Isaac's tiny hands in mine less than a year ago and swore it would be me and him always. I'd found comfort in that independence, and I had no intention of giving it up.

Isaac giggled and cooed as I reached the edge of the blanket, but he didn't crawl over to me as I expected. He was far too interested in flopping onto Adrian's chest and wriggling into his arms. His doing so seemed to be some sort of game that involved a good deal of tickling and capturing of toes.

Irritated by my own irrational frustration, I knelt across from them on the blanket, unable to completely temper my voice.

"I was wondering who had taken my son. I assumed Miss Barton brought him outside as she likes to do."

Adrian rolled onto his side and propped his head on his arm. "I believe that was her original intention." He eyed me for a moment, then tried a playful smile. "Don't be cross, Elizabeth. If you must know, I intercepted Miss Barton on her way out of the house. She looked a bit drawn, so I decided to give her the rest of the morning off. Be assured, Isaac has been quite pleased with our little arrangement."

Another spark of annoyance flashed through my core—more at my own inability to notice that Miss Barton might be in want of a break. But how could I when I'd spent a good deal of the morning fighting the mistress-of-the-house battle? Mrs. Ayles and Mrs. Coombs would not give up their assumed positions so easily. Oh, how Adrian got under my skin! It wasn't as if I wanted him to stay away from my son; I'd need his support if Isaac was to make a successful transition into society. I just trusted Miss Barton with him more than anyone else at this point.

I flicked a stray leaf from the edge of the blanket as I listened to Isaac's giggle. "I suppose he is still giving her some trouble sleeping—with his blanket missing and all."

"Still no sign of it, huh?"

"It's the strangest thing. How could a blanket simply vanish like that? Unless we actually did leave it at the inn."

"I'm fairly certain I saw it on our way to Middlecrest, but who knows. I did, however, find this near the hedgerow." He dug into his pocket and pulled out a small silver heart-shaped item with an H engraved in the middle. I was lost as to what the thing could be until he shook it in the air.

The rattle! "You found it! Miss Barton will be so pleased."

"I'm sure the other missing belongings will turn up too." Isaac plunged forward at Adrian once again, and he lifted him into the air. Isaac responded with the infectious cackle I'd not heard since we had lived at the Towers and Curtis swung him around in circles.

I couldn't help but laugh myself and join in on his joy. "I see you've found a new friend."

Adrian held him at arm's length. "You know, I believe I have as well. I missed . . ." His voice trailed off as he looked off into the woods. I was not to know what he meant as Isaac let out a yawn. It was nearing nap time, and his wild bursts of energy fled as quickly as they came. Adrian cradled my son beside him on the blanket and pointed up at the clouds. "Look, Isaac, we've quite a few puffy ones to admire today." He extended his finger to the left. "Right there. Can you see the pony? And next to it, the ship?"

I inspected the heavens as well, tilting my head and squinting into the bright light. "I . . . I don't see them."

Adrian coughed a laugh. "I daresay you haven't the right angle at all. Join us down here so you can see better."

It was a practical suggestion, but my heart constricted at the invitation. I glanced down at the pair. Would my compliance be seen as encouragement of some kind? Surely not. I hesitated just long enough to be certain of Adrian's indifference. He hadn't the time to spare me a look, as Isaac had captured his entire attention. Relieved, I shifted into place beside my son and rested backward onto the blanket. Seconds before my head hit the ground, I was startled to find Adrian's strong arm tucked nicely behind my upper neck like a pillow. He had timed the move perfectly. I bit my lip. Apparently my husband wasn't going to make this complicated arrangement easy.

He lifted his head just enough to see me over Isaac. "Can you see the ship *now?*"

Did I detect a hint of sarcasm in his voice? I stared into the sky, my gaze roaming from one puffy cloud to the next.

"No, I don't."

He pressed Isaac closer between us and pointed up. "There. Right there."

I sighed. "That is nothing but a bulbous ball, not at all ship-like to me."

His hand moved onto my shoulder. "You must use your imagination for it to take shape." His voice deepened. "Some things in life are not chiseled into perfect lines and boxes, Elizabeth. They are far more complex, messier, glorious versions of the original. You have to look hard to see what's hidden. I find such things far more interesting than a mere bulbous ball."

I froze when he said my name, then sat up. "I am not so daft as to miss your meaning, Adrian, nor as rigid as you suppose. Believe me, I can look into the heavens and see the beauty of God's creation. Beyond that is where we differ. I have to know exactly what I see, messy or not."

Adrian sat up as well, resting his hand on Isaac's soft hair before looking at me. "We both know they are only clouds, Elizabeth. Isaac and I simply see more."

My throat felt thick. I turned away. How could he possibly understand how I felt when he had no idea of the scars on my heart?

Adrian touched my arm. "He's asleep."

"What?" I looked down at Isaac's tranquil form. The poor dear hadn't even cried for his blanket. Adrian must have worn him out.

My husband moved onto his knees and gently gathered Isaac in his arms. "I'll take him to the nursery if you'll grab his shoes."

I turned to do so as he walked away, still shaky from our conversation, but everything had shifted. In that moment, when Adrian scooped my son into his arms and stopped to place his little bare feet in his hands, I was struck by the overwhelming realization that I'd made a terrible mistake.

Why had I hidden Isaac's parentage from Adrian? If he knew Isaac was his nephew, he would have cared for him exactly as he was doing now. Adrian knew Brook as well as I did. Could I not have trusted him to manage my delicate situation and protect

Isaac? My chest tightened, my skin a tingling mess of nerves. What a fool I had been—a scared fool.

But now the decision I'd made in haste wrought unfortunate repercussions. A feeling of complete emptiness plunged into my core. My omission in effect had become a lie between us. Furthermore, could I handle the uncomfortable thought of Adrian knowing about my affair with his brother?

I shook my head. Since the very beginning I'd told myself I concealed the fact to protect Isaac, but what had I really been doing?

Protecting myself? Deep down I knew the answer well. If Adrian learned of Isaac's parentage, he would never look at me the same way again. And right then and there, with my son tucked so neatly in my husband's arms, I knew I had to guard the secret forever.

L

I received an invitation to visit Mrs. Harris the following day. Adrian had estate business to attend to, which really meant he wanted to make one last-ditch effort with the French prisoner. He and Mr. Browning still hoped to reach some sort of deal. I, however, was more than glad to leave the interrogation to the men—as well as the questions surrounding my relationship with Adrian—behind for the afternoon and go see how Mrs. Harris was faring.

The Harris family had lived on the far side of Plattsdale at the Meadows for generations. The estate, though small, was immensely manicured and boasted a long, windy front drive. Gardens paralleled the entrance and seemed to stretch on forever, brimming with springtime blooms that scented the breeze.

I departed the coach at the front portico and was ushered by a servant dressed in blue livery into a bit of a garish drawing room. Though perfectly large enough, the gilded and papered room felt crowded by a sizable claw-foot sofa, rococo tables lining nearly every wall, and a white sculpted lion stood guard over a crenellated fireplace.

It took a second before I saw Mrs. Harris resting on a nearby settee. She shuffled to her feet and hurried to greet me.

"Lady Torrington, it is so good of you to make the journey to the Meadows."

Though she welcomed me easily enough, her eyes looked pinched and hollow—the result of sleepless nights, no doubt. She fretted with the trim of her black gown as she turned to offer me a seat next to the sofa. "I have never liked this particular day gown, bunching as it always does. Now . . ." She sat and attempted a deep breath, but it came out as a puff as she reached back to tug on a bell rope behind her. "Do you know, I saw Torrington in Plattsdale yesterday."

"Did you?"

"Why, yes. It was the strangest thing. I called out, and he didn't respond. I daresay, it's not like him to fob me off in such a way."

"Perhaps he didn't hear you." On second thought, Adrian had been at home all afternoon. At least I thought he had. "Or maybe you mistook someone else for him. It is my understanding he was at Middlecrest."

"Possibly." She rubbed her arms, slow to look up, her voice shaky. "Speaking of Middlecrest . . . has there been any news?"

I glanced at the closed door. What did she mean by *news*?

"There isn't all that much to say. We continue on as best we can."

She adjusted her shoulders. "I see."

Clearly she wanted details, yet it felt so wrong to give a voice to all that had happened since she left. "Everyone feels Giles's absence quite keenly, but I know it is nothing to your loss."

She tore her gaze to the window. "The death of my son has been more difficult than I can ever say . . . unbearable . . . but I did not bring you here to try to explain what I know you cannot understand." She scrunched up her nose. "How is Juliana?"

I felt her struggle. How to describe it? "Some days are better than others."

Mrs. Harris twisted back to face me, and the light from the window revealed how thin she had become in such a short amount of time. "When you believe Juliana is ready, please bring her with you the next time you call. I would have included her in the invitation, but today I wished to speak with you alone."

She narrowed her eyes, and I couldn't help but sit up. "Oh?"

Her fingers lay unsettled in her lap. "I have heard on good authority that you have a Frenchman at the house."

The servants were talking already, even when Adrian specifically told them not to. The local authorities had promised discretion as well, but they too would have a difficult time keeping the information hushed. Of course, the Frenchman was nearly recovered from his wounds. He would be off to London soon.

I decided to be frank. Mrs. Harris deserved answers. "We found the man in the kitchens. He had quite a few injuries and could not be moved until he was well."

She knitted her brow. "And has he said anything . . . about Giles?"

"Giles?" I gasped, hoping to appear surprised, but the keen look in Mrs. Harris's eyes told me she'd not believe it for a moment. Perhaps this conversation warranted a different tactic. "The man has said nothing definitive, although Lord Torrington does believe him involved if not wholly responsible for what happened to Giles."

Her eyes flashed seconds before an elderly servant entered the room with a tray of tea and cakes. He must have sensed the tension, as he set the tray on a small table before us and hurried from the room. Appearing more controlled now, Mrs. Harris motioned to the set.

"Would you pour, my dear? I'm afraid my hands are not steady enough at present."

Fearing I might make a terrible mistake but needing to learn what she knew, I leaned forward and picked up the teapot.

"Two lumps of sugar, dear."

I poured us each a cup, then began. "I do have some information regarding Giles's death . . . if you think you can bear to hear it."

"Please. I must know." A firm nod was followed by a piercing look. Her voice had morphed into that of a stranger, and I had difficulty finding the right words.

As if Mrs. Harris was privy to all my thoughts, she lowered her hands to the sofa, clenching the fabric beneath her fingers. "Go on, my dear."

"We . . ." Why did I find the truth so difficult to reveal? It wasn't as if Mrs. Harris could have had anything to do with Giles's death. Goodness, if my son had been killed, I would demand to know everything immediately. From one mother to another, how could I possibly withhold anything from her? I straightened my back and returned my teacup to its saucer. Adrian would understand. "Lord Torrington and I believe Giles was poisoned."

"Poisoned!" The word came out like a bitter afterthought.

Then her face blanched. "Then it was murder." She sipped her tea as she absorbed the information. "Tell me, what is to be done?"

"We are working to find something to present to the authorities—a definitive clue that might launch an investigation. We fear there may be more than one person involved." I measured the tone of my voice and considered my words. I still had Adrian's secret to protect. "If the Frenchman is indeed involved, and the murder has something to do with the war, it behooves me to ask you what you know of Giles. Did he ever cry friends with anyone across the channel?"

She huffed. "Certainly not! My son was on the eve of his marriage and an honest boy through and through. In fact, just a few days before the wedding he came to me distraught. Apparently on his journey from London to Middlecrest he saw someone at a coaching inn, overheard something dreadful, but he would not disclose any details to me. He was concerned for my safety, and he was afraid. What if this Frenchman threatened him?"

"It is possible. We've gleaned no useful information from him as of yet." If Giles happened upon a private conversation, it would explain his mounting concern the day I saw him in the drawing room. "If Giles was involved somehow—"

"Giles's brother died on the continent less than a year ago. My son would never, ever betray Britain."

I had forgotten about John Harris. He was so much older than Giles. Mrs. Harris had now lost both her boys. I could not bear the thought of losing Isaac.

"Please, do not take my hasty words amiss. I knew Giles well and I agree. He was not the sort of man to involve himself in something treasonous."

I slid a piece of white cake onto my saucer as thoughts swirled.

I dare not reveal what Mr. Baxter had disclosed only yesterday—some dark secret about the Radcliff family. She did not need a target for her simmering anger. But if I could keep her talking, my visit might tease out more than it had already. After all, she had lived close to the Radcliffs for years. Perhaps she might unknowingly shed some light on their history that others wished to conceal.

"Giles seemed quite anxious when I arrived at Middlecrest, and honestly there is much I don't know about my new family. Would you be willing to share what you know about them? Even some untoward hearsay might help us put together the pieces of Giles's death."

She shot me a curious look. "You're asking *me*? For all the juicy on-dits of the Radcliffs?"

I took a hurried sip of tea. What would Adrian think of my meddling into his private affairs? He would in all likelihood prefer me to pose the question to him, but he was too close to his family.

"Please understand that my intention is only to uncover the truth. Family secrets can be difficult to disclose, particularly when they involve those closest to us. What I mean to say is, I'm not certain my husband would know what might be important and what might not."

A half smile peeked from the corner of Mrs. Harris's mouth. "So you want to hear everything—the whole infamous history?" She paused. "I daresay you of anyone deserve to know."

An interminable gossip, Mrs. Harris seemed to relax into her favorite pastime. Goodness, when I asked the question, I hadn't even considered what all she might apprise me of—a great deal more than the days leading up to Giles's death, that was certain.

I lifted my chin. "I have aligned myself with the family. It would be prudent to know what I'm dealing with." My heart ticked to life.

Mrs. Harris exhaled a breathy laugh. "Then you shall have it, my dear." She settled her teacup on a nearby table before resting back against the settee. "Adrian and Florencia Ayles were married quite young. It was something of a scandal at the time. Have you heard of it?"

I shook my head.

"Suffice it to say, he was caught in a rather compromising situation—alone in a room with the gel at a ball. Thankfully he offered as any gentleman should have. They were married straight away by special license and fled London and all the gossips." She chuckled, then sobered when she caught my eye.

"It was only later that I learned Florencia's baby did not survive the birth. Torrington was never the same after that. He spent a great deal of his time in London doing God knows what, but he did return to Middlecrest on occasion. It wasn't long before Juliana and then Phoebe came along, which is when tragedy struck again. Florencia did not survive the last birth. From then on, Adrian and the girls have stayed at Middlecrest almost exclusively. His brother, Brook, was there for some time as well until he came of age, and then Ewan took his place."

I shifted in my seat, focusing on the teacup in my lap. "About Ewan, is he, well—"

"We all suspect it, my dear. Why else would Torrington take such an interest in the boy?"

Though I had thought as much myself, the truth was a dagger in my chest coming from Mrs. Harris's busy lips. "He never speaks of Florencia. It is almost as if her very name is taboo. I am no simpering miss in the throes of her first season, so tell me, Mrs. Harris, do you think my husband harbors a deep love for her?"

She dipped her chin. "I really couldn't say. I only know that he seemed quite affected by her death."

I couldn't help but think of how he hadn't changed one piece of furniture in her room, not for all those years.

"Remember, Torrington has never confided in me. And neither does *that woman*."

I darted a glare. "You mean, Mrs. Ayles?"

"Who else could I mean? She dug her claws into that house the day she arrived." Mrs. Harris released a bark of laughter that felt horribly out of place. "I would stay away from her if I were you."

A cold sensation crept up my spine as I remembered Mrs. Ayles's hawk-like stare when I'd seen her in the shadows of the hallway outside my room. Could she be the one who left the threatening note? Surely not. Adrian said he did not suspect she had dealings with the French. But someone in the house did.

Mrs. Harris leaned forward, laying her hand on my arm. "Do not concern yourself with Mrs. Ayles. She is far too old to cause any real trouble. And believe me, everyone else around these parts is so happy to know Torrington has opened his heart again. He's been so different since he brought you to Middlecrest—so full of love and joy. It is good to see."

I was surprised by her words. Afraid for his family? Nervous about his spy work? Distracted by some misplaced attraction? Yes. But in love with me? Doubtful. His acting was simply too good.

The tea I had enjoyed earlier in the visit now felt thick going down my throat. Though I'd learned a little more about the

Radcliff family, my digging had caused only further questions about my marriage—questions I didn't want to face. Adrian had a complicated past involving his first wife, his two girls, and Ewan. How did I fit into Adrian's future?

CHAPTER 21

The air turned bitter that evening as a harsh storm billowed against Middlecrest's thick walls, rattling the windows like an anxious prisoner terrified to escape. Though I fell into a fitful sleep early on, I was shaken awake by the wind's persistent howl and the ravaging bursts of hard rain.

I sat up in bed, darkness haunting every corner of my bedchamber. The fire had smoldered to ashes in the grate, and the obstinate chill of night had already crept over the floorboards and climbed the bedposts, intent on covering every inch of the room. I hugged the coverlet beneath my chin as lightning framed the window, illuminating the unseen for seconds at a time before plunging the room back into a black abyss.

I sat for a long while before I concluded I had little hope of returning to sleep. I shot a quick glance at the window. It was strange how every storm felt so eerily similar to the night my brother abandoned me at Croft Towers. It had been years since that day, but with every subsequent storm, I found myself thrust back in time, forced to relive his rejection all over again.

The thought of a book eased my growing anxiety, and I decided to seek out a candle and make my way to the library. I donned a pair of slippers and wiggled into a heavy dressing gown.

Already I felt warmer armed with a purpose. A book would be just the thing to avert my unsettling thoughts. Gathering courage to sneak through the house alone at night, I tiptoed down the corridor. A sliver of moonlight guided my path, though the occasional flash of lightning overpowered it. Thunder crashed as I descended the grand staircase, and I stopped at the last step to catch my breath.

An aura of stillness, unnatural and unnerving, seemed to fill the gaps in the storm. In this odd silence I heard a click, then another emanating from a room down the hall. Someone else was awake. Still terribly off stride from the threatening note and the memory of someone waiting for me outside my bedchamber, I sank against the wall.

The sound of a man muttering under his breath sprang from the same direction. My shoulders relaxed, and I stole a peek around the corner. Adrian.

He was in the billiards room. The clicks I'd heard were nothing more than ivory balls smashing into one another. He was also alone. The wariness that wriggled across my shoulders could not mask the sudden tick of my heart. My hand retreated to my chest. After everything that had passed between us, I dare not invade his privacy again, not tonight. I spun and took a hurried step away, but his voice stopped me short.

"Elizabeth."

I stole a quick breath before turning to face him.

He looked tired in the candlelight, the usual spark of his countenance dulled. He lifted his eyebrows, his tone sounding all too leading. "What are you doing up?"

He wore nothing but a white shirt, brocade waistcoat, and a long pair of breeches. His copper locks lay in a perfect wave on his head, not a strand out of place. Lazily, he leaned against the doorframe, his arms entwining, a billiard mace firmly in his grasp.

I tucked some of my hair behind my ear. "I couldn't sleep." It wasn't the first time Adrian had seen me in my nightgown with my hair loose about my shoulders, but for some reason it felt that way. "This dreadful storm sent me in search of a book."

"Oh?"

How was it that he could make one word a question and an invitation at the same time? Was this where he spent his evenings now that he didn't need to visit my room?

"Have you not been to bed?"

He stood quite still as he answered. "No. I come here from time to time. I never sleep well when I have a great deal on my mind."

The turn of his voice made me glance up. "I can understand that . . . all too well, I'm afraid." Caught up in his sentiment, my next words fell out of my mouth before I had a chance to stop them. "Care for a bit of company?"

Hesitation, then a dangerous look crossed his face. But he quickly relaxed. "Always."

Something coiled in my chest as he motioned me into the room, and I was forced to come to terms with a difficult truth—I wanted to be near my husband . . . every moment I could. I enjoyed his company, and he intrigued me like no other man had before.

Once my cousin Sybil tried to explain the mystery of love—how the overwhelming power of attraction could strike at the wrong time, but that when it was right, I would know; my heart would be at peace. Well, there was no peace where Adrian and I were concerned. Yet how could I escape the overwhelming connection I felt every time I came near him?

The billiards room housed a large selection of candles as well as a snapping fire. I lingered in its warmth as I wandered past the scrolled fireplace, attempting in vain to regain some of my bearings. Every inch of the paneled room had a masculine feel to it—dark woods, towering shelves, a thick rug. How could I ever be at ease in such a place?

A decanter sat on a nearby sideboard, a half-filled glass at its side. "Care for a drink?"

"No, thank you." I continued around the room before pausing at the far side of the table. "This is a lovely billiards set. Do you play often?"

As I stood near the flames, the wavering firelight intensified the depths of Adrian's blue eyes. "As often as I can."

I smiled. "You're good then?"

He twirled the mace in his fingers before making his way to my side. "Would you expect anything less?"

I allowed a somewhat anxious laugh, attempting to hide the glint of nerves climbing my spine, and certain warmth had already made over the color of my cheeks.

He tapped the end of the stick. "Have you ever played before?"

I gripped the soft fabric edge of the table and shook my head, my mouth a bit dry.

He eyed me for a second, then leaned forward against the table to fetch a ball, his arm brushing innocently against mine. "Why don't you go grab a mace? I believe I'm in the mood for a game."

A game? 'Pon rep, why had I ever asked to join him? Now was not the time to test the boundaries I'd set so carefully between us, particularly not after what I learned from Mrs. Harris.

"I have seen Lucius play often enough, but I've never tried to do so myself. I'm not certain . . ."

He cast me a wry smile. "Don't try to fob me off now. I daresay you'll be a natural. At least, I think you will . . . if you have the courage to try it." He winked. "The mace is right over there."

He meant to bait me into staying. I should have walked right out the door, but as I looked across the room I knew I couldn't do it. One game and off to bed.

I caught a whiff of his familiar cologne as I fetched the remaining long stick propped against the wall. I was playing with fire, and I knew it.

Adrian had the balls assembled on the table by the time I returned. "The rules are fairly simple. You can score a cannon by striking this white ball against each of the other two balls in succession and a hazard by driving my red ball into one of the pockets. You set up your shot like this."

Following his instructions, I angled the mace on the table. "Allow me a practice shot first." I snapped a quick glance before focusing once again on the ball, but I felt his hand on my shoulder.

"May I offer you a suggestion?"

"Go on."

He reached down my arm to the mace. "You'll have much better luck if you turn the stick around."

My skin melted under his touch. "What do you mean?"

He took the mace and swapped the scoop-shaped block on one end for the other. I could now see the leather on the tip.

"I have a pair of billiard cues at my townhouse in London, but I've been playing quite effectively with these two maces here for some time. I have found this end fairly accurate."

I readjusted my aim and took a wild pop at the ball, which, much to my chagrin, proved entirely ineffective. Having aimed far too high, the ball barely moved an inch.

Adrian leaned down near my ear, a laugh on his breath. "I hope you don't mean to rip my table."

I stiffened. "Well . . . at least I hit the ball, and I certainly don't have to play your silly game if you mean to act in such an odious way."

"Forgive me." His voice was soft, and I couldn't help but peek at him over my shoulder. He held my gaze before angling his chin. "I promise to behave. After all, I'm enjoying myself far too much to quit now."

I attempted to mirror the ease of his movements, but something shifted in my chest. I flipped my hair to my back and lined up the mace once again.

Adrian joined me in a crouch. "That's it. Follow your arm to aim."

My muscles twitched, but I managed to ignore his presence long enough to thrust the stick forward, barreling the white ball into a nearby red one.

I could feel his hand at the small of my back. "Good shot."

I turned to meet an attractive smile. I knew I had little chance of getting a hazard, but I was suddenly inordinately pleased by my performance. "Why don't you show me what you can do so I can get a better idea of how to play?"

He gathered up the balls to reposition them. "All right, but while I am doing so, I would appreciate it if you would tell me about your visit with Mrs. Harris. Did you learn anything that might help us solve this murder?"

"I did actually." At length I told him what she'd revealed, at least the part about Giles. "Her story certainly lines up with Mr. Baxter's. On Giles's way to Middlecrest for the wedding, he must have stumbled upon a private conversation, one that ultimately got him killed."

Adrian nodded in agreement. "Did she say anything else?"

"Nothing of consequence." I inspected the table and ball placements. "We ended up spending the time discussing...oh... other things." I thought he might have noticed my hesitation, so I hurried on. "What about you? Has Mr. Browning returned with any news?"

"Quite a bit. He visited the Rose Inn as we asked him to. The best the owner could tell us was that Giles kept to himself and left early the following morning. He probably just needed lodging after speaking with the rector. I tend to agree with Mrs. Harris. Whatever set Giles's murder into motion must have happened on his initial journey to Middlecrest. Did she say if he was coming direct from London?"

"She did not."

He took a shot. "There was something else Browning happened to mention. Perhaps it's nothing, but I thought you should know. I also asked him to stop by the inn where we stayed after the carriage accident." Adrian circled the table to line up another shot. "It seems your injured coachman has up and left. Not a word to anyone, just up and gone one morning. And he most certainly did not return to the Towers. I've already made inquiries there."

"How curious." I thought for a moment. "Perhaps he went to his family to recover or to a friend. He could have been afraid. At any rate, I know he would never do anything on purpose to hurt me. He was always quite close with Lucius."

"I understand, but I should like to speak with him nonetheless. His sudden disappearance leaves far too many questions for my liking." Adrian glanced toward the rain-soaked window. "I plan to send a man to ferret him out first thing in the morning."

"Do you believe it will come to anything?"

"Browning found no other clues anywhere in Plattsdale—or Reedwick for that matter. I cannot say I'm surprised. Our little French friend has been hard at work staying evasive. Each time I question him, I grow more confident he is behind the murder. Why else would he turn up at Middlecrest?"

Conscious of Adrian's steady gaze, I found myself focusing a great deal on the table. "I do agree that the Frenchman must have had a hand in Giles's death, particularly after what Mrs. Harris said. And he was in our kitchens, after all."

"Indeed."

"But again, I cannot believe he could evade Mrs. Jennings long enough to add the poison *and* ensure Giles was the only victim."

Short on space to line up his mace near the wall, Adrian swung the stick behind his back. A lift of his eyebrows and he aimed from his side to strike the white ball, plunging it into the red one, which sent both balls into the corner pocket.

"And that's a point for me."

"We weren't even playing yet." I crossed my arms. "How can you be so accurate aiming that way? I cannot believe you managed to hit the pocket at all."

Adrian laughed. "Brook always used to shoot like that. It drove me to distraction until I mastered the art myself."

Brook. My heart deflated. Why did his name sound so cold coming from Adrian's lips? Unnerved, I paced the length of the table, running my finger along the padded sides.

I had lain in bed so many nights over the past year, wondering what had happened to Brook. This was a chance to learn where he'd gone. I swallowed my pounding reserve and snuck in a question. A simple inquiry was natural enough.

"Where is your brother at present?"

"Italy, Africa? Who's to know? He calls himself the wanderer these days, but the truth is rather sad. He had a fight with my father before his death, and even though Brook returned for the funeral, he swore he could never live at Middlecrest. He has an estate in Sussex that was passed to him from our mother. I've not been there since I was a boy. Ewan says Brook's in the process of making some extensive repairs, though I'm not certain why. He's so rarely in Britain. Frankly, it's been years. I'm beginning to wonder when or if I shall see him again."

"Oh." My stomach churned. Was it Isaac's birth that kept him away? Or worse, me? I could still hear the tremors in Brook's voice when he denied any chance of being the father. How I hated him then.

I thought I saw a shiver of indecision cross Adrian's face. Perhaps it was only the unstable firelight.

"Did you ever meet my brother?"

My chest tightened as I attempted a breath. "Yes, we met at a ball in London during my second season."

"Ah." Adrian struck the white ball with his mace, sending it flying across the table. "I daresay you were smitten like the rest of London. I can see it written all over your face. But Brook never had time for women. He was always dashing off to do one thing or another."

So that's what he'd told Adrian—that he had obligations. Well, I knew the real reason he left home so frequently. He'd gone to see me.

"I still have hopes that he'll settle down one day. The ladies miss him dreadfully, I'm sure, but I doubt he has marriage on his mind. He's never been all that constant." Adrian plopped his mace on the table and rubbed his face, a far-off look in his eyes. He took a deep breath. "The hour is quite advanced, and I'm more tired than I thought. Though it pains me, perhaps it would be best to have our game another time." He reached for my hand. "You look worn down as well."

The feel of his fingers around mine couldn't mask the insidious guilt hovering beneath my skin—the burden of Isaac's secret was growing by the second.

He gave my hand a slight squeeze. "I'm glad you joined me this evening, even if it was only for a little while. We should do it again."

I nodded, agreeing all too quickly. I recovered my hand almost as an afterthought as I made my way to the door. Suddenly I craved the safety of distance, the calm of a quiet room. I suppose I refused his offer for an escort a bit too forcefully, but I needed to clear my head. Of course, I wish I hadn't stolen a glance back as I stepped into the hallway.

There, bathed in moonlight, stood a very different version of Adrian from the one who had effortlessly bid me good night. The man who watched me as I walked away bore the distinct look of weary determination.

CHAPTER 22

I found the house in an uproar the following morning, the chaos sending my heart racing. Footmen scurried about the lower floor as I descended the main staircase. It reminded me too much of the day Giles died.

Juliana came upon me, gaping at the foot of the stairs, and pulled me aside. Though her face had grown rather pale over the last few weeks, the stark white pallor of her brow sent a chill down my arms.

"What is all this?" I motioned to the room.

"He's gone!"

"Who's gone?" As soon as the words escaped, I knew whom she meant.

Juliana's hand was busy at her neck, her voice a bit choked. "The Frenchman. Mr. Browning dashed in moments ago and turned the entire household upside down."

I glared up the stairs, the threatening letter not far from my mind. I clutched her hand. "Where is your father?"

"He's gone out to look for him."

The parquet floor seemed to shift beneath my feet. Isaac. Where was he? Oh yes, Miss Barton had taken him to the rose garden.

"Young!" I stopped the butler near the front door. "Would you ask Miss Barton to bring Isaac in from the garden at once?" The shake of my voice must have alerted him to my concern, for he offered a quick nod and took off at a brisk walk.

I whirled back to Juliana. "Where is Phoebe?"

"How should I know?"

"I don't think anyone should be alone until he's found. Come with me into the drawing room at once. Young will bring Isaac to us there. I'll send him for Phoebe after that."

Though she produced a stoic nod and followed me, I was sure underneath her rigid exterior Juliana was as shaken as I was. Her steps faltered.

"Wasn't the Frenchman hiding in the house last time they found him?"

"Yes." I thrust open the drawing room door, relieved to see Phoebe already inside. "Good. You're here. We shall all stay together until your father returns."

Phoebe dropped her book onto the sofa and stood, belatedly taking a second look at her sister's face. "Whatever is the matter?"

I motioned to Juliana. "Close the door behind us, please." I moved to a nearby window to watch for Young's return.

Phoebe hurried across the rug to join me.

I looked at each worried face. "Juliana has just informed me that the Frenchman has escaped, but take heart—he likely wants to be as far away from here as he can."

Juliana revived at my side. "Mr. Browning said he found the footman out cold on the conservatory floor. The man must have hit him over the head with something."

My jaw twitched. "He was to be taken to London tomorrow."

I thought better of speaking so loudly and led the group over to the sofa. "I don't know how he knew, but it must have made the man desperate. Depending on when he left, he is likely miles away by now."

Juliana seemed to consider my words as a line formed across her forehead. "But how could he have escaped without help? His hands were tied. Papa assured us we were quite safe."

Phoebe turned back to the window. "However will Papa recover him?"

Watching her closely, I leaned forward. "It all depends on when he left."

Phoebe pressed her forehead. "Well, there is no way for us to know that."

I angled my chin. "Is there not? Did you by any chance go see him today?"

She scrunched up her nose before shooting a glare at her sister. "I suppose Juliana already told you I did."

I tipped my head to the side. "No, she did not."

Phoebe adopted an arrogance I'd not seen in her before. "I will admit that I did see him today just after sunrise, but I assure you I had nothing to do with his disappearance."

Juliana flew to her feet. "Papa forbade you from going in the conservatory! I heard him say so myself. What if you set something in motion that you don't even realize?"

Phoebe leveled her own glare. "Don't be ridiculous. I only stopped in to see how he was faring."

My shoulders fell. "You spoke with him as well?"

"Yes, I did, but I only wanted to practice my French. I don't believe him the monster the rest of you do."

I held up my hand to stave off any further outbursts. "Phoebe, this is incredibly important. You must tell me what he said to you."

She flicked her fingers in the air. "Nothing of any consequence." I thought a bit of pink crept into her cheeks, but she whirled away.

I narrowed my eyes. I was not a fool. She was young, enamored by the dashing figure he posed. But would she be willing to go against everything her family held dear to further any kind of relationship? I had my doubts.

"And you left him just as you found him?"

"Of course I did. I am not a traitor."

Juliana scoffed. "Maybe not, but you were also the last person to see him before he escaped."

"That we know of." She flicked her finger in the air again. "Don't you dare act like this is my fault. Besides, we don't know if he has anything to do with Giles's death."

Juliana's face contorted with rage. "Who else could it have been? Even if there's the slightest chance—"

The drawing room door swung open, and I was relieved to see Adrian cross the threshold. His boots were dirty, his jacket teaming with mist. His stormy gaze found mine immediately.

"The cursed Frenchman's made a clean escape."

Juliana started in at once, pinning her arms at her side. "Phoebe went to see him this morning, Papa."

Adrian's eye's widened. "What do you mean?"

Like a bolt of lightning, Phoebe tore across the room, her eyes shooting daggers at her sister. "Please, Papa. Juliana makes it sound so awful. I only briefly stopped by to check on him. Nothing more. The footman can attest to that."

Adrian clenched his hand into a fist. "You were forbidden from going there, and to do so alone—" He raked his hand through his hair. "Unbelievable." When he spoke again, the fury had dissipated from his voice, leaving a weary rasp. "Return to your rooms at once, both of you. I wish to speak with your mama alone." He waited for Phoebe by the door, stopping her progress at the last second. "You had my trust, and I can see now I never should have given it to you. I'll be by your room shortly to hear all, and I do mean all."

She nodded as she retreated from the room, a newfound hesitancy to her steps. Adrian paused for the door to close before turning back to me. He shook his head. "The man left no evidence besides the injured footman. His ropes were cut. The door unlocked. Someone had to have helped him."

"Do you think Phoebe . . ."

He cast me a sharp look. "She's headstrong and foolish, but I could never believe that of her."

"I agree. I don't think she is responsible. Foolish, but not a traitor."

He slammed onto the sofa, his hands held out before him. "Then who? This whole blasted business has taken a deadly turn. It was one thing to keep the man here at the house, but now that he's free I shan't be able to sleep at night."

"Nor I." I edged onto the sofa beside him, the rector's words echoing in my mind. I took a deep breath. "I don't want you to take what I'm about to ask you amiss."

"Go on."

"What secret do you suppose Giles learned about your family? What was he so afraid to tell you?"

Adrian fumbled with his watch fob. "I wish I had an answer to give you. I've racked my brains trying to figure it out, but I'm left with nothing. Nothing!" He looked up, seemingly surprised by his elevated voice. "Believe me, there is no great secret about Giles I'm hiding from you."

I nodded, but it was a slow one. "Is it possible that someone else might be hiding something from you?"

He lowered his head. "The thought has crossed my mind."

I knew he would never consider one of his daughters, but I would. Juliana was controlling, Phoebe a flighty mess, and then there was Mrs. Ayles. I'd caught her lurking outside my room. What part did she play in all this? We needed more information.

"It's past time we search the kitchens and I mean thoroughly."

"Mrs. Jennings has already done so. She took an extensive inventory, not to mention how she grilled the staff. Browning and I spent a great deal of time in both the dry and wet larders where we found the spy. Trust me, nothing is in there but a few ugly stains on the floor."

"I'd still like to have a second look."

"You think you can turn up something we have not?"

"Is that a challenge?"

"Take it how you will."

"Tonight after everyone has gone to bed, I'm heading to the kitchens. Something must have been missed. The murderer concocted the poison somewhere in that area of the house and our French friend chose to hide in the dry larder. There's got to be some clue everyone is overlooking."

Adrian cast me a wry glance. "Perhaps we can find what Browning and I could not."

"We?"

"The search will have to be late. I'll come to your room, and we'll do this together."

The smell of soot hovered in every corner of the kitchen. The air was icy; the room filled with a restive silence. Sleep of any kind had proven elusive, and the small hours only heightened the pervasive dread that crept over me throughout the evening. Adrian rested the candle he'd brought onto a long central table, but the wavering flame did little to counteract the gloom.

I rubbed the chill from my arms. "Where should we begin?"

Fully dressed in his evening attire, Adrian nosed his way around the cupboards. "I have spent a great deal of time pondering just how the Frenchman could have snuck in here. Earlier something I'd forgotten came to mind. I believe I may have discovered a possible scenario." He motioned to the far wall. "What if he utilized the scullery in some way to access the dry larder?"

I attempted to respond, but Adrian held up his hand. "You probably haven't seen the pass-through between the rooms, but Middlecrest has a rather large one between our scullery and kitchens. Now, if you remember, the Frenchman is slight in stature. What if he simply slipped through the tradesman's entrance from the garden unobserved, hid for a time in the scullery, then climbed right through the pass with no one the wiser? He then could have accessed the larder at just the right moment."

I hesitated, imagining how his suggestion might work. The Frenchman was certainly small enough to fit. "It does seem probable, but why would he take the risk to come inside?"

"An important question. Of course, he may have done so two days earlier to prepare the food with the poison—if he was indeed involved." Adrian appeared resolute in the dim light. I could see his mind working. "I was certain he would reveal something to tip us off while we awaited his recovery, but he knew what he was about. Sometimes, I almost think—"

My mouth fell open. "That he hoped to be caught?"

"Exactly."

I touched my chest. "You did see to his injuries. He must have known you would be inclined to send for the doctor."

Adrian dipped his chin. "I was a fool to grant him so many days here—to give him the perfect opportunity to collaborate with whomever his contact is in the house."

"But you had him watched around the clock." I inched over to the pass-through and lifted the candle to the opening, my mind alight with various possibilities. Two large sinks on the opposing wall looked like pools in the faint light. I pulled back. "What if it was more than that? What if he returned to Middlecrest for something else . . . or someone?"

Adrian looked down. "If that is true, we are wasting our time in the kitchens. He likely found what he came for and left."

I took my time, taking in the whole of the area. "Possibly, but I came down here to search and I intend to do so." I pulled open a few drawers in a nearby sideboard. "A murderous plan at some level or other was executed in these very rooms. Tell me, where does Mrs. Jennings keep the rat poison? She did mention the varmints have been particularly bad of late."

He laughed. "What do I look like, the pied piper? I haven't the least notion. The dry larder?" He softened his voice. "I do agree with you about the rat poison. Browning was unable to locate a single apothecary or grocer that sold anything of the sort for miles around. If I was the murderer, I'd find it far simpler to use what was already at hand, particularly if I was working with someone in the house."

I smiled. "To the dry larder then?"

He gave a slight bow. "After you, my lady."

I crossed the sizable main room to a door nestled between two wooden pillars and unlatched the handle. Moonlight poured through a great window on the left side of the kitchens, but the bowels of the dry larder lay as black as midnight. Adrian retrieved the candle and extended it into the small room. Light spilled on tiered shelves as they materialized from the gloom filled with breads and pastries.

Adrian rubbed his neck. "The room looks just as it did the last time I searched it."

"Maybe." I ran my fingers down each shelf, pausing to assess every compartment. "I cannot believe the Frenchman came in here for no reason. After all, if he poisoned the meat, he would have gone into the wet larder."

Adrian yanked open drawers on the opposite side of the room, kneeling to reach the lowest shelves. I could hear the shifting of items behind me. "Oh, look at these."

I spun around to find Adrian chewing with sugar dusted across his fingertips. "Now that's good," he said out of the corner of his mouth.

I tugged back his arm. "What on earth are you doing? Mrs. Jennings will have your head."

His eyes glistened with mischief as he eased down and sat on the floor. "Not likely. Besides, who would believe the master of the house snuck down to the dry larder overnight?"

"You devil. She'll think it was one of the other servants. It will cause a beastly uproar."

"I have full confidence my staff shall deny it prettily enough. After all, it wasn't them." He held a small round pastry into the light. "Care to try one?"

I knelt beside him and crossed my arms. "Certainly not. I shall wait till tomorrow and eat them with everyone else."

Adrian shot me a devilish look. "Coward. And here I thought you were mistress of this house." He inched it closer to my mouth. "Just try the one."

"I could never be so cruel to Mrs. Jennings."

"What about Mrs. Ayles? These are her favorites."

I gave him an incredulous stare. "You wretch. I would never—"

He laughed. "Don't look at me like that. I know full well the two of you have been at each other's throats since you arrived."

"I have been nothing but civil to her—"

Adrian grasped my hand, opened it, and dropped a pastry into my palm. "Now you haven't a choice. You touched it."

His fingers lingered on mine, and I fought back a smile. "You brute. Now she will think we came down here specifically to eat her favorite treats."

"Didn't we?"

I popped his arm, hesitant to settle in beside him on the floor, but at the same time glad I did. There, so close together, I couldn't help but revel in the warmth of his arm pressed to mine, a rush of nerves brought to life by his enticing smile. "They do look delicious."

He leaned his head against the shelf. "You do know they are ours. We can eat them whenever we want—even in the middle of the night if we fancy. So go on, have another."

He was right, of course. Everything at Middlecrest was his . . . and mine, even though I still felt like an intruder. The room wavered in the candlelight and for a precious moment, I relaxed. We were simply two people wholly unconcerned about murders or investigations, driven instead by the complexities of our hearts. I stole a peek at my partner in crime while I chewed. What would it have been like if I'd met Adrian before Brook?

I placed the last bit of tart into my mouth, savoring the plum flavor.

Adrian helped himself to a third, dusting his fingers off on his breeches. "Do you think we'll ever make heads or tails of this murder?"

I could feel his eyes on me, and I turned to meet them.

It may have been only a second that we sat there looking at one another, but it felt like an eternity before he reached up and touched my cheek. His fingers were a bit hesitant. "You've some sugar here."

One subtle touch and I was struck as still and anxious as I'd been in the woods after the attack. Yet this time there was something decidedly different about the wild pulse thrashing through every inch of my body. I knew then and there my heart was no longer my own.

But what about Adrian? Was he simply enjoying himself for a time? He'd had mistresses in the past to be sure, but did he mean to be a husband now? How could I possibly tell where his charm ended and his true feelings began?

My throat felt tight, my stomach a bubbling pot of nerves. I knew if I moved an inch toward him, it would change our relationship forever.

In that moment of indecision, I caught sight of the corner of Isaac's blue blanket.

CHAPTER 23

I could have discovered Isaac's beloved blanket only from where Adrian and I sat on the tile floor of the dry larder. The hum of candlelight barely illuminated the tuff of blue fabric nestled deep into a crevice between the cabinet and the corner of the wall.

"What on earth?" I drew up onto my knees and grabbed the candle from the floor.

Adrian followed me onto his knees. "What is it?"

"Isaac's blanket." My voice seemed strange amid the quiet of the room. I wriggled my free hand into the tight gap and wrapped my fingers around the soft fabric. Gently, I twisted and pulled until the blanket was free. "He shall be so happy to have it returned." I hugged it to my chest. "Do you suppose he pushed it in there himself? He is always coming down here to see Mrs. Jennings, and he likes to shove his wooden blocks into things."

Adrian scanned the room as if the larder might provide some sort of answer. "I suppose it is possible. He would have been on the floor. But I cannot imagine Mrs. Jennings allowing him in here."

I smiled. "You'd be surprised. Mrs. Jennings has a decided affection for Isaac. She lets him do all sorts of things I'd not expect her to. One time I caught her serving the soup with him on her hip." I held the blanket into the light. "It is a bit dirty, but nothing too awful." Intending to shake off the dust and cobwebs, I grasped the edge and flicked my wrist.

First there was a blur. Then a loud clang. Adrian and I both jerked our attention to the floor. Something had fallen out of the blanket. After a moment of pulsing silence, Adrian stooped to pick up whatever had fallen out. A flash of light glinted off the smooth, metallic surface in his hand.

A knife.

We both stared at it in disbelief. "Who would have wrapped up such a thing in Isaac's blanket?"

Adrian cast me a sharp look. "A murderer, I expect."

"But Giles was poisoned." I leaned in close to examine the blade. The knife was clean with no evidence of foul play. "Wait." Or was there? All at once the terrible scene formed like a play in my mind. The Frenchman. The kitchens. "What if the killer used the knife to distribute the poison in some way?"

"He cut the meat with it?"

"Exactly." I set the candle down and paced the room, shaking out my hands. "We have believed all along that the poison must have been applied to Giles's food. What if you were right earlier and the killer did use the door to the scullery? He could have utilized the room to prepare Giles's meal—including the oil-arsenic marinade he soaked the meat in. Once the poison had seeped into the food, he would need a way to slice it and present it on a plate. If this knife was left behind somehow, he'd certainly want to recover it."

Adrian took a moment to respond. "But why hide it in the dry larder?"

"Giles's death was supposed to look like an accident."

Adrian picked up the candle, his eyes bright in the wavering light. "Then he could not have taken a chance on this same knife poisoning someone else." He frowned at the blanket. "Pardon me if I don't exactly follow you in regard to this."

I bit my lip. "Perhaps someone came upon him during the act, and he needed an immediate hiding spot. Isaac could have dropped his blanket anywhere. He has a habit of doing so."

Adrian offered a slight shake of his head. "I'm sorry, but there is a definite hole in your assumptions. If the killer had to dispose of the knife quickly, he must have been seen. Otherwise, why bother—he could just take the knife with him. But since he stashed it in the pantry, we have to believe he did so with some purpose in mind or out of urgency. Either way, someone would have remarked on seeing him that morning."

I lifted my eyebrows. "Unless he has a friend in the house, as we've thought all along, someone who helped him."

Adrian fell motionless.

My heart galloped as the scene took shape in my mind. "One person in the scullery and one in the main kitchen area."

He turned away. "You mean to suggest, whoever hid this knife is one of my servants?"

"Yes, or perhaps one of the wedding party."

I allowed him time to digest all I'd proposed before taking his hand. "Come on. I'd like to check the scullery as well."

We wound our way out the kitchen door, across the small side garden, and through the scullery entrance, the moon a constant presence. An icy draft roamed the length of the stone floor. Adrian deposited the candle beside a large copper sink.

"What do you hope to find in here?"

"I'm not certain, but if the killer prepared the meat with this knife, he might have done so in this room." I stepped onto a raised mat by the double stone sinks and inspected the cistern.

Adrian took a stroll around the room. It had probably been some time since he'd been in this part of the house. He stopped short near a small side cabinet and swung open the doors.

"You don't suppose . . . Ah, yes, here we are." He pulled a container into the light. "Your rat poison, madam."

"I'll have to check with Mrs. Jennings, but I have a sneaking feeling they don't usually keep that in here." I clasped my hands and caught my husband's pointed glare. "Someone must have stolen into this room—probably our escaped Frenchman—poisoned the meat, then delivered the plate through the opening into the kitchen and the other murderer's waiting hands. That person, a resident of Middlecrest, cut and served the tainted food to Giles." My elation at finally coming to a possible theory faded as quickly as it had come. Two people . . . two devious, cold-blooded people, one of whom was likely still inside the house.

I did a poor job of covering a sudden yawn.

Adrian tugged me to him and wrapped his arm around my back. "This whole blasted business has taken a toll on everyone in the house. I daresay we've done enough tonight. I, for one, am ready for my bed."

I nodded, all too aware of my own weariness. I'd thought at one time that learning the truth of Giles's death would quench my unsettled feelings, but the loss of my dear friend, particularly in such a senseless way, would never be completely understood. Not really.

Lofty shadows christened our retreat up the stairs, the weight of truth hanging on our shoulders. Adrian must have sensed my disquiet as he followed me all the way into my room.

"Try to get some rest. I'll speak with Browning in the morning. My instincts agree with your assumptions. The Frenchman was in the scullery, but I haven't a clue who in the house has betrayed us."

"Nor I." I walked as if in a fog and dropped Isaac's blanket on the floor. It would have to be thoroughly washed before returning to his sweet hands. I'm not at all certain I saw the white flash of paper perched on the coverlet as I rested my hand on the bedpost, but I could feel its presence all too quickly. My hands quivered as I drew them up to my throat.

"Not again." Someone had been in my room while we were gone—someone had known of our wee-hour escapade.

Adrian raced over to me and seized the note. He cast me a hard look, then tore it open, his eyes narrowing in turn.

"What does it say?" My voice had become a strangled whisper.

He crushed the paper in a fist.

I couldn't take my eyes off the wrinkled ball in his hands. "Another threat? You must tell me."

He held the paper out. "I will do as you say, but I'm afraid it will only frighten you."

Carefully, I twisted it open and focused on the jagged script.

Don't make another move or your son may be forced to pay the price.

My eyes burned with unshed tears. "Isaac! We must get him at once."

Adrian hurried to the door, his fingers clenched in a ball around the latch, his muscles so tight they twitched.

"I'm sorry, Elizabeth. I tricked myself into believing I could keep the two of you safe. We are so close to solving everything."

I followed him into the hallway with the candle. "It's not your fault."

"Isn't it?"

"I don't know . . . I . . . It was my decision to stay. Whoever wrote this only means to scare us."

"And they are doing a blasted good job of it." He halted at the nursery door. "I've never regretted any choices I've made in my life until now. I never should have married you and brought you here. It was nothing but selfish on my part." His voice grew serious. "I used you to keep my secret."

I angled into his gaze, as I reached to open the nursery door. "You act as if I had no say in that decision—that I was merely a possession to be bought or sold. You have been completely honest with me from the beginning, and our marriage was ultimately my decision." My legs felt weak. "We are together now and bound by more than a signature on a slip of paper. I made a vow before God that day, and I don't intend to break it."

The candle dipped as I pushed open the nursery door, sending a wave of shadows skirting across the room. In silence we rushed through the front room and into Isaac's small bedchamber. My knees nearly buckled when I saw his sleeping form.

Adrian was right beside me, his voice a tight whisper. "Get Isaac and let us return to your room. And I don't care what you say, I'm sleeping in your bedchamber tonight."

I felt dizzy. "What do you mean?"

He turned me to face him, his eyes so terribly direct, my knees nearly buckled a second time.

"I don't mean to break my wedding vow either. We're going to fight this together—the five of us—you, me, Isaac, and the girls. We're a family now, and I won't allow anyone to frighten us from our home."

CHAPTER 24

I awoke to find Isaac cuddled up to my side, his pudgy fist smashed against his cheek. Despite the second threatening note, I'd slept better than ever before at Middlecrest, even with Adrian on the opposing side of the bed.

I took a deep breath, my heart a vulnerable drum. There had been no other choice of sleeping arrangements, not when we had the love act to maintain. The servants talked more than anyone else. It would do no good for my maid to find Adrian asleep on the rug.

Perhaps in the end, it was Adrian's presence that granted me such a comfortable sleep. When was the last time I'd felt so safe?

I glanced over Isaac to Adrian's still form an arm's length away from me. The perfect wave my husband liked to maintain in his hair had barely moved overnight, and he appeared so much younger as he slept. He had a death grip on his pillow, and I couldn't help but smile as I remembered the night he slept on the floor at the White Lion Inn.

I glided my fingers across the coverlet before resting my hand on Isaac's warm back. Over the past few years life had dealt me a bitter hand, teaching me to rely on myself alone. Abandonment had become a pattern. Time after time I was forced to build walls around my heart and face alone whatever trials arose. It was something I'd become quite excellent at. Goodness, I actually wore my stony resilience as a badge of honor—Elizabeth Cantrell, the lady who refused to let anyone hurt her again.

But last night while I lie awake in the dark surrounded by my new family, something shifted in my heart. I didn't like the person I had become. Curious how one instance can readjust a person's entire perspective. For me it was when Adrian and I rushed to fetch Isaac, and Adrian demanded to stay in my bedchamber. I realized then, for the first time in so very long, I was not alone.

Adrian stirred before raising a hand to rub his face. It took only a moment for him to focus on me. His eyes looked tired, but his easy smile was as quick as ever.

"I meant to be up early. I saw your maid come in to light the fire, but I was too tired to rise."

"I can imagine. We fell asleep so late."

He draped his arm over his head. "I actually slept quite well. You?"

"I did. Thank you for staying."

He laughed. "I don't think I gave you much of a choice."

I was certain he'd intended to return to his own bed when he was confident we were all safe. A spark of heat crept into my cheeks, and I hid my face in the covers.

He swung into a sitting position with his feet dangling beside the bed and adjusted his night shift. "I suppose I better head on to my bedchamber to dress. Browning will be pounding on my door if I linger much longer." After a quick stretch, he crossed the rug to the connecting door.

I couldn't help but notice my husband's shapely legs, as they were so nicely exposed beneath his shift.

He turned back rather quickly. "I'll only be a room away."

I dipped my chin, attempting to conceal the embarrassment inching up my spine.

"No one is going to try anything in full light with my husband so near."

He gave me a reassuring grin. "What plans do you have today?"

Was he really going to stand there half dressed as if it was nothing out of the common way? I swallowed hard.

"First, I shall take Isaac to the nursery and spend some time there. Miss Barton must be told the whole of the danger since I cannot be with Isaac at all times. And then I should like to speak with Juliana." I hoped to find out more about the mysterious Ewan Hawkins. He had been in the kitchens the morning Giles was killed. At this point everyone needed to be considered.

Adrian twisted his signet ring on his finger. "I'd rather you not leave the house, at least not alone."

His words nettled, but I understood his concern. "I won't do so without you. I promise."

"Good. I've an appointment with Browning and then some estate business to tend to, but please do not hesitate to come to my study if you need anything."

I grasped the bell pull to call for my maid. "Rest assured, you won't be able to hide from me if I decide I need you."

He pulled open the connecting door, and I thought I heard a chuckle as he disappeared inside.

I hadn't long to wait before Lilley arrived and helped me dress. Isaac woke midway through the affair, and Lilley did a passable job playing nursemaid and abigail at the same time.

Later Isaac and I made our way to the nursery as fast as his little knees would carry him. He wouldn't even consider riding on my hip. He had an independent mind like his mother—and father.

I stopped short inches from the nursery door as a thought took hold. Adrian was Brook's opposite in every way possible. Adrian, the eldest, had been left the title and running of the estate. He had grown into a planner, a man loyal to his servants, a father loved by his children. Both brothers possessed the Radcliff eyes and teasing mannerisms, but they were not the same person. Not at all. And I had somehow managed to marry the better of the two.

Isaac scooted around the nursery door, and I followed him inside. Miss Barton jumped from her seat on the sofa and rushed over to us.

"I have been waiting an age. Tell me at once why you whisked Isaac from his bed in the middle of the night."

I was taken aback by her tone and the sharp scowl on her face. "I didn't mean to frighten you. I did leave a note."

"That told me nothing."

I closed the door behind me and made my way to a nearby chair. "I don't mean to alarm you, but you must understand the gravity of our situation. Do you remember me speaking about Giles's murder?"

Her hand flew to her mouth. "Well, yes."

"I received a note last night threatening Isaac."

Her face blanched. "From the murderer?"

"We believe so."

Slowly, she turned to look at him. "Are you and Isaac to stay in this house?"

"At present, yes. I haven't had much time to think. Lord Torrington is here. I believe it's important to stay close to him."

"But you must think of your child."

My hand fell like a stone onto the armrest. "I *am* thinking of him!"

Miss Barton drew back, probably all too aware of her gross mistake. She was never to question me. "Forgive me."

My shoulders slumped. Isaac needed consistency and security. A team of people caring for him. This was no time to pick a quarrel.

"We've all been under a great deal of stress. I hope I can count on you, for I am entrusting you with my son's life. I cannot be forever with him."

She gave me a mournful look. "You know I would do anything for our boy."

"I do, and I thank you for it."

The three of us remained in the nursery for the whole of the morning, and I left only when my stomach declared it was time for lunch. I had no strong suspicions of who could have written the notes, so I was forced to continue my investigation, hoping I might turn up something. At first I thought to leave Isaac with Miss Barton; however, when the moment came, I found I could not bring myself to part from him.

So he accompanied me to a plate of cold meat and then on to Juliana's room. I found her sprawled across her great poster bed, a book in her hand. The door was ajar, but I knocked before entering.

"Have you a moment to spare?"

She sat up at once and wiped her eyes. "Come in."

This was not the Juliana I'd experienced over the last few days, neither morose nor dejected. This version had a harried look about her. Her chignon had slipped to the side and her fingers made busy work of the patterns on the coverlet. She'd been keeping her distance from the rest of the house and suddenly I knew why. Today was supposed to be the day of her marriage.

I crossed the room to her bedside. "How are you?"

She stiffened. "As well as can be expected." She avoided my gaze. "I hoped you'd come to tell me the escaped prisoner had been found."

"Not yet, but your father and Mr. Browning are working hard to locate him."

She watched as Isaac wriggled in my arms, then flopped onto the bed. "I suppose you are here to scold me for what I said to Phoebe this morning."

I found a spot beside her and took a seat, then lowered Isaac to the floor.

"What did you say to Phoebe?"

"Oh, nothing of any consequence. She just made me so angry—visiting that man the way she did."

I folded my fingers in my lap. "I don't believe Phoebe had anything to do with his disappearance."

All at once she smothered her face in her hands. "But what if I did?"

My eyes widened. "Juliana, what do you mean?"

"I had to see him."

My breath caught. "The Frenchman?"

"Please don't scold me. I couldn't bear it if you did." Fear crept into her voice as she fought the pain of her words. "And I am certain Phoebe went to the conservatory after I did. At least I think so."

I hesitated to answer, but if I was to pursue any relationship between us, I had to give her something. I eased the tone of my voice. "Tell me the whole."

Her hand quivered as she tucked a stray hair behind her ear. I could tell she still wanted to hate me, but Giles's sudden death

ABIGAIL WILSON

had scattered her emotions all over the place. Tears welled as she spoke.

"I had to see the man, to know what he looked like. I only meant to take a peek at him through the window, but . . ." A sob broke her words. "I knew him."

My voice left me for a whisper. "You knew him?"

She shook her head as she went on, her fingers clawing at the bedsheets. "From my season in London. I met him at Vauxhall Gardens one night. I remember it distinctly because he was so much shorter than me. We were not properly introduced. I assumed he was a guest of someone because he was so amiable. My friend allowed us some space, and I really wanted to see the gardens."

Silence joined us on the bed for several seconds. Adrian was right. His daughters needed a mother, but now was not the time to point out Juliana's idiocy. I shook my head. What had she done that I had not?

"Do you remember anything he said or did that night? Anything that might be useful?"

She seemed confused and flapped her hands like a wild bird. "He enjoyed telling me about the various plants, but then things turned strange. He mentioned places he'd visited so far in London, only they weren't respectable at all. Can you believe he even brought up Newgate Prison?"

"Newgate?" Isaac had pulled himself up to stand beside the bed, and I lifted him onto the coverlet.

A smile emerged on Juliana's face as he caught her eye. "He seemed to think the idea of strolling among the prisoners a joke. He said there were so many visitors at Newgate that the only way he could tell the prisoners from the regular people was that the inmates wore leg irons."

238

"Did he say anything else?"

Isaac giggled as she removed his shoes to tickle his toes, and I was glad he'd accompanied me as he proved the best sort of medicine for a young lady tortured by loss. "Not that I can remember." Her hands seemed to pause. "Oh my goodness. Look here. Have you ever noticed Isaac's toe? Oh, and it's on both feet. What an odd little duck you are. His fourth one is so much shorter than the rest. Papa always says that's a sign of intelligence."

I laughed. "A toe?"

She shrugged. "That's what he says."

Isaac rolled over and stuck his feet in the air, and I tickled his tummy before taking a deep breath.

"What about in the conservatory? Did the man say anything there? Did you go inside?"

"Yes." The intensity returned to her voice. "I was angry. Terribly angry. It was the first surge of feelings I'd experienced since Giles's death. I was not myself when I stormed in there and told the wretch I knew who he was. Can you believe he only smirked and claimed not to know me?"

"Your father and I believe he is playing some sort of game."

"Yes!" Her eyes lit up. "I got the strangest feeling that he was exactly where he wanted to be. I sent the footman away at first. He was to wait outside the door. But I got so angry with the Frenchman that I don't even remember checking to ensure the footman had returned when I left. What if something happened in my absence? However, if Phoebe was there after me . . ."

"I wondered how you knew his hands were bound. Take heart, I cannot imagine the footman walking very far away." I looked off. "In fact, think no more about it. I do not believe you responsible." In that tense moment I realized the reason behind the ice in Juliana's frosty eyes. Not only was she struggling to grieve Giles's death but she blamed herself. The buried guilt was crushing her from the inside out. Instinctively, I moved to touch her hand, and I was surprised when she did not pull away. "There is something you should know."

She'd allowed me the merest peek into her world, and I could see her grappling with the decision to continue the intimacy. "What is it?"

"I have come to believe that Giles did not leave Middlecrest before the wedding because of you. It seems he had other reasons."

She slumped back against the headboard, her eyes wide like a frightened deer. "How can you be sure?"

"I spoke with the rector in Reedwick, and he said Giles needed to handle something quite different."

"Oh?" I could almost see the weight of guilt ebb from her shoulders as her face flushed. "I thought I'd made things so ill between us that he . . ."

"Ran away?" I squeezed her hand. "Believe me, I knew Giles quite well, and the man I met in the drawing room the day I arrived was very much in love with you. One argument would never have frightened Giles. He was a gentleman of integrity."

Juliana struggled to breathe, her eyes clouding with tears. "Thank you for telling me."

I handed her a handkerchief before corralling Isaac away from the edge of the bed. "You're a grown woman, Juliana. I never came here to play your mama. I rather hoped we could be friends instead."

I could see it took quite a bit of energy for Adrian's eldest daughter to move just a few feet toward me on the bed. However, she managed to do so at last with all the dignity I'd grown to admire in her. She finally looked up.

"I've said and done some awful things, but I don't care what Grandmama says. I'm glad you came to Middlecrest. I only hope my father appreciates you."

I pulled her into an embrace, which Isaac also joined. I was relieved to finally knock down the barrier I'd been trapped behind since arrival. Yet I would be lying to say her last words didn't sting.

Adrian's own daughters had questions about his integrity.

CHAPTER 25

I decided to approach Mrs. Ayles in the drawing room following dinner. She'd been in the house for many years and knew every little thing that went on at Middlecrest. She could be uniquely situated to see something—something that could help us solve the murder, whether she realized it or not. I knew she could not be trusted, yet I thought she might be willing to divulge a few details regarding the dubious Ewan Hawkins.

When I entered, she had positioned herself in her usual chair by the fireplace, a screen positioned just so between her and the flames. Her shoulders sloped forward, her mouth resting in a scowl. I found her shrewd eyes unnaturally fixed on the door as I made my way to her side. She sat as if able to take in the whole of the room at once and had already found the ladies present wanting.

I pulled a slat-back chair close to her with some hesitation and took a seat.

"Are you well this evening, Mrs. Ayles?" The smile I affected did little in the way of appeasement. She probably knew as well as I did that it wasn't genuine. How could it be when she had treated me with such disdain from the moment I arrived?

She eyed me for a long moment. "Much you care."

Though I'd observed on more than one occasion that

Mrs. Ayles's walk was perfectly stable, she utilized a long ivory cane to great effect. Tonight she thrust it out in front of her like a scepter, her hand perched at the top like a claw.

This was going to be more difficult than I thought.

"I do realize we have been thrown together in this house under difficult circumstances, but I assure you I ask in earnest."

"Humph."

She was looking across the carpet like an eagle intent on its prey. I followed her gaze. Ewan Hawkins entered the room ahead of the other gentlemen. It was the perfect moment to bring up his name.

"Do you know Mr. Hawkins well? He's lived here for some time, if I'm not mistaken."

At first I thought she meant to ignore me entirely, but Mrs. Ayles couldn't possibly pass up the chance to flout her superior knowledge. Her chin quivered.

"He came to us from London over ten years ago. Nothing but a boy at the time. Adrian supplied him tutors, and then he was sent away to school."

There was a decided dip in her voice that perplexed me. Was it simply her disapproval or something else?

"I've found him quite amiable, and he and the girls appear to be close. I was told Adrian found him in a workhouse in London."

She shot me a sideways glance. "That is what I understand."

"And his parents?"

Her jaw tightened as she turned to face me. "There's been no revelation if that is what you are insinuating." She patted her lap with her free hand. "And I daresay it is best for everyone involved if it stays that way." Her cane swayed as she twisted her focus back to the room, her jaw clenching again then sagging.

"There's more, isn't there?"

She pursed her lips as if she'd tasted something bitter before a cynical smile surfaced. Her eyes glinted in the firelight.

"My dear Lady Torrington, let me assure you, any secrets I possess I plan to take to the grave. You can cease your meddling at once."

Mrs. Ayles raised her chin—the queen of Middlecrest, or so she thought. It seemed impossible, but she was able to straighten her shoulders a bit. I daresay she meant to give me a well-timed set-down; however, her pointed declaration had done just the opposite. She'd only confirmed my earlier suspicions.

Ewan Hawkins was not a random boy Adrian found in a workhouse. And Mrs. Ayles was not the only person who knew why he had been brought to Middlecrest. There was someone else who bore that secret.

I located Adrian across the room, dressed smartly for the evening in a black jacket and gleaming pumps. He'd sequestered Ewan near the sideboard, and the two men were deep in conversation. I took my leave of Mrs. Ayles with a curt nod and stood to cross the room. Yet I couldn't help but take one final look back to see if I'd unnerved her. She sat as stoic as before.

A quiver settled into my stomach as that hard, knowing smile chased me from her presence. I suppose she was confident Adrian would not disclose what I wished to know—in fact, she was certain of it. My steps slowed as darker thoughts dawned. Was there more to the story than I had deduced? A possible reason he could not tell me the truth? I halted near the trim of the carpet for the merest second, my focus swinging like a pendulum between the two men.

Why had I not noticed it before? Ewan Hawkins didn't look a bit like Adrian. Ewan's nose was far more slender, his eyes a deep brown. In fact, he didn't resemble any of the Radcliffs at all. I knew very well some children did not favor their parents, but there was something about the Radcliff men. Even Isaac had begun to betray their likeness.

But if Ewan was not Adrian's illegitimate son, why was he at Middlecrest?

Amid this confusion I happened to notice Phoebe's red face out of the corner of my eye. She was once again standing at the window, her focus fixed into the depths of a particularly dark night. I was startled to see her wipe a tear from her cheek. I'd come to expect such an emotional display of affection from Juliana, but not Phoebe. I continued in my turn about the room, slowing when I neared the window.

She didn't even look up at my approach. It was as if she'd slipped into a trance. After a moment's hesitation I sat at her side, hopeful my advances would be welcome. I touched her hand.

"My dear, you are not happy."

Her face flushed, and she managed a weak glance. "I'm afraid I care a great deal too much about other people's opinions." Her voice caught in her throat. "I've hurt Papa dreadfully and everyone in the house is so angry with me right now, I find it difficult to breathe."

"I see." She drew back at my tone, and I realized I'd spoken far too brusquely. There was more to Phoebe than youth and misadventure. She had a knack for seeing the good in people, and she had a layer of compassion few people truly understood. And therefore, a fragile heart.

Her hands found her face. "Believe me, I did nothing wrong—nothing untoward. The Frenchman only asked to see a few of my pictures."

245

Pictures? My heartbeat took a rowdy turn, and I struggled to form my next question. "Are you saying you brought your paintings into the conservatory?"

She nodded. "It was innocent, I assure you. He must have seen me painting in the grove. I go there often. When he asked, he did so with such artful kindness, and I thought they might bring him a bit of happiness on his final day at Middlecrest. I-I never found him the fiend everyone else seems to think he is. He was quite civil to me. Like I said before, we don't even know if he had anything to do with Giles's death." She held up her hand to halt my reply. "Oh Mama, I fully admit it is possible that he did. I don't know how to explain it. Only, I suppose a part of me thought he might enjoy one particular picture I'd made previously. You see, I'd drawn his likeness through the window a few days before. You must admit, he does have a handsome profile."

On the tail end of a long breath, I added, "Or a deadly one."

She looked away. "He didn't seem all that interested in that painting."

"Did he find any of your work to his liking?"

She fought a smile, but I could see it tugging at the corners of her mouth. "Well, yes. He was complimentary of my skill and spent quite a bit of time admiring my drawing of the town square."

"Oh?" A flutter rippled through my chest. "Would it be too much trouble for you to fetch your drawing book for me? I'd like to see that picture."

Phoebe rubbed her forearms. "If you like, but please don't put them on display. Ewan and Juliana like to tease me."

I took her hand, careful with my tone. "I shall keep the book private, but please do hurry."

I wasn't at all certain she understood my meaning as I watched her stroll from the room, her arms loose at her sides. However, when she returned, everything had changed; her eyes were pinched, her face pale. She came at once to the window where she flopped down and thrust out the book.

"Something is dreadfully wrong."

I accepted the sketches, my pulse on alert, then scoured the drawing like a mouse looking for a bread crumb. Yet all I saw was a busy town square complete with shops and sellers—nothing unusual.

"You don't notice it, do you? I suppose you haven't lived here all that long. This is Plattsdale. Do you recognize it?"

"Well, of course, but I've only been a handful of times."

Her eyebrows peaked. "Look closer." She pointed at the bottom right corner of the picture, then over a few inches. "See here, the signposts and shop signs have all been altered. That is not what I drew. This one should point to Shedmire and this one here to Reedwick. Even the blacksmith's sign has been changed."

I shifted forward, leaning as close as I could to the thick paper. She was right. All the signs were incorrect. In fact, they weren't even words, just random letters replacing the names.

"Do you have any idea who could have done this?"

"None at all."

How could someone have known Phoebe would show this particular picture to the Frenchman? I rubbed my forehead. "You said you paint in the grove frequently?"

"Nearly every day. Everyone at Middlecrest knows that."

I dipped my chin. "Including the Frenchman." I met her troubled eyes. "Phoebe, if you could see him well enough to paint his likeness, he could just as easily see you."

"But I never even had this drawing on my easel. I haven't worked on it in weeks. I'm not even certain I brought it with me to the grove."

I focused one more time on the random letters. "But someone could have."

She shrugged. "I don't see how that is possible."

"Why not? If everyone knows you paint there, no one who saw your easel would have thought anything of it." I angled the picture. "In the proper position, your drawing could make an effective message board."

She paused and then fumbled with the paper. "What do you think the letters mean?"

Slowly, I shook my head. "I'm not certain at present, but I think it prudent to take the drawing to my bedchamber to show your father tonight. He might have some idea."

She looked around as if suddenly aware others were in the room with us. "I suppose you're right. But, please, do be careful. I've caused enough trouble already."

L

Having called Lilley to come dress me early for bed, I was surprised to see Adrian assessing Phoebe's picture in the connecting room when I returned. I looked over his shoulder.

"I've been staring at those letters for the past hour. It must be some sort of code."

"Sorry I couldn't get away earlier." Adrian turned and gave me a cool smile.

I motioned for him to follow me over to the desk in the corner, where I had been working much of the evening.

He joined me, resting his hand ever so lightly on the small

of my back. "Mrs. Ayles was quite put out not to have a fourth at whist. She does so enjoy your company."

I choked back a laugh. "I daresay she managed well enough in my absence."

"Always." He chuckled for a moment, but his voice had changed when he spoke again. "Juliana graced us with a song on the pianoforte."

"I'm so glad to hear she's continuing to play." Perhaps our time together had done her some good.

He directed me into the desk chair. "So tell me what you've discovered so far about this code."

I shifted the paper I'd been working on. "See here, I've written down all the letters from the drawing in order. At first I thought it might be a directional code due to the placement of the signposts, but I abandoned that idea almost immediately. The Frenchman had no way to write anything, so the code would have to be something simple. Lucius and I used to employ all kinds of codes to send each other secret notes as children. With a strict governess and tutor, we were forced to find unique ways to hide information."

Adrian moved the second candle to the desk, then slid a chair in beside me. "May I?" He stared at the paper for several seconds.

GJCWJFIDC FYCYBTCXH NXXTWXCNS CYCJCUTYY
JICUQFSY

I pointed to the spaces between the letters. "I don't think the breaks mean anything, since that would make words that are uncommonly long. Whatever information our culprit wished to convey had to be short and concise."

"How would the Frenchman be able to keep track of the correct letters once he began to decipher the message?"

"He would have had a great deal of time. And some people are quite good at memorizing things. Lucius could do so in a matter of seconds. Take the first letter here. If it represents a letter a few spaces away in the alphabet, the rest of the code would be quite easy to decipher. I tried that approach up to ten letters off, but I cannot seem to make a word at the beginning. And I've tried at the start of each grouping."

"I see what you mean." He rested his hand on the back of my chair and leaned in close. Warmth ebbed across my skin, and for a heart-stopping second I wondered if he could feel the hairs springing to life on my arms. Goodness knew I could.

A whiff of his citrus cologne met my nose, and I closed my eyes for a brief moment, attempting to clear my head. Why did veiled interest burst so suddenly into heart-pounding attraction when he came close? I took one last long breath before inching away.

"What are you doing?" His voice was almost a laugh.

My lungs contracted as my eyelids flicked open, my mind a fuzzy blur.

"Were you sniffing me?"

If the floor opened up, I would have gladly jumped in.

"I—" Oh, that smile, that look. Why did he have to watch me so intently? Like he knew what I was going to say before I said it. "You have a particularly nice scent. I mean cologne."

Well, I suppose he didn't know I was going to say that. He stared, trying for some sort of a response, before he looked away briefly, then rubbed his forehead as his eyes returned to me.

"My *scent?*"

I buried my face in my hands, turning away to mouth the word *idiot* to an empty wall. Straightening, I affected a smile and twisted back to him. I only hoped I masked the quiver in my voice.

"You know very well I didn't mean it like that. I suppose you purchased the cologne in London. I guess I've never smelled one quite like it."

He gave me a curious look. "I believe so. I've had it for some time."

I liked the turn of his voice—a mix of novelty and expectation. I'd managed to knock him off stride and it felt nice to have the reins for a change.

"The aroma brought back a memory, that's all—when we first met in the carriage."

This time he didn't flinch. His gaze intensified. "It's amazing how much has changed since that day."

I looked down at his hand. It was an inch away from my own, yet I could have sworn he was touching me.

He tapped his finger, turning his focus back to the paper and its letters. "There are an awful lot of Cs in the message."

I propped up my elbow on the desk, my heart a mess. "Well . . . They could represent a common letter, or . . ." I gripped the paper. "Lucius and I used to use a specific letter to represent a space in our codes. We tended to utilize an *X*, but a *C* would work just as well. Particularly if the *C* represents a rarely used letter." I dipped the quill as quickly as possible, regrouping the letters accordingly.

GJ WJFID FY YBT XHNXXTWX NS YMJ UTYYJI UQFSY

"Now they look like possible words. If I'm right and the *C* stands for a rare letter, the code could be offset by either three, four, or five letters." I pointed to the alphabet I had penned across the top of the page.

Adrian's muscles tightened at my side. "You're a genius. Look, if G and J are offset by five, the first word is *Be*!"

My fingers flew to count out the next word. "And the second *ready*!"

Adrian pulled me close to his side. "I daresay you've done it."

I used the key to decipher the rest of the message, and Adrian and I simply stared at what we'd uncovered.

Be ready at two. Scissors in the potted plant.

We'd been right all along. Someone was working with the Frenchman right under our very noses.

CHAPTER 26

After our discovery I had great difficulty falling asleep, unlike Isaac who'd curled up with his clean blanket and drifted into the unfettered dreamland only a child could attain. I could see his shadowy curls pressed to his pillow from where I lay in my bed. He was so soft and innocent. Adrian and I moved his bed into the far corner of my bedchamber as we were both unwilling to let him out of our sight since the arrival of the second threatening note.

Adrian stayed in my bedchamber again as well. I'd been so frightened the night I received the second letter that I was glad of his company, but having him in my bed so close yet so far away— only unwrapped emotions I could hardly face.

Slivers of moonlight poured through gaps in the drapes and fanned out across the floor like a peacock's feathers. I stared at them for some time, up one side, down the next, but it was no use. Sleep had no intention of joining me. The details of Giles's murder were still fresh in my mind—taunting me to link the slew of seemingly unrelated events and finally uncover the truth.

I sat up in bed with a purposeful sigh and drew my legs to my chest, pressing my cheeks against my knees. There had to be a connection among the clues Adrian and I had discovered. I brushed my way back through the memories, combing out each one and examining them from every angle. The exercise, though exhausting, eventually returned to the cursed carriage accident. Somehow the events leading back to that fateful day set the whole thing into motion.

Adrian was certain someone had been on the same road as Isaac and me, transporting a document of great importance—to France? Possibly. Perhaps it had been our Frenchman himself on his way to the coast. There was no way to know. Of course, nothing was found on his person when we discovered him in the kitchens. And such a thought did little to explain why he turned up at Middlecrest, or murdered Giles for that matter. One thought was replaced by another until I settled on the night Adrian and I searched the kitchens, and the oddity of the knife wrapped in Isaac's blanket kept turning in my mind.

I scanned the room. Had we examined the knife thoroughly? Yes, the murderer likely used it to cut the poisoned meat, but what if it hid another clue? The Frenchman had risked his life to retrieve it, so why had we paid so little attention to it? My feet itched to spring from the bed, but it was far too early to dash down the stairs and demand Mr. Browning present the knife at this hour. I slumped into the covers, resigned to a long night of waiting.

I did feel a bit reassured as I plumped my pillow and closed my eyes, confident this new angle might turn up something, but I was no closer to capturing the sleep that had eluded me thus far. Soon enough, the covers felt heavy, the room small. Sometime during my reflections, a vast stillness had crept over Middlecrest. No wind, no birds—it was almost as if God had reached down and frozen time. A quiver skirted down my spine, but I wasn't cold, just transfixed by the heavy silence.

Adrian made a sound in his sleep, snapping the growing tension in my muscles. My husband lay with his back to me, his lithe form captured in silhouette. Isaac's and my protector. I couldn't help but smile, though the sentiment was followed all too quickly by a grimace.

As if Adrian sensed the thoughts at war in my mind, he turned over. I sank into the folds of the covers. Was he awake? Was he looking at me? Somehow I knew he was.

My heart sprang to life, and the words that had burned my tongue all night tumbled unbidden from my lips. "Adrian."

At first there was silence, then a tight, "Hmm?"

"I know this is hardly the hour for conversation, but I have a question I'd like to ask you."

Another idle, "Hmm."

"Who exactly is Ewan?"

The covers rustled, then a muffled laugh met my ears. "Good morning to you too."

I propped my head on my arm. "It's not morning and you know it."

He shifted to face me, and a ray of moonlight revealed the expression of amusement on his face. "You've become rather direct of late." Several seconds passed before he ran a hand through his hair and propped his head on the pillow. "I suppose I might as well answer you. You're not one to give up. However, may I ask what prompted this question?"

I didn't hesitate. "Mrs. Ayles."

He added up the situation in a glance. "I should have known."

"Everyone says you found him in London at a workhouse."

His face grew still. "That is correct."

"You wouldn't have brought him here without a reason, would you?"

His eyes appeared gray in the dim light, but no less astute. Shadows lined his jaw. The twist in his voice did not feel predatory, but I found his gaze difficult to maintain. He went on. "I don't believe lies or secrets are the least beneficial to any sort of marriage."

I instantly thought of Isaac, but I was not prepared to take the bait. We were speaking of Ewan, and I needed answers before I could find my way to trusting Adrian completely with my son.

"Is Ewan your illegitimate child?"

He gave an uncomfortable chuckle, his profile fading into the gloom. "I imagine that is what they all think, and I've allowed them to."

The tension in my arms abated. "Then it is not true?"

"No, but I'm no less responsible for him."

I watched him closely, hoping to find answers written within the lines on his face. This was no time for a misunderstanding. "How can that be?"

When he spoke next, he sounded calm, controlled. "There is only one other person who knows the truth in its entirety."

"Ewan?"

He was slow to nod, but he finally did so. "I have been concerned for some time that I would be breaking his trust by apprising you of all the details surrounding his birth, but you reminded me the other day that I made a promise to you as well. And quite frankly, as my wife, this involves you too." He rested his hand between us on the bed, and without thinking I placed mine next to his.

My subtle movement distracted him, halting his speech. A faint smile crossed his face, but it didn't last long before he looked away. Whatever he had to say would not be pleasant.

"It would be prudent to start at the beginning, but no less

difficult." He pressed his lips together. "When I was but a lad of nineteen I fell in love with a beautiful woman." His eyes glazed over, his speech dissolving into a soft pattern, almost like he had transformed into his younger self. "Miss Florencia Ayles was the toast of the season, and I thought myself her equal in every way. Ball after ball she sought me out, and my father encouraged the connection. She was the daughter of an old, wealthy family, after all—a perfect match. And I was smitten.

"One night at the Hyatt's ball, a few short weeks after we met, she asked me to go with her alone into a part of the house I'd not been before. I hesitated at first, but since I had every intention of marrying her, I gladly followed.

"She whisked me away to the upper landing, then to her friend's bedchamber, where she revealed that she had something to tell me. I don't remember if we actually said anything else to one another. Before long we were kissing on the settee, and that is exactly where her father found us."

My eyes widened.

"It was a terrible scandal. I'd ruined her and disappointed my father. The arrangements were made promptly with my full support. A license was obtained, and we were married two days later.

"I remember bringing her back to Middlecrest, watching her reaction in the carriage as we approached. Despite how we'd begun our life together, I was thrilled to finally be home—with her." He rubbed his eyes. "Sometimes I wish I could go back to that moment, when everything was still before me, when I believed people were inherently good.

"I should have realized where I stood when she barely looked out the window at her new home." He paused to look up at me, the intricate stitches of his past so evident in his eyes. "I noticed the rounding of her stomach less than two months later. She was with child and fairly far along. The baby could not have been mine, not so soon. She'd tricked me into marrying her to save her own reputation. Love apparently had not been a part of the arrangement, at least not on her end. She was angry when I confronted her. She expected me to keep quiet and play my part. Sensing my hesitation, she got to work almost immediately, informing everyone in the neighborhood about *our* joy."

My mind flashed back to what Mrs. Harris had said about an infant who died.

"I was forced to acknowledge the child straightaway or live with the embarrassment from then on. I decided to say nothing, but it wasn't for her benefit. The baby was innocent. Regardless of how I felt, I could not disown him. I had no intention of ruining his life before it had even begun.

"Florencia, however, cared nothing for the child growing within her. He was only a horrid inconvenience. The days passed, and I grew less and less able to tolerate her company. She loathed everything about me, and she did little to hide her disdain. Mrs. Ayles arrived early for the confinement, so I decided to spend the final months in London at my townhouse. I'd intended to return nearer to her confinement. But I never should have left.

"It was raining the day I arrived back home. I was met at the door with a sad story and little emotion by Mrs. Ayles. Apparently the baby boy had come into this world that very morning but died within the hour. Mrs. Ayles swore there was nothing that could have been done to save the child.

"Sickeningly, Florencia thought I would be pleased by the news, but I assure you, I was not. I grieved for some time." He lowered his eyes "It wasn't until Florencia began to talk about the child's deformity that suspicion crept into my mind. With every passing day, I became more and more certain that she'd lied to me about the day of his birth. No one had been in the birthing room but her mother and the midwife. And then she had refused to let anyone else sit with the body. The baby wasn't mine, but I never even saw the dead child. It wasn't long before I was utterly convinced the child had survived and she'd gotten rid of him, but I had no proof. She betrayed nothing."

He looked down at his own hands on the bed. "I'm ashamed to say a part of me wanted to forget the whole affair. After all, he wasn't mine. But thankfully my heart has been transformed over and over again. That's the beauty of forgiveness. It changed me, made me into a much stronger man than I ever was before. I didn't learn the truth until after Florencia's death. She'd left a letter in her private things. The child was alive, and I had every intention of finding him.

"I tracked down a farmer's wife in a nearby village who worked as a wet nurse at the time of the birth. A few guineas and she talked freely. The baby was eventually taken to a foundling home in London. After that, she knew nothing else. It took me several years and more private investigators until I stumbled upon Ewan in a workhouse. I knew at once it was him. He has her eyes— all the children do—and his deformity assured me I was right. All I can guess is that Ewan's mangled hand must have disgusted Florencia. She would have been embarrassed for others to see him. Her vanity had no limits. Her callous heart, no compassion."

I sat in stunned silence, hopeless to fully digest all he'd revealed, let alone respond appropriately.

"Do the girls know?"

"Not exactly. I'm fairly certain they believe he's my child. They

ABIGAIL WILSON

consider him a brother at any rate. I've had no reason to disclose the truth. I don't mind them believing he's mine. After all, I've been Ewan's only parent for years. He will disclose his secret when he feels the time is right."

"And Ewan's actual father?"

"To this day I don't know who he is."

I didn't know what else to say, but words, it seemed, were entirely unnecessary as Adrian covered my hand with his own. His sudden touch sent my heartbeat racing and evoked a dangerous quiet in the room. I could scarcely breathe.

Slowly, carefully, his fingers slid up my arm, and all I could think about was how terrifying and enchanting his touch felt.

"I don't believe we'll ever know the identity of Ewan's father, but I am glad you woke me. It is a decided relief for you to know the truth."

Not only had Adrian been betrayed by his first wife but he had been supporting her illegitimate child. If there was ever a moment to disclose my own secret, now was the time. Warmth filled my heart and all at once I knew he would understand. He'd made mistakes himself.

"I . . ." I glanced up, surprised to find him so much closer than I remembered, his eyes more alive, while the room felt somehow darker. Surely a cloud had blocked out the moonlight. A slight quiver swept over me, intensified by the lingering scent of a smoldering fire.

As if irresistibly drawn, Adrian tucked a loose strand of my hair behind my ear. The courage I felt only a moment ago vanished beneath his eager fingers.

"Elizabeth, I know someone hurt you." His voice felt intimate. "I can see it in your eyes every time you look at me. He shattered your ability to trust, but believe me when I say I am not that man."

My own voice came out in a whisper. "Yes . . ."

Every decision came so swiftly for Adrian. For pity's sake, he'd decided to marry me in a few hours, and here I was still reeling from that choice.

"I had intended to wait to discover whatever this thing is between us until after the threat of death was lifted and you'd had time to adjust, but every solitary minute I'm with you, it becomes harder to stay away—to bury feelings I can't help but feel." His fingers gripped my arm. "You're shaking."

It seemed I was. I hadn't even noticed. All I could see was my husband—his strength of character, his loyalty, his care.

When I didn't answer, he moved to draw back, but my hand shot out. "Don't turn away . . . please."

My words were barely audible above the hammer that was my heart. My eyes slipped closed for a long second. If I let him roll over into silence after all he had revealed, I knew I would regret it forever. My head felt dizzy. Sometime during the few short days of this marriage of convenience I'd fallen in love with my husband, and it was high time I moved beyond a past I wasn't proud of and the man who'd shattered my trust. Adrian, regardless of his unfortunate brother, had proved to be different in every way—not by words, but by actions.

It took several seconds to quiet the fear that had lived with me for so long and give a slight nod, but I did so on a wave of tingling nerves. There would be no going back now. Adrian knew what I meant when I lifted my chin. Cautiously, he drew me against him, so close I could feel the beat of his heart through his night shift.

His hand found the nape of my neck as the other arm held

me near. He leaned even closer but stopped a few inches from my lips. He was waiting for me. Oh dear, he was waiting for me. Excitement, fear, anticipation—the culmination of days of doubt and yearning surged through my body, and I moved forward to meet him. One precious inch and his mouth found mine in the darkness.

He was gentle and urgent and unforgettable. I'd been kissed before, but not like this—not by the one man who elicited such an uncontrollable wave of energy, and I knew I'd been lost since we first met.

It was if I was suddenly flying through a dense forest on the back of my horse. Nothing could have prepared me for this moment. Not the hopes of a little girl, nor an insignificant infatuation in my past.

Smoothly, Adrian inched back while searching my eyes with an aching determination. I yearned to lean forward once again. My cheeks felt hot, my shoulders relaxed.

Adrian's hand drifted down my arm until he held mine.

"There is something else I need to tell you, and I don't want to take one step further without doing so."

The air in the room turned frosty. What did he need to tell me? He took several seconds to begin.

"You've alluded to my reputation more than once." His voice sounded strained; his eyes pained. "It's true, Elizabeth. All of it. I earned every juicy bit of gossip those old crows in London recounted in such detail. I've a terrible, terrible past that I loathe.

"Florencia and I took great joy in going our separate ways. I departed for London a few months after the birth and didn't return to Middlecrest till after her death." He ran a hand down his face. "There were opera dancers, mistresses, gaming houses, and nights of heavy drink. I believed at the time I'd thrown away my life by marrying Florencia, so by George, I meant to waste every second of it."

I sat in utter silence, staring at him, every muscle numb. Questions circled my mind, but I lacked the strength to speak them aloud. I knew something of his reputation, but for some reason, hearing the truth from his lips made it real in a way it hadn't been before. My throat felt tight as I attempted to swallow.

"Several years ago, I met Curtis Sinclair in London. He offered me the chance to make a difference for Britain. He encouraged me to return home to my country estate, to reconnect with my girls and more importantly with God. Soon enough, in my spare time he put me to work spying for the crown. I decided then I would never love again, never marry. I devoted my life to the protection of Britain. I thought at the time it was a noble choice, but I realize now it was driven by fear. I was afraid that someday I would have to look into my wife's eyes and tell her the truth of who I had once been."

My arms felt heavy. A part of me wanted to reassure him, but hurt and dread lurked in every corner of my mind.

"I am glad you know everything now . . . whatever it means for us." He scooted to the side of the bed, then stood, his movements rushed. "Perhaps it's best I return to my room for the remainder of the night." He made his way to the side door before I had a chance to respond, but stopped short before passing through it.

"The next step, Elizabeth, is yours."

L

I slept late the following morning but dressed quickly. Lilley helped me into one of my best morning gowns, a tunic of blue silk. I heard Adrian's voice through the connecting room wall and my heart leapt. He hadn't gone down to his study yet.

I'd lain awake a good part of the night processing what Adrian had revealed. A man with a past was the last person I meant to trust with my heart, but I kept coming back to the same conclusion: he and I were not so very different. We'd both made mistakes, but each of us had grown from them and changed. We were no longer the people we were in our youth.

And more importantly, I loved him—I loved his honesty, his care, his compassion. Regardless of the pain I felt when he disclosed the whole of his former life, a truth far more important was revealed—he cared for me.

I hurried through our sitting room. Today was the first day I knew his actions and words were no longer an act, and I didn't want to waste one more second. A smile warmed my cheeks as I reached up to knock on his bedchamber door.

Footsteps pounded toward me. My pulse raced. The door swung open and Adrian ushered me inside, a curious look on his face.

I shrugged off any real concern and gladly walked several steps into the room before stopping dead cold in the center of the rug.

There stood Brook, leaning lazily against the fireplace wall, his arms crossed.

"Lady Torrington, I presume?"

CHAPTER 27

I seem to remember nodding as Brook bowed, and there was some introduction between us.

We were standing, we were walking. Adrian seemed thrilled to have his long-lost brother home. If Brook was startled to find me at Middlecrest, I couldn't say. He was swift to smile and laugh, to guide us down the stairs, all eyes on his elder brother. In fact, before I could even say a word, they had departed out the front door, pleased to enjoy a country ride, and I was left to the silent vacuum of the entryway, my hand pressed to my chest.

I escaped at once to the nursery. Miss Barton sensed my discomfort the minute I arrived.

"Whatever is the matter? You look as if you've seen a ghost."

"Not at all. I was just surprised by Lord Torrington's brother. He has arrived at Middlecrest most unexpectedly."

Isaac tugged on Miss Barton's skirt. "What is it, my dear? Oh, your blanket is right over here."

I had a moment to settle my nerves as she fetched the blanket for Isaac.

"I remember Mr. Radcliff from when he was younger.

Mrs. Jennings said he's a traveler now, off on adventures all over Europe. Do you know where he's been all this time?"

"No, I only spoke with him briefly this morning."

She touched her mouth. "How did he look?"

I glanced up.

Hurriedly she turned away, but I thought I saw a slight blush as she quickly added, "I mean in relation to his elder brother, of course. Mrs. Jennings and I have debated that question more than once. The Radcliffs have always been too handsome for their own good."

"Well, I met Mr. Radcliff a few years ago during my London season, but I would have hardly recognized him now. He's much thinner. Even the cut of his clothes seems different." My voice faded. "Still handsome though."

Isaac babbled as he crawled across the floor, immune to the terror pumping through my veins.

Miss Barton watched him with a keen eye. "Will there be a celebration then, for his return?"

I pressed my forehead, my eyes slipping closed for a second. "I'm not certain. Yes, I mean, possibly. I just haven't decided how to handle his sudden arrival."

She touched my arm and I jumped a bit. I wasn't certain she noticed, but she went on. "You've had much to bear over the last week. I'm sure whatever you decide will be the best for everyone."

I decided "the best for everyone" was to confront Brook alone.

I doubted he would wish to stay very long at Middlecrest now that he'd met the new Lady Torrington. It was easy enough to slip a note into his bedchamber under the guise of checking the status of his room. After all, he'd arrived quite early and with no notice. Mrs. Coombs had not been pleased.

As I requested in the short missive, he strolled into the conservatory at two in the afternoon, dressed in a loose-fitting blue jacket and tan pantaloons. I'd planned the uncomfortable liaison for the same time Adrian had a meeting with his land agent. No use taking any chances.

"Elizabeth?" Brook's voice had deepened over the year we'd been apart. His hair fell longer against his collar, his frame far more gangly. They say you can tell when a person has led a hard life. Well, Brook must have had a rough year.

Alarm numbing my movements, I motioned him behind a large potted plant where I knew we wouldn't be seen through the windows. He drew in close beside me, and I caught a whiff of his familiar snuff. It was strange how scents were tied so closely with memories—nights lying out on the grass, stolen kisses behind a tree, our first dance.

Though I'd thought so many times about how I might feel when I saw him again, I was surprised by my wealth of fortitude. My nerves were sharp, my stomach unsettled, but my core where I'd felt such deep pain now held only pity for the shell of the man standing before me. He had chosen to give up a relationship with Isaac, and for that he was the epitome of foolishness.

I measured my tone. "You surprised me this morning."

His laugh I remembered all too well. "You and me both." He always talked with his hands, and now was no different as he motioned into the air. "How the devil did you end up my sister-in-law?"

I recalled the feel of his fingers on my neck, the excitement I'd felt every time he entered a room. How different his presence seemed now. What once intrigued, now sickened me. A layer of defense crept into my voice.

"I suppose your father wasn't alive to prevent it."

The familiarity was still present between us. I could sense him resisting the urge to reach out and touch me. "That's not what I meant."

There was an inflection in his and Adrian's voices that was so alike it unnerved me. I took a step back.

"Didn't your brother tell you?" I wasn't certain how much Adrian had revealed or intended to, but I figured I should stick to our original story.

Brook always had a lazy confidence about him and fell right back into that familiar pattern as he twirled his watch fob in his fingers. "Oh, he told me he met you at an inn, but how? When?"

I tried to affect the same nonchalance. "It was by accident actually, awhile ago. We thought we might suit."

His fingers stilled, the fob dangling on its chain. "'Thought you might suit?'" He shook his head. "That's not the Elizabeth I remember."

What did he remember? A frightened girl entranced by the wiles of a well-spoken gentleman? How much I had grown since then. "I've changed."

He studied me for a long moment, then relaxed his shoulders. "I see that. Well, at any rate, I am glad it happened."

"Are you? To appease your guilt perhaps?"

He shot me a glare, obviously surprised by my sudden candor.

"All right. I confess I deserved that, but you know full well I had little choice. What could we have lived on if we'd enacted your ridiculous plan?"

"You say that so easily, having benefited from your decision.

For me, anything would have been preferable to complete aban-donment. How do you live with yourself? You left me that night, standing there on a terrace in Plattsdale at a country dance as if I meant nothing to you."

He raked his hand through his hair. "You think I had a choice? My father sent me away as soon as I told him I meant to marry you. I spent a year in India trying to find a way back—to you."

It was a nice thought. Brook desperate to find a way home to rescue me from scandal and isolation, but I knew he was spinning the only tale he thought I might find palatable. He edged a bit closer.

"What have you said to Adrian about the child? He doesn't seem to know."

"Don't worry, your connection to my son is safe at present, but I do mean to tell him."

His eyes narrowed. "Why would you do that?"

"Because he has a right to the truth."

"You know it will only hurt him." Brook struck a dead plant leaf with his boot. "Either way, promise me you'll wait until I've gone."

Brook deserved nothing from me, but I found myself nodding. The moment I told Adrian would have to be planned carefully; however, I also realized that no matter when I chose to do so, our relationship would never be the same.

ℒℒ

I found Adrian and Mr. Browning in the library later that after-noon. They'd retrieved the knife as I'd asked them to. Adrian rose at once when I entered and came to my side, but . . . was something different about his steps? He took my hand and planted a kiss on the back, his eyes as bright as before. No, I was imagining things. If only I could have managed to return such a loving gaze, but we both knew I had never been good at playacting.

Mr. Browning was the first to speak and obviously unaware of the unease coursing through my body.

"You were right, Lady Torrington. Look here." He slid the knife across the table, and Adrian pointed at the handle. They both waited for me to examine the utensil. I picked up the silver handle. It didn't take me long to see the swirling design etched into it.

Adrian shook his head. "Not a knife from Middlecrest."

I looked again, closer this time. "But . . . do you recognize it?"

Mr. Browning shook his head.

I turned the knife over, looking for anything more. "This pattern is really not much to go on, is it?"

Adrian tapped his finger on the table. "Unfortunately, it's not; however, I can't help but think I've seen it somewhere before. I just don't know where."

I heard Brook's grating voice before I turned. He strolled into the room on a booming, "Good afternoon," and I couldn't help but flinch.

Adrian must have misunderstood my reaction as he took my arm. "Don't worry, I told Brook everything about the investigation this morning on our ride. He's a mastermind at puzzles and plans to help us sort through the clues. He's also fairly good at tracking. I'm hoping he might be able to point us in the direction the Frenchman went."

My voice sounded foreign as I turned to look at Brook. "I wasn't aware you knew Giles."

Brook flopped into a chair, swinging his leg over the armrest. "I didn't, but I'm here, so I might as well assist in any way I can." He caught my attention with a pointed glare and arched eyebrows the very second Adrian turned his head, as if he'd been waiting to do so.

I hated the warmth that flooded my cheeks. "And how long will you be with us here at Middlecrest?"

Brook idly stroked the pattern on the arm of the chair, "Couldn't say. A few weeks maybe."

Adrian chuckled as he placed the knife in a box and buried it in the desk drawer. "I daresay his pockets are to let." He sent a smile for me, then walked to the sideboard to pour his brother a drink. "You are welcome to stay as long as you need to. I cannot tell you how glad I am to have you home."

Brook slanted another questioning stare at me, and I wished he hadn't. Adrian was not a fool. Soon enough he would realize we were far from mere acquaintances.

Ewan wandered into the library at that moment, and I couldn't have been more pleased for the distraction. He made his way over to Brook's chair.

"I heard you had arrived, but I had to see for myself."

Brook jumped to his feet. "Ewan! How can this be possible? You've grown into a man while I was away."

I took a seat on a nearby sofa. "And a poet."

The room laughed, and I joined in nervously. "Have you devised any poems for Mr. Radcliff?"

Ewan accepted a drink from Adrian. "Certainly not. He'll get none of that from me."

Brook rested his head against the chair. "And glad of it."

There was a moment of silence as Ewan looked around. "Did I interrupt something?"

Brook flicked his fingers in the air. "Not at all. We were simply discussing Giles's murder."

I felt something in my chest snap as Ewan's smile fell. "Murder?"

This was exactly why Adrian should not have told Brook. He never considered anyone's feelings other than his own. Adrian swooped in. "It is something of a secret and difficult to understand, but we have come to believe Giles's death was not an accident."

Brook shrugged, then sipped his drink. "Cat's out of the bag now."

I'd been itching to speak with Ewan, so I leaned forward. "We have learned it was likely poison that caused Giles to lose control of his horse that day. Mrs. Jennings said you were in the kitchens that morning. Did you—"

"Murder him! Certainly not." He made a move as if to rise.

Brook waved him back down. "Don't be ridiculous, Ewan. Let the lady finish her sentence. Still have that hot head of yours, I see."

Reeling from Ewan's reaction, I struggled to form the rest of the sentence. "Did you see anything strange that morning? Anything you can recall out of the ordinary?"

He thought for a moment. "Not really. Mrs. Jennings gave me a sandwich to hold me over till lunch. Oh, and Mrs. Ayles added one of her pastries."

I straightened. "Mrs. Ayles?"

"Yes, she was down there seeing that her orders were carried out. She's in the kitchens frequently. She can't abide strong cheese, nor too many spices. Most days she handpicks her own luncheon."

Adrian caught my shrewd glance, but we said nothing to the room.

Mrs. Ayles had been in the kitchen that fateful day, and here I had forgotten all about her hovering outside my room. Perhaps it was time she fielded some questions.

CHAPTER 28

I knew I would need Adrian to accompany me when I confronted Mrs. Ayles about the day of Giles's murder. Bitter and calculating—she'd not give up any information to me. Adrian was far more likely to get some sense out of her. In the drawing room after dinner, I decided to wait up and speak with him to make our plans. I was certain he would come by my room before he settled into his bed, particularly after what had passed between us the previous night.

With Brook in residence, however, the men made their own plans and moved to the billiard room when the ladies retired. I had no way of knowing how long they would linger. Disappointed, I settled into the covers, far too exhausted to wait them out.

I'd been asleep for some time when the knock came at my door. Still cloudy from sleep, it took me several seconds to rub my eyes.

Thankfully the dregs of my earlier fire still smoldered in the grate. I flung my arms through my dressing gown and rushed over to poke what was left of the logs. I wasn't certain how long Adrian meant to stay and my arms were shivering beneath the thin fabric.

The knock came a second time, and I realized it had come from the far side of the room, not the door connecting to Adrian's room. I paused, caught up in the grip of numb surprise before I glanced quickly at Isaac asleep in his small bed. He hadn't moved.

I inched to the door. "Who is it?"

A voice hissed from the other side. "It's me, Brook."

I was stunned not only that he had come to my room, but that he had done so in such a brazen fashion.

He whispered again. "Please, I need to talk to you, Elizabeth."

I couldn't hide the irritation in my voice. "I said all that was necessary earlier. Now go away this instant."

A heart-thudding pause. "It's about Isaac."

My fingers flew to the latch and cracked open the door. "Have you lost your mind? What if someone sees you?"

He leaned in close, and I could smell the wine on his breath. "His nursemaid said Isaac was here with you."

I frowned at the slit in the door, a cold pain seeping into my chest. The wretch had been to the nursery already.

His eyes looked feral in the darkness, his face anxious. "I want to see him."

My fingers curled against the wooden door. "I don't think that's a good idea."

"Hurry up. Your *husband* will be up shortly." One emphasis on the word *husband* and I knew the easy acceptance he'd pretended earlier in the conservatory had already waned. He seemed to sober a bit. "I'll only stay a moment. I promise you I'll not wake him. I just want to look at him." He'd edged the toe of his pump into the door crack.

Why had I agreed to keep the truth from Adrian so hastily? Brook must have figured out my weakness, and here he was ready to exploit it.

He dipped his chin. "Don't make me beg. I never beg."

"Why can't it wait till tomorrow? Why tonight?"

He wiped his face with a handkerchief. "He's my son too, Elizabeth."

My stomach lurched and I swung the door wide, pulled him into the room, and sealed it closed behind him. The alcohol had made him bold. If I wanted Adrian to learn the truth from me, I had no recourse but to play Brook's little game.

His walk turned casual as he made his way over to the fireplace, the eagerness he'd displayed minutes ago fading to disinterest.

"I knew you'd make the right decision. We both know I may be in and out of Middlecrest for the rest of our lives. If I want to see my son, you really have little choice but to allow me to do so."

My thoughts felt muddled, a kaleidoscope of feelings and truths. "Then you mean to acknowledge him?" I twisted my fingers into my dressing gown. Please, God, let him say no.

He didn't answer. He strolled over to the child's bed as if he might consider it. "Do you think he looks like me?"

I followed him to Isaac's bedside, my nerves lit with fear. "A little. He does favor the Radcliffs."

Brook stared down at Isaac's sleeping form and his gaze softened. I stood like a statue in the shadows, watching the change in Brook's face all while enduring the knife that twisted in my chest. Our family was together at last—a dream of mine, yet one from long ago. So much had happened since then.

Brook spun to face me, his words slow to come. "He loves you, you know."

"Isaac?" I whispered.

"No." His lip twitched. "Adrian." He smashed his fingers against his forehead, rolling the skin. "He can't know, not about Isaac. It would crush him."

"Adrian is stronger than you think."

His hand clenched into a fist. "Don't stand there and lecture me. I know my own brother. He's sensitive when it comes to women, particularly after that first wife of his." He enjoyed a smile. "I'd never be so stupid as to marry a harpy."

"Nor I."

The answering leer made over his face. "Why, Elizabeth Cantrell, I believe you've grown up."

In the worst way possible. I cringed. "You've seen Isaac. Now it's time for you to leave."

I'll never know what possessed Brook to grab me and pull me close. "One kiss and I'll go."

Disgusted, I reached up to slap him, but he caught my arm.

"No need for that." He laughed. "I'll go. Just remember, not a word about Isaac to Adrian." His hold slipped to my waist. "You can choose to go against me or with me. Either way, I'm fairly good at getting what I want."

He leaned forward. I recoiled. Adrian walked through the connecting room door.

My heart scrambled to find a steady beat as my chest tightened. Brook released my arm and lazily stepped aside. What Adrian had seen, I couldn't guess, but Brook and I had been standing awfully close, too close. And there was no reason I could give for him being in my room.

Brook chuckled and made his way over to Adrian. "Seems I was one door off, old man. Bit of a surprise when I found myself in here. Blasted nuisance, if I say so myself. Your lovely lady was about to take me through to your bedchamber when you popped right out." He tapped Adrian's arm. "Had a thought about this murder business that couldn't wait till morning."

"Did you now?" Adrian pushed the door wide for Brook to pass, but he never took his eyes off me. Oh, his "Good night" was amiable enough, but I knew in the depths of my soul that he'd seen something—something I'd be hard-pressed to explain.

I wasn't able to catch Adrian alone until late the following morning where I was forced to address him in the hall. He'd left his study in a hurry, and by the look on his face, I did not think he was pleased to see me.

He tarried only long enough for me to divulge a few words. "I'd like to speak with you."

Tapping his riding crop against his leg, he darted a look down the hall.

"I've not much time. Brook and I have been hard at work all morning. He's found some possible tracks and another clue. We plan to ride out at once."

His voice was curt, his manner distracted. My legs felt weak. He knew. He had to know. My hand shook as I motioned toward the library.

"It will only take a moment."

The familiarity we'd reveled in merely two nights ago had vanished. The man who followed me felt like a stranger. He tossed his crop onto a nearby table and poured himself a drink, then turned at the last second. "Care for anything?"

"No, thank you." I folded my hands in my lap and began studying my fingers. "Last night . . ."

"Was surprising, I daresay." His voice was calm as his steady gaze focused out the window. I wondered how many times he'd practiced such an indeterminate glare. Or was he simply distracted and my imagination was adding tension to the room?

My mind was awash with possibilities.

Before I could string any words together, he threw a small shrug. "I believe Brook had a bit too much to drink. I hope he didn't upset you with his carelessness."

"No . . ." My chest felt tight, and I couldn't help but stare up at him, waiting for him to ask the obvious question.

But he didn't. He only slid his empty glass back onto the silver platter. "Was there anything else you wanted to discuss?"

I was about to create some sort of a reason for Brook being in my room, but as I met Adrian's wounded look, I realized the last thing we needed was more lies between us. Adrian deserved far more than a fabricated story, but I'd need more time to discuss the whole, preferably after Brook had left Middlecrest. I paused to regain my composure.

"You said Brook discovered a clue?"

"Ah, yes." His shoulders relaxed as he spoke, the familiar roguish quality returning to his voice. "Can you believe it? He found a box of alphabet letters in the conservatory. It was an old set that used to belong to Phoebe."

My skin tingled. "You mean the Frenchman used that to decode the message on the painting?"

"I believe so. It certainly would have helped."

I looked over at the window. "And now you believe Brook can track him from some prints he found?"

"I hope so. Brook has always had a knack for such things. He already pointed out this morning broken twigs and indentations in the ground. Strangely enough, the man must be heading west. Our guess is London, but Brook hopes to follow the trail until we are certain. The Frenchman is injured from Browning's shot, mind you, so there's still a chance we might come upon him on the road. He cannot be traveling all that fast."

"It's been days. And someone must have helped him. I don't think—"

"I see no other recourse than to follow this lead. Browning has already gone to Plattsdale where he plans to alert our connections. Brook and I will attempt to track the spy."

I gripped my muslin skirt. "How long will you be gone?"

"Who's to say? This may all lead to nothing. Ewan will remain here. I've informed him of some of our concerns, but I would rest easier knowing Isaac was to remain indoors."

"He will . . . Only . . . Please, be careful."

He stood and headed for the door, then turned at the last second, his face betraying the unsettled tension between us.

"You as well."

*

I spent the early part of the afternoon with Isaac in the nursery, then took him down to the drawing room to be with the girls— anything to keep my mind off my pressing concerns. Granted, I didn't think Adrian was in any real danger, but I couldn't escape the insidious what-ifs. What if he and Brook came upon the Frenchman and there was trouble? What if I never saw Adrian again? What if he wouldn't forgive me for what he'd seen between Brook and me?

I pushed the embroidery I'd been pretending to complete off my lap and buried it in my sewing bag beside the sofa. Startled by my sudden movement, Juliana and Phoebe watched me with round eyes from across the drawing room where they were playing with Isaac.

I tried to smile. "I believe I'll head up early to dress for supper. Come along, Isaac."

The feel of the house had transformed the instant the gentlemen departed. With Ewan checking the grounds and Mrs. Ayles retired to her room for her afternoon nap, the girls and I had little recourse but to sit and wait in the drawing room. Trapped in the house, we were all too aware of our inability to help, and by the looks on the girls' ashen faces, the stress had only grown.

Juliana cast one last fleeting glance out the window. "You don't think we should have Mrs. Jennings hold supper?"

Perhaps it was our shared concern, but for the first time I truly felt like part of the family. Slowly, I shook my head.

"I did not get the impression your father would be returning today. The search may take some time."

Footsteps pounded down the hall, and Phoebe jumped to her feet before hurrying to the door. She thrust it open as if the answers to all our problems might lie just on the other side.

"Ewan!" More footsteps approached, louder this time, and then he poked his head through the opening she had vacated.

A nervous energy hid behind a pair of cool brown eyes. "Everyone well in here?" Obviously Adrian had put Ewan on alert. Though the girls knew nothing of the threatening notes, we all realized Giles's murderer remained free.

Phoebe lifted her voice. "Any word?"

He coughed. "Not yet. They hardly could have reached Canterbury by now."

I wished I hadn't let panic fester in the girls' minds, but Ewan's presence would certainly lift their spirits. I stood and made my way across the rug before hoisting Isaac onto my hip.

"Thank goodness you are here, Mr. Hawkins. I daresay you are just the person to remain with the ladies until dinner, and believe me, they are in sore need of company."

Ewan was young but also uniquely perceptive. He'd find a way to calm Juliana and Phoebe while I took a moment to myself in my room. Carefully, I lifted my eyebrows as I passed him at the door, and he answered with a knowing look.

A few steps into the hall and the drawing room door clicked shut behind Isaac and me. I instantly felt the emptiness of the main corridor and vacant rooms. Though the sun wouldn't set for another hour or more, the orange blaze that trickled in through the leaded window at the end of the hall seemed to thicken the air with dust and lengthen the evening shadows that lay in wait.

It was a warm silence that afternoon, the kind that went down my throat like gruel. I reached the central stairs and hurriedly followed the curved balustrade to the main landing. I forced my taut muscles to relax, for it was far more peaceful on the first floor. The upper halls betrayed the evidence of a house well-lived in with nicks on the windowsills, tufts in the carpeting on the floor.

I deposited Isaac in the nursery with Miss Barton, and it wasn't until my hand touched the door latch to my bedchamber that the insidious anxiety I'd been fighting all day crept over me once again. Was I alone, or had someone followed me into the family wing? I shot a quick look down both halls and another into the recessed corners. Nothing. I shook my head. It had been a long, tiring day, and the door to my room was still locked. I was being silly. I turned the key and pushed the door inward, determined to shake off the worries that had chased me into my room.

I sealed the door closed behind me and released a breath, but I'll never forget the sharp pain that clenched my chest when I became aware of an actual presence in the room. She had commandeered a chair by my window, the darkness surrounding her like a throne, her attention fixed on the door. How strange it was that I could see her eyes so clearly in the dim light.

"Mrs. Ayles? How did you get in here?"

"With a key, of course." She produced a raspy huff. "You do realize it was *her* bedchamber before it was yours." An eerie look filled every crevice of her sallow face. "In many ways I don't think she ever really left."

Florencia. A tremor sparked the hairs to life on my arm, and for a moment it almost felt as if a third person could have been with us in the room. I sidestepped across the rug, never taking my eyes off my unexpected visitor. Mrs. Ayles was old and feeble. She posed no real threat to me. Yet I had to admit there was no one else in the house who evoked the same level of trepidation.

A thought struck me cold, and I stopped short at the foot of the bed, my fingers curling around the bedpost.

"It was you who placed the notes on my bed, wasn't it?"

A line crossed her wrinkled forehead. "What notes?"

She could very well be lying, but her voice held a tone of surprise. Had I guessed wrong, or did she see me as a threat to her daughter's memory?

"Mrs. Ayles, I don't know what brought you here, but I need to dress for dinner. I would like you to leave."

Expressionless, she started speaking as if my words meant nothing to her. "I come up here most days, you know." Her finger slid down the curve of the window drape. "It's the only room left in the house where I can still feel her."

"You are the person I saw in the hallway the other day. Why didn't you—"

"We so often would be together in this room. Mrs. Coombs knows how I feel. With Adrian avoiding the room like the plague, Mrs. Coombs has allowed me to keep it just like Florencia did."

I watched as tears filled Mrs. Ayles's eyes. There could be no pain like that of losing a child. My heart softened. I could only imagine what it must have been like to live here after her only family was gone. She had no one to comfort her now but her memories.

"It must be quite difficult for you to see me here, in her place."

Her eyes flicked to mine like those of a hawk who'd finally discovered the prey it had been watching for all along. The sudden condescension in her voice felt like gravel in my ears.

"My dear, dear, Elizabeth. You're not in her place. She cared nothing for Torrington or the prison within the walls of Middlecrest. Believe me, my daughter would have left him for any one of the fathers if she could have." She folded her fingers into a bony fist on the armrest, a dangerous smile cracking the brittle lines on her face.

"I saw something, you know." She motioned with her cane. "Out this very window. Days ago." She twirled her index finger in a circular pattern. "Pity you do not possess the same clarity of mind as my Florencia. She knew everything that happened in this house. This whole time, the answers you sought were right beyond your window. All you had to do was look, but you were far too busy playing mistress of the house."

I touched the base of my neck as my mind grappled to understand what she seemed to imply. "What do you know?"

She rocked front to back in the chair before thrusting her body into a standing position. "It's a shame you thought you were so clever. Running around with Torrington, far too busy plotting to secure his affections when you should have been uncovering the truth for Juliana." She raked her gaze over me, then started for the door.

"Wait." My hands trembled as I thrust them out to stop her. "If you know something, please . . ."

Her eyes narrowed in turn. "I owe you nothing. Nor anyone else in this cursed house."

Not anyone? What about her granddaughters or Adrian, who had provided her with a place to live and pen money for so many years? Had the loss of her daughter clouded her judgment, or was hatred born within her? I stepped forward.

"Just one question about the day Giles died?"

Her gait was steady. First a tap of her cane then a sliding whoosh of each slippered foot. She didn't even look at me as she neared the door.

I came up alongside her, my voice growing feverish. "Ewan told me you were in the kitchens that morning. Are you telling me you saw something? If you don't wish to help me, won't you help Juliana?"

One more tap of the cane and she paused. "You're asking the wrong person, my dear."

Somewhere within that warped mind of hers hid the clue I'd been searching for, but I'd get no answers from her, not today. Defeated, I watched her creep from view, nothing but a decrepit vulture who'd been favored with a hearty snack. She'd only come to see me squirm.

I plodded across the rug and settled into the very chair she'd vacated moments before. What did she mean she'd seen something out my window? I slid my finger beneath the thick drapery fabric before standing and shoving the curtains aside entirely. It was a small window but provided a nice prospect of the rear lawn . . . and the conservatory.

I pressed my forehead against the cold glass, looking over every inch of the grove where I'd found Phoebe's painting. Mrs. Ayles had spoken the truth. The window was the perfect vantage point to see who had left that clever message on Phoebe's drawing, the person who in all likelihood had killed Giles.

I sat back down, teasing the edge of my lip between my teeth, my mind churning through every word Mrs. Ayles had said, when one particular sentence popped into my mind.

"My daughter would have left him for any one of the fathers if she could have."

She'd meant those words as some sort of jab at me; however, she'd said *fathers*. My heartbeat turned sluggish. I already knew about Ewan, but could what she said be true? Were none of Adrian's children biologically his? I touched my throat. He said he'd left after Ewan's supposed death and hadn't returned home until after Florencia died.

It would be just like Adrian to keep such a secret—to allow the girls the benefit of pleasant memories of their mother, to provide them with security and love. Why hadn't I noticed the disparity before? Neither of the girls looked like any of the Radcliffs I'd seen. Everything I knew about Adrian pointed to the fact that he was as decisive as he was careful.

I could not imagine him, after being so utterly betrayed, fathering a child with Florencia, particularly after what happened with Ewan. He would not have risked it. I lowered my face into my hands as a tear slipped down my cheek. My husband was ten times the man Brook ever was. Adrian had supported and loved three children who were not his own, and he was already well on his way to doing so with a fourth.

It was some time before my thoughts shifted back to the murder investigation and Mrs. Ayles's words. I sat up. Who exactly had she seen out my window? A servant perhaps?

Mrs. Jennings was in charge of the kitchens. She'd been present the day Giles was killed as well as the day we found the French spy hidden in the larder, but she had been so shocked that day, and Adrian trusted her—explicitly. What reason would she have to betray him after so many years of faithful service?

The housekeeper, Mrs. Coombs, was nowhere near the kitchens that morning. Adrian's and my theory didn't hold water unless someone else had been there, someone who could have passed Giles the poisoned meal and ensured no one else touched it. Mrs. Jennings had initially forgotten about Mrs. Ayles being in the kitchens because she was a mainstay most days, ensuring her special requests were carried out. Could there have been someone else forgotten as well?

I tapped my fist against my mouth. It was unlikely that Mrs. Jennings would forget two people on a list of such great importance. Unless . . . I flew to my feet and paced the rug. What if the murderer's name *was* on the list? What if the person was just so unremarkable that we hadn't even questioned him or her being there? Without a definite motive, it really could have been anybody.

I could no longer assume anything.

I thought back through what Adrian and I had seen and found that night we searched the kitchens. Wind beat against my window seconds before the mantel clock chimed the hour. It was getting late. It was time to call Lilley to help me dress for dinner. I walked over to the embroidered bell pull when I noticed Isaac's bed. There, swirled up in his covers was his favorite blue blanket.

His blue blanket—the one that had gone missing the day after we arrived. The one the murderer hid the knife in. Our one tangible clue that tied someone within Middlecrest to the poisoning.

The room suddenly shifted and my hands shook violently as I gripped the side of the bed. I stood there for several panic-stricken breaths before I tugged the blanket to my chest.

I could no longer assume anything.

The murderer had wrapped the knife in Isaac's blanket because Isaac was present in the kitchen that fateful day. And if that was indeed true, one other person would have been there with him. Someone I'd not even considered.

Miss Barton.

CHAPTER 29

Was Miss Barton's name on the list Mrs. Jennings had provided? I raced through the sitting room into Adrian's bedchamber, my heart thundering. I'd seen him place the paper we used to unscramble the message into the bottom drawer of his escritoire. I only hoped the list would be there as well.

My fingers trembled as I grabbed the iron handle and jerked the drawer fully open. A mass of loose papers shifted at the movement. I lifted each missive into the light. Within seconds, my eyes fell on the familiar name I'd passed over so many times without so much as a consideration.

Alice Barton.

Slowly, I lowered the list, shaking my head. Why? Why would she do such a thing?

Moments flashed through my mind. My arrival at Middlecrest—we'd connected almost immediately, like she was an old friend. And she'd connected with Isaac. Had I been mistaken in her regard for him? Or did she have a far more sinister reason for her actions?

Her position gave her free rein in the kitchens as well as the back lawns. She was so frequently out of doors with Isaac.

I looked around in confusion as my eyes watered. The afternoon sun had disappeared below the horizon, leaving Adrian's room a mawkish gray. The small clock on the mantel ticked through the thick silence. My knees ached as I'd knelt too long, but I didn't move, not yet, not when I was so close to linking the pieces.

I crossed my arms and watched the paper drift to the floor. Frustrated and alone amid the shadow of Adrian's heavy furniture and the scent of his lingering cologne, the terrible truth clawed its way to the surface. If Miss Barton was indeed involved, I had so many details to reexamine.

I could still see the interior of the wrecked coach clearly in my mind. The bandboxes and valises we'd brought inside had erupted all over the sideways interior of the coach. All the luggage had been jumbled together and brought to Middlecrest. Mine, Isaac's, perhaps even the coachman's.

Adrian had set off that fateful day to rob a carriage fitting our coach's description. He thought he'd robbed the wrong one when he found Isaac and me inside, but what if he had been right? What if my carriage matched the description because it was *my* carriage he'd been looking for all along? My coachman, who fled the inn without a word, could have easily carried a missive I was unaware of. We were headed to Dover, after all—the gateway to France. And now he was conveniently missing.

I closed my eyes for a brief moment, still fighting what I knew to be true with every passing second. Isaac and I had been used in the worst way.

Isaac.

My eyes shot open as my stomach clenched. Isaac was with Miss Barton this very minute. If she was working with the French spy all this time, she might very well be the person who'd left me threatening notes. I shoved to my feet, grappling to process each new revelation. Miss Barton knew how to frighten me and would have had easy access to my bedchamber. But could she actually bring herself to hurt my son?

Time ceased as I attempted to unlock Adrian's bedchamber door, my fingers numb with shock. Finally the door burst open and I stumbled into the hall. The corridor, though soundless and frightening, lay as empty as before. I sprinted to the far end. He had to be safe. Oh God, let him be safe.

I took the corner far too fast and crashed into the opposing wall. Off balance, I was forced to grope my way to the nursery door, gripping the wainscoting to stay upright. Twice I had to adjust the latch before the nursery door swung open and I pushed myself inside.

For a heart-throbbing moment, I stood completely frozen, scouring the room. The stillness was deafening. I screamed his name, darting first one direction then the next. The scent of dinner met my nose, and I found two trays untouched on a nearby table. The suite was empty.

Terror filled me as I scrambled back into the hallway and down the central stairs. I was steps from the drawing room when I saw Lilley heading toward the servants' wing.

"Lilley!"

Surprise was evident on her face. "My lady?"

I hurried to her side, gasping. "Do you know where Miss Barton and Isaac are? I left them in the nursery a short time ago, and now I cannot find them."

She seemed puzzled. "I saw them leave . . . in the carriage." Her voice trailed off. "She told me you were to accompany them. I didn't know you were still here."

An ache formed in the back of my throat, and it was difficult to swallow.

"It seems Miss Barton had plans of her own." The room tilted, and I extended my arm to steady myself on the wall.

I felt Lilley's hand at my back. "Are you well, my lady?"

I managed a whispered, "Help me into the library where I can think."

Lilley assisted me across the rug where I melted onto the sofa.

"I need you to fetch Mr. Hawkins at once. Isaac could be in danger."

I wasn't certain whom to trust, but I needed help. Of all the days for Adrian to leave. I pressed my shaking hand against my forehead. I knew in my heart Miss Barton would never harm Isaac, but dread gathered in my core. I hadn't the least notion where she had gone or what she meant to do.

My attention drifted to the corners of the room. I saw nothing and everything at the same time. Miss Barton's sudden disappearance proved her guilt, and oh how complete her deception had been.

I thought back about the day I arrived at Middlecrest. She had volunteered to help me in the nursery. Why would she do that when she had so many other tasks to perform? To put her in a position to murder Giles?

Giles must have accidentally stumbled upon her and the Frenchman's plans on his way to Middlecrest for his wedding. If they meant to keep the truth from me and recover the intelligence they thought I possessed, they could have killed Giles to keep him quiet. My head felt light.

Footsteps sounded in the corridor, and I was surprised to see Juliana's scared face through the door. She hurried to my side.

"Lilley was terribly upset in the hall. She's gone to find Ewan. She mentioned something about Isaac."

I took her outstretched hand. "I don't have all the answers at present, but I believe Miss Barton may have taken Isaac from the house without my knowledge."

Juliana slumped onto the sofa beside me. "Why would she do that?"

I shook my head. "I don't know exactly . . . Only, the full truth is far worse." I searched her eyes for her readiness to hear what I was about to reveal. "Miss Barton may very well have been involved in Giles's murder."

Juliana shrank back. "How? Why? I've known her my whole life."

I recounted the details Adrian and I had uncovered as quickly as I could, hoping Juliana might provide further insight to Miss Barton's involvement, anything that might give me an idea where she had taken Isaac.

Juliana seemed lost when I finished, but her voice was steady as she spoke. "You think Giles played a part in all this?"

"Not exactly. He never would have been involved on purpose. Mrs. Harris told me he saw something on his journey to Middlecrest, something that got him killed. Miss Barton must have been involved. Did Giles ever mention anything about the incident to you?"

She hesitated a bit, her eyes flitting one direction and then the next. "Not at all."

I sighed. "Yet there must be a connection between them."

"What about the knife? You said it had a design on it. May I see it?"

I stood and crossed the room. As far as I knew the knife was still in the large desk drawer from the last time we examined it. I tugged open the drawer, relieved to see the box Adrian had placed it in. I had just lifted the lid when Ewan stormed into the room.

"What's this about Isaac?"

Juliana filled him in between sobs, and I watched as his face changed.

"Do we have any idea where they could have gone?"

I rounded the desk. "Unfortunately, we do not."

His eyes latched onto the box in my hand. "What's that?"

I drew out the knife as my heart turned to ice. "Do you recognize it?"

He stared at it for some time. "It does look remarkably familiar."

Adrian had said the same.

Ewan took the knife to look closer. "I'm just not certain. And we are wasting time. We must ride out at once for Isaac!"

I grabbed his arm. "But to where? We haven't the least idea where Miss Barton is headed."

Tears filled Juliana's eyes. "Could she have left something behind—something for us to go on?"

Ewan sighed. "Unlikely."

Juliana's voice turned frantic. "Maybe we should call Lilley back. Miss Barton spoke to her before she left."

I pressed my palm to my forehead. "I don't think she'd be so foolish as to pack Isaac's luggage, then tell the servants where she planned to take the carriage."

The carriage. For some reason the word jogged a memory. The accident . . . the luggage . . . I was back at the beginning again and—the secret missive.

Miss Barton must have been looking for it in Isaac's things.

Those first days came all at once into my mind—how I'd found the nursery in such a mess, furniture moved around, papers scattered about. Miss Barton said someone else had caused the disorder, but had it in fact been her?

My lips parted. It all made sense. Miss Barton would have been forced to look through everything. But she hadn't found it, not initially at least, which must have prompted the first threatening note. I thought back through all my actions that first day. Had I moved anything? Taken any papers to my room?

No. I'd left everything there for her, never expecting her duplicity. I'd even written down Isaac's schedule on—

My breath caught, and my pulse grew stronger by the second. That first night I retrieved a slip of paper from one of the bags to pen down the schedule, then set it on the dresser. Had there been something on the other side?

Yes! Letters. It had looked like nothing but useless scrap paper at the time.

I closed my eyes for a brief moment. The information Adrian had been looking for since the accident was written in code, and I'd hidden it in plain sight.

If only the schedule was still there.

✦

The three of us plowed through the nursery door. The far wall that housed the writing desk lay bathed in evening shadows. I stared into the alcove, my heart in my throat as I raced over to the darkened area. The floorboards creaked beneath my feet as hope blurred my vision. Would the schedule still be there? Or had Miss Barton finally realized what I'd done, found it, and run?

A few wild steps and the white paper took shape in the alcove. Thank God! Emboldened by my discovery, I snatched the schedule from the dresser and flipped it over as I sat on the desk chair.

"Letters! I was right!"

I saw the repeating *X*s almost immediately. It was another alphabet code. Ewan and Juliana leaned over my shoulders as I penned out all twenty-six letters of the alphabet at the top of the page. My fingers quivered against the quill pen.

"I simply need to uncover how many letters to count over to decipher the information. Wait! There are numbers in the code too."

Times, dates? The whole grouping of letters formed a square, the numbers traveling diagonally up the shape. Could the message be a directional code as well? In our ciphers as children, my brother used to change every letter by one in the alphabet, and then follow a diagonal pattern across to display the actual message. I decided to start there, but the result formed a string of nonsense. My heart ached. I tapped my fingers on the desk. As much as I hated to take the time, I would have to be methodical in my approach. I added one more letter each time I tried. Juliana whimpered behind me and I shot her a glare.

Minutes ticked past as I attempted two letters, then three, then four when suddenly a word formed as I stopped at the first *X*.

Newgate.

I froze. Newgate? The prison? What on earth could this message be? *East Barming* was next. I focused on each letter with grim intensity and didn't stop until one utterly familiar word emerged near the bottom and stole my breath away.

Lucius.

My brother—the smuggler, the rogue, the close friend of the notorious French spy, the late Lord Stanton—was currently at Newgate awaiting transportation to the colonies.

"East Barming, where is that?" Ewan leaned in close. "And Lucius, who the devil is he?"

I closed my eyes for a second. "He's my brother."

"Your brother?" Juliana and Ewan said together.

The entire missive was about Lucius. The room blurred as I finished the code and read aloud what I had uncovered—plans to break my brother out of prison in exchange for everything Lord Stanton had revealed to him—people, information, money.

I sat back stunned. Money? Lucius had none. I wondered if Lord Stanton even told him much about his spy network. It would be like Lucius to play a trick in such a deal. Of course, Lucius and Evie had always been close before her death, and she knew all of Stanton's secrets.

The escape plan was to be executed tomorrow. Guards had been paid and keys to his shackles obtained. Though our cousin Curtis sent money regularly, Lucius had been housed since the beginning with the commoners. The message detailed how he was to be smuggled out with a group of visitors early the following morning.

I focused on the paper in my hands and shook my head. No wonder I had been able to decipher the codes. They were written by my own brother. Having lived at the Towers with Curtis, Lucius knew quite well that the mail was not to be trusted. He must have used the coded messages and couriers to correspond with the only people who would help him escape—the French.

CHAPTER 30

Ewan, Juliana, and I found Phoebe in the drawing room await-ing dinner. Her momentary pleasure at our arrival faded rapidly to fear. I could not conceal the pulsing anxiety that had overtaken my entire body.

Phoebe's hand settled on her chest. "What is it? You look a fright."

I glanced from Phoebe's wide-eyed face to Ewan, my voice a flailing mess. "Isaac has been forcibly taken from the house by his nursemaid." I paused for a moment to allow her to process my words. "I do not know what her intentions are, but I believe them to be quite desperate. We must ride out at once to intercept the French spies. I can only hope Miss Barton means to join them."

Phoebe searched my eyes, her voice filled with worry. "But how can you know which way they have gone?"

"There's not enough time to explain, but I found a note that reveals the spies have gone to London by way of East Barming, and we must follow."

Ewan stepped forward. "Adrian asked me to watch over the house. I didn't realize you intended to ride along. I can't imagine Lord Torrington would want you to put yourself in further dan-ger." There was an underlying grimace in his voice, his mind obviously hard at work. He was young and Adrian had likely given him all sorts of instructions in regard to the ladies of the house.

"You think this is your sole responsibility?" Sparks lit my words. "To protect the ladies and the children. That I should stay here?"

"It is the man's—"

"Stuff and nonsense." I crossed my arms. "My son has been taken, and I have every intention of riding out with or without you." I pushed past the group, only to turn and face the girls at the door. "The two of you must keep your wits about you. If Miss Barton returns, it is up to you to ensure Isaac's safety as well as your own."

Juliana stepped forward into the uncomfortable silence, resolution tightening her face. How much she'd grown since Giles's death.

"You can trust us to do whatever is necessary. And you mustn't worry, I shall send every available rider behind you to scour the countryside. Come along, Phoebe, we have work to do."

$\mathcal{L}$

A frigid wind tumbled out of the heavens, rattling the shadowed branches above our heads. The sun's earlier retreat had taken with it all the radiance of spring, leaving Ewan and me a bitter night fit only for scrambling animals and gloomy shapes.

I tightened my gloved fingers around Aphrodite's reins to keep her at a canter before I peeked at the road behind me. A ghostly moon, staring back at me from behind a veil of thin clouds, illuminated Ewan's approaching form.

He'd managed a steady clip over the last few hours. But even with scheduled walks for the horses, he seemed to be slipping farther and farther behind. We'd not seen a soul on the road, and I desperately hoped I'd read the missive correctly and we were headed in the right direction.

East Barming.

The name of the village was written in the middle of the message with little else to go on, so we'd set out at once toward the river Medway, hoping to come upon Miss Barton overnight. Isaac would most certainly need to rest at some point. She could not make the entire journey in one day.

Though I didn't expect rain, the shifting clouds and roaming gusts of wind kept the horses on edge and me as well. It was a night to be tucked away in bed, not out urging horses farther into the blackened countryside. I reined Aphrodite to a walk as the old stones of East Farleigh Bridge materialized in the murk before us.

Aphrodite's panting formed puffs in the night air as I waited for Ewan to pull up alongside us. I kept my voice calm and low.

"The river Medway is just ahead."

His eyes looked pale, his jaw set. "What if she is with the Frenchman? Do we have some sort of a plan?"

"Not exactly. East Barming is but a mile ahead. Perhaps once there, we should tie off the horses out of sight. I don't wish to alert everyone in the village to our presence."

"And then?"

"We check whatever inns exist. If I remember correctly, East Barming is but a small village—the perfect out-of-the-way meeting place for French spies. It's a little off the beaten path, but still centrally on the way to London."

"Agreed."

A few paces more and we were upon the weathered stones

of the ancient medieval bridge, the river Medway rushing in the darkness below us. We guided our horses along the river for a bit before turning north across the fields, keeping firmly to the hedgerows until we saw the haunting silhouette of a church with a crenellated steeple.

We darted into a nearby copse of trees, and Ewan swung from his mount. My legs felt stiff as I readied myself to do the same, knowing my first few steps would be excruciating. Not only had I ridden for hours, but fear had driven my muscles to the breaking point. Now I was afraid I couldn't trust them to hold up over the inevitable search.

Ewan helped me dismount and tie the horses. Then we walked a bit, the wind surging at our backs, pushing us on toward the few outlying buildings of East Barming. It wasn't long before we came upon the two streets that intersected at the center of the village. The circle there was deserted, but I soon caught sight of the East Barming Inn tucked neatly onto one side.

I pulled Ewan close. "Seems to be the only inn in the village."

His gaze slid over the two-story bricked structure. "Perhaps we should take a peek into the stables before we make ourselves known."

Ewan's pocket watch revealed it was just past midnight, and the residents of the inn were most certainly abed.

The relentless wind met our arrival with renewed fury. I pulled my pelisse tighter about my neck. Squinting, I strained to see anything or catch the hint of a voice above the wind's turbulent moan. Nothing. We were alone.

Ewan fumbled the rusty latch before wrenching the large stable door open. Where was the ostler? Asleep in the loft? I peered into the looming shadows as we inched inside. No movement above.

Horses shuffled as we crept along the center aisle. Loose hay cushioned our steps. Hurriedly, we searched one crib to the next before I came to a sudden halt.

"Flick."

Ewan popped around the crib's wall. "Did you say something?"

"This is one of Adrian's horses. And there"—I pointed across the aisle—"is Atlas. If Adrian and Brook were tracking the Frenchman, surely we've come to the right place. Miss Barton must have planned to meet the spy here. They have brought all of us to the same place." My heart twisted. Isaac could be inside the inn at this very moment, but we would have to be careful. "Thank goodness we shall have help."

"I agree." Ewan slipped a hand into his coat pocket, his eyes deadly perceptive. "I've a pistol as well if we need it."

"Let us hope it does not come to that. Remember, Miss Barton has Isaac."

A hard line crossed his forehead. "I won't forget."

After a reassuring nod, Ewan led me to the inn's front door. It took several rounds of Ewan's fist pounding against the heavy wood to alert the innkeeper of our late arrival. An aging man, rounded about the middle, cracked the door before ushering us inside on a stray gust of wind. He made his way over to a desk without a word, his long gray whiskers bobbing as he walked. He seemed irritated as he took a seat and fumbled to locate a quill pen.

He glanced at us sideways, then swung open a large ledger before leaning forward on his elbows. "Looks as if I have only the one room available."

For a split second I wondered if Ewan had remembered to bring any money in our hasty flight from the Middlecrest.

"That will be fine. My wife and I are tired. We'd like to retire directly." He reached into his jacket and pulled out some coins before signing the ledger.

The innkeeper eyed us for a moment, then looked down at Ewan's signature in the book. "Right this way, Mr. Hawkins, ma'am."

We followed the man's unstable gait up a wide wooden staircase that terminated at a narrow hall. The innkeeper's candle illuminated a row of closed doors as we crept down the corridor. He stopped and slid a key into the last door on the right.

Inside, the room was small but clean. A passable bed. A washstand and bowl. A cold fireplace. Ewan and I were forced to wait while the man lit our fire. He seemed a bit amused as he turned back to face us. "My wife will have breakfast in the morning. Do you require anything further tonight?"

"No . . . thank you." Ewan's voice held a hitch of concern.

"Wait," I stepped forward. "We've come to meet a lady named Miss Alice Barton. Do you know if she may have passed through this way with a baby?"

A dry smile formed across the man's face. "I don't believe so. No one here with the name Barton."

I bit my lip. "What about Lord Torrington or Mr. Radcliff? They were to overnight here at the inn as well."

He tapped his first finger against his chin, hesitant to answer.

Ewan stepped forward with a guinea in his hand. "We're friends of theirs. They are expecting us."

The innkeeper pointed to the adjoining wall. "His lordship and his brother overnight just there." He swiped the money from Ewan's hand on his way out of the room with a last glance at me before he closed the door.

Ewan turned on me at once. "I don't believe he bought our story for a second. He probably thinks we ran away together." As an illegitimate son, Ewan had likely fought for every ounce of respectability he now possessed. I couldn't help but think of Isaac's similar plight.

I flit my hand in the air. "On our way to Gretna Green? Don't be ridiculous."

He cast me a wary glance. "How do you suggest we proceed?"

"I'd like to apprise Adrian and Brook of our situation immediately."

He nodded, the intensity in his face making him look far older than his years. "Why do you think Miss Barton isn't here? She left long before us."

I tossed my pelisse on the bed beside my bonnet, determined to keep my fear at bay.

"I don't know, but the coded message meant for the Frenchman pointed us to this very inn. It must be important. I can only believe it will lead me to Isaac."

The hall lay as utterly still and deserted as before, the innkeeper nowhere to be seen. Ewan tapped lightly against Adrian's door. No answer.

I tried the latch—locked.

Ewan curled his fingers into a fist and pounded a bit harder. A creak sounded from within, then a shuffle and footsteps.

The door inched open, two tired eyes appearing in the darkness. Adrian. The tension in my shoulders released, and I could almost imagine the feel of his strong arms around me.

His face, however, dipped as he thrust open the door.

"Elizabeth?" Clearly taken aback, he seemed to waver before guiding me into the room. "Tell me at once what has happened."

I cast a hesitant glance at Brook, who had finally managed to sit up in the bed and rub his eyes. "It's Isaac."

Ewan sidestepped us into the room. "The boy and his nurse have gone missing. Shut the door. We cannot alert the inn."

Adrian looked stunned as he did so, speaking only once the door was sealed. "What do you mean Miss Barton and Isaac are missing?"

My hands shook, so I busied them at my waist. "It all happened quite quickly after you left." I took great pains to recount every detail of my startling discovery—the truth of Miss Barton's deception and betrayal before moving on to the missive.

"My coachman from the Towers must have been the one transporting the French intelligence. He was such good friends with Lucius. It stands to reason he would risk his life for my brother."

Brook sauntered over to the washstand and splashed his face. "Did you bring the coded letter with you?"

"Well, yes."

He motioned with his chin. "I'd like to see it."

Ewan fished the paper from his pocket and handed it to Brook.

Adrian pulled me aside. "And Giles? Do you believe Miss Barton had a hand in his death?"

"I do. She was on Mrs. Jennings's list. I just never even considered her as a suspect."

"Nor I."

From the corner of my eye, I could see Brook roaming the room, his fingers busy tapping the back of the intelligence in his hand. In so many ways I could still read him, his subtle mannerisms, what he looked like when he was planning something, how he faintly twisted his lips when he meant to hide the truth.

As if he felt my gaze, he stopped cold, an odd bend to his brow. "Where the deuce is my coat?"

There it was—that telltale quirk of his mouth that any other person would never even notice, but I did.

He crossed his arms. "No need for the Friday-face, Lady Torrington. I'll have a look about the inn. Make sure this Frenchman isn't hiding under our very noses."

Friday-face. He would have to call me that. An itch tingled in the back of my throat. Brook had used the descriptor as a joke throughout our relationship. He knew it riled me. Yet as my pulse climbed I knew all too quickly something more than hearing the familiar phrase had startled me. I'd heard someone else use those very words recently. But who?

For an instant I felt lost to time as the past few days flashed through my mind. Then the memory stopped me cold.

Miss Barton. She had used those words in the nursery.

My legs felt weak as I watched the lines deepen on Brook's face. She had to have heard the phrase somewhere. It was not all that common and a favorite of Brook's. I narrowed my eyes. Did he and Miss Barton know one another as more than simply passing acquaintances as she'd implied? Moreover, did they have some sort of relationship?

The day Brook arrived at Middlecrest invaded my thoughts. I'd been caught off guard by her strange question about how he looked, and even more so by the resulting blush that tore across her cheeks. They'd grown up near one another. Was Brook's own nursemaid's daughter one of his mistresses?

Miss Barton was just the sort of young woman Brook would take advantage of. And he the kind of man to do . . . What? Betray his country? Murder his niece's betrothed? The idea was no more fantastic than Miss Barton doing so. And the intelligence the coachman from the Towers was transporting was meant for someone in Dover. Could that someone have been Brook on his way into Britain from France?

My thoughts whirled to the knife we'd found in the dry larder. Both Adrian and Ewan had recognized it at once but were unable to place it. Could it have been Brook's all along?

No. Brook wasn't at Middlecrest when Giles was murdered. Or was he? Had Brook returned from the continent far earlier than he'd let on? Then I remembered Mrs. Harris mentioning she'd seen Adrian in town, only Adrian hadn't been in town that day. From a distance the brothers did look rather similar. If Brook returned to Britain earlier than we thought, someone else might have seen him as well.

Giles!

The hairs on my arms sprung to attention. It all made sense.

Giles must have come upon Brook on his way to Middlecrest for the wedding. No wonder he was upset and sought out Mr. Baxter for advice. If I was right, Giles was the one person who knew Adrian's brother was a traitor. And he'd hoped I could help him untangle the mess he found himself in. Only he never got the chance.

An icy feeling splashed over me as my eyes dropped to the wooden floor. If Brook was indeed working with Miss Barton, might she have another reason for taking Isaac? The dark thought aligned with the other pieces of the puzzle.

Miss Barton was taking my son to his father.

Brook was the instigator behind it all. The charade of tracking the French spy and leading Adrian to him was either a trap to lure Adrian away from the house or at the very worst, kill him.

I watched as Brook slid his coat onto his shoulders and pulled on his boots. This sudden interest in searching the grounds was nothing but a farce. He had other plans, and he'd brought Isaac into the middle of them.

I flinched as Adrian took my hand, his voice a whisper at my ear. "What is it?"

My eyes shot to his, startled by how swiftly he'd picked up on my discomfiture. But how could I reveal the truth without tipping off Brook?

"I'm terribly afraid for Isaac. I-I don't know why Miss Barton would take him like she did." Carefully, I motioned over and over again at Brook with my eyes.

Adrian scanned the room, the moonlight revealing a keen intensity behind his sharp gaze. "We can only hope they will arrive here sometime during the night."

My voice cracked. "This inn was the only place mentioned in the missive, but it was also intended to be delivered to someone in Dover by my coachman, someone who was meant to escort my brother back to France, possibly someone who'd just arrived."

I widened my eyes and glanced one more time at Brook. He was dressed now and heading for the door. How clever he thought he was, how devious, but he'd made a mistake. He'd not counted on how well I knew both of the Radcliff brothers.

A clock ticked from somewhere in the recesses of the room, and the wind surged against the windowpanes. My heart drummed as Adrian's eyes locked onto his brother, rage brewing beneath a piercing stare. He'd understood my cryptic words and glances and quickly formed the same connections I had.

But what now? Adrian stepped forward, his voice as smooth as satin.

"Perhaps I should go with you, Brook."

Brook paused for a moment, turned back to the room, and leaned against a nearby dresser. Lazily, he shrugged, slow to look up or speak. Dread poured into my stomach. Brook was playing it cool, but he was far too observant.

. A muscle twitched in his jaw. Had he already become aware of his place within the charged silence? I watched as his hand inched toward his pocket, and I stiffened.

He knew. My heart sank.

His fingers plunged into the depths of his jacket, and I screamed.

Adrian's pistol emerged first with Ewan's merely a second behind, both barrels aimed straight at Brook's heart.

He only laughed in response. "Quick work, brother. I must say, Elizabeth, your performance just now was a pleasure to watch. Only I'm afraid I hold the ace to this little game we've been playing, and I daresay I'm the only one here with the desperation to use it."

Beyond the window the moon shook free of its cloudy blanket and poured an eerie white light into the room. All I could feel was the pulse pounding in my throat.

Brook had his own pistol in his hand, and he'd pointed it directly at me.

CHAPTER 31

"What the devil are you doing?" The strain in Adrian's voice held so many layers.

Brook angled his chin. "For the first time in my life—exactly what I want."

Adrian shook his head. "A traitor—my own brother—and after I defended you all those years to Father. Now I know how deep your deceitfulness runs."

Brook gave a tight laugh. "So easy for you to say when everything was handed to you on a silver platter. Money, prestige, power. Father treated me like the hired help. Well, I've been rather busy on my forced tour of the continent. He would be proud. Now"—he turned to me—"Elizabeth, my dear, you are going to accompany me out of the inn. After that, I haven't the least interest where you go." He motioned into the room. "Your pistols, on the floor, please. Let's keep this right and tight. No heroics and all will be well."

Ewan shot a questioning glance at Adrian. He nodded and carefully the two guns were placed onto the floor.

Brook knew he could use me as a shield just as he'd done so many times before. But I was finished being his pawn—the trash he burned on his way out of Britain. My muscles tightened. My jaw clenched as the deep-seated pain of what I'd endured was rubbed raw by his continued deception.

A brief silence followed as Brook slowly crossed the room, his eyes so callous on mine. None of us could guess what Brook ultimately meant to do with me, but I had an idea, and it didn't include letting me go. I shook myself as I glanced over at Adrian's utter desperation. My family needed me—Adrian, Isaac, Ewan, the girls. I was now the only one who could put an end to Brook's chances of escape. Adrian would not risk my life.

Hoping any delay could prove useful, I spoke as Brook grasped my arm. "What does Isaac have to do with all this?"

Brook tried to disguise it, but I saw him flinch. I'd guessed right. Miss Barton and he were involved. His face fell into a leer, his gaze sliding ever so carefully to Adrian.

"Do you really wish to discuss this in company?"

My voice faltered, but I managed to lift my chin. "I don't care who knows. I only want my son returned to me unharmed. He must be terribly frightened."

"With Alice Barton?" Incredulous, Brook raised his voice. "Don't flatter yourself. You know quite well she's been more of a mother to him over the last few weeks than you have. They enjoy each other immensely."

His words ripped through my chest, tearing into my heart. I fought the tears filling my eyes, stunned into a hasty response.

"You never cared what happened to him before."

"Haven't I?" His voice turned grave. "Who do you think placed spies at the Towers to watch the two of you? And then later, who suggested Alice work as a nursemaid to Isaac? Me, of course." He edged in closer, the barrel of his pistol never wavering.

"I always meant to come back for him. More's the pity, I might have considered taking you with us to France, but you had to go and marry my brother. Naturally, Alice will do just as well. She's fancied herself in love with me for some time, and now my boy too."

He turned ever so slightly to Adrian, a patronizing smile across his face. "Yes, I said *my* boy. That's right, Adrian. Elizabeth loved me long before she ever thought of you."

I stared at Brook for several seconds, my head throbbing, my fingers quivering. I couldn't even recognize the man I once thought I loved, so disturbing were his eyes, so calculating his voice.

And Adrian, the man I'd given my heart to, stood as still as a statue in the silvery light, a sharp line across his brow. He knew it all now, every sordid detail of my past. I could only hope he'd allow me the chance to explain.

Brook shoved my shoulder, spinning me to face the door, before pressing the hard, icy tip of his pistol to my back.

"Time to go."

My mind raced for options—anything to give Adrian a fighting chance. I could almost feel his fingers twitching at his sides and the shocked horror of Ewan's penetrating gaze. Brook had put them in a terrible position, and he was enjoying every minute of it.

He thrust me into the hallway, my knees locking as he rammed the pistol once again into my back. I inched down the stairs, praying the innkeeper would appear. The dark entryway felt like the inside of a mausoleum. I hesitated on the last step, and Brook, tired of my halting progression, moved beside me.

I considered a scream a split-second before his curved fingers clamped down on my mouth, his other hand gripping my arm. "Not yet, you don't."

I wriggled to free myself of his grasp, but he held me tight against his chest, keeping me completely under his power. The entry room was a muddle of moonlight and shadows. A transient chill roamed the floor. Brook forced me around the corner, and I was favored a glimpse of the fireplace out of the corner of my eye . . . and the poker next to it.

A mere foot across the carpet, and I could have the iron stick in my hand.

A creak on the stairs caused Brook to shove us against the wall, his fingernails digging into my chin. Adrian was likely already following us, creeping down the stairs, but apparently Brook wanted to be certain. I felt the cold metal of the pistol as he whiffed it across my arm to direct it up the stairs.

The drum of fear pounded its way through every inch of my body. Though I had questioned it before, I knew then and there, if necessary, Brook had every intention of putting an end to his brother.

I attempted to bite Brook's fingers, moan—anything to warn Adrian—but Brook was far stronger than I was. Tears of frustration poured from my eyes.

Another creak on the stairs. Adrian was getting closer.

Slowly, I extended a shaky hand along the fireplace stones beside me until the metal poker slid into my grasp. I had only a second to enact my plan. Balancing the poker against my back, the way Adrian had done with the pool mace, I shot the blunt handle at Brook's head as hard as I could.

He moved at the last second, weakening my strike, but a dull thump pierced the silence nonetheless. Brook's body collapsed forward onto my shoulder before dissolving into a pile on the floor.

The scream I'd been fighting to produce surged from my mouth, echoing off the plaster walls. A breathless second and

Adrian flew around the corner. Two steps and I fell into his arms. Without hesitation he pulled me tight, and I closed my eyes. Despite what he'd learned moments ago, he still loved me. He still wanted to protect me.

I didn't even feel the bullet as it grazed my shoulder.

I stood in stunned disbelief for a second before Adrian forced me to the floor behind a nearby sofa, his pistol hot in his hand. A second shot reverberated from the landing.

"Ewan," he whispered.

The innkeeper's voice sliced through the room. "What's all this?"

Adrian peeked over the top of the sofa. "We need help at once, sir. A French traitor has found his way into your inn."

A shadow darted in front of the desk, and I heard a door slam in the distance. The rug gave a subtle tug beneath my knee, and I turned to where Brook had fallen.

The floor was empty.

"Brook!" My warning was a second too late.

He charged Adrian, his hand firmly grasping his brother's arm. The pistol went off at the ceiling, and Ewan threw himself into the fray. Three more shots. All the pistols had been discharged. I sought the ground for the poker I'd used moments ago, but someone else had the same idea.

The figure I'd seen before took shape in the dim moonlight. The escaped French spy. He'd been here the whole time.

He tapped the poker against the palm of his hand and angled his chin. I was no match for that hard instrument. He only laughed and turned back to the brawl in the center of the room. Fists flew in and out of the shifting shadows. I could hardly make out who had gone down and who had stumbled his way back to his feet.

All at once the poker glinted in the moonlight, followed by

a loud crack. My heart leapt, urging my feet to do the same. The Frenchman must have missed his mark, for I could easily make out four desperate fighters.

The sofa was forced across the floor and crashed into a nearby table.

I knew I could act as a distraction to give Adrian or Ewan an edge, but how? Narrowly missing Ewan and the Frenchman as they barreled across the room, I clutched an unlit candelabra and hurled it into the fray.

The men barely even flinched as the pewter candlestick crashed onto the floor. If only I could get to the door, I might find a way to help. Adrian was up now, his fists raised, but he was beat back, splayed out across the desk, blood dripping from his lip. The fight moved inward, and I circled the room.

I could see Ewan tiring, and Adrian took a swing at the Frenchman to give Ewan a moment to recover. It was the moment Brook must have been waiting for to sprint my direction.

Desperate for escape, I turned the door latch and yanked. The night air swooshed into the entryway. The fight halted just as Brook jutted his arm across the opening.

"Enough!" His hand dipped into his pocket before reemerging with a shiny silver knife that he wrenched up to my neck. He seemed to be in his cups as he staggered back a pace, tired from the fight.

"I'm afraid I have a prior engagement with this lady's brother." His lips curved up. "That's right. Good old Lucius has some information for me. I'm to meet—"

The sudden, sharp crack of a gunshot resounded through every bone in my body.

Brook looked down at his chest as blood seeped out from the

folds of his cravat. Belatedly, he looked at me, confusion lining his pained face.

"What the deuce?"

I couldn't answer his questioning gaze, which abruptly turned to terror. The knife fell from his fingers, and I eased him to the floor as Ewan and Adrian tied up the Frenchman.

Regardless of our sordid past, pain and uncertainty filled every bone in my body. Brook's face looked ashen in the shifting light, his eyes dulled. He grasped my hand as I searched the room for answers.

Who else had a gun? Who took the shot?

Mr. Browning crossed the threshold on a sweeping gust of wind, his dark hair rumpled by the breeze. "Thank goodness I returned to Middlecrest when I did. Juliana said you might need some assistance." He gestured to Brook's listless form. "Pity it came to this."

Reeling from the shifting change of events, I turned back to Brook's twisted face. He hadn't much time left in this world. My eyes filled with tears. This man had hurt me in every way possible, but as he lay on the wooden beams of the floor, I felt only sadness. What a wasted life. Our eyes met, and I managed to whisper the three words I never thought I'd say to him. "I forgive you."

And I meant it. For over a year I'd been working my way to this moment. Alive or dead, Brook could no longer hurt me. My forgiveness was not for him. It was for me.

Adrian knelt at my side, shaking Brook awake before pressing his handkerchief against the bullet hole, but it was no use. Mr. Browning's musket ball had struck Brook from behind and must have pierced his heart.

"Where is Isaac?" Adrian stared into his brother's eyes. "This is your last chance to do something right before the end. Your son deserves to be with his mother, not in some workhouse or worse. Miss Barton cannot support him without your help."

Brook's haunting gray eyes shifted from Adrian's face to mine, his voice ebbing and flowing like turbulent waves. "Room seven . . . She's waiting . . . for me there."

Neither Adrian nor I could utter a response as we watched the life drain from Brook's face. Our lives had been linked for so long that it was difficult to imagine a world without him in it.

*

We found Miss Barton in room seven just as Brook had said. She must have checked in under an assumed name. Isaac was asleep on the bed, blissfully unaware of the danger he'd been in.

Adrian wasted no time in apprising her of Brook's tragic death, and as I looked into her eyes, I saw deadening shock. Evil manifests itself in many forms; Miss Barton had yielded to its power, certain she and Brook would prevail. When she realized none of her plans would come to fruition, her strength shattered.

As Adrian passed her into Mr. Browning's hands, I stopped them for a moment.

"Why did you do it?"

She turned toward Isaac, a hollow look about her wet eyes. "I'd have done anything to keep him." Her fingers curled around a clump of her hair, twisting and pulling. "He had his eyes, you know . . . My darling, Henry . . . Oh, his beautiful blue eyes."

The name startled me. Surely she meant Brook.

"In a way, I thought he'd come back to me, my wee babe." Her scowl deepened. "Don't look at me like that. I assure you, Brook did all he could to help us at the time. He brought in the best doctors who did all they could, but Henry was never meant for this world." Her voice dropped to a whisper. "I'd have done anything to be with my boy again." Her eyes darted madly around the room. "Anything."

The *H* on the engraved rattle flashed into my mind. *H* for Henry. *And Brook*—of course. Another illegitimate child, one who hadn't survived. My shoulders sagged. As twisted as they were, perhaps Brook had his own reasons for the shock and denial he displayed when I first told him about Isaac.

Miss Barton's voice rose sharply. "When Brook asked me to kill that gentleman and passed me the plate in the kitchens, there was a moment when I didn't want to hand Mr. Harris the poisoned food. Heavens, I was so distracted I didn't even see that Brook had left his knife on the plate. But when he asked me to leave you those notes, I wanted to do it . . . among other things. Isaac needed me, not you."

The pulsing fear I'd experienced on the back of Flick came roaring to life, seizing my heart. There had been more than Giles's murder and the threatening notes.

"It was you who spooked my horse, hoping I would ride over the cliff."

I saw the hint of a smile buried in a scornful look, but it was gone before I could be sure. Miss Barton gave me no answer to that question or any others I posed. She had said all she intended to.

We would never know exactly what led her to betray her country, yet I was beginning to understand the depths of her soul.

Brook could be quite persuasive, particularly when one wanted to please him, but her hurt ran far deeper. She had lost a child and likely never recovered.

I felt only pity as Mr. Browning led her from the room. She would stand trial for Giles's murder, and I doubted I would ever see her again.

The door creaked shut on their heels, and just like that, Adrian and I were alone. He tried one of his smiles as he leaned against the door, but it was fleeting at best.

"It's done." There was a sharpness to his movements, a hesitation on his lips, but his eyes were as keen as ever.

"Thanks to you."

He crossed the room to where I stood near the bed. "I had little to do with it, and you know it."

We stood there for a long moment watching Isaac sleep. After all we'd endured, I suppose we found it a bit difficult to breach the comfortable silence of relief, but I had things I needed to say.

"Miss Barton will be transported to Newgate, then?"

He plunged his fingers into his thick hair. "Her fate is out of our hands now. Thank goodness for that." The momentary look of exhaustion across his face was quickly followed by a questioning glance. He was waiting.

Caught not only by the hold of his honest gaze but by the relentless pursuit of my heart, I let out a breath. The words were slow to come, but for the first time since I'd arrived at Middlecrest Abbey, I felt the strength to say them.

"There were so many instances in the days following our sudden marriage when I wish I'd had the courage to disclose the truth about Brook, but I was afraid." I reached for his hand, allowing my fingers to slip so comfortably between his. "Afraid of losing this. Though that difficult chapter of my life is closed, you never should have had to learn about Isaac's parentage from Brook. Not in that awful way."

Gently, he pulled me close, his voice fading into the soft firelight and the quiet hum only the late hours of the night enjoy.

"You once said that some people possess the power to control their hearts. I think by now you know quite well that I do not." After a long thoughtful pause, he settled his hand on the nape of my neck.

"Beauty of the rarest form
Hair like a golden flame;
A man could bear most anything
If she would but speak his name."

His eyes glistened, his fingers felt soft on my skin. "My darling, my love, don't waste one more single second on the past. I'm only looking to the future." A slow smile transformed his features—not the easy grin of a hardened rake, but the genuine one I'd seen only once before, the one I was fairly certain he'd saved just for me. "Somewhere between the ridiculous start of this marriage of convenience and the day I made up that silly poem, I irretrievably lost my heart."

Warmth eased through my muscles until I managed to look up and meet his tender gaze. "Oh, Adrian. We have made so many mistakes, but I've never been so glad that one of them brought me to you. I love you with every ounce of my being."

I watched him for a long moment, memorizing the curve of his chin, the glint in his eyes, the way his face, when relaxed, revealed precisely what he was thinking. Then I raised my chin. I suppose the movement must have betrayed my thoughts, for Adrian tugged me straight into a kiss. But not just any kiss. This one was freed of doubt, worry, and shame. I'd never felt anything so utterly glorious yet so wonderfully safe at the same time.

Eventually he drew away. "I have one last thing to tell you, and I hope you can understand why I did not speak up earlier." He cast a quick glance at the bed. "I've had my suspicions about Isaac's parentage for some time. I'd heard Brook mention you before in the past. It wasn't difficult to put it all together."

My eyes grew wide. "Then you knew all along?"

He gave me that maddening shrug I'd come to loathe and adore. "Not at the very beginning, but soon after. They've all figured it out too, you know."

A prickle scaled my spine. "Who?"

"The staff, of course." He raised his eyebrows. "Isaac bears a striking resemblance to Brook at that age. Besides, he also has the Radcliff toe—you know, the fourth one. It's much shorter than the rest. You had little hope of keeping the secret when you agreed to bring him to Middlecrest."

My lips parted. "What the servants must think of me!"

"They love you for who you are. Just as I do, as well as the girls."

"You mean they know too?"

"No." He ran his hands down my arms. "When or if you tell them is entirely up to you."

I leaned forward and rested my head against his chest, a bit like I'd done that day in the coach on my way to Middlecrest Abbey. Who could have guessed what our marriage would become?

I slipped my hands beneath his jacket, my arms circling his waist, and pulled him closer still. Today marked the beginning of a new journey for us, and I knew without a doubt that neither of us would ever let go.

We'd cast aside the various masks we'd hidden behind since the beginning of our relationship. At the time I'd believed the exposure of my secret would destroy any chance of love between us, but that's the funny thing about the truth—it set me free.

EPILOGUE

Six months have passed since Isaac's kidnapping, and I suppose the servants would say life has settled into more of a routine at Middlecrest. I don't believe life will ever be tedious around here, not with Adrian running the estate. An adventurous rogue at heart, my husband could not cease his covert espionage any more than he could stop breathing, and I would never want him to. He thrives as a wealthy landowner by day and a spy by night, and I can only imagine what escapades shall befall us in the days to come. I'm grateful to share the ride.

Juliana seems to view Middlecrest Abbey as her refuge for the present as she struggles through the fog of grief. However, I have seen glimmers of her wit and quick mind more and more every day. At some point she will be ready to return to London for a season, and with her unique experiences and keen perception, I know she will blossom once again. Society will not be the same.

Phoebe continues to paint and dream of the future. With a little coaxing from me, Adrian has agreed to allow her to train with a local painter in Plattsdale who has created outstanding work. It will at least keep her busy until she can finally have the season she speaks about nearly every day.

Ewan has expressed an interest in pursuing a fellowship, and with his determination, I know he'll achieve whatever he puts his mind to.

Conveniently, Mrs. Ayles has relocated to one of Adrian's smaller houses near Brighton. Though I fear she loathed to leave Middlecrest, she put up little fight when the offer was presented. On the contrary, Mrs. Harris visits quite frequently now, and we've forged a rather unlikely friendship. Of course, I am one of the few people who knew Giles for so many years. In many ways, we have strengthened each other.

Adrian spends a great deal of time at home these days, always underfoot. He doesn't want to miss one moment of my pregnancy, and I'm thankful every day for his excitement. Boy or girl, this wonderful little person growing inside me will come into the world with six people terribly anxious to love him or her.

It is strange how much can change in such a short time. I thought my life was over when I first found out about Isaac. I know now that was only the beginning.

ACKNOWLEDGMENTS

Travis, I could not write one word of my stories without your constant love and support. Thank you for brainstorming with me nearly every night and listening to my endless "what ifs." I wouldn't want to share a minute of this crazy life with anyone else. #hobbitsforthewin

Megan Besing, thank you for rescuing this story at every stage of development with your amazing ideas, your wise critique, and your heartfelt encouragement. I hope you realize just how much you were a part of this book. #iheartyou

Mom, you continue to be my biggest cheerleader and bosom friend. Thank you for your unending encouragement. There is no one in the world like you.

Audrey and Luke, Bess and Angi, thank you for sharing my joy.

The entire Wilson clan, thank you for loving and supporting me.

Nicole Resciniti, my awesome agent, you've been such a fantastic support to me this year.

My editors, Becky Monds and Jodi Hughes, you both elevated and transformed this story in so many wonderful ways. I'm blessed beyond belief to have you guys working alongside of me and sculpting my words. And to the entire team at Thomas Nelson, Paul Fisher, Kerri Potts, Laura Wheeler, Allison Carter, you guys have given me such phenomenal support. I am thankful every day I get to work with such a brilliant group of people.

And to my Lord and savior Jesus Christ. To you alone be the glory.

DISCUSSION QUESTIONS

1. After so much abandonment in her life, Elizabeth has been conditioned to rely on herself alone. Are there areas in your own life where you feel the same way?
2. Elizabeth puts her son's needs first when she makes the decision to marry Lord Torrington. Would you be able to make the same decision?
3. Elizabeth had planned out every step of her future until the carriage accident. Has an incident in your life caused a complete change of plans? How did you deal with it?
4. What type of situation would you have to be in to agree to a marriage of convenience? Or is it something you would consider easily?
5. Elizabeth keeps the name of Isaac's father a secret to protect her son. Have you felt the need to maintain a secret to protect someone else, and how did it affect you?
6. Lord Torrington believed he was unworthy of love or marriage due to his past mistakes. Have you ever felt that way about moments in your past?
7. Elizabeth comes to trust the least likely person she

thought she would in Lord Torrington. Has anyone in
your life turned out different from what you expected?

8. Would you have handled any decisions Elizabeth made
   differently? Why or why not?

9. Who do you think grew the most throughout the novel?

ABOUT THE AUTHOR

ABIGAIL WILSON combines her passion for Regency England with intrigue and adventure to pen historical mysteries with a heart. A registered nurse, chai tea addict, and mother of two crazy kids, Abigail fills her spare time hiking the national parks, attending her daughter's gymnastic meets, and curling up with a great book. In 2017 Abigail won WisRWA's Fab Five contest and in 2016, ACFW's First Impressions contest, as well as placing as a 2017 finalist in the Daphne du Maurier Award for Excellence in Mystery/Suspense. She is a cum laude graduate of the University of Texas at Austin and currently lives in Dripping Springs, Texas, with her husband and children.

Connect with Abigail at www.acwilsonbooks.com
Instagram: @acwilsonbooks
Facebook: @ACWilsonbooks
Twitter: @acwilsonbooks